QUEEN OF CITIES

ANDREW NOVO

coffeetownpress

Seattle, WA

Published by Coffeetown Press
PO Box 95462
Seattle, WA 98145

Cover design by Sabrina Sun

Contact: info@coffeetownpress.com

ISBN: 978-1-60381-076-0 (Paper)
ISBN: 978-1-60381-016-6 (Cloth)

To Ines Faiella Prario (1926-1995), the most important person in my life who was never able to see this work but whose love of knowledge has always inspired me.

Acknowledgements

This book was an odyssey that began before my freshman year at Princeton. I read an article in a magazine about the fall of Constantinople and was fascinated by the story. Eventually, I decided to write a novel on the subject. Ten years, countless drafts, and almost three-hundred pages later, the work is complete. For this creation of something from nothing I owe a great debt to a number of people. On a professional level, I must thank my publisher Paul Beidler and the entire staff at Coffeetown Press for their hard work and for believing in the project.

On a personal level I have to thank my father, Guy, and my mother, Celia, who diligently read the first bits and pieces I produced and always encouraged me to keep writing. Their uncomplaining willingness to read draft upon draft, unfinished, unordered, and unpolished was truly heroic. Gratitude is also due to my godmother, Ann Marie Hannon, who likewise subjected herself to my work in its nascent stages and provided enormously helpful and encouraging feedback. To my dear friend, Dr. Scott MacDonald, a successful author in his own right, who gave me the confidence to pursue this project. To Mrs. Valerie Galdau who first opened the world of literature and creative writing to me. Also, special thanks to Juliana Seminerio, Chris Dexter, Greg Larkin, and Michael Jago for all their hard work.

And finally, to my wife, Natalie Nicolaou. On a daily basis, she dealt with my need to write, to brainstorm ideas, to research trifling details from fifteenth century recipes to the weather of foreign countries, with grace and constant good humor. She helped me travel to distant places and to understand foreign cultures. Natalie, without you there was nothing but an idea. You inspired me to write, to work and to never give up. Your example is my inspiration, your friendship my treasure, your love my joy.

Contents

Acknowledgements: i

PART I

1—The Sultan: October 1452 1

2—The Throat Cutter: November 1452 11

3—The Cardinal: December 12, 1452 19

4—The Condottiere: January 26, 1453 25

5—The Walls: January 1453 35

6—The Court: February 1453 47

7—The House of the Podestà: February 1453 53

8—The Final Preparations: March 1453 65

PART II

1—The Siege: April 2, 1453 71

2—The Cannon: April 5, 1453 77

3—The Admiral: April 20, 1453 95

4—The Sheikh: April 21, 1453 111

5—The Plan: April 22, 1453 119

6—The Golden Horn: April 25, 1453 133

7—The Lions of Saint Mark: April 28, 1453 147

8—The Captain-General: May 10, 1453 161

PART III

1—The Miner: May 12, 1453 169

2—The Engineer: May 22, 1453 177

3—The Sail: May 23, 1453 191

4—The Icon: May 24, 1453 207

5—The Priest: May 25, 1453   215

6—The Warrior: May 27, 1453   231

7—The Emperor: May 28, 1453   241

8—The Assault: May 29, 1453   253

9—The City: May 29, 1453, 9 am   267

10—The Ships: May 29, 1453, 10 am   277

11—The Conqueror: May 29, 1453, noon   287

Character List   302

PART I

1—The Sultan: October *1452*

"Constantinople is a city larger than its
renown proclaims. May God in His Grace and
generosity deign to make it the capital of
Islam." – (Hassan Ali al Haraway, 12th
century)

Sultan Mehmed woke suddenly. His right hand knocked
over the golden chalice, spilling wine on a drawing for a new
siege tower. He cursed aloud. It was like this almost every
night. Mehmed pulled the stained parchment to the floor
and focused on a map of Constantinople, the Queen of
Cities, the object of his desire. His fingers traced the gentle
arc of the westward land walls, while his mind imagined a
way through the ancient shield that had proved impregnable
to everyone who had tried to conquer it. No man, not the
great Attila, the Shahs of Persia, the Khans of Bulgaria, not
even his father, had ever breached those walls. Perhaps *no*
man could. His nails dug into the parchment and the map
crumpled in his hand. Mehmed suddenly felt suffocated in
the room. He went to a window. Outside, he saw darkness
broken only by the flickering lights of the sentries' torches
along the walls. He turned around to the room; the evening
candles had nearly burned away. Dawn was a few hours
away, and his blood was pounding.

He took two strides to the door and threw it open. The
weary guards clattered to their feet. "Mustafa!" he barked
down the hallway. "Mustafa!"

His servant, roused in the adjoining room, entered the
hallway half asleep. "Mustafa!"

"Yes, my lord?"

"Bring me Gülbahar!"

"Yes, my lord."

The servant knew better than to question. Once before,
when Mehmed had first become Sultan, Mustafa had
questioned a command and spent a night naked sitting on

1

top of Adrianople's battlements as his reward. He knocked at the heavy oak door. There was no response. He knocked again and the door opened a crack to reveal Eminé, the maid. A hint of perfume and jasmine escaped the chamber.

"Eminé, the master desires the presence of Lady Gülbahar."

Wearily Eminé answered: "I'll prepare her." The door closed. Eminé walked over to the bed, lighting candles as she went.

"My lady, his highness desires your company tonight."

A lilting voice replied, entirely awake, "I heard the knocking, Eminé."

"Come out of bed, child."

Gülbahar's fingers stroked the long black hair that had fallen to her ivory shoulders, standing out like ink bleeding into parchment.

"He would just as soon have me as I am now."

"It isn't done, my lady. I will prepare you."

"He would have me as I am now." She repeated. "Give me the mirror."

The maid nodded, handing over a jeweled looking glass.

Gülbahar picked it up and looked at herself: cheeks un-powdered, lips unpainted, body unadorned, unperfumed, hair undone. For a moment, Gülbahar's memory carried her back to her youth, to the wild hills of Albania where she had grown up, before the Turkish pasha, hunting bear, had found her and taken her as his mistress. Before then, her only mirror had been the stream where she played, ignorant of makeup and perfumes. She remembered the pasha's voice as he held a mirror in front of her for the first time:

"Do you see how beautiful you are?" And his hands had moved to touch her... Even from that first embrace, when the sated pasha had called the servants to bring golden rings studded with rubies for her fingers, and silken robes to replace her rags, she had begun to understand. After a few weeks, the pasha would bellow like a bull and whine like a

cat in search of her embrace. So it remained now. Only the man was different, but the pattern of desire, ecstasy, diffidence, and largesse fueled by renewed desire was familiar.

A small smile from softened lips, an inviting glance, an impassioned memory, an erotic dream, any of these could prompt Mehmed to demand her presence. Gülbahar's seduction summoned him as much as his desire summoned her. Almost always, she would comply. Refusing was hazardous, but it made acceptance, which invariably came, something to be savored. Gülbahar enjoyed that power, and the luxury of being the one person who could make Sultan Mehmed wait, as he was waiting now.

"My lady?"

Gülbahar's eyes snapped to her maid. "Prepare me."

The transformation began. Gülbahar's white silk night dress was replaced with thick satin robes of red and green. Her lush black hair was combed out, straightened, and left to caress her throat and shoulders. Jeweled rings sparkled on her hands. Golden earrings draped down her neck which gleamed with an emerald necklace. Finally, Eminé clasped a veil of white silk over her painted lips. Gülbahar looked at the opulence of her appearance, her costume, taking in every detail.

"I am done, my lady."

"Go back to bed, Eminé. I will see you in the morning."

Delicate footsteps took her down the corridor towards the Sultan's apartments. Guards left by Mustafa escorted her. They reached the door to Mehmed's bedchamber. Gülbahar, fragrant, waved the guards away and entered his room. She moved wordlessly across the floor, a rustle of silk and satin. She smiled. Powder made her face even whiter in the candlelight. She circled Mehmed like a butterfly. He watched her—motionless—as she approached him.

"Good evening, my lord."

She was at his side now, staring over his left shoulder at a map of Constantinople. He covered it quickly. But, just as quickly, she took a sketch for a catapult.

"Your majesty is planning for war." He did not answer, so she continued. "At last, you are going to make the City yours." Again he did not respond. Her hands went to his shoulders; her lips were by his ear. "I am glad. There is no greater prize for any king, no greater capital for any lord, no greater glory for any man, than Constantinople."

And no greater risk for any army, he thought, but only to himself. Before he could reply, she spoke again. "But how will you take it? How will you overcome its immortal walls? How will you scale those towers which strain to the heavens?" She wrapped the words of war in seduction.

"I did not have you brought here to discuss tactics," he snapped.

She smiled. "As you command, my lord. But you will not take Constantinople without careful preparation."

"I will be ready," he responded, resolving to her and to himself.

"It *shall* be yours. A prize no man has won. A prize never claimed by Muslim arms. A city of gold, filled with riches, the capital of the earth."

He pulled away from her hands, now clasped across his chest, attempting to disentangle himself from her provocation.

"Do you want the City for me, or for yourself?" he demanded.

"For you, my Sultan, for you." She followed him, her ghostly pale hands reaching out and catching him in another embrace. This time he did not resist. He could not resist. "Once you conquer the City, you will be the greatest king in the world."

"I am already the most powerful king in the world," he said while trying to kiss her. She pulled away.

"You know that your power is mocked by this city that stands like a sword at the center of your realm, cutting Europe from your lands in Asia." His lips found her neck, and as his kisses flowed so did her words. "You stand ready to do what has never been done, to become a king greater than any before you. Greater than any after you could hope."

His mouth was moving towards hers. Her lips dripped ambrosia when she spoke of Constantinople, tempting him with the pursuit of glory, but she kept him away.

"The man I love must be greater than all men."

"You are mine already."

"I will truly be yours when Constantinople is yours."

She had pushed hard enough. Gülbahar released herself to his embrace and shuddered as the Sultan pinned her to the great vermilion bed. At dawn, the castle began to rouse itself for the labors of another day. Gülbahar's hand stroked the Sultan's chest.

"You should sleep, my lord."

"I'm not tired." He rose and went to pour himself some wine. Love had taken the edge off her seductiveness. "I'm going to summon Halil Pasha. Get dressed and go."

"Are you going to tell him that you plan to make war on his Greek friends?" She was sitting up in the bed now, agitated by the thought of the ageing Grand Vizier. Gülbahar knew the politics of the court well. Halil Pasha favored peace, counseled caution, and accepted gifts of Greek gold.

"I will speak with my Vizier alone."

"Very well, my lord. Be careful that he does not tempt you from your course. Goodnight."

He nodded. When she was out of sight, Mehmed again called Mustafa.

"Summon Halil Pasha and bring some clothes! Bring my red jacket, Mustafa, the one with the pearls."

It would be ten minutes before the Vizier arrived, more perhaps, if he had to be pulled out of bed away from a woman. A Greek no doubt, a fitting bedmate for "the accomplice of the infidels." Suitably regal in the pearl encrusted jacket, the Sultan returned to his bed and sat up awaiting his minister, the wise Halil Pasha, his Grand Vizier, his father's Grand Vizier, a man who would do anything to curtail his power and prevent the conquest of Constantinople. Mehmed did not wait long. Almost as soon as he had adjusted the covers, the doors to his bedroom opened and the servant announced that the Vizier had arrived. Mehmed signaled that he be brought in. Halil entered, carrying a bowl filled with gold coins above his head that clinked as he walked.

"Why do you come with gold, lord Vizier?"

"It is custom that when a servant is summoned by his master, he must not come empty handed. Accept this humble gift great king, from your most devoted servant."

It was formulaic but appropriate. But Mehmed was in no mood for formalities. Irritably, he waved down the Vizier's subservient words. His spies had told him that Halil had recently received gifts from Constantinople—two large fish stuffed with gold. The sight of the glittering coins in the dish made him grit his teeth.

"Put down the bowl."

The older man raised his eyes from beneath his bowed head, trying to contain an expression that held both surprise and fear. Mehmed's tone was like ice.

"Do not bring me gold. *I* have gold." The words hung ominously in the air. "*Lala*," the affectionate term of "my uncle," made Halil raise his head. Tenderness was foreign to Mehmed; warmth was a charade. What did he want? Almost as an answer, the Sultan spoke. "I want Constantinople." The words were pronounced precisely, and in earnest. The Vizier kept silent. The young man's obsession had always been known to him, but the throne could now turn such aspirations into realities. Mehmed spoke again.

"Look at this bed. I toss and turn on it all night long, from one side to the other thinking of the City. I cannot sleep; day

6

and night my thoughts turn to Constantinople. You must help me have it." Halil made no response. "Do not allow yourself to be softened by seductive gold." The eyes of both men wandered to the bowl resting on the floor. "Temper your resolve to steel and with that steel we shall fight and win the City of the Caesars."

Halil felt himself poised above the abyss. There was nothing to prevent the plunge. Opposition at such a moment would invite rage. He thought it better to agree, but could not resist offering counsel.

"As you command, my lord. I shall do all in my power to help you as duty commands. But, I must warn you of the vastness of this task. You risk bringing the entire Christian world against us: Hungary, Genoa, *Venice.*"

Halil stressed the last. Venice, supreme among the Christian states, was the most powerful, the most immediate. Her fleet could strike anywhere, and against her warships the Sultan's navy was powerless. But Mehmed cut off his Vizier as the counsel escaped his throat.

"I fear nothing, lord Vizier. My father buried the armies of Hungary! They will not rise for a generation; Venice and Genoa will never unite against me. We are going to Constantinople. Let nothing sway you from that!" They stared at each other, silent and motionless. This was not the time for a confrontation. Mehmed would get nothing further from him tonight.

Abruptly, the Sultan continued. "Goodnight, lord Vizier." Halil bowed and left the room. Mehmed's eyes moved through the emptiness of his room and the honeyed walls of the City rose in his imagination.

Halil walked slowly back to his apartments, his mind submerged in thought. He returned to his bed and lay down to ponder the trials the future held. Once again the armies would be assembled. Once more they would march on New Rome. Lying in bed, the Vizier repeated to himself that if the boy was successful, opposition could cost him his life. He must be careful in choosing the manner of his dissent. Halil feared that the determination of Mehmed might succeed in willing the army to victory no matter what the cost. Still, there were a thousand years of failure to weigh against success. The thought renewed some of Halil's confidence.

"Let him try to take Constantinople," muttered the Vizier. "It has never fallen. I shall use all my power to prevent him from taking it. When we stand before the walls there will be a thousand chances to delay him, to counsel him to a prudent course away from violence. That will give the Christians time to come to the aid of the City. Venice will come. They will sail, great and terrible from their lagoon, and strangle us from the sea. Faced with that, he will be forced to make peace. At last we will have peace. Then, defeated in his greatest ambition, he shall have more need of me than ever." Reassured, the Vizier closed his eyes.

✷ ✷ ✷

Kings, princes, and pashas came from three continents to the Sultan's court. Marching under many flags, the proud men in their opulent robes made a fine procession from the reaches of Mehmed's empire. There were black banners engraved with holy words from the Koran, the blood red ensign of Osman with the white crescent, green colors embroidered in gold with the Sultan's monogram, and wild ox-tailed standards from tribes far to the East. They came from the sands of the Gobi desert, from the mountains of the Anatolian plateau, from the lush shores of Asia Minor, and from the gloomy banks of the Eastern Danube. In their trains rode noblemen from the conquered peoples, foes made subjects, and men of every race: Serbians, Bulgarians, Thracians, and Ionian Greeks. The Eastern pashas brought with them browned Arabs mounted on proud sleek horses and black Africans from the land beyond Egypt. Some had recruited Tartars, terrifying horsemen from the great steppes whose ancestors had ridden with Genghis Khan. Their faces, deliberately scarred since childhood, carried no expression and their narrow eyes sent shivers through the souls of friend and foe. With deliberation, for the pashas were noble men unaccustomed to haste, the great cavalcade converged on Adrianople.

When all the great men had arrived, Mehmed's heralds called them together. They stood waiting, impatient to hear the young Sultan's words, to hear the reason for their peremptory summons. Heads bowed in reverence as the Sultan appeared before them on horseback. From beneath their lowered brows, the lords judged Mehmed. Many were seeing him for the first time. He was young, but a fire burned in his eyes. The same fire burned in his voice when he spoke.

"Men of my empire! It pleases us to see you, to see the strength and greatness of our realm, that empire won in battle, defended by your courage, and passed in an unbroken succession from fathers to sons and handed to me by my father, the great Murad! No prince could consider himself more fortunate than I to rule over subjects so loyal, a nation so proud, or an empire so powerful. We must prove ourselves worthy successors to our forefathers, to increase their glory and emulate their triumphs. No people have ever been as fearsome in war, or as generous in peace.

"Now, we stand at the dawn of a new age, ready to achieve what our ancestors could only dream of, the conquest of the Queen of Cities and the establishment of our unchallenged power over Europe and Asia. For generations this city has stood alone, against us. Its riches have mocked our austerity; its lies have mystified our honesty; its pretensions have parodied our power. Sitting at the center of our realm, this city of unbelievers is an arrow threatening our heart in Europe and our soul in Anatolia. How long will we allow it to insult our pride and to plot our destruction? It considers itself the capital of the world while its mayor styles himself King and Emperor of the Romans. But we know these Romans well! Our armies have driven them out of Cappadocia, Lydia, Caria, Bithynia, Thrace, Macedonia, Bulgaria, and the Morea. Their mantle, as rulers of the world, is our mantle and their capital, their city, should be our city, and our capital. They claim they are the true faith— they lie! They claim their God is the true God, but they worship idols and deny that only God is God! They defend ancient memory with ancient walls and hope by deception to keep us from the victory promised us by the Prophet!

"We are the future! That future will be shaped by our strength and will not live in the shadow of the past. I can no longer imagine an empire without this city. If we conquer it, you may be sure that all our possessions will be secure. Without it, nothing we now possess, and nothing we will ever win, can be safe. We must attack with conviction, accept any suffering, overcome all obstacles, knowing that we shall never withdraw until we conquer the Queen of Cities!"

Cheering erupted throughout the assembly. Their fiery young sovereign had stirred the blood of the pashas to war. Eagerly, their hands reached for the long curved blades hanging at their sides. The forest of banners waved wildly as the cheers of affirmation rang out.

Shouts rose above the din: "War! War!"

"Death to the infidels!" "On to the City!

Halil Pasha shivered. He closed his eyes and thought of war. His vision was not the magnificent combat that the zealots clamored for, filled with triumph and glory, but the unadorned face of battle where bravado cries were mashed to pulp by enemy axes and drowned in fire and blood. Nothing he said would make a difference now. Mehmed had set their course—war—and the objective, the Queen of Cities.

2—The Throat Cutter: *November 1452*

Word of a disaster reached the city, and Constantinople began to buzz. A Venetian galley had been sunk by the Turks while trying to bring the city grain. Rumors spun around; the crew had been tortured, murdered in cold blood, drowned with the ship. The Sultan was demanding ransom, threatening war with Venice, planning to starve Constantinople to death. Word quickly reached the *bailò** of the Venetian colony in Constantinople, Girolamo Minotto. He received the news without expression. Two weeks earlier, Mehmed's fortress north of the city had tried to sink a different Venetian galley. Now, the Sultan's gunners had succeeded, and a ship flying the Lion of St. Mark was at the bottom of the Bosphorus.

"We must have news about the crew." *Signor* Fabrizio Cornaro, a member of one of Venice's most powerful families discussed the situation with Minotto.

The *bailò*, serious, pragmatic, precise, listened intently. In his mind, he touched each course of action, discarding the rash, the impotent, and the impossible. "We must negotiate with Mehmed for their release. I cannot leave Venetian citizens prisoners of the Sultan."

"Our honor demands war if those men are harmed."

Minotto closed his eyes. "I cannot be sure of that. Nor would I have my actions push our Republic to war. The honor of Venice is delicate. It will not be served by provoking even greater reprisals against our interests in the East."

"The provocation is the Sultan's, master *bailò*." Cornaro's voice hardened at the prospect of Venetian weakness.

"We must uncover the reason for this provocation. And bring the matter to a close."

---

* Mayor.

11

"There is no reasoning with ambition or with cruelty," countered Cornaro, his voice rising.

Minotto looked at him quizzically. "For the sake of those men, and for the sake of Venice, I hope you are wrong. And for the sake of both, I want you to go to the Sultan and secure the release of the crew."

Cornaro's face turned dark.

"I do not envy you this mission. We have little to bargain with except notions of justice and mercy."

"Justice and mercy are virtues unfamiliar to tyrants."

"They are. But I warn you, *Signor* Cornaro do not try to bully this boy-king; he is already set towards war. We cannot encourage him, nor by timidity can we invite him to conspire at our destruction."

Cornaro bowed politely. "I'll climb that delicate rigging as best I can, master *bailò*. And heaven help those men if I fail."

"If you fail, *signore*, heaven help us all.

* * *

The weather was gray as Cornaro made his journey from one imperial court to the other. There was a chill in the air. Winter was coming. The ambassador arrived with due ceremony at the dark fortress of Didimotkon, twenty-five miles south of Adrianople, to complain about the treatment of the sailors. Cornaro's family was among the most noble in the entire Republic and the ambassador himself was regal in his bearing. He stood before the young Sultan, bowed slightly, and was given permission to speak.

"Your majesty, I am Fabrizio Cornaro, special emissary of the Serene Republic of Venice and his Excellency Doge Francesco Foscari. I have come to secure the release of Captain Antonio Rizzo and his crew."

Mehmed did not respond as Cornaro's words hung in the air. The Venetian continued.

"These men are free citizens of the Venetian Republic. You have confirmed the treaties of friendship made by your illustrious father. Your present actions are a direct violation of those treaties and a threat to peace. If your majesty wishes to maintain this present peaceful state of affairs, you must agree to the immediate and unconditional release of our men."

Mehmed answered without hesitation: "Your ship, *signore*, attempted to sail past my fortress in direct violation of the protocol that had been set forth in my name, and in spite of the warnings issued by the citadel commander. Your captain is at fault for not agreeing to the reasonable demands that he lower his sails and allow his ship to be searched."

"Our ships and their cargoes are Venetian concerns, your majesty. Will you release our men?"

Halil was whispering in Mehmed's ear.

"We shall consider it."

"While your majesty is weighing his actions, may I be permitted to see that the captain and crew are alive and well?"

"Very well." The Sultan turned to one of his retainers, "Ahmed, take the ambassador to the prisoners."

Cornaro bowed curtly, turned, and left the opulent throne room. There was a striking difference between the lavish court where he had been entertained and the stinking cell where Cornaro found the galley's crew. The men, about eighty in all, were in a single rectangular space with thick stone walls and a single window looking up at the outside world. There was a look of enormous relief in their eyes as the solitary figure of the ambassador entered the room. His Venetian dress was immediately recognized and the crew surged forward to welcome him.

"*Signori*, I am Fabrizio Cornaro. *Bailò* Minotto has sent me here in order to negotiate with the Sultan for your immediate release."

The men listened attentively. One of the prisoners spoke:

"My name is Captain Antonio Rizzo, my lord. We were fired upon by the Turks on the twenty-sixth of November while attempting to sail through the straits north of Constantinople. They demanded that we lower our sails and subject our ship to search. As we were carrying a shipment of grain for the City, I refused. We were sunk with a single shot. My crew and I swam ashore where we were taken prisoner and then brought here. We have been prisoners for the past three days."

"Are all your men alive?"

"Yes."

"Have you been mistreated?"

"We could do with more food and clean water, but the men are all right. All except..." Rizzo's voice broke off abruptly. He coughed.

"What is it, captain?"

"One of our crew is missing."

"Missing?"

"Yes. The son of my clerk, Domenico di Mastri, was taken a few hours after our arrival. We have not seen him since them."

"Why would the son of your clerk be taken?"

He answered in a whisper. Cornaro craned his head forward in order to hear. "We found out from the guards that he was taken to the Sultan."

"To the Sultan, for what purpose?"

Rizzo paused to suppress another cough and continued. "The Sultan developed an unnatural affection for the boy and now he is in the infidel's *seraglio*."

"Are you sure, captain?" He asked incredulously.

"Yes, my lord. Yesterday, we received a note from the boy. The lad fears for his soul."

"I shall do everything in my power to get you out of here, captain, and your crew."

"Thank you, my lord. And please, do whatever you can for Domenico's son." The two men parted.

Mehmed's guards were at the door, calling to Cornaro that his time was up.

Cornaro returned to the Sultan and demanded that the entire crew be released. He read their names aloud from the ship's register, eighty in all, including de Mastri's, which he emphasized. The Sultan replied that he would consider his course of action with care and dismissed the ambassador. Cornaro returned to Constantinople and reported to Minotto. They would have to wait and see what the Sultan decided to do. Peace hung in the balance.

For two weeks, the prisoners remained in the dungeon. At dawn of the fifteenth day, the guards came. Hard men, they spoke in rough accents as they turned the heavy lock of the door. Light from their torches flooded in and burned the eyes of the prisoners who had become accustomed to the darkness. A strong smell of grilled meat and onions entered with the guards. The hungry sailors began to salivate. They were ushered out of the cell and taken to a courtyard against the city's walls. The day was gray. In broken Greek, a guard ordered them to line up. Rizzo, whom they had come to know as the captain, was held aside from the line. A large man with a stick now went up the row pushing every other man two paces forward. The sailors looked at each other with fear while the count was completed. The forty who had not been thrust ahead were herded into a cluster aside from the center of the courtyard.

The lead actor of the drama now appeared on the stage. He was a towering man with massive arms. His sword was carried behind him by a smaller man. The executioner took the great blade in his hands as the first victim was forced to kneel. The sword cut through the neck with a single stroke. The head rolled onto the ground as the body remained erect for a moment before collapsing to the earth. One of the sailors, whose turn to die would come soon, vomited. The rest stared at the severed head and trembled in the autumn cold. Their breath was coming feverishly and streams of vapor floated from the unhappy line. Another man was pushed to his knees and the grisly ceremony was repeated again, and again, and again, until forty heads littered the courtyard.

A voice cried out to them from a tower window. "You have witnessed the power of the Sultan! Go back to Constantinople and inform your masters what you have seen here today. Tell them of the fate that awaits anyone who resists the might of the great Mehmed!"

There was now a silent terror, but also relief among the sailors. Their lives were to be spared. Captain Rizzo, whose eyes were filled with tears for the men he had lost, thought of home. Then the voice called again.

"Mohammed, impale the infidel captain!"

All eyes now shifted to Antonio Rizzo. Fear rose within his stomach crushing the breath from his lungs. Two great pairs of hands clasped his arms, wrenching him from the brink of salvation and dragging him outside the walls towards a small group of Turkish soldiers on the roadside. They were sharpening a tall wooden pole next to a small hole in the ground. The largest man in the work party stopped his task and strode over to Rizzo whose eyes were fixed to the giant spit.

"Well *gâvur*,[†] do you think your God will save you now?

Rizzo could make no response; the words were soldered to his throat.

A huge fist crashed into his face spinning his head and sending him to the ground. Opening his eyes, his gaze fixed on the ashen sky. He started to cough. A lifetime of thoughts ran through his mind. He saw the moving clouds and thought of the prevailing wind and which tack he would choose for his ship. He saw the grayness of the day and

---

[†] Infidel.

thought of the mists in Venice during the celebrations for *Carnevale*. He remembered once as a little boy when his older brother Giovanni had dealt him a blow that had similarly sent him crashing to the earth. A thousand memories flooded to him, his ship, his father, his mother and the soft lips of his wife that smelled of the cinnamon he would bring her from his voyages.

The enormous hands wrestled him to his feet and stripped him. The cold December air struck him and he gave an involuntary shudder. His heart pounded from fear as his mind jerked back to reality. Surely, this could not be the end of his life, impaled like a lamb on a spit for attempting to run a blockade. It was happening so quickly. Naked, he was pushed to the ground and the guards once again took an iron hold of him. His legs were taken and forcibly spread. He shuddered and felt something sharp touch him beneath his waist. He heard someone walking forward and the loud thwack of wood striking wood. Instantaneously, a fiery pain shot up from his lower back through his entire body. He heard a voice, hoarse and ghastly that sounded like his own, vomited from the pain, and again saw the sky. He coughed and this time blood came from his mouth. His body twitched as the muscles began to spasm uncontrollably. He could not draw breath. Numbness spread up from his lower body. But in his mind, he could breathe freely again, and cinnamon filled his senses. With a jarring thud the pole came to rest in the earth, and the naked body of Antonio Rizzo hung in the air, his blood dripping from the wooden pole onto the packed earth of the roadway below.

3—The Cardinal: *December 12, 1452*

"Hoc est enim corpus meum!" The voice of Papal Legate, Cardinal Isidore, rang out in the cathedral of *Hagia Sophià*, pronouncing the unleavened host above his head the true body of Jesus Christ. The Latin consecration jarred upon the ears of the Orthodox congregation. This mass, announcing the union of the Catholic and Orthodox churches, was not welcome by all. In protest, many of Constantinople's priests and monks had refused to attend. Acquiescing for the sake of Western soldiers and gold, Emperor Constantine Palaeologos, King and Emperor of the Romans, stood silently through the ceremony. At his side, Grand Duke Lukas Notaras, one of the staunchest opponents of union, glared at the Cardinal. Notaras's eyes fixed above Isidore's flushed, time worn face, to the gleaming miter which glittered in the candlelight. He could feel his anger rising at the provocation of abandoning their church and temporal power to barbarians from the West, to the court of an Italian prince styling himself the "Vicar of Christ on Earth."

"It would have been better for us to see the turban of an infidel Sultan, than the miter of a Latin Cardinal," he hissed.

Constantine ignored the Grand Duke's goading and kept his eyes upon the altar. Notaras had lost his battle to prevent the union and his words reeked of impotent defeat. As the court's leading minister and Admiral of the Fleet, he was still the second most powerful man in the empire and had to be respected. But, "the silver lord" was also a constant frustration to his sovereign. The nickname derived as much from his flowing hair as from his enormous wealth – wealth that he kept hidden in Italian banks as a shield from imperial taxes.

The Emperor shifted his gaze from the Grand Duke to Cardinal Isidore. Like Notaras, the Cardinal's motives were never entirely clear. Constantine knew the man's history: a Greek by birth, a convert to Catholicism, an ardent believer in the union of the two churches. At one time, he had been the Orthodox Metropolitan of Kiev. His acquiescence to Catholic demands at the Ecumenical Council of Florence a decade earlier had so enraged the people of Kiev that they had driven him out and into the arms of the Catholic Church. Now, a Cardinal and the Legate of his Holiness Pope Nicholas, Isidore's presence in Constantinople raised as many questions as it answered. Ostensibly, the Cardinal had come to formalize the Union of Florence. His presence also represented a promise from the Pope to aid the City in her hour of need. The Cardinal had brought two hundred bowmen and gunners recruited at the expense of his master in Rome. The Constantinopolitans greeted the much-needed military aid with open arms, and were encouraged by the Cardinal in the belief that this was merely the vanguard of a larger force. Furthermore, the sinking of Antonio Rizzo's galley had caused a panic among the citizens and made the need for alliance with Rome and the West more urgent than ever.

Even with this new impetus, union would prove hard to maintain. As part of the Catholic delegation, the Pope had sent Leonardo of Chios, Archbishop of Mytilene. Constantine's eyes moved to the archbishop, who stood next to the Cardinal. Men like the archbishop complicated union immeasurably. Leonardo, a citizen of Genoa, thoroughly distrusted the Greeks. He was uncompromising and dogmatic in his faith and had no respect for the Greek people, their church or their traditions. To him, the Greeks were cowardly and deceitful heretics whose professions of union with the Catholic Church were mere lip service paid in order to secure military assistance. Their theological contentions were the expressions of inferior minds and their intransigence the resistance of a stubborn and stiff-necked race.

Constantine sympathized with the Cardinal. Isidore's task would not be an easy one. Not only had he to contend with closed-minded Catholics like Leonardo, but also with the zealots within the Orthodox Church who regarded him as a traitor and a heretic. Traitor or not, the Emperor knew that the Cardinal's mission would only be successful if he could secure enough help from the West, particularly from Venice and Genoa, to prevent the City from falling to the Turks.

The Emperor's thoughts re-entered the church as Isidore reached the most politically charged moment of the mass. To the assembled congregation, he read the decrees of the Council of Florence proclaiming the unification of the churches. Prayers were offered for the Pope and the absent Patriarch Gregory who had fled into exile in Rome the year before, driven from Constantinople by enraged citizens who saw him as a tool of the Catholic Church. With a final blessing, the mass was concluded. Isidore invited the congregation to go in peace. Many of the Orthodox Constantinopolitans departed hastily, but the Emperor and his court remained. There were important political matters to discuss.

Leonardo approached the Cardinal.

"Your countrymen fled the church so quickly upon the conclusion of mass, your Eminence. I did not have the chance to offer my congratulations on their reunification with the true church." The archbishop had an arrogance that the Cardinal was hard-pressed not to answer. It took all of his tact to maintain civility.

"I'm sure they have much to do."

"Yes. No doubt they have run to their spiritual advisors to debate what actions they should now take against us. Even now that we are here as saviors, they show us no respect and would just as soon plant daggers in our backs as drink Christ's blood with us."

The archbishop, obnoxious though he was, was correct. Isidore knew that he was right and this made him even more miserable. Leonardo's manner was such that even when he spoke the truth, Isidore, against all Christian feelings, wanted to ram the words down his throat. The Cardinal was spared the necessity of a response by the approach of the Emperor and his ministers. Isidore descended from the altar and moved to greet him.

"Thank you, your Eminence, for the mass."

"You are welcome, your Majesty. I hope that it will serve as a landmark for the reunification of our faith."

"And as a formalization of our alliance against the enemies of our faith, your Eminence," added Yiorgos Sphrantzes, the Emperor's secretary.

"We remain sympathetic, as always, Master Sphrantzes to the threats we face."

"That threat has never been more immediate than now," said Constantine.

"His Holiness is aware of that, your Majesty. That is why he gave me the authority to recruit two companies of bowmen and gunners at his expense."

"Two hundred mercenaries will hardly be enough to turn back the armies of the Sultan," retorted Lukas Notaras.

"Indeed not, your Grace," replied the Cardinal calmly. "But that will not be the extent of his Holiness' support. At this very moment he is engaged in negotiations with both Venice and Genoa for men and ships to come to the defense of Christendom."

"We are in need of both," answered the Emperor attempting to take the sting out of Notaras's words. "With regard to ships, Venice has several large ships already in our harbors. It would be a true sign of our unity if you would intercede with the captains on our behalf and convince them of the necessity of staying with us until the Turkish threat has passed."

"I will speak with the Venetians, your Majesty. I will do what I can."

"Thank you. Good night." As he spoke, Constantine turned with Sphrantzes in tow, leaving the Latins alone in the grand cathedral. Lord Notaras followed close behind. He came up next to the Emperor and whispered to him.

"Is it for these allies that we have abandoned our faith and put ourselves under the sovereignty of the bishop of Rome?"

Constantine turned to his Grand Duke with weary eyes. "The Latins will fight with us."

"It is a sad day that the Emperor of Constantinople begs for help from heretics."

"It was the same with my brother and with my father before him. You can remember that because you were there." The Emperor's temper was rising. "Our divisiveness has brought us to this nadir, Lord Notaras, spiteful infighting of which the disrespectful criticism you level at your Emperor is just a lonely symptom. That is what has brought us to this position, where we must plead, and beg, and offer compromises, in order to survive. Had our ancestors put aside their differences to fight together against our common foes, instead of fighting for their own petty advancements, we should not be in this position!" The world-sick eyes were alive, the Palaeologos temper awakened.

"It is a heavy burden, my lord, sleep well on it." Constantine turned, leaving the silver lord to think on the situation. With great strides, the heir of Augustus left the glorious cathedral whose sanctity he could no longer protect without the aid of the foreign men who remained inside debating the future of his empire.

4—The *Condottiere*[*] : *January 26, 1453*

There was cheering along the sea walls. The citizens of Constantinople thronged the ramparts to see the two ships as they arrived. It was late January, and though the day was cold, the banner flying above the ships' decks warmed the hearts of the citizens. The top half of the standard bore the emblem of a crowned eagle against a golden sky. At the bottom half stood a gate with three towers on a crimson field. It was the coat-of-arms of the Giustiniani family, the Genoese lords of Chios. A century earlier, the family had won the island during the civil wars and the chaos that had plagued the reign of Emperor John V. They remained a nominal province of the Empire and paid a small tribute every year. Under its Genoese masters, Chios had become a land of warriors and scheming merchant families. A cartel of such families, the *Mahona*, was the true master of the island. And as the *Mahona* ruled Chios, the Giustiniani family ruled the *Mahona*.

The ships docked in the harbor, lowering their sails, throwing in their towlines and dropping anchor to the jubilant ovation of the populace. As the gangplank was lowered he arrived in glittering armor. He had intentionally worn full armor to impress the citizens. Likewise, he had ordered the seven hundred men under his command to appear on deck fully armed. Giovanni Giustiniani, citizen of Genoa, one time *podestà*[*] of Kaffa and master of urban defense, set foot on the dock and surveyed the city he had come to save.

The people continued to cheer as four hundred men-at-arms and three hundred archers disembarked with their equipment and supplies. Help had arrived. Some of the soldiers came from Genoa, others had been recruited by

---

[*] A mercenary war-leader common among the city-states of Italy during the fourteenth and fifteenth centuries.
[*] Governor of a Genoese colony.

Giustiniani in Chios. They had a distinctly professional air
that gave comfort to the cheering citizens.

A delegation of Byzantine courtiers stood on the dock to
welcome the *condottiere* as he stepped off the ship. He was a
man of average height with a medium complexion and wavy
brown hair. Those who saw him in the crisp sunlight of that
winter day, in his dazzling armor, no doubt found his face
handsome. He was thirty-six and still at the peak of his
physical powers. After being warmly greeted by the
Byzantines, to whom he spoke in excellent and fluid Greek,
he was told that he was to be conducted to the presence of
the Emperor. Constantine's emissary suggested that he
might be more comfortable out of his armor. The
condottiere agreed, returned to his ship and disappeared
below the deck. He emerged half an hour later. The steel
plates and mail had been removed. Beneath a dark blue
cloak ornamented in gold, he wore a red arming jacket and a
pair of dark blue tights. His steel *sabatons* had been put
aside in favor of soft, leather boots trimmed with fur.

Coming off the boat, the *condottiere* was brought to a
waiting horse. He swung himself into the saddle with
elegance and strength. There was a younger man
accompanying him. Imitating his commander, he also had
removed his armor and likewise mounted one of the waiting
horses. The youth resembled the warrior. Like the
condottiere, his face was handsome, but possessed
something of adolescent innocence. He was not more than
twenty years old. There was good reason for the
resemblance. The youth, Marco Giustiniani, was the
condottiere's nephew. At the request of the boy's father,
Giovanni had brought him along. It was time to begin his
education. The famous name brought with it the
responsibility for each generation to perpetuate the family's
glorious legacy through action, heroism and
accomplishment. Such was the way of the world.
Constantinople would be Marco's first taste of war.

Out of his armor, Giustiniani cut an even more dashing figure. As the party rode towards the imperial palace at Blachernae, the eyes of many of Constantinople's women traced his progress with interest. They rode west along the sea walls passing harbors and churches. The commander was pleased to see that the sea walls were strong and in good repair. He began to count the ships at anchor and make note of their flags. He saw ships from Genoa and Venice, as well as a handful of Greek ships under the Emperor's double headed eagle. There was enough of a navy that by the time Giustiniani reached the imperial palace he was feeling confident and hopeful about the defense of the City.

Marco, on the other hand, had not given much thought to the state of the sea walls, nor to the ships at anchor. His eyes were filled by the City itself. It was winter, and there were a few clouds, but they did not obscure the magnificence of the churches or the bustling buildings of the Phanar quarter through which they rode. Approaching the imperial palace, they had a slightly veiled view of the northern land walls around Blachernae. Giustiniani examined them with professional curiosity.

They passed through the gates of the imperial palace, dismounted, and were led up a winding stairway, then through rooms filled with chattering diplomats and courtiers. Giustiniani did not hear them, nor did he care to. He had already had his fill of courtiers. There were far too many of them and far too few soldiers. His mind focused on the task at hand—the defense of the City. He was anxious to meet the Emperor and to discuss details for the preparation for the siege. He also wanted to see the state of the land walls. From what he could glimpse around Blachernae, they were not in as good shape as the sea walls. The silent escort led him into a small and finely decorated room. There was a fire in the hearth which warmed it considerably. An icon of the Virgin Mary stood against the far wall with candles flickering in front of it.

"Please make yourself comfortable, my lord. His majesty will come shortly." His companion had been far from loquacious and after a bow left the soldier and his nephew alone in the room.

There was a ceramic pitcher filled with wine and ceramic drinking cups. They were cream colored with pictures of seabirds in green and blue painted on them. Marco moved to fill the cups. Giustiniani motioned that he didn't care for any wine.

"It's excellent wine, Giovanni. Are you sure you wouldn't like some?"

"No, Marco. But thank you." Giustiniani was more interested in the cups. While the painting and glaze work was fine, he had expected cups of gold, or at least silver in the Emperor's palace.

"It's quite a place. What did you think of those walls? And the towers! I've never seen anything so splendid in my life."

"Yes. It is a marvel of a city."

"It is indeed a marvel of a city, the finest in the world." The voice that came from behind Giustiniani was cultured and refined. It had in it a familiarity of command that the *condottiere* recognized from a life of soldiering. The Italian, while not native, was clear and well-spoken. The speaker, the Emperor Constantine Palaeologos, paused to give the startled Italians a chance to turn and bow. They quickly did so in great humility as if moved by a force greater than any of the individuals present. "The City is dear to me. It is my mother, wife, and empress all at once."

Giustiniani and Marco gazed into the royal visage that had appeared before them. The Emperor was a strong man only two weeks away from his forty-eighth birthday. His well-defined features were made all the more distinguished by his finely groomed beard. His hair was dark brown interspersed with strands of silver and his complexion the same rich honey as the City's walls. So captivated was the *condottiere* that he spoke directly to the Emperor without noticing the suite of attendants who had likewise entered the room.

"Your majesty, I am Giovanni Giustiniani Longo of Genoa. This is my nephew, Marco. We have come with two ships and seven hundred men to the service of your majesty in defense of the City against your enemies. We place ourselves under your command for the glory of Christendom and the honor of God."

"Thank you my lord. We greet you with open arms. You have our sincere gratitude for coming here in our hour of need. With your help, we are certain of victory against any foe. We know you to be among the finest soldiers in the world for the defense of cities. Stay with us and defend our city. In return, I appoint you commander of our land defenses with the rank of *protostrator*. When the Turks are successfully driven off, you shall have the island of Lemnos to govern, with our thanks."

"Your majesty, I am most grateful. I humbly accept your charge and will defend Constantinople until victory is won."

The formalities had been completed smoothly and with a swiftness that took the *condottiere* by surprise. Giustiniani was graciously introduced to the Emperor's suite, to Lukas Notaras the Grand Duke and Admiral of the Imperial Fleet, Cardinal Isidore the Papal Legate, Demetrios Cantacuzenos the Imperial Marshal, and the Emperor's cousin Theophilos Palaeologos. Admiral Alvise Diedo represented the Venetians and commanded the fleet. The leaders adjourned to a larger room so that they might better discuss the situation. It was the first council of war that Giustiniani attended. When it came his turn to speak, his professionalism and skill took center stage.

"I appreciate the honor your majesty has bestowed upon me by making me commander of the land defenses. You must all know that I have come to fight. I will not leave until the battle is won and the Turks are driven away. First, I would like to see the state of the land walls in order to determine where our weak points are and at the same time to see which areas are most in need of repairs."

Lukas Notaras frowned visibly. The presence of Giustiniani vexed him. Was it necessary to make this soldier of fortune the commander of the land defenses? Was it necessary for a foreigner to be brought into the Emperor's council?

"From my experience, I think it advisable for us to defend the outer wall. First, it is my impression that the outer fortifications are in better repair. Second, it will allow us to use the inner wall to deploy artillery, archers and gunners, and as a fall back position. Finally, if we defend the inner wall, the enemy will be able to use the outer wall for cover."

"The inner walls are taller. Do you not think that we should make our stand there?" The question was posed by Notaras.

Constantine responded.

"I believe the *condottiere*'s arguments for defending the outer wall are valid. After all, it was the course pursued by my brother, the Emperor John, against Sultan Murad. I appreciate your reasoning, but I cannot contemplate abandoning any part of the City, even the outer wall, to the enemy."

The *condottiere* continued: "Since your majesty has graciously given me the command of the land defenses, I would appreciate if you could tell me the exact number of men presently under arms within Constantinople."

"Sphrantzes, my secretary, will gather this information for you today. Yiorgo, please also provide Lord Giustiniani with an account of the number and types of weapons in our armories."

Sphrantzes nodded.

"Lord Notaras, as Admiral of the Fleet, will be responsible for the command of the sea walls and for our reserve, including our mobile cannon." Constantine sensed tension between Giustiniani and Notaras. There was no time for such things now. He would have to be careful that their budding rivalry did not interfere with the defense. "Admiral Diedo will retain supreme command of the Fleet and our naval operations. He can explain the situation at sea to you, *protostrator*."

"Thank you, your majesty," said the Venetian. "There are thirty-three vessels in Constantinople. Ten belong to the imperial fleet, there are six Venetian, five Genoese, nine from our colony of Crete, and one from each of Ancona, Spain and France. We Venetians have pledged to stay, and we are trying to convince the other captains to do likewise. With these forces, I feel confident that we can hold the Horn against anything the Sultan will bring."

"Lord Cantacuzenos, what is the situation on the land side?" asked the Emperor.

"We are clearing the foss‡ and continuing to repair the walls wherever we can. Finding enough stone is a problem and working during the winter weather is difficult. I am particularly concerned about Blachernae, sire, near your palace. That area is defended by a single wall and has no foss at all. When the ground softens in the spring we should extend the foss to protect the entire land side."

"Agreed. And we will have to move quickly, my lords. Mehmed will not wait once winter ends. At the end of March, early April at the latest, the Turks will arrive. We have two months to prepare. I thank you all for your council. Our *protostrator* must be tired after his voyage. Today's light is failing. We will reconvene tomorrow morning and show the commander the full scope of our defenses."

Giustiniani thanked the council and departed with Marco. The two captains were walking along back to their ship and the young man turned to his companion with a smile.

"Commander of the land defenses! *Bravo*, Giovanni! And the island of Lemnos, that was a bonus you could not have

---

‡ A ditch or dry moat dug in front of a defensive wall to impede enemy attacks.

expected." The initial success with the council coupled with seeing the fantastic City for the first time had put Marco in an ebullient mood.

"It will be a lot of work, Marco." The *condottiere*'s sober reflection was lost on the unbloodied youth. Giustiniani did not have time to press his case because over their shoulders they heard the sound of hurried footsteps trying to catch up with them.

"*Signori*," cried a Greek voice.

They turned and stopped. It was one of the Emperor's officials. He was out of breath. Obviously not a soldier, thought Giustiniani. Then he saw the face clearly and recognized the man as Sphrantzes, the Emperor's personal secretary.

"Greetings, *protostrator*."

"And to you, Master Sphranztes." The diplomat paused for a moment to catch his breath before continuing. Giustiniani and Marco exchanged a subdued smirk.

"I would like to thank you personally for coming to Constantinople. We all appreciate what you are doing and have every confidence in you and your men."

"Thank you."

"We are truly honored by your presence and encouraged by your great reputation."

The courtier's flattery was beginning to irritate the warrior. He responded without a hint of diplomacy.

"I wish the Grand Duke shared your opinion."

Sphrantzes grinned coyly.

"Not everyone agrees with Lord Notaras."

"I was under the impression that he was a man of importance whose opinion carried a great deal of weight."

It was now Sphrantzes' turn to allow the mask of courtly manner to fall.

"Lukas Notaras is an arrogant man. He resents your appointment as the commander of the land defenses. Even though he has never commanded a battle in his life, he feels that that honor should have gone to him." The secretary paused for a moment as if afraid that someone loyal to the silver lord could have overheard his words. Moving closer to the *condottiere*, he continued.

"I can tell you that not everyone sees eye to eye with his Excellency and that the opinions of other men also are highly regarded."

"Like yourself, Master Sphrantzes?"

Again Giustiniani saw the sly diplomat's smile. This time, it was accompanied by a hint of joy behind the dark eyes.

"It would be a lie to say that the Emperor does not value my opinion, or to argue that I have any great affection for the Grand Duke when you know that I do not. Still, he is a powerful man, and he must be respected. Were I in your position, *protostrator*, I would be careful of his Excellency."

"Thank you for your advice. I doubt there is anyone among the Emperor's court so qualified to give it."

Now, the *condottiere*, having absorbed the first verbal onslaught with such delicacy and effectiveness, turned to the offensive to extricate himself from the verbose secretary. At the same time, he decided to use the situation to play a joke on his nephew.

"Master secretary, I would ask one matter further of you. I heard the Emperor ask you about the number of men available for the defense. I would appreciate it if you could involve my aide, Marco, in this undertaking. I feel that it will be a useful learning experience for him, and at the same time he can help you and become familiar with the City."

The panic in Marco's expression almost made Giustiniani regret what he had done. Still, once an order is given, a commander cannot retract it. So Marco, devoid of scholarship as any sailor, and even more awkward in the matter of sums, was suddenly swept into conversation about the mini-census by the secretary. Giustiniani bade them both farewell and, chuckling to himself, walked away down the corridor for some much needed rest.

5—The Walls: *January 1453*

Giustiniani awoke at dawn, as the first rays of sunlight entered his cabin. He dressed immediately and went to wake his nephew. Marco was incoherent as his uncle shook the sleep from his foggy mind. "We're going on a tour of the land walls. Be ready in ten minutes." Marco just made out his uncle's shadow exiting the room as his eyes opened. With an enormous yawn, he launched himself out of bed and prepared for the day.

They began in the north, around Blachernae and the imperial palace, where the defenses were weakest. At the Kerkoporta postern, the double wall began, running south past the Chora Monastery and the Gate of Charisios, which opened onto the broad avenue of the *Mesé*. The walls were straight from this point until the Fifth Military Gate just above the River Lycus. From there, they bowed outwards to the Gate of Saint Romanos and the Fourth Military Gate. Here the battlements arched back in to the Gate of Rhegium. The roadways from all three points of entry converged on the single south-easterly road towards the Forum of Arcadius. To the south, the walls continued to the Third Military Gate, the Pegae Gate, the Second Military Gate and finally the Golden Gate that opened onto the quarter of Studion. Beyond this, the land fortifications met those of the sea at the Postern of Christ. The circuit made almost fourteen miles of stone. It was an enormous front. Worse, there were sections that were in poor repair and could hardly be considered ready for an assault. They had ridden the entire distance and returned to the Blachernae quarter to meet with the Emperor when Marco turned to his uncle with disappointment.

"The walls are in a rather poor state. They look run down up close."

Giustiniani was frowning as his nephew spoke. Marco was right. The scars of centuries were worse than he had expected.

"We've got to find something to patch them up with, and quickly. It's a pity there are no masons in our family. There'd be enough work here for two generations," said the younger man, trying to lighten the mood.

Giustiniani was still frowning and responded impatiently.

"I doubt that the Emperor has a supply of large cut stones just waiting to be lifted into place."

"If we don't do something to repair the walls, the City has no hope of standing a siege."

It was the first truly pessimistic statement that Giustiniani had heard from Marco. Oddly, Marco's adoption of his uncle's realism struck the contrarian nature within the *condottiere*. He snapped back:

"We're not dead men yet. We'll find a way to stop the Turks, whatever they throw against us."

Marco did not respond, but Giustiniani had given himself an idea. There was in fact a great deal of stone within Constantinople, cut stone lying around and being used for no structural purpose at all—tombstones. It was hardly an auspicious source, but it just might serve the purpose. There were few alternatives. He would bring the idea to the Emperor. Perhaps his majesty would be able to convince the priests that removing the headstones was not a violation of the tombs themselves. It was worth a try.

Marco detected something in his expression. "What is it, Giovanni?"

"I have an idea. Come." The *condottiere* said nothing more but spurred his horse to the north, towards the area beyond the imperial palace. Marco went after him.

"Are you going to tell me?" he shouted over the pounding hooves of the cantering horses. "Are we going to see the Emperor?"

But Marco's words were scattered by the wind. The riders moved along the walls and past the imperial palace, but Giustiniani kept riding. The two horses were nearing the northernmost point of the walls, near the church of Saint Mary in Blachernae before the *condottiere* slowed to a walk. They were on holy ground.

"What in God's name is on your mind, Giovanni?" demanded the young man.

Giustiniani had leapt from his saddle and was moving with powerful strides into the cemetery next to the church. Marco did not understand, and dismounted to follow his uncle.

"What are we doing here? I thought you said we weren't dead yet?"

"The tombstones, you fool. Look at the stones."

Giustiniani was right. Marco understood. Together, the two began to examine the stones. Those graves not marked by simple crosses had headstones. The majority of these were large and solid blocks of cut stone. Most would serve very well to fill in and patch the ancient walls. It wasn't the perfect solution, but they were sure that it would work.

"Are you going to tell the Emperor?"

"I will ask him this morning when we meet with the council."

"It's an excellent idea, Giovanni." They smiled and spurred their horses towards to imperial palace, where they were ushered into Constantine's presence.

"Welcome, *protostrator*, I hope you slept well."

"I did, your majesty. I have just come from riding along the land walls and have come to the conclusion that they are in dire need of repairs. New stones are needed for the work. Is there any supply of stone available for this purpose?"

Constantine shook his head knowingly and led Giustiniani towards the council table.

"We are aware of this problem, *protostrator*, but unfortunately, there is no stone in the City that can be used, and we have little capacity to venture outside to supply you with the materials you surely need."

Giustiniani thought of how best to phrase his idea. "Sire, there is a possibility that might have been overlooked."

The eyes of the council fell upon the soldier. Notaras's were the most critical.

"What is that?" demanded the Grand Duke. The Emperor cast the silver lord a glance but did not reprimand him for his abruptness.

"With your permission, we can use tombstones to repair the walls. The stone is of good quality and already cut."

"That is an irreverent suggestion!" exploded Notaras.

"Irreverent or not, my lord, I see no other source of stone with which to repair the city walls. Let me make it clear that there is no intention to touch the tombs themselves, merely the stones marking the graves."

Constantine responded.

"This is a difficult question, *protostrator*. I will consider it." The Emperor turned to his councilors and asked them to leave him alone with the *condottiere*. Giustiniani told Marco to return to their ship and await further orders. Sovereign and soldier were now alone. Constantine's expression was drawn. The warrior sensed that there was something on his mind.

The Emperor stood motionless at a window, gazing into the City. Constantine saw small clusters of houses and open fields. Different quarters appeared distinct and separate. The once homogeneous metropolis had become a patchwork of individual cities divided by pastures and even a few makeshift walls. *"Constantinople, where has your glory gone?"* he thought. *"This is all that remains."* He turned to Giustiniani.

"Come to the window, lord marshal." The *condottiere* obeyed, and the two men stared out in silence. "This City is the last bastion of my empire. It is the heart of my empire. I am enormously grateful that you have come to help me defend it. The City is the only important possession left to us Romans. You Latins call us Greeks, just as we call you Franks, but I cannot forget that Constantinople has passed directly from Saint Constantine to me. Our history stretches back in an unbroken line to the Emperors of Rome, all the way to Augustus. It was long ago that St. Constantine founded this City. He built it to be the capital of imperial Rome, the capital of the true faith, a glorious capital for one empire under one emperor and one God. For over one thousand years, it has been exactly that."

The *condottiere* did not answer.

"I was born here, *protostrator*. It is the only home I have ever known. I love this City more than anything in the world, and once more, our enemies are coming to destroy it. I fear that, at last, they may succeed." There was a pause as both men confronted the future, before the Emperor pulled the conversation back to the present. "Have you ever had an enemy come to destroy your home, *protostrator*?"

"No, my lord. But then again, no place has even been so much a true home for me as Constantinople is to you." The Emperor nodded, pleased with the answer.

"You have traveled much in the world and seen a great deal. I would like to ask you something, but you must answer honestly—will you?"

"I shall, your majesty."

"As I have said, it was many centuries ago, over a thousand years, that my namesake founded this city. So much has changed since then. The empire has crumbled, bit by bit. Turks, Franks, Venetians, and even your countrymen have all taken parts of it. Of all the lands we once controlled, now there are only a few islands, my brothers in the Morea and the City. No, my lord, do not seek to defend the actions of your people. I am not accusing you. The past is buried. But I wish to ask you if you think that our time is ending."

There was silence.

"Sire, this is not a question I can answer." The *condottiere's* response was slow, his words weighted with uncertainty.

"We are an ancient civilization *protostrator*, an ancient people. I wonder if our vigor has not been diluted by the generations. Have we been corrupted by greed and civil wars? I wonder if it is not time for us to pass away."

"Why do you say that, your majesty?"

"I have seen other peoples, Venetians, Genoese, the Turks, rising and conquering. They brim with life and confidence. You and your men have come here, seven hundred strong, to fight for Christendom, for *our* City. The Venetian captains have pledged their lives and their honor to the defense. Many of your countrymen in Pera have come here, freely offering their lives and fortunes when they know that we have nothing to give them for their efforts. *Bailò* Minotto has written to Venice requesting that the *Signoria* send a fleet. Everywhere, people are making sacrifices for the sake of the City. And today, Sphrantzes tells me that there are no more than five thousand Greeks within these walls to bear arms in our struggle."

Giustiniani heard the appallingly small figure. Shock registered in his eyes. Involuntarily his mouth opened to speak, but there were no words.

"You are surprised. The population of our city has bled away for three centuries. There are few young men here to fight for our freedom. Too many have left or been killed. Others have chosen to follow a path to God as monks or priests and cannot be expected to fight. Still, I have ordered the monasteries to send anyone who can, with second-hand weapons, to protect the southern sea walls where the natural defenses are strongest in case the Sultan tries to surprise us. This information about our numbers must not become known to anyone. With your men, the Venetians, the two hundred soldiers of the Cardinal, the citizens from Pera, and the other foreigners who have stayed to fight, our total for the land defense will hardly amount to eight thousand men."

Giustiniani was downcast. The odds were enormous.

"Eight thousand men, sire? With so few, it will be impossible for us to man the perimeter of the entire City."

"It will be difficult. So, my lord, I ask you again. Has God decided that the Empire should be no more? If, at this moment, when the enemy is upon us, we have so few citizens to defend their homes and must rely on the generosity and strength of others, do you think it is because our energy as a people is spent?"

Giustiniani thought for a moment. How could he answer? He agreed with the Emperor that the fighting spirit of the Greeks had certainly declined since their days of glory. The legacy of the recent past was one of defeat and suffering, diplomatic duplicity and dynastic intrigue. He responded in the only manner he thought appropriate.

"Your majesty is a man of great courage and a just ruler. I cannot believe that God has willed it that you would lose your crown and your city."

The Emperor smiled, knowing that the question had been turned aside rather than answered. The *condottiere* would not be maneuvered into giving a direct response.

"I thank you for your compliment *protostrator*. The coming months will test its truth. If we survive, I believe it will only be through the mercy and grace of God."

Giustiniani seemed unmoved.

"That is something else I would ask you."

He paused and assessed the younger man before him, a man of war and action. Yet the Emperor felt a strange camaraderie and understanding with this man. There was comfort in the direct simplicity of the warrior that made him the one person Constantine wished to open his heart to.

"Do you believe God will help us in our time of need?"

Giustiniani was not a religious man, but he knew the Emperor was and hoped his words would carry sincerity.

41

"God has been very kind to me throughout my life, your majesty. I cannot say that He has ever failed me in any meaningful situation. I believe that He will not abandon the City now."

"Then we shall continue to pray to Him—you and I, *protostrator*—and hope that our prayers will be answered."

Silence reigned over the two men as they gazed out at the City in the dying afternoon light. Evening was approaching rapidly. Giustiniani had eaten only a bite in the saddle while looking over the walls, and was hungry. The Emperor seemed content to leave the conversation as it stood. Sensing that the *condottiere* was eager to leave, Constantine spoke once more:

"One final thought, my lord. If you have not done so already, make yourself known to your countrymen in the colony of Pera. Perhaps you can convince them to lend us their support. Goodnight, lord Marshal."

Giustiniani excused himself and returned along the northern sea walls to his ship. His mind dwelled on what the Emperor had said. Eight thousand men. What chance did they have? He had come to fight and to triumph, not to sacrifice his life in a cause that was already lost. The instinct for self-preservation, which had kept him alive in a score of battles, was awakened by the Emperor's words. Doubt began to creep into his mind about whether he had made the right decision in coming. Voices in his mind began tempting him to leave and to survive. But how could he leave now? He was the commander of the City's defenses, a warrior admired for his courage and honor. And the City was still strong. The walls had never failed in a thousand years. He would see to it that they did not fail now.

* * *

Battling these thoughts, Giustiniani returned to his ship. Marco greeted him anxiously with a smile.

"Welcome home Giovanni. I waited for you to eat." He paused. "Is something the matter?"

He did not want to speak, to burden his nephew with the news, or to ugly the evening with a confession of his doubts.

"I'm tired. It's been a long day. Let's eat."

The two men sat down to their table. Dinner was a chicken, a small bird from one of the local farmers, all Marco had been able to buy, and a couple of small fish that the crew had caught and offered to their captain's table. There were a few preserved olives from the ship's stores and onions from another Constantinopolitan farmer. The chicken had been roasted with crushed almonds and fennel. They ate hungrily, speaking little and picked the last bones clean. When everything had been consumed, Giustiniani stood:

"I'm going across to Pera. I must meet with the *podestà* and ask for his support personally."

"I'll come with you."

"No." Already Giustiniani was shielding his nephew, protecting him from discovering the desperate odds. "I'll go alone." The tone left Marco no room to argue, and the commander was quickly gone, shouting for a boat to take him the short distance across the Golden Horn.

Giustiniani watched Constantinople recede as the rowboat pulled its way to the Genoese colony of Pera. The magnificence of the city was gradually restored as each stroke of the oars blurred the imperfections with distance. But Giustiniani was not deceived by appearances and felt the need for cooperation with his countrymen was greater than ever. But would they help? Could he convince Genoa to join the side of the Greeks and the Venetians, risking war and destruction at the hands of the world's most powerful empire? The boat was approaching the dock. Sight of the *condottiere*'s banner had already caused a small commotion, and a representative of the *podestà* was waiting to greet him. And then he saw her. She was standing toward the back of the crowd, two dozen yards away, her long dark hair, as

unmistakable as her charcoal eyes, and the long slim nose
that led invitingly to her full crimson lips. A shiver passed
over him as those eyes caught his, held them for a moment
and then turned away, exuding hatred and regret. Caterina
Luccio, the woman Giustiniani loved, the woman he had left
all those years before. Caterina Luccio, here in Pera, a few
yards, and a lifetime, away.

"Lord Giustiniani?" The voice of the *podestà*'s secretary
wrenched him to reality.

"Yes."

"I am Antonio di Michiele, the secretary of *Podestà*
Lomellino. His Excellency is eager to meet you. Please follow
me."

Giustiniani turned, searching for Caterina, but she was
gone. He began to wonder if she had been an illusion. The
secretary led him away from the crowd to the governor's
palace, through the vestibule and up the marble steps to the
podestà's audience chamber. Angelo Lomellino greeted his
famous countryman courteously and immediately delved
into the intricacies of their situation. At first encounter, the
podestà of Pera seemed a decent man. A small figure with
brown hair, matted down with sweat and watery gray eyes.
He spoke with great concern for the safety of his colony in
the event of war. They were speaking of international
politics, war, and the rise and fall of empires, but
Giustiniani's mind could not focus on Angelo Lomellino and
his diplomatic machinations. The *podestà* would not commit
the colony of Pera to the fight, so Giustiniani had turned
deaf to the banal and convoluted explanations for the
decision. His eyes wandered the room aimlessly: the table,
the servant bringing candles for the evening, the glowing
logs in the fireplace, the window. His mind could only see
her and his body yearned to feel her.

"Do you agree, my lord?" The *podestà* was asking a
question.

"I sympathize with your position, your Excellency. It is a difficult one. But, I think you will find—if you examine the situation—that a Turkish victory will bring suffering to your colony."

"I agree that this is not the result we would prefer, but consider our situation. As subjects of Genoa, we have no desire for Constantinople to survive only to become a tool of Venice. Better to have a Sultan who we can negotiate with. As a Genoese, you can surely understand that."

"Caution in this situation is understandable and commendable, but we must think about the future. Pera will not remain free if Mehmed conquers Constantinople. Our entire position in this region will be reduced. Our trade will suffer. Ships going to and from Kaffa, to anywhere in the Black Sea, will have to pass through the Bosphorus and be subject to the Sultan's taxes and inspections. Success here will embolden Mehmed like nothing else. His power will spread throughout the Aegean and threaten every colony we have."

"But expanding Turkish power may balance the power of Venice and, if we stay in the Sultan's good graces, provide us opportunities for profit. I know that Genoa has no desire to court the possibility of war with Mehmed."

"This war, *podestà*, may not be our choice. Our choice may not be between war and peace but between destruction and survival."

"I see no need to overly dramatize the situation. We will deal with war when it comes, if it comes. Until then, I cannot act in any official capacity that might jeopardize the neutrality of Genoa or the safety of Pera."

"Perhaps, in a less official way, you could inform your people of the odds we face and at least allow them to cross over if they wish to fight with us."

"That is a possibility, my lord. The citizens of Pera are free individuals. I will offer them this choice. Dine with us next week and we will speak about this further."

"It will be my pleasure, *Signor* Lomellino."

The *condottiere* suppressed a yawn. Fatigue was starting to overtake him. It had been a long day.

"Are you tired, my lord?"

"My apologies, *podestà*. I am. I have had a tiring day." Giustiniani wished to leave, and so he continued: "You are busy as well. Please excuse me. The next months will be difficult, but together, I am sure we will persevere."

"I wish there was more I could do, my lord, but as I have tried to explain, my position is extremely difficult."

As the oars pulled Giustiniani back to Constantinople, two objectives rose in his mind: to win a woman and to save a city. Caterina Luccio would not leave his thoughts. How her gaze had humbled him and torn at his soul. He had still not recovered from its sting. He had been wrong to leave her, wrong to abandon her, wrong to choose the way he had. Her last words to him were rooted in his brain. *"I loved you like no other. I loved only you. But you have chosen a different life and I am no part of it. I will never forgive you or see you again."* His eyes closed around her vision.

6—The Court: *February 1453*

The palace apartments were in an uproar; Sultan Mehmed had disappeared. Mustafa ran through the corridors, peering into one empty room after another, but there was no sign of the Sultan.

Halil Pasha came out of his apartments swathed in a rich, green night robe. "What's all the commotion, Mustafa?" he demanded.

"The Sultan, Lord Halil! The Sultan has disappeared!"

"Allah protect us," lamented the Vizier. "When did you see him last?"

"A few hours ago. I served him his dinner, and he told me to leave him alone."

"Find him, Mustafa. Find him. Take fifty of the Janissaries, comb every street from here to the city walls and find him."

Just then, Gülbahar entered the corridor. The noise had awakened her. Across the torch-lit hall she saw the Grand Vizier. There was a moment of uneasy silence before she turned on Mustafa.

"What's going on?" she demanded.

"Nothing, my lady. Please return to your room."

"I wish to see the Sultan," she commanded.

Before Mustafa could answer, Halil closed the length of the hallway, interposing himself between them. He turned to Mustafa. "You have your orders."

Gülbahar smiled scornfully. "Have you lost him?"

"Go to bed, Lady Gülbahar," answered the Grand Vizier calmly. He turned to leave.

"What are you afraid he will see out there, Vizier?" His title escaped her lips like a curse.

"I am concerned for his safety."

She laughed cynically. A chattering, mocking laugh which shivered the Grand Vizier.

"Afraid for him? I doubt it. You are afraid for yourself. Afraid that he will see the sewers and shacks of Adrianople for what they are. Afraid that he will see that this is no city for a king." Each sentence brought her closer to him. Now she was practically touching him. He could feel the jasmine-scented breath from her mouth on his face as she spoke. The moon-white face was looking up at his with its glittering eyes. "And you are most afraid that you are losing your control over him. Every time he sets foot outside of this palace without you, you feel your grip on him slipping away."

Halil listened to her words without reacting.

"But *I can* control him, Lord Vizier. I can shape his desires. Because desire is what I know. His," she was touching him now, the taut young body next to his own, "and yours."

Halil half-smiled; that fire had gone out, rendering him impervious to her charms. "I am flattered, Lady Gülbahar, that a woman of your age would be interested in an old man like me."

She recoiled. "The old men of this palace," she replied, "would do well to remember that this is an empire of young men. It is driven by their desires and not by a burnt-out illusion of peace clung to by men reaching the end of life's road. Our lord will achieve his destiny with or without you, Halil Pasha."

"His destiny is to rule a great and powerful nation, to bring it peace and prosperity."

"His destiny is an empire greater than the world has ever seen with Constantinople as its capital. His destiny is glory and conquest that a weakened old man like you no longer even dreams of."

The words finally stung Halil Pasha's pride. Looking down into the olive-black eyes he answered: "You are driven by an ambition worn out of you by a lifetime in this world, by a lifetime of seeing agony, hatred, and suffering. Yours is

48

an ambition that can never be quenched because it seeks to overcome itself. Your ambition is like you, born in the pig-pens of Albania. No glory, no riches will ever wash that stench from you."

She struck him, a powerful blow across the face.

"One day I will hold your head in my hands, Vizier, and I will pull congealed blood from the hairs of your beard!" She screamed the words in anger and rushed to strike him again. He caught her hands as they reached for him and turned them aside.

"Good night, my lady. The smell of swine in this corridor is too strong for me."

Furious, Gülbahar turned back to her room overturning tables, scattering clothing, and spilling powder on the floor. With the Vizier's insult ringing in her ears, she tore at silken gowns and shattered mirrors. The Pasha, her Pasha, in his rages, had mocked her the same way, but the years had failed to dull her sensitivities. She craved revenge against the Vizier, but there could be no confession to Mehmed. For the Sultan to know of her humiliation at Halil's hands would satisfy nothing. Halil's words would diminish her in an instant. So she brooded in her room, waiting for her Sultan to return.

* * *

With only one bodyguard, Mehmed had sneaked away from the palace and into the city of Adrianople. The ceremony of the court was driving him mad. In the darkness, he walked the streets of his capital taking in the ordinary events that he so rarely saw, trying to bring peace to his restless mind. He had played and replayed the siege in his mind. His drawings of siege engines, harmless on the page, mocked him with their promise. The pashas had returned to their provinces to raise armies that grew fat and soft during a winter of inaction. Would it never be spring? Allah alone commanded the earth and the heavens, and Mehmed, so accustomed to exercising authority, could not stand something so much out of his control. Too proud and powerful in his youth, too confident in his own gifts to pray, he cast his eyes to heaven and demanded that Allah bring the campaigning season early.

There was nothing for him in the streets of Adrianople, made lonely by the winter wind. It was a poor city, a capital unworthy of him. Boiling over with disgust and impatience, Mehmed had returned to the palace. Entering his apartments, he dismissed Mustafa and threw himself on the vermilion bed. He had no desire to sleep. He rose from the bed, left his room and moved swiftly down the corridor to Gülbahar's apartments. Without hesitation he opened the heavy door to her bedroom and stood, expectantly, in the doorway.

Gülbahar rose immediately and came towards him. "My lord, I was not told to prepare myself. I did not know you wished to see me."

"I did not tell anyone to prepare you," he said, not moving from the doorway.

"Come in, my lord," she answered, sensing his unease. "Sit with me a while."

"I have come from the city." His voice was still distant.

"I know. Mustafa was searching everywhere for you. And Halil Pasha too."

"Halil Pasha?" Anger brought his mind back from far away.

"No one knew where you were." She led him from the doorway and they sat together on the bed. "Why do you waste your time with such trivial things? You are a king. Kings do not walk through slums in the dead of night."

"I have been working too hard. I couldn't go on. My mind has not rested since you spoke to me about Constantinople. What have you planted in me? I cannot free myself from it.

Now, in winter, with spring so far away, I'm losing my mind."

Gülbahar had not seen Mehmed this way before. There was no trace of his usual arrogance or self-assurance, Constantinople was weighing on his soul. Wisely holding back her sarcasm, she offered him comfort.

"Spring will come, my lord. And when it does, you will be ready to fulfill your destiny. Constantinople is your destiny. It is for you, not for the broken down Greek pretenders or their Italian mercenaries. Spring will come, I promise, and Constantinople will be yours."

"It has never fallen."

"You have never tried to take it."

"But what if I fail?"

"You will not fail. You will not allow yourself to fail."

"And Halil Pasha?"

"Your Vizier is a cautious old man. He will not oppose you openly. He cannot oppose you openly as long as you are careful and successful. He must wait for you to give him an opportunity by making a mistake. Once you are victorious, you will deal with Halil Pasha."

"My father made him my Vizier, but he acts like my jailer, like an inflexible, old schoolteacher."

"You must have patience, my lord."

"You counsel patience as he does," answered Mehmed accusingly.

"Not as he does, my lord. Halil counsels patience to thwart your desires; I counsel patience to turn your desires into reality. And you have loyal men, Zagan Pasha, Shahabeddin. They will support your war."

"But why will they support me? Not from love, but from greed. I don't trust them."

"You do not have to trust them or their motivation. For now they are yours, yours to use to achieve your goals. That is all that matters. Victory is all that matters."

Seduced by her voice and her logic, Mehmed took her in his arms, feeling himself alive again.

"Victory *is* all that matters," he responded. "And victory will be mine."

7—The House of the *Podestà*: *February 1453*

The last days of January slipped away in work, and Giustiniani remembered the dinner he had promised the *podestà* of Pera. He had little desire to leave the preparations for the defense to spend an evening in the tiring company of Angelo Lomellino and the tortuous explanations about why he could not help. However, on the small chance that something might be accomplished, and because it was not wise to insult his countrymen, the *condottiere* sent a message accepting the *podestà*'s invitation for dinner. In his heart, he knew there was another reason—against every hope, he dreamed that by some trick of fate he would see Caterina in Pera.

An hour after sunset, Giustiniani and Marco were rowed across the Golden Horn to Pera. Antonio was on the dock to greet them, and they were led to the *podestà*'s official residence for dinner. Lomellino was in the dining hall which was formally decorated for the occasion. He rose to greet the *condottiere* and his nephew.

"Welcome, Lord Giustiniani, welcome. I'm so glad you were able to accept my invitation. We have much to discuss. Let me introduce you to our other guests." Lomellino made a circuit of the half-dozen notables from Pera and Genoa who had been invited. "This is Captain Bartolommeo Soligo. He has two ships in the harbor and is adamant about staying to help Constantinople."

"A pleasure, Captain Soligo. Any help that Pera offers to us is truly welcome. You must come with me to Constantinople and speak with Alvise Diedo, commander of the Venetian ships. The Emperor has appointed him commander of our fleet."

Soligo, a tall man of thirty with curly light brown hair nodded his assent and added, "I can only speak for myself,

53

but will offer any help I can for *signor* Diedo and his majesty the Emperor."

"This, *condottiere*, is my nephew Imperiali and his wife, the lady Isabella."

"I am honored, my lady."

"Imperiali, I'm afraid, agrees with Captain Soligo. Tonight, I fear, I will be outnumbered in preaching caution," said the *podestà* wearily. "They are younger men and crave excitement."

Giustiniani indulged in a slight smile. "I know what your Excellency means. This is my nephew, Marco Giustiniani. I'm sure he and Imperiali will have much to discuss. Shall we sit?"

"In a moment: there is one other person I would like you to meet. Once I find her." Lomellino scanned the room. Suddenly, she appeared, "Ah! Lord Giustiniani, this, is my wife, Caterina."

She was wearing a dress of red and black velvet, high-waisted and opening wide towards the floor. Her cinnamon hair was pulled back tightly in the current fashion, and the front strands had been removed to open her face and extend her forehead. She wore a black velvet band on the back of her head which fit three perfectly curled locks that reached to the middle of her neck. There was a single string of pearls, tight around her throat that glowed white hot against her skin. Her lips seemed to throb in the candlelight, more seductively than Giustiniani had ever seen them.

"This, Caterina, is the famous Giovanni Giustiniani."

They stood opposite each other for a moment, a passing moment which would not end, with neither of them able to speak.

"My lady," Giustiniani bowed formally and turned to the *podestà*. "You are a truly lucky man, your Excellency."

The *podestà* smiled, gratified, familiar with the reaction of men to Caterina. "I am."

"And he has the good sense to recognize his luck, *signore*," said Caterina. Her voice was edged with scorn detectable only to Giustiniani, half angry, half regretful.

"I have learned, in a lifetime of soldiering, that the ability to recognize the nature of a situation is a skill of enormous importance."

"And what is your present situation, *condottiere*?"

"Strong, my lady."

"Lord Giustiniani is a master of the defense of walled-cities," volunteered Lomellino. "If anyone can hold Constantinople, it is he."

"Then, as an expert in such matters, how would you characterize our situation here in Pera?" asked Caterina, unwilling to let anyone else dictate the conversation.

"I would say that it is precarious."

"Precarious because our safety depends on a man like you who fights for money?" Lomellino frowned. The bitterness in his wife's voice was now less latent.

"My dear, the *condottiere* does not fight for money, he has come out of duty."

"Forgive me, Angelo." She had no desire to appear rude in front of her husband, or to hint that there was something between her and the *condottiere*, but she refused to back down. "So, *condottiere*, if you are here for duty, then you are willing to die in Constantinople?"

"My dear, please, do not speak of death. Lord Giustiniani is a soldier."

"As a soldier, then, he should be comfortable with the subject. Are you willing to die here?" she pressed.

"I am willing to fight here, Lady Caterina. And being willing to fight is to be willing to die. But I am not eager to die. Presently, I am eager only to eat."

"Indeed," interjected Lomellino, happy for the conversation to shift. "Let us eat."

"Let us eat," echoed Caterina. "As tonight's hostess, I would be remiss if I stood in the way of the desires of one of our guests."

Giustiniani's eyes caught hers for a moment. The word "desires" struck a chord between them, suggesting both the *condottiere*'s selfishness and the feelings that they both still shared but willfully submerged.

At dinner, Caterina was separated from Giustiniani, sitting to her husband's left, while the *condottiere* occupied the seat of honor on his host's right. Soligo sat on Giustiniani's other side and the two spent much of the evening in practical discussions about the City's defense. Lomellino, for his part, remained unmoved by Giustiniani's efforts to gain more overt support for the fight from Pera, but the *podestà* did agree to allow anyone who wished to cross over to fight. The Emperor would be given permission to deploy the ancient defensive chain across the mouth of the Golden Horn and attach it to the walls of Pera. All Genoese ships would be given a choice about fighting with Diedo and the fleet. It was not everything that Giustiniani wanted, but it was something.

After their initial exchange, Caterina remained remarkably quiet, making polite conversation with her husband and with Marco, who sat to her left, but saying nothing further to Giustiniani. As the dinner finished, Giustiniani thanked his host, invited Soligo to Constantinople in the coming days to make further preparations, and with a slightly tipsy Marco, left the *podestà*'s home.

"They seem decent fellows, eh, Giovanni?"

"Decent enough. Some of them will help. Soligo and Imperiali at least."

"Lomellino's wife's a beautiful one, isn't she?"

"Very."

"Oh, don't sound so wistful, Giovanni, she's probably a cold one. Too philosophical. The way she went on at first, she was worse than that fellow Notaras."

"She's a woman of unique talents."

"It sounds like you wish she wasn't married to the governor of Pera?"

"Marco, you've had too much to drink. The wine is giving you delusions," responded Giustiniani with feigned seriousness.

"The *podestà* has an amazing cellar, but if I had to chose between his wife and his cellar, ha-ha! And you would make the same choice, because you don't even like wine. Even if she is a bit cold."

"Hot and cold are relative things, Marco. Perhaps you said nothing she found interesting."

"She's not my age, after all."

"As if she would have you at any age!"

"Hot and cold are seasonal too, uncle. And while she turns me to winter, it seems you are in the heat of summer. Speaking of seasons, you are both by now in the autumn of your lives. Perhaps that explains the affinity."

"Autumn? All right, nephew, enjoy your little joke, but you've mistaken autumn for a cool summer night. And if you're not careful," teased Giustiniani, "you will be spending the rest of this winter with the Emperor's secretary checking the number of arrows in the imperial armory."

"I repent, wholeheartedly, uncle. I pray God that I age as gracefully as you," responded Marco in mock apology.

They smiled. The boat arrived in Constantinople and they disembarked.

"I'm going to our ships for a while, Marco. There are a few matters I need to attend to. You should go home to the house in Blachernae. I will meet you there in the morning, and we will see the Emperor to give him our news. Goodnight."

"Goodnight, uncle."

* * *

There was a breeze growing, as Marco arrived in the Phanar quarter, walking from the dock further east where the ship had landed. Pulling his cloak about him, Marco turned and walked towards his billet in Blachernae, passing the Venetian quarter as he went. Though it was late, he detected movement. Something was going on at the quay. His curiosity piqued, he moved towards the harbor. Nearing the sea, he felt the wind again. Beneath the flickering light of torches, he saw goods and provisions being loaded onto a galley. The ship, which looked ready to sail, bore the standard of the red and gold lion of Venice.

"What's going on here?" he demanded.

No one saw fit to respond. He went over to a sailor carrying a large sack and interposed himself between the man and his ship.

"Where are you going with that?"

"Out of my way," hissed the Venetian.

"I asked you a question, friend. Why will you not answer me?"

"'Friend,' who are you to call me that? I don't even know who you are."

"My name is Marco Giustiniani of Genoa. And you?"

"Ha! A Genoese. Go about your business. What we do here doesn't concern you."

"If you are leaving Constantinople, it concerns me very much. I have come here to fight for the life of the City. Have you chosen to abandon us to the mercy of our enemies?"

"We are free men. We do as we wish."

"Then you *are* leaving. I cannot believe it. What of your countrymen? Hundreds of Venetians have pledged to stay and fight."

"That is no concern of mine. Let me pass."

"Where is your captain? How can he have decided to flee? I demand to speak with your captain!"

"I said out of my way, boy!"

The Venetian bulled his way past Marco. Fury took possession of him and the youth grabbed the Venetian's arm and sent his right fist crashing into the man's jaw. The sailor staggered back and dropped his bundle. Regaining his balance, the sailor lowered his head and charged, hammering the wind from Marco's lungs as he butted forward. Marco grabbed the man, and the pair fell to the quay where they became a tangle of strained arms and legs attempting to gain advantage. Immediately, other Venetians noticed the commotion and moved forward to stop the two combatants. An officer pulled them to their feet.

"What is the meaning of this?" He looked at Marco. "Who in hell are you?"

"Marco Giustiniani."

"Giustiniani? Are you a relation of the *condottiere*?"

"He's my uncle."

"Why were you fighting with one of my sailors?"

"Why has Venice decided to run away from this fight?"

"Were I in your position, young man, I would not presume to ask such questions. Your name and your famous kinsmen do not give you the right to judge other men who have seen so much more of the world than you have."

"You have seen so much in the world, *signore*, but would leave this battle without a single sight of the enemy?"

"We are leaving to live our own lives. Fears that may or may not be realized are not our concern. Stay if you wish, but this is not our fight." The officer turned to leave and walked up onto his ship. The gangplank was pulled up behind him. From the dock, Marco shouted into the darkness: "The Sultan will come, and God curse you for a coward when he does!"

59

The captain of the ship, Piero Davanzo heard the voice calling from the quay as the officer came to his side on the bridge.

"What was the commotion, Matteo?"

"Nothing captain. One of my men had an argument with some Genoese soldier."

"An argument? Over what?"

"It was nothing captain."

"Stop trying to shield the man. What was it about?"

"The Genoese objected to our leaving."

"Your tone suggests you share that view. Don't look away from me; I want an answer."

Matteo bit his lower lip. "Our countrymen have all chosen to stay, sir. *Bailò* Minotto called for help, and Alvise Diedo has stayed to command the fleet. It seems strange that we should leave."

Davanzo smirked. "You recite to me a litany of famous names, but you don't put your own on it. If departing is such a dishonor for you, why don't you remain here? I, for one, have no intention of sacrificing my life for a cause that is not mine, for a sovereign who is not mine, in a land that is not mine. If you wish to fight this vainglorious battle to protect foreigners who are already doomed, I will not stand in your way."

Matteo did not answer his captain so Davanzo pressed his argument. "Do you honestly think that there is any chance for victory against the Sultan? No power on earth can stand against his army. Certainly this fetid shred of ancient glory cannot escape him. And even if the Turks should fail this season, what will stop them from taking the prize next year or the year after that? There is no reason for us to stand against this tide. You do not answer me. I should have known that there was no conviction behind your ostentatious words. We are merchants, not soldiers, not heroes. Let the Diedos of this world, the Cornaros, the Minottos, the well-bred patricians with the glorious names spill their blood in these foreign quarrels. What can such actions bring us except suffering and loss? What will it bring them, except a foreign grave?"

"Leaving like this will bring dishonor to our names forever."

"It is no dishonor to me to put my duty to my home and my family before Constantinople."

Silence took hold of both men. Within Matteo, the contending forces continued their battle. Was it right to die so far from home in a battle Venice had not sought and did not want? Was it honorable to leave Maria, his young wife, and their baby girl alone in the world? Pulling his cloak about him to ward off the cold, he turned away and walked to his cabin. Davanzo watched him leave, confident from his victory. He stood alone at the back rail of the ship's stern castle, threw back his head to look at the stars, and felt the breeze float through his hair. He took a deep breath.

There was a decent wind. It would be more than enough to fill the sails of his ships and take them to safety. This night had been long in coming. He breathed in the cold air again, letting it refresh and invigorate him. The captain was something of a hedonist. He enjoyed breathing in the fresh air, letting it fill his lungs languorously and then passing it through his lips. Occasionally, the men chided him for his voluptuousness. It was well known that he kept a mistress in each of the ports where the ship docked: Elena, the slim and tidy tavern keeper at Tenedos; Olympia, the voluptuous widow of a merchant in Negroponte; Lauretta, the farmer's daughter at Modon whose half-shut eyes made her look forever tired. Even here in Constantinople, there was Anastasia the courtesan, free with her love for any man who was free with his money. Davanzo went to her whenever the ship came to Constantinople. That night, he wondered whether he had seen Anastasia for the last time. Well, what did it matter? The world was full of cities, ports, and women.

Perhaps before returning to Venice he would stop the ship to re-supply at Negroponte and visit Olympia.

He felt the wind again. He took pleasure in feeling the unsullied sea air breeze through his long hair. The crew chided him for that, too. He was extremely vain about his hair. The night was a little overcast with the clouds moving swiftly, driven on in their journey to nowhere by the wind. Seven ships were leaving. Davanzo's own Venetian galley and six smaller ships from Venetian controlled Crete. The Cretan merchants had nothing to do with Constantinople. Their captains had not been asked by the Emperor to remain, and their ships were too small to be of any real use during the fighting: there were fewer than a hundred men on each vessel. Davanzo's departure would be a surprise. He might argue, with pedantic precision, that he had not personally been asked to stay, but everyone in the City knew about Constantinople's desperate plight and the fact that the Emperor had asked the trading fleet from Tana to remain to help the City. His actions would be viewed by those who stayed as cowardly. But what did he care? They could call him a coward if they dared, if they survived. It was not as if he was abandoning the City in the face of the enemy. Matteo was a fool for trying to convince himself to stay. It was pointless. Though he was convincing himself, a feeling of emptiness froze like ice in Davanzo's belly. He wanted to leave immediately.

"Are we ready?" he called to the sailing master.

"Not yet, sir. A few more minutes yet."

Davanzo snorted in frustration. He wanted it to be done with. He wanted Constantinople behind him. He wanted to be done with the cursed domes, the towering walls, the quarreling priests, the supercilious *bailò*, the noble *signori* and their talk of honor.

"Bring me word when we are ready to sail."

"Yes, sir."

He looked out at the City once more in the darkness. In the night he could see nothing of importance. Constantinople as a whole was not important to him. It was not worth his blood or the blood of his crew. They could have chosen to stay. Each man among them could have refused to set sail, but their captain was giving them the chance for life, and they could not reject it. Davanzo smiled at the thought. In choosing between life and death, the smart man will always choose life.

"We're ready sir."

"Raise the anchor. Set our course east-southeast."

The anchor came aboard, dripping with the clear water of the Golden Horn. The sail billowed. The wind pushed them swiftly towards the Acropolis Point. There, they would turn south for Tenedos and freedom. Davanzo looked to his right as the ship cut through the waters. Under his breath he muttered:

"Farewell Constantinople. God have mercy on the souls who stay there."

8—The Final Preparations: *March 1453*

"Again!"

The swords rang edge against edge.

"Again! Come on! Strike harder! Force me to defend the blow!"

Marco lowered his blade and stared at his uncle, grimly dressed beneath his armor, his reassuring eyes hidden by his helmet. He lifted the sword and struck again, but his uncle's guard remained immobile.

"You have to attack with more strength than the enemy."

Marco lowered his blade again. Wearily he asked: "What if the enemy is stronger?"

"If the enemy is stronger, then you must be faster; if he is faster, you must be smarter."

"And what if he is smarter?"

Giustiniani paused: "If the enemy is smarter," he said, "you had better have help. Now, back to work. Ready?"

Marco nodded, and Giustiniani immediately swept forward cutting in short, powerful motions, driving his nephew backwards. "Why are you only defending!" shouted the *condottiere* as he continued to cut. "If you parry, *riposte*! Always *riposte*! You can't hit me if you're only defending yourself." He took off the helmet and stared at his nephew. "Listen to me. When you force the enemy to defend, you are forcing him to react. If he is reacting, he has uncertainty, and if he has uncertainty, you have the advantage."

"But we are defending the city."

"Yes, in this battle we are defending the city, but every battle is composed of a thousand individual combats, and in each one of those we can attack and force the enemy to react! Again!"

Marco's eyes drifted behind his uncle to the approaching riders. The Emperor.

"Good morning, *protostrator*."

"Good morning, your majesty."

"How is the repair work going?"

"Very well, sire. The walls will be ready."

"I am pleased. As you suggested, we are digging a foss in front of the Blachernae quarter. I would appreciate your opinion on its design."

"I will come, sire." Giustiniani gave his sword to a squire, mounted his horse, and rode after the Emperor.

Within Constantinople, February had become March. The pink and white almond trees were beginning to flower. Little hints of spring sprouted everywhere. At Blachernae, Giustiniani saw the crews from the Tana fleet digging furiously. Three work parties, each watched by their captain, competed to dig the greatest length of trench. "Diedo's ditch" grew rapidly, swiftly approaching its desired depth and length. Though exhausted, the sailors continued their work through the afternoon, not wishing to allow their comrades to surpass them. All three captains encouraged their crews under the pleased gaze of Diedo, Giustiniani, and the Emperor.

Giustiniani surveyed the work and turned to the Emperor. "It will not stop the Turks, your majesty, but it will make their approach more difficult."

"Anything that can be done must be done," replied Constantine. He turned to Diedo, "I am grateful, Admiral, for the work of your men. Please inform me immediately if there is anything you and your sailors need." The Emperor and his suite departed, leaving the Italians alone.

Diedo watched the Emperor ride away and turned to Giustiniani. "It will be more what you need than what I need, *condottiere*. I know I have enough ships to hold the Horn, but do you have enough men to hold these walls?"

"We will hold."

"For how long?" prodded the Admiral.

"Long enough," answered Giustiniani calmly.

"Long enough for what?" Diedo insisted.

"Long enough for a Venetian fleet to arrive." There was a moment of silence, then Giustiniani suddenly brightened and faced Diedo. "But don't let them come too soon; I have a reputation to advance."

Diedo smiled his wry smile. "I'll see what I can do."

Giustiniani turned his eyes to the Venetians laboring in the ditch. "How do your men enjoy digging?"

"Less than yours. They are used to the freedom of the sea, not the weight of the land."

"Do you miss the sea?"

Diedo looked at Giustiniani, the glibness deserting his eyes. His voice suddenly filled with feeling. "I miss the quiet of the open sea. I miss its sounds too, the waves, the birds, the spray of the water against the ship. I miss its harmony and its peace."

"Do you miss the storms?"

"I have been on land too long to remember the storms. The sea is my love affair, *condottiere*. I have forgotten her faults." Diedo's eyes reached out to the men digging, to his sons Marco and Vittorio, buried in the ditch below them. "Do you have any children, *condottiere*?"

"No, captain, I don't."

"Children are man's greatest freedom and his greatest prison." Diedo continued as Giustiniani questioningly raised an eyebrow. "They free his soul to aspire to immortality and are a prison for his heart, which is always captive to them, their feelings, and their safety."

"Are you worried for them, captain?"

Diedo's wry smile returned, "Since they were born."

Giustiniani looked at the two youths, younger even than Marco. "I wish I were that age again." Diedo did not respond. "Fear was not something that we knew at that age. Life was simpler then. We had neither families nor commands. All we had were orders to follow and a feeling of invincibility as we followed them."

"I hope that they live to see an age when they will have responsibilities such as ours," Diedo said forlornly.

"Do you regret having stayed?"

Diedo looked directly at the *condottiere*. "No. I don't regret it, but I do regret that my sons have stayed as a result of my choice."

"Did you ask them to leave?"

Diedo shook his head. "No. They are old enough to make their own decisions. And how can I tell them to leave and with the next breath encourage the rest of my men to stay."

"The City will be safe, captain. We will hold it. Your *Signoria* will send a fleet; there is no reason to fear. I wish you a good evening."

The *condottiere* departed, leaving Diedo silently watching the men at their work as the last daylight drained away. With the darkness, the sailors stopped their work and trudged back to the ships. There was only a little more to be done. Alone, Alvise Diedo descended from the battlements, preoccupied with his thoughts. He did not know what the future would hold and doubted if he had made the right choice. The end and only the end would exonerate or condemn his reasoning. He hoped that that end was not foretold in the walls above him, patched with gravestones, transforming the entire City into a tomb.

PART II

1—The Siege: *April 2, 1453*

"Tell them to march faster!" shouted Mehmed.

"Zagan Pasha's vanguard covered twenty-one miles today, your Majesty. Just before sunset, his forward scouts came within sight of the city walls."

"I want his entire division in front of Constantinople by midday tomorrow. Send a rider forward with that order."

"Yes, sire."

"Lord Vizier, what news of Venice?" Mehmed's tone was tinged with scorn.

Halil answered patiently, "There is no news from the *Signoria,* as yet. But there is information from the city that several powerful Venetian ships have remained to help in its defense. The Venetians within Constantinople have pledged themselves to its defense as well. We will goad Venice by fighting these men."

"They have made their choice to stay. They remain at their own peril and through their own responsibility."

"It is a dangerous game, your Majesty."

Mehmed smiled his raptor's smile, "A king's ventures cannot be otherwise, Lord Vizier. A sovereign must not deal in trivialities."

Mehmed bent his head over the command table, laid out with flags and wooden blocks as the army marched on behind him. He called another courier forward.

"Give Lord Zagan my orders: he is to encamp outside of the walls when he arrives, but he is not to engage the Greeks, neither in the outlying fortresses nor in the city itself. There will be no reversals, no small triumphs for them. Nothing is to happen until I arrive. Make this clear to him."

"Yes, your Majesty."

He turned to Halil Pasha again. "Lord Vizier, what do your spies say about the City's defenses?"

"They are strong, your Majesty. Substantial resources at sea, perhaps thirty sail, including the five Venetian ships I mentioned before. On land there are several thousand Greeks and several thousand Italians, including the famous Giovanni Giustiniani of Chios."

"Famous? I have not heard of him." Laughter came from the young-bloods of the Sultan's suite. Mehmed smiled at them and turned to his Vizier, "Perhaps I can make this man's reputation by permitting him to die in defense of Constantinople."

Halil bowed. "Reputations are made in many ways, sire."

"True. But no one values a reputation for cowardice."

"Cowardice is reserved for those who abandon the field of battle; it is not a term for those who strive to avoid it through good sense."

Mehmed snapped a miniature flagstaff in two. "Enough words! Zagan will have his forces before Constantinople's walls in a few hours. More divisions will follow tomorrow. I will arrive in three days with the Janissaries and the heavy artillery. Lord Vizier, you may return to the march."

"As you command, your majesty."

Mehmed looked at his army strung out along the road, a serpent stretching beyond both horizons, whose fangs, at long last, could almost touch the Queen of Cities.

✳ ✳ ✳

Einai edo! Einai edo! The Greek cry interrupted the war council in the Imperial Palace. A messenger burst into the room and bowed. "Your Majesty, the Turks are here."

The emperor stood. "How many are they?"

"Twenty-thousand men, sire, at least."

"The Turkish vanguard," said Giustiniani. "Cavalry and infantry?" he asked the messenger.

"Yes, both."

"Guns?"

"Not yet."

"We must settle our dispositions along the land walls, bring in all citizens from the surrounding countryside, and destroy everything outside of these walls which could help support Mehmed's army."

Constantine continued the *condottiere*'s planning: "Once those people are safely in, I will order the bridges across the moat destroyed."

"Then we are resolved to a defensive battle," muttered Grand Duke Notaras.

"The odds, my Lord, do not allow us any other choice," replied Giustiniani. "The villagers must bring inside their families, their livestock, everything. And they must move quickly."

Constantine nodded. "Begin the evacuation immediately. Lord Cantancuzenos, once the last person is inside, destroy the bridges over the moat." He turned back to Alvise Diedo, "Admiral, the Turkish fleet will not be far behind Mehmed's army. Prepare your ships for battle. Speak with Bartolomeo Soligo in Pera and have him deploy the great chain to protect our harbors and the Golden Horn."

"It will be done, sire."

"Then we are ready for the enemy. I leave you to your preparations. Go with God."

The captains bowed and went to their companies. Giustinani ordered his men to arm and take up their positions along the walls. In less than an hour, Marco, the *condottiere* and most of their soldiers were at the walls. The banner bearing the crowned eagle and the three towered gatehouses waved above them in the spring breeze. Giustiniani was in full plate armor. He carried no shield because the quality of his armor made it superfluous. On his head he wore a typical Italian barbut. The helmet evoked the classical helmets of the ancient Greeks. It had large cheek pieces and wide horizontal openings across the eyes joining a more narrow vertical slit in front of the mouth and nose. It provided the wearer a maximum combination of visibility, freedom of breathing, and protection. He had a sword in a scabbard at his left side and a dagger behind his back. Though only Marco and Giustiniani wore complete suits of armor, all the soldiers present wore breastplates and helmets that glittered in the morning sunlight. The right cheek piece on the archers' helmets was unique, folding away from their faces to not interfere as they drew back the bow string. Some of the men had plate guards on their elbows or knees. Their arms and legs were covered in bright red, orange, and yellow fabrics tied tight to their bodies. Many had tied scarves to their arms for the sake of patron saints or sweethearts, and these fluttered in the breeze. Professionalism hung in the silent air. There would be no battle today, but Giustiniani wanted his men armed and on the walls, a visible show of strength to the people.

Below them, the Lycus Valley brimmed with Turkish soldiers. Two and a half miles away, a sea of tents and banners enveloped the landscape. Horsemen and foot soldiers covered the plain and the hills. Soon, the cannon began to appear. Teams of oxen dragged the massive guns that had come from the foundries of Adrianople. As they were unloaded, engineers began to plan and construct the gun platforms and palisades that would allow the cannon to turn their destructive fury against the City. After such an eternity of inaction, it was all happening so quickly. For months, the defenders had waited for an enemy that was remote, a rumble of distant thunder, but no more. Now the men in Constantinople saw the force that was arrayed against them.

The bridges over the moat were destroyed. The heavy gates of the City were closed and locked. Near the Acropolis Point, from the Tower of Eugenios, the iron chain boom was extended across the Golden Horn to Pera to close up the harbor. There, Bartolomeo Soligo oversaw the fixing of the boom to a tower along his city's sea walls. With this accomplished, the captain moved to his ship and took position along the chain. Alvise Diedo had detached Soligo with ten ships, mostly from Pera, to defend the boom. Sealed by land and sea, the Queen of Cities prepared for the onslaught to come.

As the sun waned, Marco stared out at the Turkish camp. The hillside above the Lycus came alive with torches and campfires. Beyond the walls was an army greater than anything the young soldier had seen before. Thousands of fires threw a red hue across the evening sky. It reminded Marco of blood. He shivered. There was a chill in the air this night. He pulled his cloak around him. Spring had yet to come in full force. He wrapped himself in the cloak and stared to the west. More troops were still marching into the camp. How was it possible for the defenders to turn back such a tide? Could the ancient walls withstand the power of the Sultan's armies and his new weapons of war? Perhaps God would help them. Marco began to pray. *"Pater noster, qui es in caelis, sanctificetur nomen tuum. Adveniat regnum tuum...."** Soon, he had drifted off to sleep.

---

* The Lord's Prayer: "Our Father who art in heaven, hallowed be thy name. Thy kingdom come..."

2—The Cannon: *April 5, 1453*

It was the fifth of April when Mehmed arrived at Constantinople with the remainder of his army. The Sultan galloped the last few hundred yards, imagining that he could smell the City. The horse, driven by the Sultan's spurs, charged up Maltepe Hill and the great walls rose before his eyes. Beyond them, he could make out the domes of churches and monasteries, the ancient obelisks and the distant hippodrome. An overwhelming desire took possession of him. In the valley below, his army bustled with activity. Soldiers unpacked their loads, unburdening themselves of tents, weapons and supplies. Engineers brought forward their siege equipment: catapults, mangonels, and cannon. He allowed himself a small smile at the sight of Constantinople ringed by his army. Mehmed could feel their power, the power that was now his to command: one-hundred and twenty-thousand men ready to do his bidding, ready to drive forward against the City. It too would be his.

"I want my tent here, Mustafa, beside the river, opposite the area between those two gates!" Mehmed thrust his hand towards the City, pointing halfway between the Gate of Charisios and the Gate of Saint Romanos. "Prepare a table and summon my war council."

"Yes, your majesty."

Mehmed's heart was racing. His eyes were fixed on the walls before him, already probing, seeking a way through to victory. He wanted Gülbahar, but she was far back along the road. It would be a day, perhaps two, before she arrived in the camp. His mind danced between his two desires as slaves set out a great oak table, placing upon it maps of the City and painted wooden blocks representing his armies and those of the Emperor. When the Pashas had arrived, Mehmed dismounted and came to the table. He scanned their faces, testing their resolve with his eyes. Halil Pasha, blank and unmoved, awaiting his chance to counsel inaction. Zagan Pasha, fiery and eager for battle. Karadja Pasha, unquestioning, skilled, imbued with a steady, soldier's loyalty. Ishak Pasha, a graybeard, worn, a servant of his father's, a friend of Halil, a man of moderation. Shahabeddin Shahin, trustworthy, zealous and shrill, the court's Chief Eunuch. And Orban, the Hungarian gun-maker, an imported mercenary bought for his skill in designing huge cannon, the man whose gun designs had triumphed at the Throat Cutter.

"Here is our battle plan," he said. Though he had rehearsed this speech, his voice betrayed a hint of excitement. His mastery of the subject, however, was complete.

"Lord Zagan, your army will cross the Gold Horn to the north and occupy the ground to the West of the Genoese colony of Pera. Do not press them; their neutrality is to be respected and encouraged. You will control the Valley of the Springs and link with the fleet once it arrives."

"As you command, sire."

"Lord Karadja, deploy our European armies opposite the area called Blachernae in the north. This is the location of the Imperial palace. Stay alert and be prepared in case the enemy should launch attacks to sever us from Lord Zagan's forces." Karadja Pasha nodded his assent.

"I will be in the center," continued the Sultan, "opposite the area between the gates of Charisios and Saint Romanos. To my right, you, Ishak Pasha, will deploy our Albanian troops." Another heavy wooden block came down on the map. "Mustafa, tell the commander of the Bashi-Bazouks that his men are to take their positions behind the main army. They have no place in the front line."

"Yes, sire."

"You have your orders, my lords, to your positions." The rest of Mehmed's council remained by him. "Orban, you will be in charge of the placement of the guns. Choose their locations well. I want my army to have a breach as soon as possible."

"As you command, sire."

Orban set about his task. Along the entire length of the land walls, the siege engines were deployed. The pride of both the engineer and the Sultan was an enormous cannon constructed after the success of the guns built to command the straits. It was the largest gun the world had ever seen, made especially for use against Constantinople's walls. Construction had taken weeks, but the finished product was a masterpiece. The barrel was almost twenty-seven feet in length and had a diameter of forty-eight inches. It fired a stone ball weighing over half a ton propelled by one hundred and fifty pounds of powder over a range of more than a mile. Two hundred men and a team of sixty oxen had taken two months to drag the barrel from Adrianople to Constantinople with a special team of engineers detailed to level and clear the road. Mehmed had christened it *basilisk*, a fire-breathing monster to topple the walls of Constantinople. It was a king of guns to conquer the Queen of Cities.

Mehmed stood at the oak table, impatient to see his guns in action. Runners were bringing news as the army set its positions. Staff officers detailed the specific deployments from each commander. Workmen labored feverishly to construct the camp wall that would protect the cannon and the troops from fire and sorties from the City. Trees in the nearby countryside were already being felled and brought in. The engineers were building beds of wooden planks on mounds of earth as gun platforms. In front of where the gun was to be laid, a door was placed that would be lifted by a system of ropes and pulleys when the piece was fired. Orban had set *basilisk* to the north, opposite the solitary Blachernae wall. Two other large cannon were brought to support it. Along the entire line of the walls, Orban placed nine of his own large cannon, plus an additional fifty-six guns of various sizes, most acquired for a price from princes in Europe.

Mehmed had wanted *basilisk* at the center of the line, opposite the *Mesoteichon* and near to his tent, but Orban was the gunner, and Mehmed trusted his skill—at least for now. The red and gold tent was pitched, but the Sultan could not tear himself from the walls. Halil Pasha and Shahabeddin remained with him, studying the map as the situation unfolded. Then, Constantinople erupted with cheering. Everyone's eyes were drawn to the walls which had suddenly come alive. Soldiers, glittering in armor, were parading along the walls under huge silk banners.

"What is it?" demanded the Sultan.

"The Venetians are here," whispered one of the courtiers, versed in heraldry. One by one, he read the roll of illustrious families to Mehmed as the ensigns passed. To him, the crests were as familiar as the celebrated names, the colored bars and symbols as easily readable as letters. Finally, his eyes fixed on the winged-lion, sewn in gold on a crimson field, and read the inscription held in the lion's right claw: *"Pax tibi Marce evangelista meus.* Peace unto thee, Mark, my evangelist."

After hearing the Latin verse translated into Turkish, Shahabeddin muttered.

"Peace indeed! We shall give you war and death."

In a subdued tone, Halil Pasha answered him.

"Weigh your words, my lord. The power of Venice is more than silk banners and painted lions; it is men and ships. The West is coming to rescue Constantinople."

Mehmed's blood quickened. If Halil was right, there was not a moment to lose. The City must fall before the Venetian fleet arrived. Everything would hinge on the appearance of the red banners of Saint Mark on the Bosphorus skyline. As the sailors completed their trek around the walls, word was brought to him that the guns were at last in position. Despite the failing afternoon light, Mehmed gave the order to fire.

The pulleys turned, lifting the great wooden doors which protected the guns. Matches struck the touch-holes and the cannon flamed forth. The siege had begun.

* * *

The explosion of *basilisk* was colossal, shaking the earth around it. The walls of the City shuddered as the enormous stones struck home, shattering themselves into a thousand pieces and bringing down great chunks of the battlements. The men on the walls saw the Turkish line come alive with smoke and fire and watched as boulders hurtled through the air from behind the wooden palisade.

The arms of catapults snapped, the leather and cloth slings of mangonels swung and the barrels of the massive cannon jetted flame. These engines of destruction tore at the walls as long as light held. Shot after shot smashed into the ancient fortifications, chipping, disfiguring and finally breaking them down. Near the Gate of Charisios, an entire section of wall was badly damaged and in danger of collapsing. Never had so much firepower been brought against the City. The defenders were taken by surprise at the power directed at them, and at the inability of the walls to withstand the torrent of stone.

Reports of massive damage reached Giustiniani and the Emperor. The ancient masonry seemed incapable of stopping the new weapons of war. At the heart of the storm stood *basilisk*, pounding the weak single wall of the Blachernae with its enormous power. Giustiniani, having spent much of his life defending obsolete fortifications against modern weapons, was less concerned than Constantine. Still, he was disappointed that the famed walls were not faring better. The *condottiere* had made contingency plans to repair the City's defenses and would put them into action when the time came. For the present, he withdrew the troops from the walls themselves, placing them in the open space between the inner and outer fortifications. Lookouts on the towers of the inner wall watched the Turkish lines for any sign of movement and were prepared to raise the alarm. The noise made it difficult for the defenders to speak. Rather than leaving his men at the mercy of the guns' intimidating thunder, Giustiniani busied them with the task of bringing barrels of earth and large timbers from within the City to their position. When the Turkish bombardment stopped, they would move forward to their repair work.

Basilisk fired again and again, but the very size of the great gun was proving a limiting factor. That first day the Sultan's men only managed five shots. After every blast the barrel was sponged and cooled with buckets of water. One hundred and fifty pounds of powder were pushed and bundled into the great void followed by an enormous polished stone. When the spark ignited in the touchhole, the massive gun shook its carriage and spewed the ball against the walls of Theodosius. It took half an hour just to reset the cannon from its exertions before the loading process would begin again. Mehmed looked on impatiently as Orban, begrimed by the endless gun smoke that engulfed him, barked orders in his accented Turkish. The little Hungarian was doing his job well, and the great walls were already crumbling under his assault of stone.

Satisfied with the progress, the Sultan's mind moved to other matters. Outside of the walls, there were two small castles still in enemy hands. Before Mehmed moved against the walls of Constantinople itself, he decided to eliminate the two bastions. The first was Therapia, on a hill above the Bosphorus. It was far to the north, beyond even the citadel of the Throat Cutter, but Mehmed did not want to take any chances. It was near enough that the garrison could disrupt communication between the Sultan and his fleet. Several heavy cannon and three thousand troops were detached from the division of Zagan Pasha with orders to reduce the citadel.

The pasha, with an interpreter and a handful of horsemen, approached the fortress under flag of truce and called out to the commander to surrender. There was no response. Zagan turned to the interpreter.

"Tell them that their lives will be spared and that they will be allowed to return to their homes upon surrendering their weapons to us."

The interpreter conveyed the words. A single word was shouted in reply.

"Never," came the translation.

Zagan wrenched the bridle of his horse furiously and gave orders for the bombardment to commence. The guns battered at the walls of Therapia. They were not made from as stern stuff as those of the City, and after forty-eight hours the castle was in ruins. Both nights, the Turks advanced against the devastated walls without success. Two score of the defenders clung to the rubble trying to survive.

With their fortifications shattered, and having no weapons with which to continue the struggle, there was nothing left to do but throw themselves on the mercy of the Sultan. The men surrendered. Blackened with smoke and grime, the vanquished were marched past the Valley of the Springs and across the pontoon bridge to Mehmed. The Sultan ordered them impaled immediately. The stakes were to be erected in front of the Sultan's tent, within plain view of the men in Constantinople. The sharpened stakes were brought, the men stripped, and the grisly ritual performed. Their cries brought the defenders to the walls. They turned away in horror as the twitching figures rose above the colored tents.

The castle of Studios, near the Marmara coast and opposite the City's Studion quarter, fell the same day. There were thirty-six survivors and they too were brought before the Sultan to meet the fate of their comrades from Therapia.

A forest of human flesh now stood around Mehmed, who focused all of his intentions upon the City itself.

As the Sultan's forces took Studion and Therapia, fire continued against Constantinople's walls. In three days of incessant firing, the terrible guns succeeded in tumbling a section of wall near the Gate of Charisios. During the nights, Giustiniani put his repair plans into action. It was impossible to make direct repairs to the Theodosian masonry. There was simply no stone left in Constantinople. Besides, Mehmed's cannon were pulverizing the ancient battlements into dust. The defenders made due with the materials they had. The *condottiere*'s men patched up the damage using wooden or wicker barrels filled with earth and rocks and supported by timbers.

Giustiniani's defensive skills were at the fore. The soil within the barrels proved highly effective at absorbing the shock of the Sultan's projectiles. The *condottiere* was everywhere, advising on the repair work and bringing forward barrels, rocks and timbers with his own hands. Each night, the defenders exhausted themselves until the makeshift palisade stood as proudly as the ancient ramparts had done. Then Giustiniani and his men would return to their quarters for a few hours of sleep before renewing their battle with the Sultan's war machines the next day.

Constantinople's walls, however, were not Mehmed's only concern. Before those impervious barriers could be reached, his warriors would first need to cross the deep foss that shielded them. They would have to descend to its floor, cross the bottom and then climb out to scale the counter scarp just to reach the base of the outer wall. All the time, they would be under fire from the defenders. Once in the depths of the foss, Greek fire would be poured on them from the walls. This terrifying weapon was an imperial invention, first used with great success against the Arab invaders of the seventh century. Its exact recipe of naptha, sulfur, pitch, and tar remained a state secret. Imitations were never as successful as the original. The compound was pumped from pressurized copper containers and ignited with a single flame. Soldiers could also carry small projectiles of the substance in clay jugs that they threw after igniting a small fuse. Water spread the blaze, which could only be extinguished with sand, earth, or urine. The Greeks used their liquid fire with equal success on land and at sea.

For any assault to stand a chance of success, the foss would have to be filled. Mehmed set his warriors to the task. The Turks cut down more trees, brought branches, sacks of earth, lose stones, anything that could be used to fill the great ditch. They marched forward carrying their loads and dumped them into the foss. The defenders fired at them, but the Turks moved on impervious to the rain of arrows, stones, and lead bullets. They refused to allow the bodies of the dead to lie by the walls and came forward to pick them up and bring them back to the camp. Many of those who carried the bodies were themselves shot and fell, but more men came forward picking up their comrades so that no one was left behind.

Day after day, the fire from the Turkish lines continued. Orban was in his element. The gun maker was directing the laying and firing of his creations and was successfully bringing down great portions of the ancient walls. At night, he would confer with the Sultan and pore over maps and plans for the next day's targets. In spite of the defenders' ingenuity, Orban remained confident that soon a breach would be ready for assault. He tried to convince his master to be patient and let the guns do their work. Mehmed demanded more speed.

Around noon on the third day of the bombardment, *basilisk* was re-laid for its second shot. The powder and shot had been brought and loaded down the great muzzle. The flame struck the touchhole and a blast, louder than usual, shook the air. The gun disappeared in smoke. There was a shattering metallic crash. The iron stays along the barrel burst loose. The massive stone shot was propelled crazily forward spinning and crashing well short of the walls into the foss where it buried itself in the earth. The gun crew and its maker were enveloped in the explosion. Those immediately around *basilisk* ran for cover. As the smoke cleared, they came forward to inspect the smoldering debris and to see if they could do anything for their comrades. The bodies were charred and smoldering. Merely cinders of the men remained. Orban was dead, *basilisk* destroyed.

Mehmed accepted the news without a hint of emotion. His only concern was that the siege should proceed with all speed. Immediately, a replacement was found to take the Hungarian's place in charge of the bombardment. The cannon had already been built, so the engineer was no longer entirely fundamental to the siege. The loss of *basilisk* was more important to the Sultan; he would have to make due with the other guns that Orban had made.

Free to choose his own targets, the Sultan decided that the focus of the cannonade should be shifted away from the Blachernae. Success had been too slow in coming in that area, and the ground made it difficult to bring troops forward for the assault. Mehmed had been studying the ground and decided that the terrain between the Gate of Charisios and the Gate of Saint Romanos, the *Mesoteichion*, was the best area to direct the attack. The largest guns were repositioned to the south. These would be the final emplacements for the guns. Mehmed chose his objective with care, and the siege began in earnest.

* * *

The Emperor and Giustiniani attended to the positioning of their troops. They agreed that, to achieve the maximum cooperation from their disparate forces, the various nationalities should be separated. The Emperor called a council of war to portion out the various areas of the City to his commanders.

"Our enemies have shifted their strength to the Gate of Saint Romanos. It is there that the weight of their assault is likely to fall. It is there that we must make our most resolute stand. Who among you is willing to take this spot as their position?"

Silence enveloped the Emperor. Neither Greeks nor Italians moved. No one, Greek or Catalan, Venetian or Genoese, Latin or Orthodox volunteered to step into the lion's mouth. The men were proud and courageous; they had come to and stayed in the City at its most pressing hour of need. Now, to be asked to step into the most perilous part of the field, their nerve failed them. The Emperor, ashamed by their reluctance, was moments from accepting his own challenge, but hesitated, knowing that his place was at the rear, commanding the defense of the whole city, rather than on the walls. It was then that Giustiniani stepped forward. The *condottiere* had come to Constantinople to protect it—to fight. If the Saint Romanos Gate was the most threatened then that was where he would stand. As the commander of the land defenses, it would be dishonorable of him to fight from any other position. He spoke calmly, his voice resonating with conviction.

"My lords, I am ready to stand there with my men. With God's help, I shall defend the gate."

The assembly cheered in gratitude. The Emperor declared that his headquarters would be to the *condottiere*'s left, behind the Lycus River, so that he could support him. The positioning of the rest of the commanders was then decided.

The far northern corner, around the Gate of Caligaria fell to Girolamo Minotto and his sons, Zorzi and Polo, and the Venetians who were residents of Constantinople. To their left, near the Emperor's palace at Blachernae, the Genoese from Pera took their stand. Behind them, in reserve to reinforce the thin walls of the Blachernae, was Grand Duke

Notaras with a complement of mobile cannon. The Grand Duke also commanded the sea walls and from this position supported Alvise Diedo, who commanded the fleet in the Golden Horn.

To defend the harbor, the Venetian captain deployed ten of his largest ships along the chain itself. Because of the position of the boom (attached as it was at Pera) Diedo had entrusted this squadron to the Genoese captain, Bartolomeo Soligo. Five of the ships, including Giustiniani's flagship and an enormous merchantman commanded by Zorzi Doria, were from Genoa. Of the remaining ships, three were from Venetian-controlled Crete, one was from Ancona, and the last was from Constantinople.

At the far end of the City, on the Acropolis Point, Cardinal Isidore stood with his escort of two hundred archers. To the Cardinal's south, beneath the hippodrome and the old imperial palace, stood Péré Julia and a company of Catalans. By the church of Saint George of the Cypresses, monks from the City's monasteries would guard the sea walls if they were threatened. Jacobo Contarini, a member of one of Venice's most noble families, also defended the sea walls, linking the monks with Demetrios Cantacuzenos. The imperial *protostrator* stood at the southwest corner of the City, with his left resting on the sea. To his right, Maurizio Cataneo of Genoa defended the Golden Gate. Next came more Venetian troops under Filippo Contarini in defense of the district around the Pegae Gate. To the right of the Venetians, the Emperor's cousin, Theopholius Palaeologos defended the Pegae Gate itself. More Genoese troops were positioned to the imperial cousin's right, linking with the forces under the Emperor and completing the ring of defenders. All was ready for the assault.

On the Turkish side, the re-laying of the guns was now complete. April the eleventh dawned overcast, but Mehmed gave the order to commence firing and the great cannon tore at the ancient walls beneath the gray sky. Before noon, it

began to rain. It was not long before Mehmed's gun crews
began to have difficulty with the mud. The ground
supporting the gun emplacements was becoming soft and
the great iron barrels were pushing their wooden supports
into the earth. Only Herculean strength could lift the larger
pieces back to their firing positions. An unexpected hand
was stirring difficulties into the Sultan's plans. While
Orban's cannon seemed to dominate the triumph of
Theodosius' architects with surprising ease, Nature, with an
effortless shower, mired science in muddy chaos. The
Sultan's fury could not contend against the gray sky, and it
was not until the next day dawned bright and clear that the
guns resumed their bombardment.

The rain had delayed more than the Sultan's siege; it had
also delayed the arrival of his mistress. Gülbahar, unwilling
to have her arrival dampened by the storm, had waited for
the sunshine to appear at the side of her lord. It was
afternoon when she entered the camp, her carriage draped
in thick green silk and drawn by a pair of white horses.
Veiled, she moved swiftly from the carriage to her tent, set a
few yards from the Sultan's and already prepared for her.
Her maids, except for Eminé, who was always at her side,
had arrived days before and put everything in order. A
company of Janissaries, sixty strong, stood guard around the
tent to ensure her safety.

Mustafa noticed the carriage and immediately set off to
find his master. Mehmed had ordered him to report
Gülbahar's arrival immediately. He found the Sultan at the
gun battery opposite the *Mesoteichon*. Approaching,
Mustafa whispered in his ear, "Sire, the Lady Gülbahar has
arrived."

Mehmed nodded, gave a few commands to the battery
commander, mounted his horse and spurred it towards his
mistress's tent. He stormed in. "You were supposed to have
arrived yesterday!" he shouted, half reproaching, half
demanding an explanation.

"The rain muddied the road, my lord. I could not travel in the storm," she explained. "A Sultan can command the earth, but he cannot order the heavens."

"My command was for you to be here yesterday, not for sun or rain."

The cannon and the armies had filled him with energy and power, she thought. It would not be well for her to begin with an argument.

"I apologize, my lord. I came as soon as I could. I am here now. Here for your pleasure." As she spoke, she unclasped the right side of her veil, letting the silk fall away to reveal her lips. He moved forward to kiss them.

"Send your maids away," he commanded.

She smiled, clapped her hands and signaled for the servants to go.

"Then you still desire me." It was half a question. He answered with a barrage of kisses. When they had lain together, she repeated it, now as a fact: "You still desire me. And you still desire Constantinople."

"We are here to conquer it and will not retreat until that is accomplished. You should see the guns, the greatest cannon in the world! Mine! Battering the walls to dust."

"And what of Halil Pasha?"

"What of him?"

"Do you think he will allow you to continue this war that he opposes all the way to victory?"

"We will be victorious with or without Halil Pasha."

"With or without Halil Pasha, my lord, you must conquer this city and take your place on the throne of the Caesars." She was beating the drum again, driving him towards action. "Think of it, my lord, the throne of Constantine, the church of Justinian, the home of emperors for a thousand years, yours." Mehmed's eyes caught fire from her words. The glittering throne and golden domes rose in his mind. "Rooms of gold and silver, chalices crusted with jewels,

columns and arches commemorating the triumphs of
centuries, yours."

He rose, stung into action. "I will order an assault
tonight!"

"Assault? My lord, the siege has only just begun; your
guns have not had time to do their work."

"Tonight!"

"Patience, sire. An assault will leave the City, your city,
devastated. Do not forfeit your right to the prize!"[§]

Mehmed remained unmoved.

"Do not risk your army so soon. Any setback will give
power to Halil and those who would hold you back from
your destiny."

"Would you hold me back from my destiny?" he snarled
at her.

"No, my lord. I want you to fulfill your destiny. If I am
cautious, it is out of concern for you."

"I will not be ruled by fear. The army attacks tonight.
Constantinople will be ours by morning!" and he stormed
out of her tent.

* * *

The warcries tore the shroud of darkness from the City's
walls. The attack came unexpectedly, driven onward by the
blaring of trumpets and the menacing sound of castanets.
Neither Giustiniani nor the Emperor had thought that the
Sultan would order an assault at this early stage. Worse, they
had not even considered the possibility that any attempt
would be made in the confusing darkness of the night.

Giustiniani and his men were repairing the damage made
by the Sultan's guns when howls erupted from the Turkish
line. It was two hours after dark. Giustiniani rushed to the
nearest battlement and peered into the darkness. He was

[§] Under Islamic law, the attacking army had a right to sack a city
which refused to surrender and was taken by assault for three days.

trying to make out the shapes of the enemy. Someone at the section of wall where the first contact had been made had thrown a few torches down from the walls. The foss below was faintly lit by the flickering orange light. Giustiniani could see some Turks trying to scale the rubble of the breach while others attempted to put out the firelight with blankets.

The *condottiere* calmly ordered the repair work halted and sent word for the every available man to come to the walls. Runners were also sent south to the Emperor at the Gate of Saint Romanos to inform him of the attack. Time was short. The defenders not on duty fixed the clasps of their armor. With hurried hands made unsure by the need for haste, they tied on their helmets as they ran to the walls. Giustiniani called for Marco, and the young man appeared out of the darkness.

"Are they attacking?"

"Yes. It looks like a small night sortie. I think they're trying to catch us asleep."

"I hope it doesn't develop into something more than that. I'm not sure the defenses are ready for a full-scale assault."

Giustiniani looked at his nephew for a moment, but did not respond. Unfortunately, the young man was correct. They were not ready yet. The repair work had not progressed far enough.

"Stay by me, Marco. Make sure to keep your men in close order."

The two captains had assembled thirty armored men-at-arms to lead to the breach where the Turkish attack was falling. With a single word, "*Avanti*,"** Giustiniani led them to the battle. They ran north along the parapet to the section of wall under attack, raising their own cheer as they threw themselves upon the Turks. The enemy was engaged at the top of the rubble of the breached wall. The only light came from a few torches mounted on the walls or thrown

---

** "Forward."

haphazardly into the contending forces. Giustiniani slashed down a lightly armored foe before him and with his left arm pushed a second off the crest of the rampart down into the rubble. His men had arrived at the breach and now stood like a wall of steel between the Turks and the City. Beneath them, the enemy was reforming.

"Bring more torches forward!" he called back into the darkness.

The castanets and trumpets were still playing. Before the light arrived another assault struck. Screaming, the Turks scrambled up the rubble from the foss attempting to gain the top of the ruined wall. The Genoese met them with swords and spears, furiously beating away the light wooden shields of the Sultan's warriors. Some of the Genoese were marines, trained to fight at sea. They were armed with axes and used these weapons as they would against enemy boarders, hacking off arms and heads. The open ground at the crest of the crumbled wall was littered with human debris, but the Turks continued to press on. Giustiniani was concerned about his young nephew. He could not see Marco in the darkness, and the enemy in front of him held his attention.

A Turkish officer was shouting back into the darkness ordering the reserve companies forward to the breaches. A group of marines moved towards him, but the Turks rushed forward to protect their leader. The armor of the Italians was too strong for the Turkish spears and they cut their way through, sending the enemy, officer and all, into the darkness below. Beneath the walls, the Turks huddled in the foss, unwilling to move up against the breaches. The Turkish officers could do nothing to force their men into the assault.

Along the breach, Giustiniani directed fire from the defenders' handguns and crossbows against the enemy massed in the darkness. The shouts of battle were dying out. The sporadic crack of gunfire and the cries of the wounded soon replaced the battle cry of the Turks as they withdrew from the battle. Giustiniani found his nephew. He put a steel encased glove on his shoulder and asked:

"Are you alright?"

"Yes." Marco was short of breath. "I'm fine. You?"

"No wounds."

"Are they done?"

"I think so. At least for tonight. Find water for the men and ask the company commanders to report their casualties to me by sunrise."

Marco nodded.

Giustiniani was tired, but he needed to report the night's engagement to the Emperor. Constantine was at his headquarters behind the Lycus.

"Has the Turkish assault halted, *protostrator*?"

"Yes, your majesty. The enemy has been repulsed with heavy losses."

"And our losses?"

"The company commanders will report their exact casualties in the next few hours, but they are mercifully small. The line held very well."

"Thank you, *protostrator*. Get some sleep."

Giustiniani nodded and headed back to his quarters. It was nearly morning, and he needed to sleep. He made his way to his headquarters and looked at the battlefield map. Seeing the disparity of forces, he understood why Mehmed had attacked, testing, probing for weakness, and eager for victory. But the Turks had been repelled, at least for now, and they had survived this first test. With a few more men, Giustiniani felt he would be able to hold the City against anything. He dozed off to sleep, awakened a couple of hours later by the distant thunder from the west as Mehmed's cannon greeted the day. That night, as always, there would be more repair work to be done at the walls.

3—The Admiral: *April 20, 1453*

It was night, and the three Genoese ships sailed north through the Sea of Marmara under a veil of darkness. They had been commissioned and outfitted at the expense of the Pope, who had ordered them to defend the City. For days, they had languished off the island of Chios praying for a favorable wind, but none had come. While at Chios, the three Genoese were joined by an imperial transport ship bound for home and loaded with grain from Sicily. Soon after the arrival of the Emperor's ship, the wind changed, and the four vessels set sail together. In the early hours of April the twentieth, they moved through the Dardanelles, hoping to slip around the Acropolis Point and into the safety of the Golden Horn before daylight announced their arrival to the enemy fleet.

A fresh wind from the south carried the ships swiftly on their course. Antonis Patanelas, the captain of the imperial transport, strained his eyes into the darkness relentlessly examining the sea ahead of him for Turkish sails. His ears searched the black void for any sound that would indicate the enemy. It would be a matter of timing and luck as to whether his ships would pass undetected. Captain Antonis cursed his blindness but had every confidence in the abilities of his own crew and in the Genoese. They were professionals and more than equal to the task of battle.

In spite of the favorable wind, the ships were somewhat later than they had hoped, and though the hour was still early, the first rays of dawn were lifting the blackness. If they did not reach the safety of the chain boom soon, patrol boats and observers from the coast would surely spot them. There was even a chance that the Turks would have time to intercept them before they could enter the Golden Horn. At this point, they could neither stop nor turn back. Their supplies were urgently needed. An engagement would have to be risked. As these thoughts filled Antonis' mind, a flame-

tipped arrow streaked up from the starboard side of the bow
no more than fifty yards away, another followed in rapid
succession, then a third. They had been spotted. Light from
the arrows momentarily illuminated a small patrol boat.
Shouts of alarm sounded; cymbals and drums crashed as
signals announcing their arrival to the Turkish fleet. Antonis
took stock of the situation. If the wind held, the ships might
yet make the safety of the Horn before the Turks could arm
their ships and intercept them. It was a race.

As soon as the flares lit the murky, pre-dawn sky, the
Turkish fleet at the Double Columns began to buzz with
activity. The Sultan, who was present in the camp, was
quickly roused by breathless messengers who announced
that four ships, three flying the red cross of Genoa and one
flying the double-headed golden eagle of the Emperor, were
swiftly sailing north through the Sea of Marmara. The Sultan
quickly grasped the importance of the situation, and it was
not long before Baltoghlu Suleiman Bey, Governor of
Gallipoli and Lord High Admiral of the Turkish fleet, was
summoned into the royal chamber. When he arrived, bleary
eyed, his master, who never seemed to suffer from fatigue
like an ordinary man, spoke quickly.

"Lord Admiral, four ships are approaching the City. You
are to take our fleet and capture them. We want the captains
and crews in chains before the day is out!"

The Sultan's voice rose as he spoke. Baltoghlu, his mind
clearing from the haze of sleep, understood and appreciated
his master's urgency. The ships were no doubt crammed
with supplies for the garrison: arms, ammunition, and food.
Beyond the physical aid, the ships would supply the garrison
with an enormous emotional encouragement if they were to
elude him.

"It will mean your head if you fail! These infidels have
made fools of us long enough!"

The retainers around the Sultan were shocked when they
heard him make this threat. No one spoke, but several pairs

of eyes among his Magnificence's inner circle looked up in surprise and sought the eyes of their comrades. The admiral was well known both for his bravery and his ability. Moreover, he was an extremely senior commander and was well respected by his peers. To threaten such a man was a clear indication that the strain caused by the siege's failure was beginning to affect the young ruler. Worse, the boy Sultan did not understand the intricacies of war at sea. The admiral was aware, even if his sovereign was not, that the four ships were not easy prizes. Many men would die before the banners would be struck from those high decks. With the ominous warning ringing in his ears, Baltoghlu boarded his flagship and prepared to lead his fleet into battle.

Dawn was coming rapidly. Visibility improved with every minute. From the stern castle of his command ship, Baltoghlu could see four distant silhouettes coming up the straits under full sail. Though moving swiftly, they still had some distance before they would reach the City. If he acted quickly, he would be able to bring them to battle in the narrows before they could round the headland and enter the safety of the Golden Horn.

Baltoghlu had taken measures to improve the fighting readiness of his fleet. He lined the sides of many of his ships with shields to protect the crews from the hail of arrows, stones and javelins that were hurled at them during combat. The cannon on board his larger ships were raised on platforms to better reach the high decks of the Italian-built ships and rain deadly fire on the crew.

Now four of those ships, their high decks appearing clearly out of the light of daybreak, were approaching him. Every available craft was called to action and prepared for battle. Marines strapped on their armor. Elite soldiers who had accompanied the Sultan to the Double Columns were loaded onto transports from which they could board the enemy ships and engage the sailors hand to hand. That was to be the essence of Baltoghlu's strategy. Since his primary

97

orders had been to capture the ships and their crews, his fleet would approach under the power of their oars, they would use their guns to wear down the enemy, then board and take the survivors prisoner.

For the defenders in the City, the sight of the four ships was a ray of hope. Their arrival meant that the world had not abandoned Constantinople to its fate. As the sun appeared, they recognized the banner of Genoa and the standard of the Emperor and cheered. From the eastern and southern sea walls, from the Acropolis, even from the roof of the decayed Hippodrome, the inhabitants of the City, and all soldiers who could be spared from the land defenses, watched the scene as it unfolded in the waters beneath them. But as the Turkish fleet sailed in strength from *Diplokionion*, the scenario began to look bleak to the untrained eyes of the people on the walls. Brutally simple mathematics made the issue hopeless. Four ships were facing the oncoming tide of a hundred and forty. There seemed to be no chance. Desperation forced a hushed silence over the onlookers.

The same wind from the south that drove the Christians towards the City worked against the Turks sailing south from the Double Columns. In addition to the wind, the oars of the Turks fought the current every inch of the way. Nevertheless, the Ottoman sailors were euphoric; the enemy had stumbled, like helpless prey, into their entire fleet. At last they would be able to exact revenge for two weeks of failure and frustration. The rowers pulled in a frenzy to reach their foes, who seemed to wait helplessly for the slaughter. The Turks clashed cymbals and blew trumpets as they rowed towards their victims, confident of victory.

Antonis called his crew to battle stations. The commanders of the three Genoese ships did likewise. They would have to fight it out. Preparations for the impending assault were swift and controlled. The sailors armed themselves with axes to swing at the heads and arms of boarders, with pikes or spears to force the enemy back from a distance, and with swords and knives for close combat. There were large numbers of archers, bows at the ready, quivers full of arrows, as well as a few hand gunners. The men put on their helmets and tightly fastened their chinstraps. Catapults loaded with large stones were made ready to fire. Archers strung their bows. Aboard the imperial vessel, heated and pressurized barrels containing the famous Greek fire were brought to the bronze siphons that would release the deadly concoction.

The strong current prevented the four ships from staying in closer formation. Antonis and the Genoese did not fight it, as separation at that moment gave them a superior field of fire. The current and the angle of Baltoghlu's attack meant that the imperial transport was the first engaged. With the nearest enemy ship in range of his catapults and archers, Antonis gave the order to fire. The catapults aboard his ship snapped into action hurling stones in an even arc against the sailors on the Sultan's ships. Archers lofted their arrows so that death rained down upon the deck. Casualties began to mount. Baltoghlu's sailors tried to keep the decks clear of the bodies of the dead and wounded, but they themselves fell to the well-directed fire from the imperial ship. Many aboard tried to protect themselves with shields and bucklers, but the heavy stones from the catapults smashed through their light defenses cracking open skulls and shattering limbs. The longboat shuddered as stones struck the deck. Oars were smashed to splinters. The mast was struck and collapsed.

Captain Antonis ordered more stones brought on deck. The arms of the catapults bent back as ropes were pulled. The crews in the lead Turkish ships were suffering greatly. Two ships had sustained such extreme casualties that they were compelled to break off their assault. The mass, however, continued forward and opened fire with their own archers, catapults and cannon. Baltoghlu had equipped his ships with another weapon, too—incendiary lances. These were massive bolts, the length of a man and nearly a foot in diameter. These were covered with cloth and oil, set alight, and fired from enormous crossbows mounted on the bows of the largest ships. As the Turkish ships advanced, these missiles streaked through the air to bang against the hulls of the Christian ships. Baltoghlu cursed. Like his cannon, these missiles lacked the necessary elevation to reach the sailors clustered on the decks. They were not propelled with sufficient force to damage the solid wood of the hull and fell harmlessly, steaming, into the sea. On horseback from the land, the Sultan watched the proceedings. Impatiently, he chewed his lips and twitched the reins of his horse, cantering up and down the shore to view the action.

The Turkish ships closed with the imperial transport, and the prows of their vessels touched the high sides of the ship. The longboats bumped against each other, and in the confusion many oars were snapped by friendly craft jockeying for position. The three Genoese ships were also heavily engaged. The Turkish sailors threw grappling hooks in an attempt to fasten their ships to Antonis' vessel. From the lofty decks the Greek sailors fired arrows, stones, and javelins into the mass beneath them. One longboat succeeded in attaching itself to the imperial ship. No one cut the ropes to disentangle the ship, and the enemy deck below became a killing ground.

Antonis also had a surprise in store. "Release liquid fire!" he commanded.

Sailors manning the great bronze siphons, protected under iron-sheeted shelters, now went to work pumping the deadly concoction through the tubes and onto the decks of the grappling enemy ship. The effect was sudden and devastating. The compound was ignited by a small flame as soon as it left the tubes, and a liquid fire rained upon the Turks. A cry of agony, the cry of dozens, pierced the air. Some jumped overboard in an attempt to extinguish the flames in the water of the sea, but water alone could not accomplish the task and the scorched bodies continued to burn as they floated motionless on top of the churning waves. More fire was poured into the Ottoman ship until it was completely ablaze. Antonis now ordered that the longboat be cut free and the imperial ship released the burning hulk the way a spider releases, to its death throes, prey that it has bitten and filled with deadly venom.

From the deck, Antonis could see that the Genoese ships had also shrugged off their attackers. The four ships moved forward once more, their sails filled with the southerly wind that now carried them beyond Baltoghlu's vanguard and towards the City. The citizens on the walls cheered as the four sails broke free. On shore, Mehmed was irate. That fool of an admiral was letting the infidels escape! Furiously, he galloped along the shore screaming at the top of his lungs that his admiral was to close again and capture the infidel ships.

With the wind at their backs it seemed that no effort, no matter how superhuman, could catch them. Baltoghlu barked orders at his rowers for more speed and signaled the rest of his fleet to angle their pursuit so that they could potentially cut off the ships before they reached the Horn. The clashing cymbals and trumpets of the Turks had stopped. The only sound was now the cheering of the Constantinopolitans, willing their comrades on to safety.

Then suddenly, the sails in all four vessels went limp. The friendly breeze died, and with it the cheering from the City. The four great sheets of cloth flapped uselessly against their masts. The last impetus of the wind was spent, and the ships bobbed helplessly on the waves. Worse still, the ships had reached that point, just beneath the Acropolis, where the current strengthened. They were frozen in the water with the Turks bearing down on them furiously. Captain Antonis and the Italians were making every effort to generate speed, but with no wind, and in direct opposition to what was rapidly becoming a strong current, the ships drifted helplessly until they were practically touching the walls of the City. From this position, they were slowly forced by the current out into the straits and towards the Sultan's ships. It seemed that the admiral would have another chance to claim his prey.

Mindful of the damage that his foes could cause with their catapults, and the deadly power of the imperial transport's Greek fire, Baltoghlu disengaged his smaller ships and held his large vessels at a distance. Again, he tried to use his cannon and flaming lances to wear down the enemy, to shatter their ships with his superior firepower and burn them to cinders. The Sultan, on seeing his fleet disengage, shouted at Baltoghlu to push forward. Why was the fool pulling back? Why was he not advancing? Was his admiral, the commander of so many ships, afraid of four?

When the ships drifted into the range of his cannon, Baltoghlu gave the order to open fire. Many shots fell short, the stones plunging into the sea and sending up sprays of water. A few reached the ships where they thudded weakly against the heavy wooden hulls and fell into the water below. No shot made it as high as the decks in order to cause casualties. Baltoghlu ordered an increase in the elevation of the guns, but the second sporadic volley met with as little success as the first. Burning lances whizzed forward in a spray of flame. Patches of fire broke out, but these were quickly put out by the disciplined crews using blankets and water.

It was clear that no progress was being made. Reluctantly, aware that he could neither set fire to the ships nor kill off the crews from this distance, Baltoghlu gave the order for a general assault. He would hurl his entire fleet forward to grapple and board the enemy ships.

The ships continued to drift northeast, away from Constantinople, closer all the time to the impatient Sultan. Baltoghlu was well aware of the fact that his master would have an excellent view of the engagement that was about to take place. His ships were closing rapidly with the enemy. Once again his sailors raised their fearful war cries and launched an avalanche of noise from their drums and cymbals. From the stern of their ships, the enemy fire was light. They were conserving their stores until each shot would be most effective. Baltoghlu admired their professionalism, and cursed it. His own men were firing furiously and doing little damage, but they could not be controlled, not now. They had come too far to be stopped. For an entire day they had played at cat and mouse with these four ships. He gave the order for his ship to increase to ramming speed. Now, in the late afternoon light, the issue would be decided.

The admiral's flagship closed the final few yards rapidly, and its ram caught the imperial craft squarely in the stern. The impact jarred the crews of both vessels and sent many tumbling to the deck. By taking the ship in the stern, Baltoghlu had nullified the awful Greek fire mounted in the ship's bow. In the face of a torrent of arrows and javelins, his men hurriedly clambered up the stern of the imperial ship. Bodies flew from the boarding ladders and tumbled into the sea, but more men kept coming. Other ships now grappled with the transport, and their crews likewise moved to board her. Some came too close to the bow and suffered attack from the Greek fire, but the majority continued to unload more and more soldiers into the battle. The fight became desperate.

The imperial sailors waited along the sides of the ships and sliced off the heads and arms of attackers as they appeared. The number of assailants became so great that they were forced away from the sides of their ship and fought on the decks, in the open, against an endless flood of Ottoman warriors. Arrows were falling into their midst, hitting Greeks and Turks indiscriminately, but the imperial sailors were better armored and suffered less.

At the forefront of the battle was Antonis. The commander, glittering in armor, was everywhere. At the stern of the ship he defended resolutely. Slashing to his right, he cut off the arm of an assailant. He saw a head appear in front of him and brought his sword across, severing the skull from its neck. Blood jetted into the air. Struggling to save his ship, he fought like a man possessed. Stepping back from the mêlée, he ran down from the ship's stern castle to the deck. Breathless, he reached the bow and directed the aim of the liquid fire until two enemy ships were ablaze. The rest, he noticed, fearful of sharing the same fate, were holding back. Detaching ten men, he hurried back to the stern to continue the fight. Another craft had succeeded in sending boarders and Turks were now swarming over the side of his ship, taking the places of the first wave which had retired to make way for these fresh troops. He and his escort were confronted with a dozen Turkish marines armed with axes. One swung for his head and he felt the jolt of the blow against his helmet as he thrust his sword forward at the foe. The blow glanced off, leaving his head ringing. His attacker lay on the deck. Breaking into a run, he forced his way over another Turk and once again to his position at the stern.

He shook his head to stop the ringing and to clear his vision, which was blurred. Dizzily, he grabbed at a rail to steady himself. Still there was no wind, no hope of breaking free. The Turkish ship, the large one to his stern, held them tight unwilling to let go. There was no quarter, no mercy. Looking around him for a moment, Antonis saw the three Genoese ships were likewise besieged. They were completely surrounded but were offering fierce resistance. He could hear the din of battle coming across the water and see smoke rising from their decks. A gun exploded next to him, sending a bullet through a Turkish head that had appeared. His own head rang. The grapples from the most recent attacker were cut, and again the transport was free except for Baltoghlu's flagship, which still had its ram imbedded in its stern and continued to harass them with fire and wave after wave of boarders.

Antonis knew he had to collect his thoughts. He called an aide and instructed him to report the status of his commanders: active troops, wounded, stores of arrows, ammunition and other weapons. The report was not encouraging. Casualties in terms of deaths were few, but half his men were fighting with some kind of wound. The situation regarding weapons was more desperate. The gunners were nearly out of ammunition. There were practically no more javelins. Many men had broken spears, swords and axes in combat and were using weapons that they had picked up from the dead. Archers scrambled about the decks ripping arrows from motionless bodies.

Then the Turks struck again. The ship under the aegis of the double-headed eagle was clearly the prize they desired most. More grappling hooks, more boarders. Again the axes and swords went to work. Hands, arms and heads littered the deck, which was splashed with blood. Men slipped on blood and were covered by it. Mangled bodies floated in the water around the ships as they struggled for victory. Baltoghlu directed covering fire for the boarding parties and urged his men into the vortex. The deciding moment was approaching. The captains of the Genoese ships were aware that the imperial ship had become the sole target of the Ottoman assault. Realizing that the crisis of the battle had arrived, they maneuvered their ships against the enemy, the current and the dead air until their ships, all three, reached the imperial vessel. Antonis understood what the Genoese were attempting and moved his ship to join them. They could not allow themselves to be destroyed in detail. Orders were given for the four ships to be lashed together. To the eyes of the people in the City, a great four-towered keep rose like an island in the middle of the Turkish sea. Under attack, the ships drifted towards the Sultan on the shore.

The sight of the three crosses joining with the golden eagle made the Sultan go wild with rage. He was now uncontrollable and hurled abuse and nonsensical orders at his fleet. Livid with rage, he savagely spurred his horse forward into the waves screaming at his sailors to slaughter the infidels. As if seeking to join the battle, he pushed his horse deeper and deeper into the sea until his robes were wet from the waves. With the ships coming so close to the shore it seemed that he might in fact reach them, but he could not. Mehmed's retainers followed their sovereign's example and they too spurred into the sea towards the ships that were but a stone's throw away. They joined their master in a chorus of abuse, reproaching their comrades as cowards, dogs, and useless women.

On this day, it was they who were powerless, and the "cowardly dogs" aboard the Sultan's ships were contesting every inch of the blood-red sea, flinging themselves again and again, unflinching, into the battle. Baltoghlu heard the shouting from the men on the shore and the orders of his master but ignored it all. With the ships joined, Baltoghlu had only one target, and he attacked it with all the ships he could bring to bear. No sooner could they grapple than they would find themselves cut loose by the relentless axes. Too many ships were crippled, their oars smashed by catapult stones. But for every one of the Sultan's ships that was disabled, another took its place. The men on board the ships bound for Constantinople were weary. The afternoon was wearing on, and having fought since sunrise, their stores of weapons were nearly depleted. Exhausted and blackened by smoke, they were thirsty. Many were wounded, and still they fought. They struck with their swords, with their axes, with their spears. Stoically, they loaded and fired the last bullets from their handguns and notched the last arrows to their bows.

Now the admiral threw himself into the battle. Brandishing a saber, he vaulted onto the stern of the imperial ship and led his men against the foe. His sword glanced off armored chests and helmets, shattered a wooden shield, and found an unprotected side with a thrust. A gun fired in his direction, but the bullet struck a man behind him. He was conspicuous at the front of the fighting, a long red velvet jacket fastened over his mail and plate armor. To protect his face, his helmet had only a long nasal guard that ran from his forehead down over the end of his nose. He wore no visor because he insisted that he needed to see the battle and be recognized by his sailors and marines. The sailors saw their admiral fighting at their side and clawed and hacked their way forward with renewed strength. The four-ship fortress was surrounded. Stones and arrows rained on the crowded decks from all sides. The crews of all four ships were now intermingled as parties rushed across the lashed decks to support their comrades where the fighting was heaviest.

The Turks poured new men into the struggle, relieving those in action. Baltoghlu's assault party had retreated to make room for fresh troops, and the admiral was standing at the front of his flagship shouting orders to the next wave when a stone struck him in the face. Blood came hot on his check, and he reached a mailed hand up to wipe it away. There was a moment of shock. Then the pain nearly made him collapse. Half the world was black. The assault was going forward, but those close to him on the deck quickly rushed to their admiral as he staggered back. His face was a mask of bright red blood. Hastily, he tore at his iron gauntlets trying to free his hands so that they could touch the wound. The admiral's bared hand clapped over his left eye. With his right, he could see blood running between his fingers and down to his elbow. He felt blood soaking into his beard. His left eye felt like hot yogurt.

"My lord, you are wounded, let us disengage."

"No! We must press them! Continue the assault!" His voice was harsh, filled with pain, but still commanding.

Baltoghlu staggered up to the deck and watched with his right eye as the onslaught continued. Again, there was no progress. As if this latest failure sapped his strength,

Baltoghlu slumped to the deck. The physician on board had been killed, so the admiral's aide put a tunic as a pillow under his head. Nor was there fresh water at hand, so another sailor scooped salt water from the sea and used that to wash to wound. The aide tore some bandages to cover the bloody gore that had been his master's left eye.

The battle raged on. The stone and arrow fire between the ships was still heavy. New boarding parties tried to force their way onto the decks. Suddenly, the four sails came alive. A wind from the south. It took Antonis and the Genoese only a moment to notice the breeze. Instinctively, they knew that now was perhaps their last chance to make a run for the City. Shaking off the most recent assault, they separated their ships and made for the Golden Horn, their great sails swelling with the wind. The Constantinopolitans came alive with the sails and cheered as their heroes began to move away from the enemy fleet. Driven by the wind, the four large ships crashed through the small Turkish boats in front of them and headed for the safety of the harbor.

Frustrated at again having lost contact with the enemy, the Turks tried to pursue. Baltoghlu regained his senses with the breeze and thought of pursuit, but his fleet was fought out and dispersed. Night was rapidly approaching. His wound throbbed. Countermanding the will of the Sultan, he ordered a retreat back to the fleet's base. His officers concurred. The fleet had lost two hundred killed, four times as many wounded, and a dozen ships. They had failed.

Mercifully, the cover of evening was swift approaching. After shaking off their pursuers, the four ships were lost in the velvet gray dusk. Seeing their approach, the Emperor ordered the lifting of the chain boom. Three Venetian galleys under the command of Captain Trevisano, blasting trumpets and cheering to sound like thirty, sailed out to escort the four weary craft into the safety of the harbor. From the walls, the cheering citizens ran to the docks to greet the new arrivals. The Emperor and Giustiniani rushed forward to offer their congratulations for the day's heroics. Giustiniani spoke affectionately with the Genoese captains. The Emperor congratulated Antonis, who formally bowed before his sovereign and reported the successful delivery of his cargo of grain from Sicily.

The state of the vessels revealed the full extent of the trial they had surmounted. The decks were covered with broken arrows and shattered spears and splashed with gore. Many men were wounded, but only about thirty had been killed. Comrades lifted the distorted and bloodied bodies of their mates from the decks with reverence. The smell of fire and blood hung heavily in the air. Physicians from the City were brought to treat the many wounded. Every sailor was blackened from head to foot, but they were alive: alive and victorious, smiling so that white teeth shone through charcoal faces. Antonis and his crew felt an enormous relief at returning alive to their families and comrades. Their mission had been accomplished. Now, it would be their task to help in the defense of their City.

Giustiniani's Genoese men came from the walls to speak with their newly arrived countrymen. They went to see if the ships carried any friends or relatives from home and then asked for the latest news. Pope Nicholas had hired the three Genoese ships to support Constantinople. His Holiness continued his negotiations with Venice for the purchase of ships on his behalf and for the *Serenissima* itself to send a fleet. Genoa still entertained hopes of remaining neutral and had no intention of risking open war with the Sultan. It was hardly encouraging news. An important battle had been won, but the fate of the City still hung in the balance.

4—The Sheikh: *April 21, 1453*

The Turkish sailors returned to their base at the old Roman columns called *Diplokionion* in silent sorrow. No fanfare greeted them. The Sultan had changed his robes, taking a black cloak in place of the white robe he had dragged into the sea. Lord Baltoghlu was summoned once more into his presence, but the admiral's wound prevented him from appearing. Orders were given that, regardless of his condition, the admiral was to present himself before the Sultan at dawn. Alone, Mehmed retired to his tent to brood, refusing both food and Gülbahar.

Later in the evening, a message was brought to him, a letter from Sheikh ak-Shemseddin, one of the holiest and most respected religious authorities in the camp and a formidable and dangerous man. The Sheikh's desire to take Constantinople and blot out the infidels was as strong as his sovereign's. The day's failure would not sit well with him. Bracing himself, Mehmed read. As he looked over the words, his face turned red. He slammed his fist against the table. A servant came in and asked if he would like to prepare for bed. Mehmed dismissed the man with a burning stare. Tonight he could not sleep. Again and again he read the letter. The words of condemnation endlessly replayed themselves through his mind.

.... Many are convinced that your highness's misjudgment and lack of authority are responsible for the continued failure of our forces on land and at sea... I cannot urge you firmly enough to severely punish those who have failed you, Allah, and our most holy mission.... If you do not exact punishment for the outrage of today, I swear by the Prophet that this army will cease to respect your highness's authority and that similar disasters will soon befall our troops on land as they have befallen them at sea....

What did the Sheikh mean by this? Was it a threat? Mehmed had threatened Baltoghlu with death before the battle. Would he now be forced to take that promised course? Harnessing the sheikhs to his cause in a holy campaign against the City of the infidels had filled the army with strength. If Shemseddin and men like him abandoned the cause now, the strength of the army would vanish.

Mehmed became furious. His mind filled with fear and anger. A curse upon the City that still defied him! Defied *him*! And now that defiance was stronger by the cargo of those four ships. Four ships had made fools of his entire navy and reached the City against the efforts of his whole fleet. What would happen when the Venetian fleet, ten times greater in number, appeared in the straits? He would have to withdraw, humiliated in front of the entire world. Withdraw, he, the Sultan, the king of kings and successor of the Prophet! Those cursed Christian ships stood untouchable behind their chain just as those cursed Christian soldiers stood untouchable behind their walls! How long would this army, the army of his father, stay in the field with only failures to nourish it? How long could he stay in front of the walls of this accursed City before the great lords of the West sent an army to relieve the siege? How long would it be before men in his own council, Halil Pasha at their head, would turn against him openly and begin to move for the abandonment of the siege? His youthful spirit rebelled at the thought of failure.

"I have come to conquer, and I will not allow us to fail," he said to himself. Tomorrow, I shall make an example of Baltoghlu, he thought. I can only allow my commanders to fail so many times. Yet, what else could he have done against those four monsters? He made every effort a man could make. For a moment, compassion displaced his predatory instincts. But they re-asserted themselves abruptly. "No!" he said aloud. The admiral must pay for his failure! He will pay and then Shemseddin will perhaps give me some peace. Mehmed then spoke aloud again.

"I will break Baltoghlu, and that will warn others of the price of failure. But beware Sheikh, I am Sultan! You cannot call for too many heads before I serve you your own!" Reassured by the thought of the admiral's impending ruin and his own strength, the Sultan moved to his bed and soon drifted off to sleep.

When the sun rose, guards came to Baltoghlu's bed and awakened him. He had spent a painful and sleepless night receiving treatment for his wound. The physicians were certain he would never see with his injured eye again. The great exertions of the previous day, compounded with the enormous loss of blood, robbed him of almost all his strength. A bandage, stained red, covered the eye and the left side of his face. When he spoke, his speech came slowly, as if the terrible wound had taken more than just his eye. The guards helped him up from the bed and took him wordlessly to the Sultan. The resignation of a man who has failed and must pay a terrible price for his failure was stamped on the admiral's face. He felt numb.

Upon entering the tent, he found it full of commanders from both the land and sea. His subordinates, who had suffered in the previous day's action, looked at him with pity through exhausted eyes. Some had wounds of their own, but nothing as serious as their commander's. The army generals who knew him and knew his courage glanced with compassion. Others, political rivals and those who simply disliked him, looked at him with irritation, knowing that his failure would mean greater hardship for all of them.

The Sultan paced the length of the tent listening as various strategies for the next action of the siege were put forward. Sheikh ak-Shemseddin stood to one side, and the Sultan's eyes continuously met those of the cleric as he marched back and forth. There was accusation in those dark eyes and a zealotry that made even Mehmed uneasy. The eyes of both men now came to rest on the wounded admiral. Those of the Sheikh began to burn with indignation.

113

The Sultan's first question before the august company shamed Baltoghlu, as it was meant to. "Lord Admiral, where are the ships we commanded you to capture yesterday?"

"Sire..." The Sultan cut the weak voice off.

"Where are they?" he demanded. The assembly stood stiffly as the scene played out before them.

"We were unable to capture them, sire. The cannon on my ships could do no damage to their vessels. Our efforts to board met with unyielding resistance."

"We saw the engagement! From the shore we viewed your feeble attempts to capture four ships. *Four*, my lord! What cowardice are we to find in our own Lord Admiral? What indolence? You have made a mockery of our fleet. You have ridiculed our power, embarrassed us before our enemies, before our allies, before our army and before Allah."

The mention of God made the Sheikh's eyes blaze even more brightly. Mehmed continued.

"The responsibility for this catastrophe is yours and yours alone." The Sultan paused to catch his breath before pronouncing sentence. "You shall be taken from here and beheaded in front of the army which you have failed and the navy which you have led so poorly."

As soon as the Sultan spoke, the commanders of the fleet erupted in a spontaneous defense of their admiral.

"Sire," a senior galley commander spoke. "I beg your majesty to reconsider. Lord Baltoghlu did everything in his power to gain victory yesterday. You saw the battle. We met the infidel ships again and again. For the entire day we threw ourselves at them. No effort was spared."

"Yet, captain, the failure remains."

"Your majesty," this from a subordinate officer from the admiral's flagship, "I was present aboard the admiral's ship. He fought in the front himself with a courage that surpassed anyone in the entire fleet. With his own sword he fought a score of Christians. Have mercy sire."

"Yes! Mercy sire!" the officers present pleaded in chorus. The Sultan felt his heart forgiving the admiral, his courageous warrior. The Sheikh noticed that his master's face had softened. He spoke.

"Sire!" He had a deep voice that commanded respect.

He had hoped that his letter would have been sufficient to secure the head of the admiral. His master was relenting and would have to be pushed again to action. The Sheikh did not speak often in council. Out of respect there was a hushed silence. The proud and brave commanders feared this man and the tempest of zealotry that he could unleash.

"This is not an issue of the failure of the fleet. It is deeper. In the face of this infidel foe we have failed both on land and at sea. Against great odds this accursed city has stood and endured every assault we have prepared. Our fathers, our grandfathers, generations of our people have fought and died in front of these walls. It is written in the book of the Prophet that one day we shall be victorious here. We shall climb over those walls and make the City our city. Our Sultan will sit on the throne of the Romans. So it is written, but we continue to fail.

"Sire, to your soldiers it seems that Allah has deserted them. Failure breeds failure, and failing the Sultan must be punished. The admiral must pay for this disgrace with his life. Then your army will not fear the enemy. They will not say that the admiral was not punished because victory was impossible. Shall you be known as one who orders the impossible? Let Baltoghlu live, and tomorrow, when your soldiers march against the walls, they will know in their hearts that victory is not expected, that failure will not be punished."

There was silence after he finished. No one seemed prepared to take up the admiral's defense in the face of the Sheikh. Then an old captain, with a bandaged arm stepped forward. He bowed formally and, with his eyes still on the ground, he spoke.

"Your majesty, noble lords, I have been a soldier for many years. I fought beneath these walls with the late Sultan, Allah praise him. I have seen hundreds of battles, cowardice, bravery, victory and defeat. Men do not fight because they fear, Sheikh. Fear is man's enemy. Perhaps our slaves fight from fear, but we cannot. We cannot. Courage, sire, cannot be punished." The captain raised his head, meeting Shemseddin's eyes. "I was in yesterday's battle—I, Sheikh, not you. I faced the Christian arrows and stones, saw my men spitted on their pikes, watched their blood flow over the decks of our ships and spill into the sea. Lord Baltoghlu was there, too, my lords, saber in hand, struggling with the Christians. Look at him. He can barely stand from his wound. He will never see again with his left eye. He has given everything a warrior can give, except his life. And, more often than not, it is better to live and fight again rather than to die." He was winning nods from the other commanders, and this gave him courage to continue. "The Sheikh speaks of the morale of the army. There can be no morale if courage and service are punished by death. Lord Baltoghlu's execution would hurt this army, sire, and endanger our siege."

Shemseddin moved to respond but Mehmed cut him off.

"Enough!" The Sultan's fury at being told what to do from all sides boiled over. He made a decision, a compromise, and would now enforce it. "It is ordered that Lord Baltoghlu be relieved. He is hereby stripped of command of the fleet and removed from the governorship of Gallipolis. All his possessions are forfeit. Let them be divided among the Janissaries. In further punishment for his failure he is to be *bastinadoed** in full view of our forces. Then he is to be removed permanently from this camp and from our forces."

The Sultan met the single bloodshot eye that was focused on him, held it for a moment and turned. The commanders

---

* Beaten upon the soles of the feet.

hung their heads. The captain with the bandaged arm moved towards the admiral as he was being led from the tent and touched his arm, but only for an instant, before he was led away. The commanders were shocked. They had known that the Sultan held them completely in his power, but to see the Lord High Admiral, the Governor of Gallipoli, broken so thoroughly made them realize that no one was safe. Their lives and positions hung on the success or failure of the siege.

The admiral was downcast. The thought of his own death had never troubled him. He had resigned himself long ago, as a warrior does, that his life could end in any second on the battlefield. This life he had been granted was a humiliation. His lands, his fortune, his titles, were carried away on the wind that had propelled those four ships past his fleet. What else could he have done? What more could he have done?

He was tormenting his mind with these questions while the guards brought him out of the Sultan's tent and to an open space before the assembled troops. He was laid on the ground. The sky was blue. Strong arms lifted his legs up. Ropes were tied around his ankles and drawn tight. Two men stood on either side of him. He could not see the one to his left, but heard him. The numbness in the side of his face became lethargy and weakness which spread throughout his body. His head hurt. It throbbed from having to support its own weight. He closed his eye. Something was being read out to the troops: perhaps his sentence, perhaps a warning. The two were the same in either case. The throbbing in his head made it impossible to hear.

Then the beating began. Strong arms alternated blows with switches from the left and from the right. The blows struck sharply and painfully into soft and tight skin on the bottoms of his feet. One after the other they came, endlessly. His feet began to redden and swell, but still the blows came. He grimaced. The spasm of the muscles in his face sent pain from his wound shooting through his entire body. He felt a warm wetness on his feet. The skin had cracked. His feet had begun to bleed. The blows continued. A tear came to his right eye. He could feel the blood dripping from his feet. Then the beating stopped. His legs were released and collapsed to the ground. Roughly, Baltoghlu was lifted up from the earth and made to stand. The agony of the action made him clench his teeth and swallow. His breath was ragged. They led him to a small tent away from the Sultan, away from the bustle of command, away from the fleet. He did not know how long he waited there before men came, took him to the shore and bundled him into a small boat that set sail for Anatolia and obscurity.

5—The Plan: *April 22, 1453*

Mehmed's great cannon greeted the dawn with their customary salvo. The failure of the previous day had not altered the Sultan's intention of reducing Constantinople's walls to rubble. There was no respite for the weary defenders. Like all days since the beginning of the siege, the twenty-second of April began with thunderous fire from the Turkish lines. Constantinople trembled as the impact of the colossal cannon stones against the ancient walls sent shockwaves through the City. The bombardment was concentrated against the area around the Gate of Saint Romanos. The victory of the Genoese seemed to have redoubled the desire of the Turks to take the City. It was as if the frustration of the previous day was being given vent as the guns drove stone after stone against the walls. The shots shattered themselves on the ancient masonry, chipping away at the City's shield until the Bactatinian tower was brought crashing down. With the tower, the barrage swept away an entire section of wall more than a dozen yards in length. The wreckage tumbled into the foss so that the ditch was nearly filled. Fear took hold of the defenders as the positions along the *Mesoteichion* were laid bare.

Giustiniani was immediately at the scene giving orders. Whatever building material could be found was raced to the gaping wound and assembled into a makeshift stockade. Drums and wooden barrels filled with earth and stone were propped up with timbers on top of the rubble. A few courageous men braved the enemy fire and ventured into the foss to clear it of debris and deny the Turks a level causeway to the defenses. Behind Theodosius' ruined bulwark, Giustiniani set the men to dig a second ditch that would further impede the enemy assault. The defenders were losing ground, and the *condottiere* did not like that. They were now defending a crude palisade on top of and behind the original rubbled wall. He glanced hurriedly at the men

119

scrambling to make the repairs while scanning the Turkish lines for any sign of an impending assault. He had sent Marco to the workshops in the Venetian quarter for *pavises** and anything else that could be used to provide protection during the assault. The assault, however, did not come. The Sultan was at the Double Columns, brooding like his hero Achilles over the failure of the previous day, and punishing his failed admiral; he was not in the Lycus Valley to order the troops forward.

The disgrace of his admiral weighed heavily on Mehmed. Though Sheikh ak-Shemseddin had not convinced Mehmed to execute his admiral, he had convinced the Sultan that Baltoghlu's defeat was in many ways his own. As the Sheikh had said, it was a symptom of a larger illness. Continued failure was beginning to strangle the Turkish camp. The Sultan sat alone in his tent, weighing the course he would pursue. Despite the enormous odds in his favor, the siege was not going well, and time was growing short. Many soldiers had had enough and wanted to go home. Soon the enormous burden of feeding his host would become an issue. Unless the situation was drastically altered in the next few days, they would be compelled to withdraw.

Mehmed racked his brain. What could be done? The Sultan had no intention of leaving the City unconquered, but "wiser" heads among his courtiers would no doubt advise caution and work for an abandonment of the siege. Halil Pasha was foremost among those moving for an armistice— the coward. The Greek-loving Vizier was so easily corrupted by their gold, their flattery, and their talk of peace. Mehmed chaffed at the thought of his dream dying because of the resistance of the shrewd old man. But Halil Pasha was not alone. There were others in the camp who would take the Grand Vizier's side. How could all of them be overruled? Defeat would disgrace him in the eyes of Gülbahar. Never

---

* A large rectangular shield, usually placed in front of slow-firing crossbowmen. Widely used during sieges.

again would she cast her spell at him with those bewitching eyes or inspire his embrace with talk of glory. He could see her eyes, if he failed, glazed with boredom and disappointment, reluctantly giving in to his embraces until he went mad from her insipid love.

What could be done? Every assault against the land walls had failed. No matter how much of the walls his cannon brought down, those inside the City managed to make repairs and hold their line. And at sea... in the name of the Prophet! At sea, that fool of an admiral had failed to capture four ships. His anger was building. How could the fleet hope to force its way into the Golden Horn and threaten the sea walls against a score of Christian ships sheltered behind an impenetrable chain? Mehmed's mind was racing. That cursed chain! His armada had no chance to even come to grips with the enemy while they remained behind the boom. How could he force his way past it? Past it... through it... around it.... Perhaps there was a way around the chain. It was then that the solution came to him. It filled his brain with an image of victory. In his imagination, he saw his ships moving around the boom, pouring into the Golden Horn, riddling the Christian fleet with gunfire and raking the sea walls with a relentless barrage. The warm feeling of confidence that it gave him traveled from his head down through his entire body. His heart began to beat rapidly. The full red lips parted in a smile. Around.

"Around." He murmured the word out loud now, rolling it off his tongue gleefully and smiling broadly as he pronounced it. He leapt up from the desk and called for one of the guards. Within him, anger was transforming itself into energy.

"Send Hamza Bey to me immediately! Bring Zagan Pasha too!" He would reveal his inspiration to the new admiral and the commander of the land forces on the Peran side of the pontoon bridge. He would need their cooperation to turn his inspiration into reality.

The two commanders were not long in coming. Each entered the Sultan's tent with several staff officers, bowed and looked at their sovereign. Mehmed was still smiling. He explained the plan to them quickly with rapid sentences and excited gestures. He pulled them over to the maps and traced the operation out with his hands. When he finished, the officers stood in shock. They had no comprehension of what the young Sultan was demanding. It was impossible. They looked at each other and their master with blank, uncomprehending expressions. Did the young ruler have any idea what he was proposing? It was a ludicrous idea that would cost time and energy for no result.

There was a tense moment of silence. The Sultan was irritated with his captains. The fools did not see his plan! They could not comprehend it. For their part, Hamza Bey and Zagan Pasha looked at their fierce young ruler and wondered how they could refuse his wild scheme and keep their heads. It was at this moment that one of the foreign advisors intervened to break the awkward silence.

"The plan is possible my lords. It can most certainly be accomplished."

The eyes of the assembly turned to the speaker. A few among them, including the Sultan, had no idea who he was. He was one of Karadja's Pasha's European advisors. That was all any of them knew. But, for the moment, he commanded the floor of the distinguished assembly.

"How are you so sure?" demanded Zagan Pasha.

"It has been done before. I have heard that the Venetians succeeded in a similar operation during one of their wars in Italy. What your majesty is proposing would follow the same principles. It is possible."

Mehmed leapt at the reinforcement of his proposal. "Then, my lords, it is settled. Make the necessary preparations. We move immediately."

The commanders stood dumfounded. There was nothing left to debate. They would act to make their master's impossible idea a reality. Possible or not, it was the Sultan's will. Mehmed and his commanders began to work out the numerous details. The plan slowly took shape. If it succeeded, the entire complexion of the siege would change.

Above the Valley of the Springs, behind Pera and at the Double Columns, the Turks worked furiously. Speed was of the essence. It all had to happen swiftly, before word was brought to the City by sympathetic Genoese in Pera or by spies in the Sultan's camp. Any information that leaked would compromise the element of surprise and lessen the effect on the Christian forces. Much wood was needed for the plan, as well as ropes and pulleys. Batteries of cannon would be set up above the Valley of the Springs so that their covering fire could be directed against the Christian ships along the entire length of the Golden Horn. Timbers were brought to build the gun platforms. Within the camp, lambs and oxen were slaughtered and their fat rendered into grease for the ropes. The ground behind Pera was leveled so that it could be more easily trafficked. A long ditch was dug from the Double Columns all the way to the Pera basin beneath the Valley of the Springs. Wooden planks were laid out in the trench as a sunken highway to connect the two points. Along the edges, rails were installed to steady the traffic that would soon pass. Men and oxen were assembled so that the operation could begin as soon as the sun set. Secrecy was paramount. The success of the Sultan's plan hinged on achieving complete surprise.

As the day wore on, the defenders along the *Mesoteichion* continued their repairs. The wall was being rebuilt with earth and timber. At night they would complete their work and move forward to clear the foss. In the late afternoon, a new battery of guns next to the Genoese colony of Pera opened fire. Their bombardment was concentrated against the chain boom and the ships in the Golden Horn. The fire was heavy. Shots fell not only among the Christian ships, but within the walls of Pera itself. The Sultan had specifically

ordered that some shot fall short so that any curious
Genoese would be kept away from lookout posts along the
town's walls. Along the chain boom, an imperial vessel was
struck by a cannon ball and sank. Soligo moved the other
ships under his command out of range. Thick white smoke
obscured the Genoese colony from the view of the defenders
along the sea walls and the dull bangs of the cannon drifted
over the calm waters of the Golden Horn. The failure of the
fleet during the previous day's engagement had obviously
spurred the Sultan to a new pitch of action, but the
defenders could not have imagined the surprise that the
young ruler had conceived.

* * *

No one in the City knew how it happened, but the ships
were sailing across the land. They came in a great procession
as if at a review, their brightly colored sails billowing
proudly in the wind. It was an impossible sight, an entire
fleet crawling along the ground like a caravan. Fishermen
who had set out for the morning's catch in the waters of the
Golden Horn were the first to see the strange cortege.
Drums, fifes and trumpets were playing, enhancing the
surreal aura with their music. A single longboat led the way.
It negotiated the steep slope from the Valley of the Springs,
and, supported by ropes and pulleys, dragged by oxen and
steadied by a team of marines, was lowered with a splash
into the basin of Pera. The crews cheered, and before the
fishermen had packed their nets to return to port, a
succession of longboats followed the first, taking possession
of the hitherto impenetrable Horn. Like ducks, the fleet
slipped back into the water. By now, the defenders along the
sea walls were awake and viewed the outrageous events
unfolding beneath their eyes with stupefaction. Nothing
could have prepared them for what they witnessed. Panic
began to spread.

Now that the Sultan's armada was entering the Horn, he could bring assault parties against the sea walls. He could attack the fleet from two directions at the same time. The crews of the Christian ships were forced to stand at arms, ready for action, through the entire day and night as the Sultan continued to pour ships into the basin. In all, seventy-two long boats and transports were brought across the land and lowered in behind the Christian fleet. At the same time, Mehmed was throwing a pontoon bridge from the Pera basin towards the City so that direct assaults could be made against the sea walls. On this bridge, made from enormous barrels covered over with wooden planks, cannon were already positioned and had opened fire on the Christian ships. Soon the bridge would reach the sea walls bringing them too under attack.

The paralysis of shock soon wore off, and Minotto called a meeting of his Venetian war council. With Alvise Diedo in overall command of the Christian fleet, the crisis was primarily a Venetian concern. Giustiniani, due to his position, was also invited to attend. The men met in the church of Santa Maria to try to determine how they would deal with the new threat. The presence of the Turkish fleet in the Horn had compromised the safety of their ships. The sea walls were now in serious danger. Decisive and immediate action was needed. The *bailò* called the council to order.

"As you all know, the enemy have somehow managed to bring their ships into the Golden Horn. In a single day, the defense afforded our ships by the chain boom has been rendered almost useless. I have called you here so that we may settle on a course to neutralize this new threat." The assembly remained silent. "Does anyone have a plan to suggest?"

Giovanni Loredan, a member of one of Venice's richest and most powerful families spoke first: "The ships lie close to the Genoese colony of Pera. The Sultan's guns fire from behind Pera, over the city. The Genoese must realize how precarious our position is. They must realize how precarious their position is becoming. Surely, the time has come for them to put aside their pretenses of neutrality and wholeheartedly take up the sword for Christendom. Their ships, joined with ours, will be more than a match for the longboats currently in the Golden Horn." There were murmurs among the council. "I do not mean any disrespect to Master Giustiniani. He is a brave man and fine soldier, but the cowardice of his countrymen must cease!"

Fabrizio Cornaro replied. He was not wholly hostile to Genoa, as were many of the other men present, and his diplomatic background brought a voice of moderation.

"My Lord Loredan, whether the Genoese are cowards or not, you must recognize the practical difficulties of what you suggest. First, Pera has absolutely refused to take sides officially for the duration of the siege. It is unlikely that they would abandon this position now, when the Sultan's grasp is tighter than ever around their throats. I would also suggest that we do not have the luxury of time necessary to negotiate for their cooperation. Such a diplomatic effort would take days, and time is pressing. I do not think that Genoese cooperation is a reasonable solution. What do you think Master Giustiniani?"

Giustiniani smiled. He had ignored the slur against the courage of his countrymen in the interest of the council's success and because time was precious. He knew that cooperation for this operation, even if Pera agreed in principle, would occupy too much valuable time. He concurred with Cornaro.

"My fellow Genoese would indeed need much convincing if they were to abandon their neutrality for the sake of this attack. As for *signor* Loredan, he seems to have forgotten yesterday's display of Genoese courage and the fact that many citizens from Pera and from Genoa are part of the City's defense. Nevertheless, I do not think we have the time we would need to persuade them." He paused for a moment and then continued. "I would, however, make a suggestion of my own. It might be possible to slip a party of several hundred men across the Horn in small boats so that they could attack the Turkish camp west of Pera. These men would assault and destroy the guns positioned at the Valley of the Springs and disrupt the bridge that the Sultan is using to bring the ships across the land."

It was Minotto who responded.

"Master Giustiniani, we appreciate your courageous and daring suggestion, and under other circumstances would agree that it is an excellent course. But I for one feel that we do not have enough men defending the City to risk the number needed for such a bold attack."

Cornaro took the part of the *bailò*.

"Indeed. There are too few defenders on the land walls as it is. I don't think a single man could be spared, let alone several hundred. The Emperor would never allow it."

"Noble sirs," Alvise Diedo, the commander of the fleet now spoke, "We may have few men, but we have many ships. With the addition of the Genoese ships that arrived, we are even stronger. At sea, our skill and the superiority of our ships make us more than a match for the enemy. Every engagement has shown our fleet to be completely dominant. I believe that the Turks have presented us with an opportunity. They have divided their fleet and presented us with a large part of it in confined space. Let us attack them with all our ships, with or without the help of Pera, and crush them in an open fight!"

"Courageous words, captain," answered Minotto, "but too ambitious, I think. We cannot hope to win this siege at sea; all we can do is lose it, and a failure in the engagement you suggest would spell disaster for the City. I believe the risk is too great."

"The *bailò* is correct, *signore*," added Fabrizio Cornaro. "And the Sultan's batteries on the heights above present too much firepower for our ships. We cannot risk it." Diedo, unwilling to challenge the consensus, responded with a weary nod and the assembly drifted into silence once more.

It was Giacomo Coco, the intrepid master of the galley from Trebizond, who broke the silence: "Sirs, I know the course we must pursue. Let us prepare a small group of ships and with them set fire to the Turkish fleet now inside the boom at night. We would need only half a dozen ships. Two large vessels to move in the lead supported by two swift galleys and finally some small longboats equipped with incendiaries. We will approach the Turks under the cover of darkness and engage them with the fire-ships. I would consider it an honor to lead the attack personally."

The plan quickly won the assent of many in the council. It was daring, but would also not endanger a great number of ships. The operation could be planned in a short time and had the potential to develop into a substantial success without enormous risks. It would take place at night and therefore would neutralize the firepower of the batteries along the heights. Coco's plan was accepted.

Preparations were in full swing along the harbor. There was an attempt to put a veil of secrecy over the operation, but the docks buzzed with excitement. Excitement soon became gossip that some attempt was being planned to break the Turkish control of the Horn. Night fell, and the preparations continued in the darkness. It was midnight when the commanders taking part in the attack assembled on board Alvise Diedo's flagship. It was decided that the captains of the merchantmen from the Tana fleet, Silvestrio Trevisano, Girolamo Morosini and, of course Giacomo Coco, would command the longboats. Gabriele Trevisano would lead the supporting light galleys. The final details were being discussed when a clamor was heard along the dock. The pronunciation was unmistakable—Genoese voices. A group of about ten Genoese entered the cabin.

"Captains! What is this we are hearing about Venetian plans to burn the Turkish fleet tonight?" The Venetians

128

turned, searching each others' eyes for explanations of how the Genoese had heard of the plan. "No sooner do we arrive in the City, stained with battle and covered in glory, than you immediately seek to outdo us and steal glory for yourselves!"

Alvise Diedo calmly answered the accusation.

"Sir, we had no intention of 'stealing' any glory for ourselves. As commander of the naval defenses for Constantinople, it is my duty to organize a response to the new Turkish threat. Your ships have only just come to the City. As you have said, you were in action the day before yesterday, for the entire day. In my judgment your ships are not yet ready to face the enemy again."

"Captain Diedo, we demand that Genoese ships be included in your operation. We are allies in this battle. You cannot act alone. Inform us of the details of your plan and allow us to participate in its implementation." Diedo did not recognize this man who was obviously the spokesman for the Genoese.

"Where are the captains of the ships that came in two days ago? I would like to speak with them and see if their vessels and crews are ready for such an operation."

"I speak for those men, captain. I can assure you that they and their crews are ready for battle. The only necessary delay would be for us to prepare the ships to your specifications for the attack."

Diedo's position was difficult. As commander of the fleet he could not simply ignore his allies. All eyes were upon him. The captain was feeling uneasy again. The burden of command was weighing on him. It was feasible that the Genoese might use their exclusion from the operation as an excuse to abandon the defense entirely. Compromise was the only feasible course.

"Very well." He paused. The eyes of the Venetian commanders registered disbelief. Coco's gaze smoldered with anger. Diedo continued. "My captains and I accept the offer of Genoese assistance in our endeavor. Sit, and we will discuss the plan."

More chairs were brought to the large table. The spokesman and two of his companions sat. The rest remained standing. When they had settled in, Diedo explained Coco's plan.

"Tomorrow night, we hope to send two large ships, padded with bales of cotton, forward from our lines against the Turkish cannon. These ships shall cover the movements of a pair of light galleys, three longboats, and several small craft equipped with Greek fire and other incendiaries. This force will engage the Turkish fleet within the Golden Horn and set fire to as many ships as possible." The Genoese nodded. "What support can you offer?"

Puffing himself up proudly, the emissary answered. "The Republic of Genoa volunteers one large sailing ship to be used in the vanguard of the attack and will prepare three fire-ships."

"When can your be ready?"

"Thank you, *signor* Diedo. I must ask the captains, but I am sure everything will be ready in only a few days time."

"A few days time?" exploded Coco.

Diedo glanced at him. Coco answered the eyes that pled moderation.

"After a few days, *signore*, it will be out of the question for us to surprise the Turks! We must attack tonight."

There was a moment of silence as Coco's words hung ominously in the cabin. Diedo had an uneasy feeling that his friend was correct. There was no going back now, not without irreparably offending the Genoese. It would have to be a cooperative effort. God willing everything would be ready in twenty-four hours. Diedo turned to the men from Genoa.

"Make your ship ready as quickly as possible. Time is of the essence."

Bowing, the Genoese delegation left the cabin and departed for the shore to prepare their ship for the attack. As soon as they were gone, Coco erupted.

"Captain Diedo, why did you agree to their demands?" He was furious.

"I had no other choice, Giacomo. We cannot hope to be victorious if there is continued enmity between Venice and Genoa. We must work together."

"How can we be victorious if we wait for them to be ready? My ships are prepared. The other captains are ready to attack tonight! We cannot wait. The Turks grow stronger every hour that we delay. Every hour gives Mehmed more time to uncover our plan with his spies! What have you done?"

"Calm down Giacomo, please. There are many considerations to be made. We must not be disunited at such a critical moment."

But Coco was beyond allowing his commander to calm him down. "By heaven, Alvise, do not take your position as admiral so seriously! You dislike and distrust the Genoese as much as I do. You are jeopardizing the entire plan and the lives of my sailors."

"Do not forget yourself Captain Coco! I command here. The sailors you speak of are not yours, but the servants of our Republic of Venice. It is my decision that we shall wait for the Genoese to prepare their ship." Coco would have responded, but Captain Morosini restrained him.

"Calm yourself Giacomo, we are all in God's hands. His will be done." Morosini's voice was composed.

Coco responded desperately. "Girolamo, you know better than I the position we are in. Our success depends on complete surprise. This delay will mean failure and death for us all. My plan was not for us to lead our ships against the Turks after they had days to prepare, but for us to attack now, tonight!"

"We will wait. Perhaps everything will be ready by tomorrow. Let us hope that our Genoese comrades prepare swiftly." Morosini now spoke to the entire assembly. "Now, I think we need to address our plans and how the partnership with the Genoese will affect them." The council continued their discussion through the night. It was not until dawn was breaking that the captains left Diedo's flagship and returned to their quarters to get some much needed sleep. As the sun peaked above the horizon, Mehmed's cannon thundered their daily greeting.

6—The Golden Horn: *April 25, 1453*

The Genoese had assured Diedo that the crews of the newly arrived ships were ready for combat. This, however, was not the case. The sailors were exhausted by their long battle. Fully one half of the crewmen had some sort of wound. No attack was possible on the twenty-fourth or even on the twenty-fifth. Delay followed delay as the captains requested more time to ready their men for the attack. The preparation of the fire ships was also slow. As each day passed, Giacomo Coco became progressively more anxious, but there was nothing he could do. Alvise Diedo had regretted his acceptance of Genoese aid almost as soon as it had been made. Now that the attack was suffering a significant delay, he was beside himself with apprehension. Diplomacy and his authority made it impossible for him to go back on his word. They would have to wait for the Genoese.

In the meantime, the Sultan had not been idle since penetrating into the Horn. More guns had been brought to the heights above the Valley of the Springs and the pontoon bridge was moving forward from the basin into the water. Additional cannon had been mounted on it. Mehmed was consolidating his gains. Undoubtedly there would be some attempt to dislodge his ships from their new position, and he would be ready for it. His spies in Pera would inform him of any operations that were being planned. The Sultan decided to remain at the Double Columns to make certain that the Christians would not try to win back what had been lost. Along the land walls, the barrage continued. In Mehmed's absence, however, there were no assaults, only the now routine task of rebuilding at night what had been destroyed during the day.

The empty hours weighed on Giustiniani. For the first time since the siege had begun, his mind found itself thinking of Caterina. She had been so cold to him that night:

133

few words, mere polite formalities to prevent arousing her husband's suspicions, thinly-veiled insults, and glacial silence. Now she was so close, a thin ribbon of water away. And now Mehmed had thrown a fleet between them. Whatever hopes the *condotierre* had of seeing Caterina were dashed by the Sultan's daring. He would not be able to see her until the siege was over, and then only if he was victorious. Much of the chance for that victory hung on the sails of the Italian ships that would move against the Sultan's fleet in the Golden Horn. As the *condotierre* made his way to the imperial palace the longing to enter the fight built within him, until nearly bursting, he found himself in the presence of the Emperor.

"Good evening, *protostrator*."

"Good evening, your majesty."

"How is the repair work proceeding at the *Mesoteichon*?"

"Well, sire."

"Are you lacking any supplies?"

"No, sire. We have sufficient barrels, stones, and earth to patch the wall, shields and wooden *pavises* for shelter. The new line will hold. But, if your majesty could spare a few small cannon, the extra firepower would be appreciated."

"Lord Notaras?" Constantine's eyes moved questioningly to the Grand Duke. Notaras commanded the City's reserve, including the cannon.

"It is not prudent sire, to deploy our reserves so early. We will have need of them against the larger Turkish assaults to come. I don't see why they should be chopped up piecemeal."

Giustiniani responded directly, even though Notaras had spoken to the Emperor. "It is clear that the Sultan is concentrating on the *Mesoteichon*. That is where the assault will fall, and that is where the reserve is needed."

"There are enough men there to hold that position, under the proper command," added Notaras bitterly.

134

Constantine intervened, diplomatically attempting to maintain the balance. "We cannot ignore the possibility that Mehmed will shift his attentions somewhere else. The reserve will remain intact, for now." He paused, silent for a moment and then changed the subject. "I have word from *Bailò* Minotto. The assault against the Horn will take place tomorrow in the hours before dawn."

"Yes, sire." Giustiniani's voice was distant, sailing with his Genoese to the battle.

"I pray that they are successful, but no matter the result, this siege will be decided by the men at the walls. That is why I need you there, *protostrator*. There is no man better." And suddenly, to the complete astonishment of the assembly, Constantine put his hand on the *condotierre*'s shoulder. "We will summon you with news of the engagement as soon as we know anything. Good night, *protostrator*."

"Good night, your majesty."

✳ ✳ ✳

The spy slipped out of Pera easily and moved towards *Diplokionion*. He mounted a mule and rode off, approaching the Turkish camp with caution. It was not uncommon for traders to visit the base trying to sell supplies or information, but he did not wish to take any unnecessary risks. He was soon spotted by the guards on sentry duty. They did not recognize him. He told them, in broken Turkish, that he wished to see Hamza Bey immediately. The admiral's secretary, he added, would recognize him. There were a few tense moments as Faiunzo waited. The secretary arrived, bleary eyed with fatigue. He had been working extremely hard to bring the ships into the Golden Horn and had not slept much during the past week.

"Who is this man?" he demanded of the guard.

"A citizen of Pera, lord, who claims that he needs to see Hamza Bey on a matter of immediate importance."

The secretary looked quizzically at Faiunzo. The thin wrinkled face was familiar to him, but he could not place it.

"What is your name?"

"Faiunzo, lord Ahmet. I am a Genoese citizen of Pera and a servant of his most gracious majesty the Sultan. I have important information to convey to Admiral Hamza Bey. Your lordship and I have met before."

The secretary searched his memory, then nodded. He remembered. Ahmet turned to the guard.

"Bring him to the admiral's tent in ten minutes." The secretary walked away to prepare his master to receive the guest. Faiunzo stood with the sentry and arranged his clothes, attempting to make himself more presentable in front of the Sultan's admiral.

Hamza Bey was a short and fat man. He was an intimate of the Sultan's and had been the chief cupbearer of Mehmed's father. A compliant piece of clay in the hands of his master, his unfailing obedience had won him a fortune in court appointments and now, after the disgrace of Baltoghlu, command of the fleet. Like his secretary, he had been working madly during the past days. He stood hunched over maps of Pera and the highway being used to transport the ships. The charts were stained with bits of food and drops of wine. There was a silver tray full of chicken bones on the table. They had been picked clean. He looked up and saw Faiunzo.

"Is this the Genoese informer?"

"Yes, my lord." The secretary pushed the merchant forward.

"Lord Hamza, I am Faiunzo of Genoa, a merchant from Pera. Tonight I overheard plans for an attack against your ships in the Golden Horn. Tomorrow night, or perhaps the day after tomorrow, a small group of Venetian ships will sail out from Constantinople and attempt to set fire to your fleet. They plan to attack before sunrise."

The new admiral listened wordlessly prompting Faiunzo to volunteer more information.

"Your lordship should prepare to meet the assault with as many cannon as possible. The larger vessels in the lead will be padded with bales of cotton so that your cannon fire will be less effective. Smaller ships will follow and they will be armed with Greek-fire and with other incendiary devices."

The admiral looked at the small man who was bringing him this news. "Are you sure of your information?"

"Yes, my lord."

"And why do you bring such information to me? What do you hope to gain?"

"I felt that it was my duty, my lord."

"Ha!" Hamza laughed sarcastically. "Duty indeed. You must truly despise the Venetians if you are so willing to see them killed by us infidels. Such enmity and hatred exists between you Christians. It is astounding that your faith survives." He paused. "Your loyalty is appreciated." As he spoke Hamza threw a bag of coins across the table. A few of the golden florins spilled out. "These should be more to your taste than Venetian ducats."

The merchant pushed them into the bulging purse and buried it in his cloak. The two men stared at each other over the table for a moment, then Hamza motioned to the secretary with his hand.

"He has his money, take him away."

Faiunzo bowed awkwardly and withdrew. Guards escorted him to the edge of the camp where the traitor carried his gold back to Pera. In the tent, Hamza still pored over his maps. Without looking up, he spoke to the secretary.

"So, Ahmet, do you believe him?"

"Yes, my lord. I know the man. His information is reliable. He hopes to profit from our victory and from the defeat of Venice."

"The defeat of Venice? Does he care nothing for the final smothering of the Empire of the Romans?"

"The Greeks are heretics, Lord Hamza. No one seems interested in helping them. Venice and Genoa are here to protect their own interests."

"Well, for the moment that is not our concern. We must inform his majesty and prepare. I shall not fail the same way as Lord Baltoghlu."

Ahmet nodded. Hamza picked up a sheaf of papers and strode as swiftly as his stocky legs would carry him to his master's tent. Coco's plan was betrayed. The Sultan would be forewarned, and the doom of the Venetian sailors was sealed.

* * *

It was two hours before sunrise on April the twenty-eighth when the attack force finally set sail. They slipped silently from the harbor into the darkness of the Golden Horn. The two large ships, one Venetian and one Genoese, each padded with cotton and wool, were in the lead, followed by two galleys commanded by Gabriele Trevisano and Sir Zacaria Grioni. Behind these came the three longboats and finally the fire-ships with pitch, brushwood and gunpowder. The Greeks had supplied several of the craft with siphons of liquid-fire that could be used both against the Turkish fleet and to burn the pontoon bridge.

Coco was anxious. He had waited for nearly a week to make this attack. Now was the moment of decision. It was important that he push any distractions away from his mind. The argument with Diedo, the postponements of the Genoese and the interminable days of waiting needed to be forgotten. But he could not clear his brain. The concerns weighed heavily on him as the rowers silently dipped their oars and moved the ships on in the darkness. His worries transformed themselves into impatience. The transport ahead of him was moving so slowly! Was it not enough that the Genoese had delayed the attack for days, now they were impeding his progress during the operation? The great ship had only forty rowers on each side and was not as fast as Coco's longboat. They were crawling forward. At this speed they would not be able to surprise the Turks. The black of night would soon resolve itself into a gray that hinted at the dawn.

"What are the Genoese doing?" He hissed under his breath. "Haven't they slowed us enough already?"

Andrea da Ruodo, the captain of the ship, replied. "Their ship is not as fast as ours, sir."

"They're not even making an effort! How can we hope to surprise the Turks at this speed? The Genoese are deliberately slowing the attack so that the Turks will be forewarned. They are betraying us!" Coco's temper had been roused.

"We must proceed at their speed, sir. They are our cover," advised da Ruodo. "We cannot run beyond the rest of the fleet."

"To hell with their speed! They are leading us into a trap. We must be the first to engage the enemy!" Coco's temper had boiled beyond his ability to control it. He turned to one of the ship's mates, Polo Catanio.

"Full speed!" he ordered.

Catanio looked at him uncomprehendingly and turned to da Ruodo for reassurance. The ship's master nodded. The longboat's seventy-two rowers began to pull with all their strength. The ship's slender hull cut swiftly through the black water. Coco had waited too long for this moment. There would be no more delays. Soon, his ship had outstripped the padded transport and was moving in the lead against the Turkish fleet. Coco encouraged the rowers to pull with greater strength. The smooth splashing of the oars propelled them into the night. In the darkness, they had lost touch with the rest of the fleet, but Coco was confident that they could not be a long way behind. He could hear the faint slapping of oars. The other longboats, fire-ships, and even the two galleys were not far away. Coco was confident that the night would soon be lit by the burning of Turkish ships.

Suddenly, a streak of flame came from the Turkish position illuminating the ships as they made their way forward. Out of the darkness, a flurry of cannon shots shattered the rhythm of the oars. Cheering erupted from the Turkish lines. A shot struck Coco's longboat just behind the mast. The ball had been fired over a long range and did not penetrate the hull. Other shots plunged into the sea, splashing water on the deck. The soaked oarsmen continued to pull. Andrea da Ruodo looked at Coco, apprehension plain on his face. The Turks were prepared for them. They had sailed into a trap.

"Giacomo, we are betrayed!" exclaimed the captain.

"Keep your post captain!" shouted the commander. He thrust the tiller into da Ruodo's hands and ran forward, down from the stern to see the extent of the damage.

The ball had smashed the handles of three oars. Two rowers were dead and another three wounded. Coco slipped on their blood and had to steady himself against the mast. The ship was still sailing forward, but the element of surprise had been lost. The Turks fired again. This time, a shot struck the *fusta* amidships and punched through. Water plumed through the shattered hull, flooding the deck. The force of the blow threw Coco to the ground. He felt a sharp pain in his left leg and looked down. A large splinter had imbedded itself in his thigh. Already there was a pool of blood beneath him. Dutifully, the femoral artery continued pumping, carrying his blood into the sea. The deck was tilting into the water. Coco, facing the stern now, felt himself sliding into the waves. His leg was afire with pain. He could hardly move, but knew that he had to get off the ship quickly if he wanted to avoid drowning. Arrows and gun shots were now striking the ship as flares illuminated the target for the Turks. The crew was in chaos. Coco saw that Catanio, the mate, was near him. He could hear the voice of Antonio da Corfu, one of the ship's partners, but the shouts were incoherent and desperate. The Turkish cannon roared again, churning the waves around them. Catanio was over him.

"Captain, are you hurt?"

"Help me up."

But the mate could not. An arrow shot through his neck and he crumpled to the deck. The ship was sinking. Desperately, Coco tried to raise himself and swim free of the wreckage. He could not move his left leg, so he reached with his right hand for a rail or an oar on the ship's port side to lift himself up. He managed to plant his right foot. But the wounded ship rocked again and sent him tumbling to the deck. The water was rising and lapping over his legs.

For the first time in his memory, the bold captain began to feel fear. There was no way out; he felt he was going to die. Other crew members were already flailing in the water as they tried to climb the sloping floor of the ship to no avail. His breath quickening to the pace of abject terror, Coco began to pray. *"Ave Maria, gratia plena, Dominus tecum. Benedicta tu in mulieribus, et benedictus fructus ventris tui, Iesus. Sancta Maria..."* then an upsurge of water momentarily submerged him. He surfaced again, but it was only for a moment. He spat salt water from his mouth and in desperation spoke the final words of the prayer: *"Mater Dei, ora pro nobis peccatoribus, nunc et in hora mortis nostrae. Amen."* The proud Giacomo Coco could do nothing as the waves closed over him and the broken vessel for the final time. It was only a few moments before the ship had disappeared beneath the waves taking all hands with her to the bottom of the Golden Horn.

In the darkness, the other ships did not realize that Coco's longboat had been sunk. The large sailing vessels pressed forward. The Turks continued their heavy and confused fire with cannon and catapults. Flame-tipped arrows burned a fleeting light over the engagement. Stones struck the padded hulls repeatedly. The thick bales of cotton and wool soaked up the damage and the great ships pressed on.

The escort galleys also came under fire. Gabriele Trevisano's galley was hit once, then a second time. Turkish stones slammed into the ship's sleek beauty. She was taking water. A wounded sailor bundled his cloak into the hole to stem the flow of water. One of the small incendiary boats had reached the pontoon bridge and was pouring liquid fire onto it. The bridge came alive in sparks and flame. The blaze threw wild shadows across the Horn. In the glow, the Venetians could see Turkish longboats moving forward to engage them. Gunfire from the shore batteries tore at the fire-ship that had reached the bridge and sent it to the bottom of the sea. The crew flailed helplessly in the water. A Turkish longboat picked up the sailors who had fallen into the water. An unmanned incendiary boat reached one of the Turkish longboats and the two vessels were soon burning, mortally entwined.

The sea was pouring into Trevisano's galley. She was half submerged. With dawn breaking in no more than an hour, the captain realized that to go forward was suicide. He gave orders to return to port. Someone had betrayed them to the Sultan. The two transports, the two remaining *fuste*, and the small escort boats followed Trevisano's example and disengaged. It was only through the superior seamanship of the Venetians that the ships were able to disentangle themselves from the debacle without further loss.

As the sun rose, the retreating ships clearly saw the trap that they had so narrowly escaped. The batteries above the Valley of the Springs bristled with new cannon. Many more guns had also been mounted on the bridge. Two dozen longboats sat at anchor with their broadsides facing the oncoming attack, their decks lined with cannon. From the stern castle, Trevisano looked back and saw the captives being pulled from the water and onto Turkish ships. The attack had been a complete failure.

Defenders from the sea walls ran down to meet the ships as they came back. Alvise Diedo and Minotto were there, along with Giustiniani, the Cardinal and the Emperor. The men could say nothing as the tired sailors pulled into the harbor and docked their ships. Trevisano came running onto the land.

"We have been betrayed! The Turks knew of our attack and were prepared for it. As soon as we moved against their ships we were struck with cannon fire. Captain Coco's ship was the first hit. She sank almost immediately. We could not find any survivors."

It was the Emperor who responded. "Captain, please accept my heartfelt regret for the loss of life among your crews. Your attack was courageous. If the Turks were forewarned, there was nothing anyone could do." He turned to Alvise Diedo. "Captain, can you still hold the Horn against the Turks?"

"Sire," the voice was extremely tired and pained. "I, and my crews, shall do everything in our power to hold the Horn. I swear on my honor." Diedo's mind was far away, trying to comprehend the death of his brave friend, Giacomo Coco. The captain was so young, so daring. His charisma had almost made the admiral believe that he was invincible. Now he was dead.

Minotto began to talk about the events of the night in greater detail with Gabriele Trevisano, while Giustiniani questioned Morosini. There were rumblings of anger.

"Master Giustiniani, the delay caused by the Genoese irreparably compromised our operation!" Morosini, usually moderate, could not control his temper in the face of the disaster.

"I would not put it past the Genoese in Pera to have notified the Sultan of our attack personally!" added Trevisano aggressively.

"My lords, I beg you," Minotto was trying to mediate, "this will solve nothing."

"We have been betrayed!" prodded Silvestrio Trevisano.

The opinion of the Venetians appeared to be unanimous. Hasty words of reproach were fired at the Genoese crew disembarking from their ship, which had not been seriously damaged. Giustiniani and Minotto tried to reconcile the two parties. Not even the Emperor couldcontrol them, but the raging argument was brought to an abrupt halt by a rider from the walls.

"My lords!" The messenger sounded desperate. "Noble sirs, please come at once to the land walls. The sailors captured by the Turks are being brought onto Maltepe Hill."

Forgetting their differences, for the moment, the party quickly rushed to the land walls to behold the spectacle that was unfolding at the Turkish lines. The prisoners, forty-two in number, were being marched up the hill in full view of the City, their hands bound behind their backs. They stumbled forward, prodded by the shafts of spears and with whips. One man fell, but the guards dragged him back to his feet and pushed him onward. Venetians, Genoese, and Greeks alike strained their eyes to see. Among the prisoners, almost every Venetian had a comrade, relative or acquaintance. Horrified, the defenders watched as the swordsman came forward. The executioner was naked to the waist. He approached the first prisoner, who was pushed to his knees, and with a single stroke cut off his head. The body sat erect for a moment, blood streaming from the severed neck before it collapsed limply to the earth. The defenders watched in horror as, one after the other, all forty-two heads were sent tumbling down Maltepe Hill.

Impotently, the captains watched the spectacle. Some turned their eyes away in disgust as the severed heads littered the ground. Others ground their teeth and angrily grasped at the handles of their swords. The Emperor's calm façade was shattered. The volatile Palaeologos blood ignited in his veins. The barbarity of the enemy had infected him. Angrily he called one of his retainers.

"Manolis! Bring our prisoners forward to the walls immediately. All of them." The servant ran off.

"What are you going to do sire?" Minotto, wary of bloody reprisals, dared to pose the question.

"Do not trouble me now with your chivalry master *bailò*!" replied the Emperor and descended the tower to the parapet below.

The Turkish prisoners were being brought forward. Like the Venetians they came with their hands bound behind their backs. Their once brightly colored costumes were filthy from the fighting, stained with blood and grime. Constantine ordered them lined up along the walls from the Gate of Charisios to the Gate of Saint Romanos. The two hundred and sixty prisoners were positioned one man every six feet along the third of a mile between the two gates. Minotto rushed down to the Emperor.

"Your majesty, what are you going to do with these men?"

By way of reply, Constantine raised his arm. His hand was clenched violently. He turned to the *bailò* who drew back when confronted with the blazing eyes. The visage of the Emperor was hardly recognizable to him. The fist snapped down to the Emperor's side. At the signal, Greek soldiers began to behead the Turks all along the line. The *bailò* could hear foreign murmurings of prayer interspersed with cries begging for mercy. There was none to be had. Blood ran down from the embrasures staining the ancient masonry. To the warriors in the Turkish camp, the walls seemed to glow red as the morning sun cast its brilliant rays on the Queen of Cities.

7—The Lions of Saint Mark: *April 28, 1453*

They were arguing at a fevered pitch. All decorum had been abandoned. The ancient antagonism between the men of Genoa and Venice boiled to the surface and overflowed, feeding the flames of hatred. Shouts and insults poured from both sides as anger and frustration manifested themselves in loud and vociferous recriminations. The captain of the galleys from Tana listened to the tempest swirling around him with two minds contending against each other. Alvise Diedo was a tired man. His last stores of energy were dwindling. His patience was deteriorating. The events of the past week had hardly been conducive to sleep or a placid temperament. First, the Turks had appeared out of nowhere behind his ships. He had seen his attempt to neutralize them shattered with the loss of one of his galley commanders and the entire crew of a longboat. Fifty more good men were gone.

The tragic death of Giacomo Coco weighed heavily on Diedo's heart. Giacomo had been his friend, a companion from a dozen voyages, someone the commander had known personally. Silvestrio Trevisano and Girolamo Morosini lived, but their comrade was gone. How many more would be lost before they would return home to Venice in peace? He had thought it shameful to leave in December. If it had been a disgrace to leave then, it was certainly unconscionable to leave now. Honor compelled him to stay. Honor compelled him to fight. But was there honor in the death of so many good men in a foreign land, dying to save the city of a foreign prince? Was Constantinople worth the lives of his sons? Surely, he did not owe such loyalty to the Emperor.

No one was safe from danger. Death could come at any moment. He had known some of the men who had died. Others, he would never know. Their families would never see them again, their wives never kiss them again, their children

147

never hold them again. And his wife? Would his Laura ever see him again? Love him again? Would he ever be enfolded in her thin white arms? Caressed by her delicate fingers? Loved by her sumptuous lips? A terrible fear took hold of him. For whatever small life he had left, his soul would only be nurtured by memories. To him, it was as if Laura, Venice, love, and happiness were already dead. They were only memories, isolated instants passing through his mind in times of weakness or conjured in moments of desperation. When would Death come for his boys? They were young and strong, just as Captain Coco had been, and now he feared that, like the captain, they were not invulnerable. His heart was trembling. He felt himself drowning in an endless sea of questions, recriminations and self-doubt. He wanted to escape.

"Leave. Leave while you can, while there is yet time," murmured the demons of comfort and self-interest. The temptation of self-preservation was creeping forward in his mind. Diedo shook his head, trying to clear the spirits away. He had to push them back. It was weariness that brought them out. If he rested, they would recede from the open, back into the gloomiest places in his soul, back into the buried evil within all men. The duty at hand was the preservation of Constantinople. Coco's failure threatened not only the safety of the City, but also the strength of Venice's partnership with the Genoese of Pera. The eternal enemies had been reluctant allies at best. Now, every one of the commanders was exhausted. They were inching ever closer to a point of physical and mental collapse. Diedo thought it miraculous that the "alliance" had held as well as it had. The contending voices came into focus once more, blotting out the turmoil in his soul. Minotto was speaking out against the Genoese.

"You delayed our attack! The responsibility for the death of Giacomo Coco is yours!"

Diedo had hoped for a more cooperative attitude from the *bailò*. Minotto had been essential in maintaining cooperation. Now, it seemed, no one in the Venetian camp trusted the Genoese.

"The captain was himself to blame for his death. Did he not move ahead, alone, beyond the cover of the other ships in order to engage the Turks first? He was a hotheaded young man, hungry for glory, like all Venetians. He hoped to steal the laurels of victory for himself!" responded a Genoese captain from Pera.

"Better to be hungry for glory than hungry for the Sultan's gold!" blasted Gabriele Trevisano.

"Answer that accusation with your sword Captain Trevisano!" shouted the Peran captain, drawing his own blade and spitting at the Venetian.

The other Genoese rushed to stop him. On the part of the Venetians, Diedo entered the fray interposing himself between Trevisano and the Peran captain.

"Nothing could have saved our ships from destruction. The Turks were forewarned!" Diedo was trying to stem the conflict, but instead, his words provoked a new rush of accusations.

"Yes, forewarned Alvise, and we all know by whom!" It was Trevisano.

The Genoese captain went for Trevisano again, but was held back by his lieutenants. The captain of the light galleys stepped forward to accept the challenge. Mastering his fury, the Genoese captain shrugged off his companions and replied acerbically.

"The attack would not have been so disastrous, Captain Trevisano, if your crews possessed sufficient experience in battle. Captain Coco was an untested commander. He was too young and therefore ill-equipped to lead such an operation."

"Only if you refer to experience in duplicity was Captain Coco inferior to you Genoese!" Giovanni Loredan answered for Trevisano. The failure of the cooperative attack had done nothing but confirm his hatred and suspicion of the men from Genoa.

Zorzi Doria, who was master of the largest Genoese ship defending the City, replied.

"How dare you speak of duplicity, *signor* Loredan, when the Venetian captains never miss an opportunity to send their ships away from the action and to the safety of the City's harbors? The neutral merchant ships of our brothers in Pera have drawn more fire from the Turks than your combat vessels supposedly defending the Golden Horn."

"We are well acquainted with the neutrality of Pera, *signor* Doria. It is that neutrality which has killed Captain Coco and the entire crew of one our longboats!"

"Pera is neutral for its own safety. Nevertheless, it has sent almost all of its able citizens to fight within these walls for the safety of Constantinople. If our brothers there profess neutrality, it is only so that the Sultan does not wipe them out with a single stroke. We are here to fight and have been so since the beginning." This, from Bartolomeo Soligo.

"Since the beginning, indeed, Captain Soligo. But will you remain here till the end? Or will you make a separate peace with the Sultan and join your neutral brothers in Pera?" Loredan again.

"Do you dare suggest that we would leave the City while she is yet besieged? Did you not demand of the Emperor, before the Turks even came before these walls, permission to load your ships with their cargoes? Was this not so that you could slip away more easily if the battle turned against us?"

"That was done because those goods are ours. We have the right to do with them whatever we please. And now, *signor* Doria," countered Minotto, "we have unshipped the rudders and sails from our galleys so that they cannot leave the City. Why do you not demonstrate your goodwill by doing the same?"

"A foolish Venetian solution. You have made your ships less effective. Not that they were so effective to begin with," snorted Doria contemptuously. "We have no intention of reducing the fighting capacity of our vessels."

Trying to glide past Doria's insult, Soligo added, "It is also that we have wives, children and relatives in Pera. We cannot abandon them in the case of tragedy. Our ships must remain fully equipped."

Loredan interrupted furiously, "No doubt it is from concern for your families in Pera that you continue to negotiate a separate peace with the Sultan!"

The captain from Pera responded, "All overtures of peace that we have undertaken have been with the complete knowledge of his majesty the Emperor. His interests, at least, are similar to our own."

"Do you dare to suggest that we do not share the interests of the Emperor in preserving the City from conquest by the infidel?"

"I question the sincerity of an ally that months ago promised to send a relief fleet that still has not arrived! Even a Venetian navigator could have found his way to Constantinople by now! If the City falls, it will be because you and your *Signoria* have no sincere interest in coming to her aid!"

The final barb was too great for the Venetians to bear. Trevisano and Loredan drew their swords and rushed at the Genoese. Diedo attempted to stem the tide, throwing himself between the two parties once more.

"Put down your swords! This is not the time for us to quarrel among ourselves. There is much that we need to do. We can only accomplish it together."

His actions took the combatants by surprise, and cooler heads soon had the men under control. The eyes of the would-be duelists continued to blaze, but the situation was calming down. Mastering his emotions, the *bailò* took charge.

151

"I have written to Venice. The fleet will come. We must hold out until it arrives. When the Captain-General comes, the Turks will be turned back." Minotto paused. There was a tense silence before he continued. "Brothers, we are all tired. Let us meet tomorrow and discuss what must be done." He spoke with extreme politeness, but the *bailò* was clearly dismissing the Genoese.

"I agree, let us discuss the situation again tomorrow." Soligo spoke for his compatriots. There seemed no point in continuing.

The Genoese departed, more resentful of the Venetians than ever. Alone, the Venetians looked to each other with weary expressions of concern. They had been promised a fleet, but no sails flying the ensign of Saint Mark broke the horizon. None of them dared to voice the doubt that must have been felt by all. The *Signoria* would send a fleet. But where was it? What was delaying it? Still, they were sure that the ships would come. Until then, they would fight, with the Genoese, with the Greeks, alone if necessary, but they would fight.

Freed of the Genoese, the council began to discuss their present situation. A knock at the cabin door interrupted the Venetian deliberations.

"Enter!" commanded Diedo.

It was a courier from the Emperor. The Greek stood silently in front of the Venetians for a moment. Their eyes were raised to him expectantly.

"A message from the Emperor."

"What is it?"

"His majesty requests the presence of captains Diedo and Trevisano as well as *signor* Minotto. There are important matters he wishes to discuss with you."

The Venetians looked at each other. Minotto spoke for the group.

"Where is his majesty?"

"At the Blachernae Palace."

"Please relay to him that we will be there shortly."

The messenger bowed and left.

"Why do you think the Emperor wishes to see us, master *bailò*?" asked Trevisano.

"I'm not sure, Gabriele, but we shall find out." As he spoke the *bailò* rose. "Gentlemen, we shall speak again after our return."

The three noblemen left Diedo's flagship and moved along the sea walls towards the imperial palace. The suffering of the previous days preoccupied their thoughts. What they observed betrayed the hardships of the siege. Along both the land and the sea walls, houses had been abandoned. For the most part, the streets were deserted. There were no patrons at the small ground-floor shops. The owners would have boarded the counters up, but all available wood had been taken to build the makeshift stockade that was rapidly replacing the battered walls. As a result, the small shops stood eerily deserted, open to the world and smothered in darkness. In the Venetian quarter, a few workshops were busy preparing weapons. Occasionally, the company passed a haggard soldier or a harried monk. No one wished to be out of their houses, and the figures moved swiftly and silently past them.

Diedo thought of the odd juxtaposition within the walls. May was near, and the City was in the full blossom of spring. The flowers and plants were burgeoning with life, swelling with fruitfulness. At the same time, the human vitality of the City was waning. Day by day, the citizens grew weaker; Constantinople's spring could not rejuvenate them. The captain thought to himself about the irony of it all: a town coming alive amidst a dying population. The harvest of life that the City was preparing would be reaped by another. The Sultan would take Constantinople in its most delicious spring bloom, at the apex of its beauty.

In a flash, Diedo's mind traveled south through the Aegean, west through the Mediterranean, up the narrow channel of the Adriatic to Venice. It would be spring there, too. In Venice, the sun would be glittering over the canals. Its brilliance would illuminate the Piazza San Marco. The air would have the delicious bouquet of the sea as the breeze came in from the Adriatic. Beyond Venice, the captain's mind wandered to his country home, away from the bustling canals to the pastures of Treviso. There, his Laura would be in her garden, or walking along the covered porticoes, surrounded by blossoming trees and the sweet-scented country air. She would be waiting for him, her Odysseus, buffeted by the Gods, but triumphant over their perils, always returning to her. He felt a shudder of fear, uncertain whether he would return from this trial. The Blachernae palace loomed in the distance, wrenching Diedo from his dreams.

The commanders were silently ushered into Constantine's presence. As always, Giustiniani was at the Emperor's side. Constantine was seated, examining a map of the land walls. The *condottiere* was behind him. The Emperor stood to greet the Venetians as they entered.

"Welcome my lords of Venice."

The magisterial calm had been restored. No trace was left from the eruption of the previous day during the execution of the prisoners. The Emperor's expression was once more serene and dignified. Fatigue was becoming painfully apparent around Constantine's eyes. They had become pink and the skin beneath then was puffed and blackened from lack of sleep. The Venetians bowed. Giustiniani nodded.

"Thank you for coming."

The Emperor motioned to one of his attendants. A side door opened. Soligo, Doria, and the Genoese captains from Pera were brought into the room. Immediately, they began to speak out against the Venetians, but a glance from Giustiniani silenced them. The Emperor now addressed both parties with a weary voice.

"*Signori*, truly disturbing news has been brought to me that you captains, both from Venice and Genoa, have quarreled openly. There have been harsh words spoken on both sides. I need not remind you of the perilous situation of our City or of the responsibilities that rest on you for its defense. We cannot hope to win if we ourselves are divided. I beg of you, make peace among yourselves. We have war enough from beyond our walls without waging one within them. Do not add to our troubles by fighting between yourselves on account of the woes God has sent us."

The two sides glared at each other. These were proud men, unaccustomed to rebukes, but the presence of the Emperor demanded their acquiescence.

Bartolomeo Soligo spoke first. "Sire, we citizens of Genoa will try our best to cooperate with our neighbors from Venice and shall continue to serve your majesty in defense of your city. That has always been our foremost concern."

Minotto nodded his assent and added, "We shall abide by your majesty's wishes. For our part, nothing further shall be said of the matter." The *bailò* and Bartolomeo Soligo shook hands. Each of the representatives from the two Republics followed their example.

"Thank you *signori*. Now I should like to speak with the Venetian captains alone."

The Genoese bowed and disappeared. Their suspicions remained, but they acquiesced to Constantine's request. The Emperor now turned to the three Venetians.

"Thank you, gentlemen. The peace between you is essential to the survival of my City." Constantine's voice was heavy. "I cannot emphasize too strongly how desperate our situation is becoming. Many citizens within the walls are now running short of food. The soldiers are low on weapons and ammunition. Now the Turks are in possession of the Golden Horn. I have asked to speak to you in private because I do not want the Genoese to hear the question that

I must ask. Where is your Captain-General and the Venetian fleet?"

Diedo looked at Minotto. The *bailò* had written to the *Serenissima* months ago. Other than the three Genoese ships hired by the Pope, no relief ships had come to Constantinople.

"Your majesty, I have written to the Senate. The fleet will come. I have every confidence that our *Signoria* will send help."

"We have put our trust in Venice, master *bailò*. Our very lives depend on it. We cannot survive without your help. I have heard that your Captain-General, Giacomo Loredan, is a courageous man and a good Christian. Surely he will lead your fleet here soon."

"Help will come, sire. I swear to you on my honor, as God is my witness, the Captain-General shall bring the fleet here to our aid."

"I pray, master *bailò*, that your fleet will not arrive too late and find our City already taken." Constantine's voice echoed death.

"The winds are contrary this time of year, your majesty. It will take our ships some time to beat their way north through the Aegean against them," volunteered Captain Diedo.

"It is also possible that the Sultan may have discovered the *Serenissima*'s intention to send a fleet and dispatched some of his own ships to intercept them," added Trevisano.

The Emperor nodded. "All that you suggest is possible. Uncertainty is often harder to bear than ill tidings. We must find out the truth. We must be aware of the realities of our situation, no matter how painful they are." Constantine turned to Diedo. "Could you prepare a small boat to send out into the Aegean to see what has become of your ships?"

The captain nodded his assent. "We shall send a *bregantino* out immediately to find the fleet of the Captain-

General, to tell him of our plight and of the need for immediate action."

"Thank you *signori*. I pray that the fleet is found and brought here quickly." Constantine turned and returned to his seat. The audience was over.

The Venetians bowed and departed. They returned to the sea walls and their ships. Diedo bid farewell to the *bailò* and the other captains and hurriedly boarded his ship. As he walked the small gangplank he called out for Niccolò and the sailing master soon appeared at the doorway to the captain's cabin.

"Yes sir?"

"The Emperor has requested that we send a *bregantino* out towards Negroponte to make contact with the relieving fleet of the Captain-General."

"Yes sir."

"The ship will cruise the Aegean and try to find signs of the fleet. I need twelve volunteers for the crew."

"Understood."

"Give orders for the ship to be prepared at once. Choose it carefully. Pick one with a solid hull and good sails. I don't want some decaying piece of junk that will sink before it reaches the Dardanelles."

"Yes sir. Don't worry, I'll find a sturdy one."

"And Niccolò, make sure only reliable men volunteer. The mission is extremely important."

Niccolò nodded. "Yes, captain." The sailing master was leaving, but Diedo called after him.

"And find some Turkish clothing for the men on board! They'll need to be disguised to slip through the Sultan's fleet. The ship leaves as soon as I have a chance to speak with the crew."

The sailing master returned with a smile. "Yes sir. I don't know how the men will feel about putting on those flea-ridden rags, but I'll see what I can do."

The sailor disappeared. He's a good man, thought Diedo. Steady. I wish I had a thousand like him. With a thousand like him we would force back the Turkish ships in a single day. Still, the other lads are brave enough. There's nothing to complain about except that there are too few of them.

"And fewer all the time..." he whispered aloud. "Fewer all the time."

It was not long before the small brig was ready to sail. The men aboard, in their Turkish disguises, were storing provisions for the voyage. The sails were ready and had only to be unfurled. Diedo passed on orders for the crew to come aboard his ship so that he could speak with them.

Emerging onto the deck, Diedo saw the sailors before him. They looked odd in the Turkish costumes. He quickly looked among the faces to see if he recognized anyone. They were familiar in that he had seen them before, but he could not remember names. Now, he doubted that he would ever get to know any of them. What a waste, he thought. Seeing the men in front of him, he thought how precious life was. In each face, he saw the features of his sons. Would they find the fleet, and if they did would they make it back alive? Would he be alive when they got back? He was counting as he looked at them. Nine, ten, eleven. Eleven? Where was the twelfth? Niccolò stepped off the gangplank onto the flagship.

"Here they are, sir. Twelve volunteers as requested."

"I only count, eleven, Niccolò."

The sailor flashed his teeth in a smile.

"Well, sir, I was hoping that you would allow me to be the twelfth."

"You want to go?"

"Yes sir."

The conviction with which the sailor spoke indicated to Diedo the futility of trying to dissuade him, but he tried all the same. Coming closer so that they spoke only to each other he whispered.

"Why Niccolò? This is an extremely dangerous mission. I beg you to reconsider."

"No, sir. I'm sorry. My mind is made up."

"But I need you here. You're the sailing master of the flagship."

"This little ship," he said motioning to the brig, "will need a sailing master too, someone who knows the Aegean and who knows a thing or two about running blockades. Didn't you say you only wanted qualified volunteers? Besides, I'd really like to give the Captain-General a talking to for making us wait so long."

Diedo forced a smile to his lips. He was feeling very tired again. There was a pain against his temples like the hands of a vice.

"Very well," he said softly. Then, more loudly he added, "I'll miss you Niccolò. Bring back the Captain-General as quickly as you can. Don't let him lose a minute."

"Yes sir. And thank you."

Diedo then addressed the entire company:

"You men know what is expected of you. When it gets dark, we'll slacken the chain-boom for you and you'll sneak out past the Turkish fleet. Be careful of the current as you sail into the Sea of Marmara. Don't get caught by it and get washed up against the City's southern sea walls. Once you are through the straits, choose your course with care. Stay in the Aegean and try to find our fleet. If you can, make for Tenedos and see if they have any news of the fleet. If the fleet is not there, head in the direction of Negroponte. The Captain-General may choose to assemble the fleet at either place. You all know how desperate the situation is here. I don't think we can hold here for more than a month if the fleet does not come, so plan accordingly. You're all brave men. You would not have stayed to defend the City if you were not. I have every faith in you. Good luck, and God speed."

The men went to their stations and waited for night to fall. As the sun disappeared, the small ship, flying its Turkish ensign, unfurled its sail and made slowly for the chain. The boom had been loosened and the brig glided over the great iron links. The sailors held their breath, waiting to hear a challenge in the darkness from the Turkish patrol boats, but none came. The ship rounded the headland and sailed south towards the Dardanelles and the Venetian fleet beyond.

8—The Captain-General: *May 10, 1453*

Giacomo Loredan tapped the hilt of his sword and stared up at his ship's sails. To the eyes of the sailor, the great cloth triangle looked relieved to be filled, at last, with the sea breeze. The commander was a patient, meticulous man of fifty-five. Venice did not appoint hotheads to the command of her fleets. But, even so, the losing battle against time was beginning to needle its way through his composed nature. He had been waiting too long for this moment. Everything had started in February with the letter from the *bailò* of Constantinople. That desperate plea for help had prompted a flurry of concerned debates in the Senate. Still, that august body of pedantic indecision wrangled for two months before commissioning Admiral Alvise Longo to relieve the City. The Senate voted two large sailing vessels, each filled with four hundred soldiers, and fifteen galleys for the operation. The resolution passed on April thirteenth and the sailing date of the fleet was scheduled for the seventeenth. Of course, there were delays, and the departure was postponed until the nineteenth when definitive word finally reached Venice that the Turks had arrived at Constantinople.

Even after setting off, Longo was not allowed to go as swiftly as possible to the City. Instead, the admiral was given a tortuous set of instructions for his progress. From Venice, he would proceed to Modon, a port in the south of the Peloponnesos. There, his galley would stop for a day to re-supply. Then, Longo would sail to Tenedos and await the arrival of the Captain-General who would bring several other galleys and take command of the expedition. Together they would sail north to Constantinople, force their way through the straits and relieve the City.

It was not until the seventh of May that the Senate gave Loredan his orders to leave Venice. Again, receiving orders to leave and actually sailing were two very different propositions. On the eighth, the Senate decided to send a

161

special ambassador with the Captain-General to negotiate with the Sultan. The addition of Bartolomeo Marcello had caused further delays. Before allowing their emissary to sail, the Doge and leading senators conveyed to him a long and complex list of instructions. These negotiating points covered every eventuality that Marcello might encounter.

Loredan had his own orders, which likewise mapped his actions depending on the possible events. That was another characteristic of the Senate; they did not give their representatives, military or diplomatic, much leeway in terms of personal initiative. The Captain-General's orders were clear. Their first destination was the island of Corfu. Loredan had orders to stop there and wait for the island's governor to escort him to Negroponte where he would link up with two galleys from Crete before proceeding to Tenedos. The Captain-General thought it a completely unnecessary delay, but the Senate had been insistent that the galleys from Crete were an essential addition to the fleet. He stared up at the sails again and wondered how long it would take them to carry the ship through the Adriatic to Corfu. The wind was fair, not strong, but at least they were moving. His thoughts were interrupted by the sound of feet on the deck behind him.

"Greetings, captain." Loredan turned. He recognized the voice of Bartolomeo Marcello.

"Good afternoon *signor* Marcello."

Despite the warmth of the spring day, the diplomat was swathed in a cloak. The brisk sea air did not seem to agree with him. He tilted an ignorant eye to the ships sails. "How is the wind for Corfu?"

"Fair. We should arrive tomorrow by midday."

"Then the governor will take us to Negroponte?"

"Yes. Swiftly, God willing."

"Let us hope that Admiral Longo will wait for us before attempting to relieve Constantinople."

"He has his orders, just as I have mine. If we move to Tenedos and the admiral is not there, he is to leave behind a galley to tell us that he has already sailed."

"I'm sure he will wait for us."

"He has orders not to stay past the twentieth of this month. If we do not reach him by then, he is to move towards Constantinople alone."

"Will we reach Tenedos by the twentieth?"

"I don't know. It will depend on the wind and on the galleys from Crete. At this time of year, the wind makes it difficult to sail north through those waters."

"Forgive me for my questions, my lord, but I am a diplomat and not a sailor." Loredan smiled slightly. He was entirely aware what Marcello was. "Would you mind if I asked you something?"

"No."

"Do you believe our fleet will be enough to relieve the City?"

Loredan looked the diplomat straight in the face.

"Yes, *signor* ambassador. Our ships combined with those of Admiral Longo will be more than a match for the Turks. We bring food, weapons, supplies and fresh men to the battle. If the City is still in danger, we will turn the tide."

"I am glad to see that you are confident. It is very important that Constantinople not fall. I have been in correspondence with many of our noble families. Almost everyone has a kinsman in Constantinople, yourself included."

"Yes, a cousin of mine, Giovanni Loredan, is in the City."

"There are also representatives from the Contarini, Venier, Dolfin, Cornaro, and Morosini families, among others."

Marcello impressed himself more than Loredan with the recitation of the names. Every mentioned family had placed at least one of their number on Venice's ducal throne. The families were the most patrician and highly respected in the Republic. The Captain-General's face was expressionless.

"We are making a great sacrifice in coming to the aid of the City." Loredan gave no sign of hearing, but the diplomat continued all the same. "Much is at risk. We are involving ourselves in a potentially explosive situation. We face the possibility of open war with the Turks."

"We have fought the Turks before, and we will fight them again." The prospect did not worry Loredan.

"His Excellency the Doge is not convinced of the necessity of fighting the Sultan at the present." With this, Marcello finally seemed to capture Loredan's attention.

The Captain-General thought of the Doge. Francesco Foscari was an old man. He was seventy-nine and would turn eighty in October. He had been at war for most of the three decades of his reign. His primary policy had been to increase the power of Venice on the Italian mainland. For thirty years he had waged war against the duchy of Milan for control of Lombardy. Of course, there had also been tension with Genoa, and Venice's maritime colonies in the Levant always faced the expansion of the Turkish sultans. Doge Foscari did not strike him as the kind of man who would back down from a fight. The diplomat's statement disturbed him.

"*Signor* ambassador, I was in the Senate on the day it voted to send us to Constantinople. One hundred and twenty nine Senators voted in favor of our action. Only three voted against it. I have heard *bailò* Minotto's letter begging for our assistance. My cousin is in the City with the brave gentlemen you have mentioned. How would the Doge not desire that we sail to the rescue?"

"I simply mean that in this case, the Doge and the Senate would rather that we avoid war and achieve our ends through diplomacy rather than combat."

"Do you mean to tell me that the heathens know a language other than violence? What other than swords will turn the Turks back from Constantinople?"

Marcello grinned thinly at the soldier's bluntness. "I only mean, my lord, that we can all hope the Sultan has decided that he cannot win and withdraws before we arrive. If he withdraws *before* we arrive, the Republic is in the pleasant situation of avoiding open war while at the same time maintaining her position in Constantinople, all without the loss of a single sailor, a single ship, or a single extra ducat."

Loredan answered impatiently. "Our mission is clear to me, *signor* ambassador—to save the City. To fight our way in if necessary and to offer our unconditional support to his majesty the Emperor. Brave men must act and cannot let others fight their battles for them." The Captain-General looked longingly at the sail, as if somehow it could rescue him from his predicament.

"Indeed, my lord. Indeed. But wise men will know which battles are to be fought and which cannot be won." There was a tense moment of silence. "If you will excuse me, whatever the outcome, I have a great deal of work to do before our arrival."

The diplomat bowed and left. The Captain-General was glad to see him go, but uneasiness remained with him. Loredan was a soldier, proud, brave, and direct. Still, he was shrewd enough to realize that all men did not share those vices and virtues. There were other men, men who made war with words and pieces of paper, men who toyed with the truth until pure intentions had been wrought into hideously hidden motives. These were the methods of the Marcellos of the world. He had no patience for such creatures, but he knew that, more often than not, their methods would decide the issue. Against such a man, his weapons were powerless.

Loredan began to understand. Deciphering the diplomat's words, he began to see what was happening and what was going to happen. It was Marcello's intention to leave

Constantinople to her fate. If the Emperor were successful in defending his City, that was fine. If the Sultan triumphed, there was no difference. Marcello would simply negotiate with him instead. There would be more delays. Marcello would manufacture more delays: at Corfu, at Negroponte, even at Tenedos, if they made it that far. Loredan tried to think of a battle plan. Something to counter the diplomat's intentions, something that would allow them to reach Constantinople before it was too late. As his mind grappled with the problem, the Captain-General looked up at the sails and hoped that they would bring them swiftly to the rescue of the City.

PART III

1—The Miner: *May 12, 1453*

The sun awoke and began to dim the evening stars, peeling back the darkness blanketing the Turkish camp. In the torchlight, surgeons set shattered limbs, patched mangled bodies, and tried to sooth flesh scorched by Greek fire. The wounded still screamed; no one slept. The Sultan's assault, the first since the middle of April, had failed. Constantinople's walls stood bloodied but unbroken by the evening's four hour battle.

Many of Mehmed's warriors had advanced with hooks attached to the tips of their lances so that they could tear down the barrels of earth and wooden planks that formed the makeshift stockade. They were shot down as they advanced. Arms and hands were severed as they appeared over the wall. The Turks forced their way up the breaches and fought the defenders hand to hand, but somehow, the Christians held. Amir Bey, the Sultan's own standard-bearer, had been killed, cut in two by the sword of a Greek soldier. The Turks had closed around the champion and hacked him to pieces, but nothing could disguise the fact that they had suffered another defeat.

Mehmed was furious. In spite of constant bombardment, the defenses were still strong enough to repulse a frontal assault. The night's debacle had made a mockery of his hopes that the infiltration of the Golden Horn would turn the tide. If only there were something to circumvent the strength of the ancient walls! But Mehmed could think of nothing. He could feel victory slipping from his grasp. He reached out and took a cup of wine, drained it, and refilled it. The rigors of life in the field had intensified his passion for alcohol.

Drinking pushed away the last restraints on Mehmed's conscience. Sodden with wine, his mind indulged in its darkest thoughts and greatest fears. The present situation called for action. He could sense Halil Pasha growing in strength. The Vizier had not made his move, but this latest failure would provide him an opportunity to argue that the siege should be abandoned. Mehmed could see it in his Grand Vizier's eyes. How he wished to see those eyes glazed and blank looking at him over a severed, bloodstained neck!

That decision had been made some time before, but politically, it could only be accomplished on the surge of euphoria following the taking of the City. Then, no power would be able to shield the meddlesome Halil from his proper fate. The young Sultan tried to control his thoughts, to master his desires and focus on Constantinople. He was pacing in the tent, alone. He had taken to being alone during the siege. Mehmed felt better that way, free from the provocations of Gülbahar, free from the conflicting advice of his ambitious generals and from the nauseating expression of disapproval in the gaze of the *gâvur ortagi*. He vainly searched for inspiration, but relentless failures had hardened his mind to lead, and he could think of nothing. The young Sultan needed ideas and summoned his senior commanders to a council later that morning.

Zagan Pasha had his own ideas about a solution. The Sultan's father-in-law had overseen the construction of the causeway behind Pera. During that operation, he had discovered a number of professional miners—Serbians, from the silver mines of Novo Brodo—among his troops. There had been some attempts to undermine Constantinople's walls, but thus far they had achieved little, and the efforts were all but abandoned. The discovery of professionals, however, encouraged the Vizier to restart work. He decided to suggest that operations be stepped up under the auspices of his Serbian miners. Success would certainly ingratiate him to his son-in-law, and at the same time it would silence cowards like Halil Pasha who were calling for peace.

As Zagan prepared for the council, the commander of the Serbian miners was at his side. He had decided to take the man with him. Once more, Zagan turned to the Serbian for affirmation.

"You're sure it can be done?"

The Serbian was a short man of stocky build. He was middle-aged and pale with his short brown hair that had begun to gray. He had a long nose with a rounded tip. Zagan thought he looked like a badger. Since the animal was a renowned digger, the man's odd looks reassured the Vizier.

"Yes, my lord. My men are all professional miners. They can tunnel through anything."

"They had better." The Vizier looked intently at the Serbian thinking of their chances for success. "Be prepared," he continued, "to explain to his majesty and the others exactly what you intend to do. The operation will not go forward unless we can convince the council of its certain success."

Zagan Pasha paused. He did not wish to go further than this and explain that another failure could well endanger the whole siege. At the very least, failure would bring Halil Pasha clamoring for an end to the war. That was the last result Zagan wanted.

"I'll do my best, my lord."

"Your best had better be good enough."

The Serbian frowned, but made no reply.

"Come, we must go."

The two men mounted, and with the rest of the Vizier's staff, they set out across the pontoon bridge towards the Lycus Valley and Mehmed's great red and gold tent. Zagan rode easily, but the Serbian, accustomed to working under the earth, bounced about miserably. As a result, they were among the last to arrive. The Sultan was already surrounded by most of his commanders: Ishak Pasha, Karadja Pasha, Sheikh ak-Shemseddin, Shahabeddin, and Hamza Bey. Halil Pasha too was in his customary place.

The Grand Vizier was silent while Karadja complained about the conditions of the assault during the previous night. It had all been heard before. The walls were too strong. The defenders were able to concentrate their strength. They were better armored. Mehmed listened and bit his blood-red lips as the commander made his litany of excuses. Shemseddin had his eyes closed and tapped his thumbs together impatiently. When the excuses ended, Mehmed's eyes moved among his commanders and asked if anyone had an idea of how to proceed. No one responded. Zagan could tell that Halil Pasha was biding his time. If no one came forward with a productive suggestion, he would step forward and move for peace. Picking his moment with a soldier's precision, so that the Grand Vizier had not yet raised his voice, Zagan spoke.

"Sire, noble lords, I have an idea." All eyes were upon him. "We have tried to batter the walls down. We have tried to attack over them and through them. We have moved the fleet into Pera in order to move around them. There is only one direction we have not explored—down. We must try to mine under the walls."

"Lord Zagan," answered Ishak Pasha, "we have already tried to mine under the walls. We have been digging since the beginning of April. There have been no results. The earth is hard. Constantinople is built on rock."

"We have been digging since the beginning, Lord Ishak, but I have something new to add to our efforts—professional miners among my troops from Serbia."

A low murmuring broke out. Mehmed silenced it with a stare, then nodded at Zagan to continue.

"Digging is the livelihood of these men. They tell me that it is possible to tunnel under the walls of Constantinople and bring the ancient masonry crashing down so that our troops can enter the City. But I will not explain this to you. Mining is not my business. I ask your permission for the commander of the Serbian miners to address our assembly himself and explain what will be done."

The young Sultan's interest had been piqued by the prospect of circumventing the strength of the great land walls. He nodded that it would be acceptable for the *gâvur* to address the council.

The badger came forward. Shemseddin's nose wrinkled noticeably. Halil looked at the stranger with concern. He did not like the fact that yet another stratagem would be proposed to take the City. He wished the Sultan to withdraw, the siege to be over, and peace restored. As long as the army remained in front of Constantinople, he could feel the shadow of the executioner's sword across his neck.

"My lords, Lord Zagan has explained the proposal to you. I will only add the details." He was speaking slowly, methodically, as if each word were a shovel of dirt. "We shall begin digging well behind our lines opposite the Caligarian Gate. The ground there is excellent for mining, and the single wall around the Blachernae quarter makes our job easier. When the tunnel reaches several yards under the wall, we'll pack it with explosives and blow it up. The masonry above will collapse, and you will have a breach for your assault troops. There's very little that the Greeks can do in order to defend such a sudden gap in their position. They will be unable to refortify the area, either with stones or timbers. The assault that follows the detonation of the mine should encounter nothing except a few shocked troops that your warriors can easily overcome."

Sheik ak-Shemseddin bowed his head to the Sultan's ear.

"We have nothing to lose sire. If they fail, you have lost nothing except the lives of a few infidel miners. Let the other operations continue as they are, with no further assaults against the walls and give them permission to go ahead."

Halil Pasha remained silent, his face expressionless. Mehmed looked fleetingly in his direction and then nodded his assent to Shemseddin. He had listened to the Serbian, but he directed his response to Zagan Pasha.

"Lord Vizier, we agree to the plan. Begin at once."

Halil Pasha blinked. There was nothing to say now. Zagan had planted yet another idea in the young Sultan's head. The Grand Vizier and Constantinople both would have to weather the storm of this latest inspiration before it would be safe to broach the topic of peace once more.

"Thank you, your majesty."

The Vizier bowed. The Serbian captain did likewise. They left the tent. Zagan and his suite crossed back onto the northern shore of the Golden Horn.

"Get your men and have them begin as soon as possible. You will report to Ibrahim Bey." One of the riders spurred forward to the Vizier's side. Zagan raised his hand indicating the man. "Lord Ibrahim will be in charge of the operation. Bring any problems that you encounter to his attention."

"Yes, my lord."

The Serbian bowed again, once to the Vizier and a second time to the bey. He looked over his new commander. The bey was tall, tanned, and thin. The thinness accentuated his height but did not do justice to his physical strength. The Serbian knew nothing about the man's abilities and hoped that he would be allowed to do his job properly without too much interference.

It was several hours before the miners and their equipment crossed the pontoon bridge. They made camp behind the main Turkish position opposite the Blachernae quarter. Work began well behind the Turkish lines. They did not wish to attract the attention of the defenders. A small palisade was erected at the entrance of the tunnel to shield it from view. It was not more than a few hours before the tunnel was inching towards the City.

The Serbian captain, with Ibrahim Bey at his side, was overseeing the work. The badger wore only a tunic of plain dirty-white wool and a pair of worn, baggy tan trousers. He was giving commands in Serbian to the miners as they worked. They emerged from the tunnel with narrow eyes, squinting even in the failing daylight, carrying sack after sack of earth. What the great guns and the armies of a score of conquerors could not accomplish, these humble, dirt-covered badgers would achieve.

2—The Engineer: *May 22, 1453*

Johannes Grant knew he was going mad. The strain was too much for him to bear. The Scottish engineer, like so many others, had come to Constantinople to help the City in its hour of need. He was the commander of the mining defenses, thirty-seven, short and squat, with wavy red hair and pale skin further whitened from his subterranean work. Though the Turks had been mining since the beginning of the siege, it was only during the last few days that their attempts had become a serious threat. Grant detected a troubling new purpose and professionalism in their endeavors.

On the sixteenth of May, a mine had been discovered under the Blachernae wall near the Caligarian Gate. Grant dug a countermine, entered the Turkish tunnel and burnt its wooden supports. The mine collapsed, burying the Turkish sappers. That arrested the enemy progress for a short while. Now, less than a week later, Grant knew that they had resumed operations. He could hear them, once more near the Caligarian Gate, scratching like trapped rats at the earth under Diedo's ditch. They were creeping closer, hour by hour. The noise had begun to torment him. He could hear the scratching in his bed, at council, even staring out at the sea. The claws never stopped. It had reached the point that he was no longer able to sleep.

On the morning of the twenty-first, he discovered a new mine. It had almost reached the single Blachernae wall. By that evening, the Turks would complete their digging, blow up the mine, and bring a huge section of wall crashing down. Now Grant was awake, even earlier than usual because two hours before sunrise the Turkish fleet had moved out against the chain-boom. The noise from their castanets and tambourines had awakened the entire City. The ships in the harbor had gone to battle stations prepared to fight them off, but the Turks had changed their minds and retreated to

Diplokionion. Rather than returning to bed, Grant decided
to examine the Blachernae quarter for signs of renewed
enemy operations. Most of the enemy's work was done
during the night, anyway. With sunrise still an hour away,
perhaps he would catch them at it before morning. He
yawned. He took a torch, lit it, and moved out into the
deserted streets towards the imperial quarter. Deliberately
he made his way along what was left of the once tall walls.
Every ten yards he had set a barrel filled with water. When
the Turks dug in the vicinity, the water would vibrate. A ring
would ripple inwards from the edge. He peered into the
barrel at the Xyloporta Gate and saw his reflection,
illuminated by the orange torch light. The water was as
smooth as fine glass. He walked south towards the
Caligarian Gate. This was where the Turks seemed to
concentrate their work. The scratching rats in his mind grew
louder. He stood motionless at the barrel immediately
behind the gatehouse. The water was calm. He waited for a
moment—nothing. There was a Greek guard nearby.

"Has this water moved at all today?"

"Sir?" The man was half asleep. In any case, he did not
seem to understand the engineer's concern.

"The water," he repeated wearily, "has it moved at all?"

"I couldn't say, sir."

Grant rubbed his eyes. He yawned again and ran his
fingers through his hair. The rats were scratching again,
fatigue was wearing on him. He looked at the bucket. This
time, the water moved. It was a single ripple. The engineer
thought he had imagined it. Perhaps it was a trick of the
light. He moved nearer, bringing the torch so close that he
could feel his face growing hot. A moment later, the water
rippled again, then a third time. He turned to the guard.

"Come here! Do you see how this water is moving? It
means that the Turks are digging somewhere around this
gate. Go and bring as many barrels as you can to this area."

The guard hustled off. Grant rushed away too, his fatigue melting from excitement and apprehension. The engineer ran to tell Lukas Notaras what was going on, the scratching noise, throbbing in his head. It did not take him long to find the Grand Duke. It was just before dawn and Notaras had risen and was at his headquarters in the Phanar quarter, just behind Blachernae. The engineer burst into the room gasping for breath.

"My lord, the Turks are tunneling near Caligaria!"

Notaras stood up from his seat. Grant had interrupted his breakfast. "Are you sure, Master Grant?" His tone was devoid of emotion.

"I am certain, my lord."

Notaras exchanged glances with one of his lieutenants. Five days before, this man had succeeded in destroying one of the Turkish mines. Despite the fact that he was a Frank, the Grand Duke respected him. Besides, at this moment, his work was essential to the survival of Constantinople.

"Then we must act. How will you proceed?"

"The mine has probably progressed quite far, but I think it will be possible to flood it with water or fill it with smoke. In either case, the Turks will be forced to abandon it."

Notaras thought for a moment.

"Very well, Master Grant. Do as you think best. We are in your hands."

The engineer returned to the walls immediately with a force of about one hundred men. The guard had done his job well, and there was a score of Greeks unloading barrels from several wagons. These, the engineer set up in an arc around the gatehouse. He had to find the exact location of the tunnel. Day was breaking and, like a madman, he ran from barrel to barrel checking the size and frequency of the ripples before beginning his own digging. Time was of the essence. With dawn approaching, the Turks would soon stop their operations.

When Grant had made all the necessary calculations, the shovels and picks went to work. For the rest of the morning, Grant and his sappers dug. As the day grew hot, most of the men stripped to the waist. Their bodies became blackened with dirt. Ignoring the relentless thunder of the Sultan's guns, they dug deeper and deeper. They were below the wall now, and Grant could sense that they were very near the enemy. The mine was somewhere close. Grant divided his sappers, splitting his tunnel in hopes of finding the Turks more quickly. Spades carried away great heaps of soil to be loaded into barrels or sacks and sent to strengthen Giustiniani's palisade. No effort would be wasted.

Grant was inspecting the northern branch when the foot of one of his diggers went through the floor of the tunnel. The thin layer of earth beneath him had given way. The Turks were below. Grant reacted quickly. The southern branch was abandoned. He brought the men into the northern mine and ordered them to bring liquid fire and brushwood. The sappers dropped into the Turkish tunnel below with the combustibles. It was empty. The Turks were waiting for the night to finish their work. Fear of being discovered during the day had made them cautious. Grant's men brought branches and straw. They packed these materials along the supporting timbers and connected them with a cord fuse. When everything was prepared, Grant ordered the fuse lit. The men hurried out of the tunnel as the Turkish mine began to blaze. They had all reached the fresh evening air when the earth beneath them trembled. The enemy mine had collapsed.

The news was quickly brought to Ibrahim Bey and the Serbian commander. Another mine had been destroyed. There had only been a handful of casualties, but the tunnel that had reached so close to the City's walls was ruined. Ibrahim Bey struck the table in front of him furiously.

"Another failure! We've been at this for more than a week and have nothing to show for all your empty boasting!"

An accusing finger was pointed at the Serbian captain. The badger was silent. As usual, he was dressed in his mining clothes, which were stained with earth and smoke.

The bey continued. "Lord Zagan will not be pleased."

"My lord, the engineer in charge of the enemy's operations is obviously very skilled. As I have said before, there is little we can do to prevent him from detecting our mines. We must have some luck and hope he does not find them. When they are found, we must fight to defend them more effectively."

"Are you daring to shift the blame for this to my men?"

"No, my lord."

Ibrahim, who himself had some idea about mining, knew that the Serbian was telling the truth. They were doing everything possible, but Zagan Pasha, and certainly the Sultan, would not see it that way. The badger had come over to the table and was examining the map, already planning which mine to push forward next. His face was shadowed in severity.

"We will continue digging. This mine in particular is nearing the walls," he said tracing a charcoal line with the black nail of his thumb. "*I* will lead the digging party and will not leave the tunnel until I pack it with explosives and light the fuse myself."

The bey was moved by the man's courage. His life was at stake as well.

"I will go with you."

The badger nodded.

The mine they spoke of was also near the Gate of Caligaria. In fact, it was a branch of the tunnel Grant had destroyed earlier. It was dusk when Ibrahim Bey and the Serbian, dressed for battle, descended into the mine behind their lines. Hunched over, they made their way through the damp darkness of the earth towards the work crews. The bey had a long knife in the sash around his waist. The Serbian had tucked a short-handled axe into his belt and a knife behind his back. As they crept further, the sounds of the picks and shovels became apparent. The men were surprised to see their commanders among them. The officer in charge saluted.

"How far are we from the wall?" asked the badger.

"Quite close, sir. No more than twenty yards."

"How long?"

"A few more hours. We might be ready to lay the powder before daybreak."

"You must, lieutenant. We can't risk leaving this mine overnight for the enemy to discover."

The Serbian turned to the bey. Ibrahim nodded. The two men took charge of the work crew. The badger himself lifted shovel and pick, driving into the earth with an atavistic fury. The bey moved up and down the tunnel checking its supports, listening for the sound of counter-miners, and encouraging the diggers. The work was faintly lit by a handful of torches alternatively held or propped into the freshly dug earth. The hours passed. Above them, the great guns fell silent. The sun set, but beneath the earth the miners remained oblivious in their gloomy world. Suddenly, when the badger was carrying some dirt away from the tunnel's front, the left side of the mine collapsed. Figures appeared in the darkness.

"The enemy!" he screamed.

The workmen turned, drawing their knives and short axes. A few rushed forward with picks and shovels. Grant's sappers began to pour into the tunnel. The Serbian threw down the sack of dirt and drew the axe from his belt. An enemy came at him with a knife, but the Serbian stepped back and then brought the axe sweeping through the narrow tunnel and severed the man's arm. His victim shrieked and fell back in shock. Ibrahim Bey rushed towards the gap at the head of a group of Serbian miners, shouting orders that no one heard. The two forces clawed at each other with knives, shovels, and fists. The reddish-orange light from the torches flickered around the deadly dance. The Greeks were trying to reach the wooden props in order to set them on fire and collapse the tunnel. The Serbians and Turks tried to defend their work and hold the enemy back. Soon, the supports were alight. The tunnel began to fill with black clouds. Beneath the earth, amidst the swirling smoke and flanked by raging flames, the men fought in hell.

The Sultan's miners were overmatched. Outnumbered, taken by surprise, assailed by fire and smoke, they died in their underground tomb. Coughing and half unconscious from the fumes, Ibrahim Bey and the Serbian commander were dragged from the inferno by Grant's engineers. They carried the bodies away from the carnage as the last supports gave way, bringing the mine in on itself. The two captains were carried through the countermine and up into the early morning light. The men that emerged were blackened from head to foot, and the bey and his companion were still unconscious.

Day was breaking in Constantinople, and the miners' eyes slowly accustomed themselves to the emerging sunlight. Johannes Grant was at the entrance to the mine. The rats, at last, were silent, but the engineer was exhausted. He was covered in smoke and grime and was sweating profusely. It had been hot business. His eyes were bloodshot from lack of sleep and constant exposure to smoke.

"Are those the enemy commanders?" demanded Grant wearily.

"Yes, sir, as far as we can tell," replied a Greek covered in dirt and blood.

"Revive them and bring them to Lord Notaras."

The engineer set off to clean himself and inform the Grand Duke of what had happened. If these men were senior officers among the Sultan's miners, they would know the location of the remaining mines. If he knew the positions, destroying the tunnels would be simple. But would these officers speak?

The Greeks had some water and used it to splash the faces of their two captives. The badger was the first to come to his senses. His eyes opened slowly. He was not wounded, but had passed out from the smoke. The Serbian coughed immediately, then sat up and stared straight ahead. He hoped that his eyes did not betray the fear he felt. The thin officer in charge asked him, in Greek, if he wanted water. He nodded and drank. Ibrahim Bey had also regained consciousness. His eyes opened suddenly and darted from one captor to another like a frightened animal. Then his gaze came to rest on the badger. The bey held out his hands to his companion for water. The Serbian gave him some.

"What will they do to us?" whispered the badger.

"I don't know. We mustn't tell them anything."

"There's nothing for us to tell them."

A man was approaching the group. "Are these Master Grant's prisoners, captain?" he demanded.

"Yes, sir," responded the officer.

"Have them follow me."

The officer turned to his guards. "Have the prisoners follow the secretary." He then motioned to the captives. "Get up, please."

The badger and the bey rose. They slowly regained control of their bodies and stumbled after the secretary, guarded on both sides by Grant's miners. They were led into the heart of the Blachernae quarter, away from the walls. After being in the darkness for so long, their eyes were having a difficult time adjusting to the sunlight that grew brighter with every moment.

The group entered a grand building near the imperial palace. The guards moved into a large room filled with people. Runners came and went with messages. Everyone wore armor. At the back of the room, an older man in full armor, sat at a desk speaking with several standing officers. He wore no helmet, and his great mane of silver hair reached almost to his shoulders. The party at the desk heard them enter and turned, and a younger man approached and addressed them in Greek.

"Sirs, my name is Johannes Grant, I am the commander of the City's mining defenses. I would appreciate it if you would tell us where you have dug your other tunnels." The Serbian and the bey exchanged glances but remained silent. "Please, gentlemen, understand the gravity of your situation. Our position is a serious one. We need the knowledge that you possess."

Again there was no response. Grant changed his tone, it was now colder and in earnest. "I urge you to recognize the fact that we will use any means in our power to extract the information that we know you possess."

The bey now spoke. "Sir, I am Ibrahim Bey, son of Suleiman, an officer from the staff of Lord Zagan Pasha. There is nothing that I can tell you about any mining operations."

"And you?" Grant asked the badger.

"This is a Serbian from my command," replied the bey. "He cannot tell you anything, either."

Lukas Notaras had risen from the table and now approached the two men. He turned to Grant.

"Master Grant, are these your prisoners?"

"Yes, my lord."

"Are they willing to cooperate with us?"

Grant turned to the two men. "Will you tell us where you have dug your other mines?"

"No, sir. We do not know," answered Ibrahim.

Grant turned to Notaras. The silver lord spoke.

"Then there is no choice." He paused. "Grigoris! Take the prisoners away and question them."

A well-muscled man with raven black hair stepped forward and took charge of the two prisoners. He had a large fleshy face that, to the engineer, seemed perennially glistening with sweat. Grant turned to leave; the man and his work made the engineer uneasy. Grigoris called after him.

"Master Grant, Lord Notaras insists that you are present for the questioning of these men. You will understand better than anyone the nature of their information."

Grant's heart sank. He shivered. He was an engineer, not an inquisitor. Grigoris noticed his expression.

"Lord Notaras *insists*," he said again.

The engineer looked up and nodded. "Very well, I shall follow you."

Guards took hold of the prisoners. The party left the large room and went down. Down further, thought Grant, than any mine he had ever dug. Stair upon twisting stair, they moved beneath the great stone palace, beneath the world of court, beneath God's creation to a realm purely of man and the devil. A cool, damp air struck them as they moved into the earth. The guards opened a small iron door that Grant noticed was almost a foot thick. It revealed a large room with a low ceiling, not more than seven feet high. Grant's eyes hurriedly scanned the instruments that stood mute and terrible, waiting for their victims. The room terrified him. He remained at the door, not wanting to enter the chamber. The Turk and the Serbian involuntarily moved closer together, trembling with fear. Grigoris moved with confidence in his world, strutting to the center of the room before addressing himself to the prisoners.

"Gentlemen, everything that happens after this moment will be your fault. It will be the result of your foolishness and your unwillingness to tell us a few simple things. We want you to make the situation easier for all of us. Master Grant will find your mines whether you tell us their locations or not. But if you tell us freely, now, you will save yourselves extraordinary pain and suffering."

The captains made no response.

"Very well gentlemen. Perhaps you do not understand the true extent of your situation. Let me explain, so that you fully comprehend what is about to happen."

The torturer moved towards the rack. His words now became punctuated with gestures. "First, you will be stripped and placed on this bench. Your wrists will be tied here, and your ankles there, with thick leather straps. One of my men will then turn this wheel, pulling these ropes until they bring the leather straps tight. As the straps tighten, your limbs will become taut. My man will continue to turn it slowly until your muscles and sinews begin to stretch. As he continues, the muscles connecting the bones around your elbows will begin to tear. Eventually, the bones will be pulled apart from each other. If you still refuse to tell us what we want to know, he will go on until your arms pop free from your shoulders. Usually, the knees are pulled out next, and last, your legs will come out from your hips. We can make this excruciating process take hours, during which time you can think about why you are choosing to suffer so much."

Grant stood motionless by the door, hoping that the prisoners would speak, but they said nothing.

"I encourage you to recognize the futility of silence. Eventually you will tell us everything we ask for. No? Very well. Vassilis, we'll take the Turk first."

An enormous guard moved towards Ibrahim Bey, undoing the leather thongs at his wrists and pushing him forward towards the rack. A second guard grabbed him immediately and removed his shirt, trousers and leggings. He was laid out, and felt his wrists bound again, as well as his ankles. A moment of silence hung over the group, broken only by Ibrahim's irregular breathing.

"Begin," commanded Grigoris.

The rack creaked as the wheel began to turn. The leather restraints pulled, biting into Ibrahim's ankles and already scarred wrists. After a quarter turn from the wheel, he was stretched to the limits of his length and felt himself raised slightly above the bench.

"Where are your tunnels?" asked the interrogator.

Ibrahim made no response. The Serbian chewed his lips in terror, as he felt the pit of his stomach churn in panic. The wheel began to turn again. Ibrahim felt the extensor muscles along his lower arms straining. The pain moved powerfully to his elbows. His ankles and the Achilles tendons began to ache. Everything became tighter as he felt himself lifted up and stretched. The rack was creaking, and his bones began to crack as they shifted in their joints. His entire body broke out in sweat.

"Tell us. There's no reason for this," murmured Grigoris. "Tell us."

Vassilis had slowed the wheel for a moment while his master spoke. Now he renewed his work suddenly, with vigor. Ibrahim chaffed against the restraints, which now began to cut into his flesh, drawing blood. There was a sickening noise of snapping muscles and popping bones. Ibrahim screamed and shook bodily as his arms were mutilated by the force of the ropes and pulleys.

Grant turned away in disgust. The badger's eyes stuck to the ground.

Grigoris approached the Turk's head and whispered, "Ibrahim, can you hear me? Don't do this. There's no reason to do this. Tell me where the tunnels are. Yes? You can do that so easily."

The bey was drenched with sweat. His breath was coming in short, spasmodic gasps. He did not answer. His arms had been broken, his body hideously disfigured, like a broken marionette. The interrogator nodded to Vassilis who again turned to wheel, straining and twisting the mangled limbs once more. The bey shrieked again. Vassilis did not stop—he continued to slowly turn the wheel. Grant was struck dumb by the horror of it all. The humanity within him wanted to cry out for the torture to stop, but the lives of his men and perhaps the safety of the City were at stake. The suffering of a single Turkish soldier, grotesque though it was, could not tip the scales. He could feel his heart pounding. He leaned his head against the damp wall. The rats were scratching again. The cool stone refreshed his burning forehead. He began to pray for the ordeal to stop.

As if in answer to his prayers, Ibrahim was trying to speak. Grigoris motioned for the torturer to stop. The bey was panting uncontrollably.

"Do you want to tell me something, Ibrahim?" asked the interrogator tenderly. "You only have to nod."

Ibrahim nodded in the affirmative.

"Will you tell me where the tunnels are?"

Ibrahim nodded again.

Grigoris signaled Vassilis to slacken the wheel. The distorted arms and legs came to rest on the bench. The bey was sobbing softly, trying not to cry out loud. Grigoris quickly moved to get some water and as he did, went to Grant and told him to come over to the rack. The engineer and the inquisitor knelt over the broken body. Grigoris gave the bey some water and whispered:

"Ibrahim, Master Grant is here. Tell him everything you can."

The bey's voice, hoarse from screaming, came in irregular gasps that were difficult to understand. Grant knelt with his head by the Turk's mouth and listened intently. Occasionally he would ask the bey to repeat what he had said or to explain a location in greater detail. Body and spirit had been so completely shattered that Ibrahim complied without complaint. When Grant rose, he knew the exact positions of every Turkish mine. He did not have time to see what they would now do with the Turk. The man needed medical attention. He looked up at Grigoris.

"Bring him a surgeon. If he dies you'll have to answer to me. Send the other prisoner to Lord Notaras."

Grigoris raised the thick eyebrows above his cold black eyes in surprise.

"You heard me captain. Get a surgeon immediately."

He walked towards the door, passing the Serbian with a hurried side-ways glance. The man had escaped a terrible fate. Grant thought him lucky. He almost ran from the terrible room, and burst up the stairways before exploding into the mercifully fresh air of the world above. Twice today, he had been in hell. Now, he would have to enter it once more to destroy the last of the enemy's mines.

3—The Sail: *May 23, 1453*

After informing Grand Duke Notaras that the Turk had broken under torture, Grant returned to work and during the rest of the day proceeded to destroy each and every enemy mine. The Turkish miners, shorn of their commanders, could do nothing as tunnel after tunnel was filled with fire and smoke and brought crashing down. The defenders behind the walls were elated as they heard the earth tremble time and again with the collapse of the enemy mines. Grant's sappers, covered in dirt and smoke, were cheered as heroes. Constantine, with Giustiniani at his side, watched as the men celebrated their victory. Notaras was with them. He spoke to the Emperor.

"Your majesty, Master Grant has done an excellent job."

"Indeed, my lord. You too, have done well in this matter. We are grateful."

Notaras glanced proudly at Giustiniani. This was his triumph, not the *condottiere*'s, and he relished it. But Giustiniani was disarmingly gracious.

"I offer my congratulations too, Lord Notaras. This is an important victory."

The Grand Duke nodded curtly. He did not need the foreign captain's approval, but he still felt buoyed by the compliment's necessity.

"Still, my lords," continued the Emperor, "our position remains precarious. What is the condition of the defenses, *protostrator*?"

Wearily, Giustiniani replied.

"Sire, there is significant damage along great sections of the *Mesoteichion*. Several breaches have been made in the walls. We've done our best to patch them back together, but I don't know how well they will stand against another major attack. We need the help of the Venetian fleet."

Constantine looked at his marshal. He had not seen the *condottiere* look so poorly. The confident and bold exterior, like the walls, had been battered almost unrecognizable. "We will hold, Lord Marshal. We will hold. See to the defenses."

Giustiniani nodded. His thoughts were drifting away from the beleaguered City to Pera and Caterina. His single encounter with her during the dinner in Pera was no more than a dream now, but he could not shake her from his mind. What would become of her if the City fell? During the last few days, Giustiniani had begun to recognize that the fall of the City was actually a possibility. The walls were crumbling beneath the relentless assault of stone. The men were short of food and weapons and nearing exhaustion. There was no sign of the Venetian fleet. Giustiniani had not allowed his prejudices free rein, but he was becoming increasingly suspicious about why the City's Venetian allies had yet to arrive. It was hard to understand. There were so many Venetians fighting bravely within Constantinople. Did their countrymen not wish to save them from death and slavery at the hands of the Sultan?

His thoughts were interrupted by a breathless messenger. The boy, still in his teens, had run a long way and was panting furiously for air as he knelt before the Emperor.

"What is your message, my boy?" asked Constantine.

The young man swallowed hard and managed to gasp out two words, "A sail!"

"A sail?" asked Notaras, not sure if he had understood the breathless words.

Mastering his strained lungs, the youth replied, "Yes, my lord, a sail."

Everyone present knew the potential magnitude of the two words. Within his tired chest, Giustiniani's heart raced: a sail, a ship from the outside world, perhaps a courier from the Venetian fleet bringing news of salvation.

"Bring our horses," commanded the Emperor.

With all speed, Constantine, Notaras, Giustiniani and their retainers galloped off across the City towards the Acropolis Point to see the single sheet of cloth that promised so much. The sighting had stirred a commotion along the sea walls where desperate hopes raised a breathless desire.

The noblemen pushed their way to a place where they could view the events as they unfolded. There was silence as weary eyes strained to see the ship. It was a brigantine flying Turkish colors, but it was moving north through the Sea of Marmara with all possible speed. There were Turkish ships in hot pursuit, but the brig was too fast for them and was using the wind and current well. The observers held their breath as the tiny boat rounded the headland and made for the relative safety of the chain boom.

It was late in the afternoon when the brig lowered much of the sail that it carried and hung silently waiting for the cover of night to cross the boom. The proximity of Soligo's ships along the chain kept the little boat safe until darkness allowed the boom to be slackened so that the brig might enter the Golden Horn.

The notables of the City had come down to meet it: the Emperor, Notaras, Giustiniani, Minotto, and Diedo stood on the dock in silence as the brig threw in its tow cables and lashed them to the pier. One of the crew vaulted over the ships side onto the dock. Even in the torch-light, Diedo recognized his sailing master. Niccolò had not shaved for three weeks. A scraggly brown beard, beaded with sweat, had sprouted beneath a pair of haggard eyes. Diedo rushed forward to his friend.

"Niccolò, did you find the Captain-General?"

The weary eyes were cast down at the pier.

"Did you make contact with the fleet?" repeated the captain.

Niccolò looked up. There were tears in his bloodshot eyes. "No sir. We saw nothing."

"Nothing at all?" demanded Diedo incredulously.

"Nothing, sir."

"And you came back?"

"It was our duty, sir." Niccolò was hurt.

Diedo bit his lips. He felt hollow as an enormous
emptiness rose within him on a tidal-wave of fear. Surely all
was lost.

Minotto pushed his way forward. His glance shot between
the commander of the Tana fleet and the sailing master.

"Did you find the fleet?"

"There is no fleet, Girolamo," answered Diedo. "They saw
nothing."

"And there was no word of the fleet? In the straits? At
Tenedos? At Lesbos?"

"Nothing, master *bailò*."

Minotto turned pale. All hope escaped him with that
breath. He could not believe it; he did not want to believe it.
It had been so long since he had sent word to Venice about
the plight of the City. How could they have abandoned it to
its fate? Minotto looked at the sailor and suddenly realized
the magnitude of the sacrifice that the twelve men had
made. They had come back when they knew that the City
was hopelessly besieged, now with no hope of rescue.

"You bring heavy news," said the *bailò*. "I thank you for
your courage."

Minotto turned to the Emperor who had arrived with
Giustiniani.

"Sire, the ship that has arrived carries the men we sent
out at your request three weeks ago to find the Venetian
relief force. They were unable to find the fleet of our
Signoria."

Constantine was visibly crushed by the news. The lofty
and magisterial calm, which had been momentarily dropped
during the execution of the Turkish prisoners, was again
breached in the face of this most terrible news. Minotto
moved towards him, reaching out his hand in comfort, but
stopped himself. Instead he repeated the message.

"There is no fleet, sire." Then, prompted by the Emperor's
despair, he added, "At least there was no fleet a week ago.

I'm sure the Republic has sent aid. We must hold out until it arrives."

Constantine, however, was disconsolate. His reply was barely audible, a prayer mumbled as if to a priest performing the last rights.

"I fear, master *bailò*, that if the fleet does not arrive within the week, only God will be able to save our City. It is in the hands of Christ that we must place ourselves, in those of His mother Saint Mary, and in those of Saint Constantine who will defend his City. This is what we must do since the world has been unwilling to help me against these faithless Turks, my enemies and theirs."

There was more than a little bitterness in Constantine's final words. It was true. It seemed that the western powers could not see beyond the confines of their prejudice to recognize the threat that the Sultan posed to all of them.

Giustiniani looked at the Emperor, who spoke with the resignation of a martyr. He felt an enormous emptiness in his heart. Constantine was willing to fight for this lost cause, this now hopeless battle in which the victor was known before another blow was struck. What hope had any of them now? There was no Venetian fleet. Their fate was sealed. And what of Caterina? Giustiniani's mind returned to Pera and his love. What would her fate be? Mehmed would destroy Pera after he took Constantinople. Like the Constantinopolitans, the Genoese would be humbled, robbed and raped. Anger and fear took possession of the *condottiere*. With every part of his being he wanted to go to Pera that very moment. He needed to see Caterina, to feel her, to reassure himself that she lived and could escape. But there was no way to go.

"Sire, I must return to the walls." He choked the words out to Constantine and, turning his back on the heavy news, spurred his horse hard towards the *Mesoteichon*. Marco saw him coming.

"Is there news, uncle?"

The *condottiere* growled at his nephew's curiosity. He had no desire to share the sorrowful news, but he could not lie.

"A Venetian ship returned; they found no sign of the fleet."

"Nothing at all?"

"I'm afraid not. We are on our own." Because he wanted to inject some hope, he added: "There is a chance that they will still come. Perhaps the ship barely missed them and the relief fleet will be here by the start of June. We can hold until then."

Marco nodded silently, unwilling to let his uncle hear the fear in his voice.

"I'm going to check on the Turkish positions," said Giustiniani abruptly. Mehmed's guns were still thundering, but the *condottiere* paid them no heed and headed for one of the unruined towers of the outer-wall.

Marco shouted after him: "Don't go there, Giovanni, the Sultan's guns have been firing at these positions all day. Those towers are dangerous places! Wait until darkness ends the bombardment."

Giustiniani would not listen. He wanted to be alone, alone to confront his enemy, to conquer his fear and to think, by himself, how he could reach Caterina. He was scanning the endless sea of tents when a shot from one of the Sultan's huge guns tore into the tower, sending pieces of stone and wood into the air. The tower shook to its foundations, and Giustiniani found himself on the floor beneath a pile of rubble. He staggered to his feet and limped from the battlements. Reaching the flat ground behind the wall, he could see Marco running toward him with a few of his soldiers. Then he collapsed. Opening his eyes, Marco was above him.

"Are you hurt?" The *condottiere* was dizzy and did not respond. "Bring Doctor Colombo! The *condottiere* is injured."

Giustiniani was shaking his head. "Don't... don't..." he mumbled.

"Surgeon! Here!" commanded the young man once more.

Momentarily, the *condottiere*'s surgeon was at his side, checking his condition.

"What happened here?"

"He went into the tower to look at the Turkish positions, and it was hit by cannon fire. He came out on his own, but then collapsed here." Marco was speaking quickly.

"We can move him," responded the doctor, interspersing his examination and his words. There doesn't seem to be any structural damage. Nothing broken. Let's get him home and out of sight."

They carried the *condottiere* from the field, across the open space between the walls and through the Gate of the inner-wall a few hundred yards more to the house near the *Mesoteichon* where he was living. The doctor completed his exam.

"He needs to rest a little. He has some muscle damage from the accident, and he'll have a headache for a couple of days. Nothing's broken, so that's good, but he needs rest." The doctor made a brew of medicine and forced the *condottiere* to drink it. "That will make him sleep a while. Try and keep him from the battlefield for twenty-four hours, more if you can. I'll go to the ship and bring him some more medicine this afternoon when he awakens."

"Thank you, doctor. Do we tell the Emperor?"

"Only if he asks."

"Good-day, Captain Marco."

Marco nodded as the doctor left and turned his eyes to his uncle. The men around waited for his command. He turned to the soldier at Giustiniani's side: "Michiele, stay here with him. Get him anything he asks for. Wait until Doctor Colombo gets here and then take your instructions from him. The *condottiere* is not allowed back to the field today. Those are the doctor's orders so make sure that he obeys them. Hopefully the doctor's potion will keep him asleep and make your job easier. I have to return to the walls." Michiele nodded.

Marco hurried back to the walls to survey the damage. Tonight's repair work would be arduous, and he would be in charge. He prayed that no assault would come, that Giustiniani would recover and that no one, no one, would hear of his uncle's injuries.

* * *

Word that the *condottiere* had been wounded at the *Mesoteichon* flooded the Italian community in Constantinople. Passed from the men at the walls, the news reached the ears of the Genoese defending the Blachernae quarter, spread through the Venetians at Phanar and finally made its way to the corridors of the palace of Angello Lomellino in Pera as he finished his evening meal.

Antonio di Michiele whispered the news in his ear.

The *podestà*'s eyes opened wide. "Is he badly hurt?"

"He cannot be well, my lord. He was in the tower when it collapsed and had to be carried from the scene by his guards. He has not been seen on the walls since."

"This does not bode well for the defense of the City."

"No, my lord."

"We must act carefully." Lomellino paused, trying to analyze the situation. "How many of our citizens are in Constantinople?

"More than four hundred, sir. The Bocchiardi brothers, the crews hired by his Holiness, even your nephew, Imperiali."

"Find out what you can, Antonio. If he dies, I must know immediately. It changes our positions dramatically. We will have to pull our men out of Constantinople and try to reach a compromise with the Sultan."

"Is Giustiniani worth so much to us?"

"He is worth that much to the siege. Constantinople will fall without him."

"Has something happened?" the voice of the *podestà's* wife disarmed him for a moment. It was unusual for her to interrupt him while he was working, but the commotion had obviously disturbed her.

"The Genoese commander in Constantinople has been gravely wounded."

The blood drained from Caterina's face. Even her luscious lips became pale. "*Signor* Giustiniani?" Her voice was a whisper.

"Yes."

"You spoke as if he were dead." She was speaking quickly now, contending with herself as anger, fear, and anguish turned within her.

"We don't know." He turned to Antonio. "Bring me news when you have it. Goodnight." Antonio left, leaving the couple alone. "Don't concern yourself, my dear. We are in no danger." But his words, instead of soothing her, sparked her volatile emotions into flame.

"If we are in no danger, it is because my husband is a coward who will not lift a hand to help the brave men who would sacrifice their lives to keep us free from the Sultan's yoke."

He recoiled in shock. "Caterina, how can you say that?"

"Am I blind? Haven't I seen the enemy's ships off our shore, the guns a few yards from our walls, the field of tents and banners? Have I not heard their cannon day upon day and been kept from the walls of my own city because of their firing?"

"We are not at war, Caterina," he pleaded.

"We are a part of this war. When your home is attacked, you are at war whether you wish it or not!" and she fled from the room.

As she left, Lomellino grabbed his hair in exasperation and pounded his first upon the table. Caterina ran to her apartment, slamming the door behind her and bolting it. She had no desire to see her husband again tonight. She was furious: furious that her husband would not fight, furious that her city stood on the verge of conquest, furious that Giustiniani had been wounded, and furious at herself for caring that he had been wounded. She had sworn, sworn to never speak to him again, sworn to never let him back in her life, sworn that she had forgotten him and no longer loved him, but the thought of Giovanni Giustiniani lying on his deathbed was too much for her to stand. She was trying to avoid the thought, trying to push it aside with reason, with explanations, with deceptions, but knew that she could not. Sobbing, through teeth gritted in anger, she decided to do what her heart commanded.

* * *

Giustiniani lay in his bed, a little dizzy and covered in bruises. The sleeping draught had worn off, and Doctor Colombo was by his side with medicines to dull his pain.

"I must be at the walls tomorrow."

"Drink this, get a good night's sleep and tomorrow you may return to your post."

The *condottiere* tried to choke down the hideous tasting concoction. "I can't drink this! A pig wouldn't drink it!"

"Drink, my lord. If you wish to return to the walls tomorrow, you will do as I say." In his element, the physician would not be deterred by his master's complaining and thrust the cup towards him once more. Giustiniani drank through a grimace of agony. "Well done, commander. I'm going to leave you for the evening. The sleeping draught is very powerful and you are almost recovered anyway, so I will not give it to you tonight." He smiled subtly. "Besides, it would seem you have had enough of me and my medicines. Goodnight." As the physician made his way to the door there was a knock.

"A messenger from Pera for the commander."

"You have business, at so late an hour, my lord?" asked the physician.

"None that I know, but I should see what the message from Pera is. It could be important."

"As you wish, but do not go to the walls again tonight, my lord, not if you can avoid it. Goodnight."

"Goodnight doctor. Send the messenger in."

A cloaked and hooded figure entered the room. Giustiniani raised a candle from the table by his bed and peered across the room. "Come in, man. The doctor has said that I must stay in bed until tomorrow. You have news from Pera?"

The messenger closed the door and moved forward cautiously. The *condottiere* was losing patience. "Damn it man, I'm not contagious, it was a fall I had, not the plague. Come and give me your news."

In response, the messenger stopped, turning slightly towards the bed, the hood was pushed back. Caterina Luccio stood before him. The shock left them both speechless. The *condottiere* leapt up from the bed, the sudden movement straining his damaged muscles so that he bit his lips from the pain. "Caterina," he whispered, breathless.

"You are hurt," he could sense the concern in her voice. "They feared you dead."

"And you? Did you fear me dead?"

Her eyes fell to the ground. Silence commanded them once more.

"There were times when I prayed for you to die. Times when I prayed that we had never met, when I prayed that you had never been born."

He did not answer.

"Have you nothing to say?" she demanded, harshness returning to her voice.

He opened his mouth to speak, but nothing came.

"Surely you can say something. There was a time when you were full of words, pretty words, compliments, flattery, poetry, words that promised so much and in the end were worth so little. But I know your silence too. That silence you had the day you left me. That silence when you could not explain why you were leaving me, why you were abandoning me for a life in pursuit of gold and glory. How often I have had that silence echo in my mind and thunder in my soul."

"You are married."

"Yes, married. Did you think that I would wait for you to come to your senses? To go back and decide that love was more important than battles, cities, or titles? You are where I feared you would end, where I knew you would end a heartbeat from death in this life you've chosen, this life of war and struggle. The life you chose instead of me."

Giustiniani hesitated before responding as her words bled his resolve to answer with strength. "I can't explain the choice I made. My reasons are lost, buried by time. I cannot defend them. I was a different man."

"Is that all? You would have me be satisfied with that. After living through losing you for ten years, you would try to placate me with lies like this?"

"What should I have done? It was my duty to go. I had a duty to my family. Should I have betrayed that? Should I have stayed with you and become a trader, peddling bangles and bolts of cloth for money? Or perhaps you would have preferred a laborer breaking stones or digging ditches. I could not have stayed, and you would never have come with me."

"You broke my heart, Giovanni. You took from me my dignity, my self-respect, part of who I was," the harshness in her voice was decaying into bitterness and sorrow.

"I didn't want to do that," the excuse sounded pathetic, even to the *condottiere*.

"What did you want?"

"I wanted you. I always wanted you. I just never had the courage to make you mine."

"Oh! The great Giovanni Giustiniani lacked the courage!"

"There are many kinds of courage, Caterina," he responded desperately.

"And you spare yours for people who do not love you." She turned abruptly. The word had escaped her lips, the beautifully cruel word that had inebriated her life all those years ago, the word she had told herself again and again that she would not use in front of him.

"For me, Caterina, there has never been love in this world without you." He rose from the bed, slowly, moving toward her one step at a time, approaching as he might approach a deer, afraid to frighten it away.

"You have no right to say that. No right." She pulled away, but not far enough and he had her in his arms.

"There is no love in this world without you. Ten years of journeys and battles, and cities--I have lived more than a lifetime, but I have never found love away from you."

"I am married."

"You are here."

"I thought you were dying."

"You hoped I was alive."

"I prayed for it."

She was in tears. His heart was ready to explode. "God forgive me, Caterina." He kissed her. "The Devil may have me. I would burn in Hell for one taste of your lips." She kissed him again. He pushed her cloak away, running his fingers through the long, dark hair that caressed her shoulders. Her neck came alive in the torch-light, glowing sensuous and golden, inviting his lips. Her crimson mouth burned his cheek. He kissed her, intoxicated by the perfume that was her mouth as they moved to the bed to recapture the passion they had been denied for a decade.

Giustiniani awoke before dawn and stared at the woman next to him, so peaceful, so beautiful. But reality returned harshly. She was in danger. In Constantinople she was endangered by the Turks; if she did not return quickly to Pera there would be trouble with her husband. He awakened her with a kiss. "Caterina? *Amore*, wake up." Her eyes opened suddenly. The serene expression evaporated and her countenance registered dismay.

"I should not have stayed," she whispered.

"Sshhhhh." He held her.

"I must go, Giovanni."

He knew she was right. "I'll help you get back to Pera."

She was dressing. She turned to him and asked: "Why don't you come with me?"

"I cannot. You have a husband, and I have a city. Neither will fare well without us."

She frowned at him. "This was a mistake."

"Mistakes are judged by the ending alone. We may know some day." He took hold of her hands.

"Oh, if only we had more time!"

"I know. We cannot hold time captive, not with swords, not with love. With you, Caterina, there are moments I wish would never end."

"And others I wish would never come. I cannot say goodbye."

"My nephew, Marco, will take you to Pera. You can trust his discretion. Stay here a moment."

Giustiniani went to Marco's home, which was next to his own, and woke his nephew. "Marco, wake up," he whispered.

"What's going on Giovanni."

"I have an important and delicate mission for you."

"Are you recovered?"

"Never mind that. I'm fine. Now listen." He explained the situation briefly. Caterina had come on a skiff with two trusted servants. She would lead Marco to them, and the four would cross over to Pera along the chain boom since that was still under the protection of Diedo's fleet. The skiff would then bring Marco back across before finally returning home.

"I'm glad that you've recovered... your strength. Next time I'll make sure to be the one who has a tower fall on him."

"This is no time for your jokes, Marco," snapped the *condottiere*. I will bring the lady here in ten minutes. Be ready to leave." He returned to his house. Caterina was dressed and ready. As she moved to raise her hood, Giustiniani went to her to kiss her once more.

"I have always loved you, and only you." His eyes were on hers.

"Is there no chance for you to escape?"

"There is nowhere for me to go. We will fight here and we will win. I will come again to Pera after we are victorious to celebrate."

They left the house together and entered Marco's room. He was ready.

"Marco, take the lady back to Pera. Guard her with your life."

"I will."

He turned to her once more. "God be with you, *amore*."

"God be with you, Giovanni." She turned as the tears came to her eyes.

"Farewell, Caterina."

"Farewell, my love."

Giustiniani kissed her once more. At first she resisted, then relented. In that last kiss he tried to drink in the perfume of her lips so that he could keep it with him always. As she and Marco rode away down the lonely street, he hoped that the taste of her mouth would remain with him until he saw her again. But, by the time she was out sight, her delicate fragrance had faded completely from reality into memory.

4—The Icon: *May 24, 1453*

Father Athanasios whispered his evening prayers in the flickering candlelight. Finishing, he crossed himself and stared at the great icon of Mary. This night, like every night since the siege began, Athanasios would pray, staring at the painting of the Mother of God, asking her for protection. The priest was thin, and the thick white beard that covered his face concealed a worn countenance. Time had drained the strength from his body, but he felt his soul buoyed by seventy-four years of faith. He was kneeling in front of the city's holiest icon, the *Hodegetria*, painted by St. Luke. With Easter week past, the icon had returned to the Chora Monastery and the small chapel that acted as its shrine next to the splendid *Hagia Sophià*.

It was late at night, and the day had brought bad news. The Venetian fleet had not been found. The city would be alone to face the Sultan's assault, and that assault would come soon. One hundred thousand men, shouting their war-cries to heaven, would be sent against the City. Suddenly, he heard the screaming. Terrified cries suddenly shattered what little peace the citizens had found during the night. The priest rose and went to a window, but he could not see anything amiss. Surely there was no attack. No alarm had been sounded by the church bells. The cries came again. He heard the sounds of running. Exiting the shrine, he still could not tell what the matter was. True, it was dark and he could not see well, but nothing seemed different. Then he realized what it was—the darkness. Tonight was the full moon, but no light shone from the sky. Father Athanasios raised his eyes to the heavens and saw blackness. The moon had disappeared. There was nothing discernable in the sky except for a faint reddish shadow where the moon had been. The people were panicking. A man saw the priest and came running up to him.

"Father! Father! The moon has vanished! We are lost!"

"Calm yourself my son. God is watching over us." But the terrified man had already run off down a side street.

Athanasios walked down the *Mesé*, past the ruined Hippodrome and towards the Forum of Constantine trying to think of a way to counter the terror that was taking hold of the citizens. The people had come out of their homes to see the eclipse and now stood huddled together, spectators in the eerie darkness. Voices cried out in the darkness.

"God is abandoning us."

"The moon has turned red like blood! Our city will be drenched in blood!"

"We are lost!"

"We are not lost my children! God will save us. He and his mother are with us always." Athanasios was among the horrorstruck faces, wading into the frightened crowd, but his words were swallowed by the darkness. "The mother of God will save us!" he cried. "Do not fear!"

But the people were afraid. They had already abandoned the streets and gone back to their houses. A ghostly calm descended over the City. The Constantinopolitans sat trembling in their homes. Mothers held their children to their breasts and prayed. Even as the shadow inched its way off of the moon and the pale blue light returned, the people remained terrified behind their doors.

The priest would not accept the defeat. Father Athanasios returned to the shrine and resumed his vigil. "Blessed Mother, now we need your glorious help more than ever. Tomorrow morning I shall take you around the walls on my shoulders. We shall restore their confidence and bring victory to the Emperor. Surely you will stand by us now."

Like a squire keeping vigil over his armor the day before his knighthood, Father Athanasios prayed to the *Hodegetria* until dawn. As the first light of day streamed into the shrine, he rose and moved through the cloister preparing the other priests and monks for the procession. Father Athanasios adorned himself in his most splendid vestments. The glittering robes were encrusted with gold and precious stones. The large icon in its gold frame, which was likewise adorned with gems, had been removed from its recess and towered above the procession on a large platform borne on the shoulders of four deacons. The men would carry the icon the entire day, and beneath the giant dais the people would pass. As they crowded under the *Hodegetria* they would cross themselves and murmur their personal intentions to the mother of God. She would hear them.

Emerging from the shrine, Father Athanasios intoned, "Holy Mary, be our guide. Bring victory and peace to your people and your City." The procession began.

The sun drenched Constantinople with its radiance. The golden vestments of the priests and the gold frame of the *Hodegetria* reflected the light brilliantly, casting a shower of auburn light all around. The spectacle was awe-inspiring. Father Athanasios was in the lead, swinging an incense burner and intoning a hymn. People came out of their houses and crossed themselves.

"It is the *Hodegetria!*" they shouted.

"The Virgin Mary has come to lead us to victory!"

The people thronged the streets, pouring from their houses to join in the holy procession. They began to push their way forward so that they could pass beneath the platform. The icon stood above them like a divine aegis.

"Bring light to your people who live in darkness!" cried Athanasios. "See, people of Constantinople, the mother of God brings you light and shows you the path to victory and salvation!" His cry was taken up by the grateful people.

"Blessed art thou, mother of our Lord!"

"Protect us, holy queen!"

"Queen of Heaven, guide us on the path of victory!"

The procession grew in size as the people crowded around the icon. Thousands of worshippers jostled and pressed around so that they could pass beneath the dais. They were cheering, delirious in their joy when the sky began to darken. This time it was not an eclipse, but clouds, black clouds coming swiftly from the east. The sun was blocked out. A chilling wind began to blow. The procession was checked, momentarily shocked by the sudden change in Nature's mood.

"Forward my children. It is nothing but a passing summer squall," encouraged Father Athanasios. But, at that moment, the summer squall broke. The rain began to fall. At first, some of the people were pleased.

"God is washing away our sins."

"Heaven weeps for our suffering." They continued to cross themselves and pass beneath the dais in prayer.

Then the wind picked up. The icon, spattered with water, swayed on its high perch. A dozen hands reached to steady the holy *Hodegetria* as the procession tried to continue in spite of the weather. It was raining hard now. The downpour was driving into the people. The drops bit at them with all the fury of Turkish arrows, and they were forced to lift their cloaks to cover their heads. Eager to pass beneath the icon, they pressed forward on all sides trying to squeeze between the four bearers. There was space for no more than two or three penitents to pass at a single time, but because of the rain, they crammed in four and five abreast, and the platform began to sway. The deacons holding up the supports were driven outwards by the human wedge. It took all their strength to keep the *Hodegetria* aloft.

Father Athanasios' beard was dripping wet as he squinted through the storm and tried to think of what could be done. Was there absolutely no mercy in the world? What else would God send to challenge them? He turned to see the wavering platform and shouted at the bearers to steady themselves, and for the people to not press through. His words were scattered by the wind.

Now the rain became interspersed with hail. Enormous chunks of ice, some the size of walnuts, hammered down from above. They battered at the helpless citizens and drummed furiously at the earth. Some struck the holy icon itself. The wind knifed into the mass again, and the helpless people were seeking refuge from Nature's assault beneath the dais. The procession clogged to a halt. The rain continued to pour. Rivers ran through the streets. Earth was washed away along the avenue. Small children lost their footing as the rivers swept away the earth beneath them. A few of the very old were likewise sent crashing to the ground. Panic took hold of the crowd. Those who kept their heads tried to help the injured back to their feet.

On its pedestal, the icon swayed. Hands reached up to it, but this time, could not steady it. Everything was slippery from the rain. Water was in the eyes of the monks and priests, blinding them as they reached to secure their Holy Mother. The entire platform rocked with the redoubled wind and from the people huddled below. The *Hodegetria* twisted from its holder and fell. The heavy icon caromed off of arms and hands that tried to keep it aloft, bruising and battering the faithful, before crashing into the muddied street. Immediately, the priests reached after their fallen idol, slipping and stumbling over each other. The podium was thrown off the shoulders of the four deacons and collapsed into the morass. The people who had crowded beneath it to shield themselves were assailed by the elements and cried out as the rain and hail struck them mercilessly. The *Hodegetria* lay trapped in the mud.

"Lift it up!" screamed Athanasios. "Holy Mary, forgive us!" he shouted, throwing himself forward to retrieve the holy painting.

It was too heavy for the old man. Others were with him. Their hands covered with dirt as they tried to raise the *Hodegetria*. It was stuck fast to the ground. They scooped at the mud around the edges trying to dislodge it. Priests dug their fingers underneath the holy portrait until they bled, but the icon would not budge. A mysterious power from the ground had taken hold of it, as if the earth were clutching it for its own protection.

Athanasios' golden vestments were saturated. His frail body began to sink under the weight of the soaking material. He was on his knees before the icon crying, exhorting the men to lift the Virgin and save her from the flood. His tears mixed with the rain and ran over the face of the painting so that Mary herself wept at the scene.

"Father," a voice called to Father Athanasios over the tempest. "Father, let me help you lift the holy icon."

Through the torrents, Father Athansios could make out an enormous young man. Rainwater had beaded on his short-cropped black hair. His arms were burly. His body was a hard tangle of muscles, but the eyes were soft. There was a hushed pause among the crowd as he bent his massive frame to reach the icon. Not daring to use anything but his hands for fear of damaging the sacred relic, he took hold of the two opposite ends and heaved with all his strength. Rivulets of rainwater ran down his brow interspersed with sweat from his exertions. The crowd held its breath.

The sound of the whistling wind and the driving hail was broken only by the grunts of the giant as he willed the icon to rise with all his strength. The mystical power of Nature holding the *Hodegetria* fast to the earth contended with the power of the young colossus. He gritted his teeth and pulled with all his might to lift the holy icon, to save it from the quagmire. The mud clung resolutely to the icon's back, but after one more massive effort, the sludge gave way, and the giant stood holding the *Hodegetria* reverentially in his arms. Others now rushed forward to his aid and the icon was finally free. Father Athanasios and the priests began to clean the relic with their hands and even their vestmests. Women came forward offering their veils; men gave their cloaks. The rain made the work easier, and soon the icon was cleansed and returned to its pedestal.

It was a fruitless victory. Rain and hail continued to pelt the citizens until their spirits were broken. The dais had been destroyed and with it, the determination of the people. Many had already returned to their homes. The procession could not go on. The priest turned to the giant.

"Thank you my son. May God and the Virgin protect you."

The young man helped Father Athanasios to his feet. The priest placed his hands on the youth's forehead and blessed him. The man smiled faintly.

"I will help you carry it back to the church, father."

As he spoke, the youth shouldered the great icon and began the arduous march back to its sanctuary. He carried it with great strength, but gently, as he might have borne his grandmother. The young man was bent double beneath the weight, and the priest crossed himself, standing in awe as the young man moved wordlessly through the driving rain to return the holy icon to its proper place.

5—The Priest: *May 25, 1453*

By the time he returned to his chapel, Father Athanasios was soaked to the bone. Lovingly, he removed the drenched vestments, dried himself, and dressed in his plain black robe. The rain was falling gently as the priest knelt before the icon, redoubling his devotions. He was mumbling the prayers again when heavy, booted feet sounded behind him—soldiers. The foot-falls were steadily becoming louder. Lighter, swift steps sounded, overcoming the soldier's tramping. Father Athanasios rose and turned to see what the commotion was. A young monk with a panicked expression burst into the shrine.

"Father, soldiers of the Emperor are coming! They want to see you! They are asking where you are." The monk was out of breath.

"Stay calm, my son. I shall go to them." He rose. "Did they tell you what they wanted?"

"No father. You should leave. What if they are angry about the *Hodegetria*?"

Father Athanasios blinked at the suggestion, but responded calmly.

"There is nothing to fear. I shall speak with them."

The young man stood trembling in front of the priest.

"Don't go to them father," he whispered.

Athanasios smiled at him, a warm smile, full of love and understanding.

"You are afraid for me, my child. Do not be troubled. Our Emperor is a good man, a good Christian. No evil shall befall me."

As he spoke he placed his hands on the monk's head and blessed him. Then he strode out from the sanctuary to meet the loudening boots in the corridor. There were two men, both thin and tired. They had been fighting for almost two months. The priest felt compassion for their suffering. The eyes of the officer in command met the priest.

"Are you Father Athanasios, the guardian of the holy *Hodegetria*?"

"I am Father Athanasios. But I am not the guardian of the icon, as you say. It is my guardian."

"You are to come with us," responded the officer. "The Emperor wishes to speak with you." He turned and began to walk away. The other soldier took his place behind the priest.

"Is the Emperor displeased with me?"

"I do not know, Father," replied the officer. "We were only told to bring you to the imperial palace immediately so that you may speak with his majesty."

Those were the last words that passed between them. The men walked solemnly onto the *Mesé*. Horses were waiting to take them to the palace. The rain had slackened and was now only a mist. Father Athanasios began to pray. They rode to the palace where the priest was turned over by the officer to a steward who brought him through a series of corridors until they reached the Emperor's council chamber. Father Athanasios had not seen the Emperor so close before. The humanity of his sovereign was apparent from such a short distance: the eyes, worn and tired and the pained expression. There were black rings under the Emperor's eyes. Above the rings, the flesh was swollen through a lack of sleep.

The priest looked anxiously at the noble men around him. He knew the Grand Duke, Lukas Notaras, old and dignified with long silver hair and rich robes. He saw the Latin, Cardinal Isidore, who had abandoned the true Orthodox faith. Then there were the foreign captains in their smoke begrimed armor and a host of other nobles and leading citizens. The priest bowed humbly before them before throwing himself on the ground in front of the Emperor and kissing his hand.

"Rise, Father Athanasios."

The priest remained rooted to the ground. The ability to move had deserted him. The Emperor was smiling, looking into his eyes attempting to bridge the gap separating a monarch from his subjects. Constantine motioned Sphrantzes to help the priest to his feet. The secretary moved forward and took Father Athanasios by the arm.

"Come, father. Let me help you."

He was standing again and Sphrantzes continued speaking to him.

"There is a messenger here from the Turkish camp, father. He claims to be your nephew. His name is Ismail. He says that his father, your brother, found service in the army of Sultan Murad. Is there such a man?"

Father Athanasios was taken aback. His reply came slowly, after he had had a chance to gather his thoughts.

"Yes, my lord. There is such a man."

"And would you recognize him if you were to see him?"

"Yes, my lord. I think that I would. It has been a few years since I saw him last, but I'm sure I would be able to identify him."

"Then tell us if you recognize him." As Sphrantzes spoke, two guards came in on either side of an exquisitely dressed young man.

Father Athanasios examined him intently, staring deeply into his face. The visage was familiar. It was his brother's son. He turned to Sphrantzes.

"Yes, my lord. It is he."

Sphrantzes looked warily at the Turkish emissary.

"Very well. Tell us your terms." The secretary took the envoy by the arm and led him towards the Christian council.

Ismail Bey prepared to speak. The Sultan had chosen him as his envoy for the simple reason that the young man's father was a Greek. Mehmed wanted the City, and if he could get it without the destruction involved in a sack, so much the better. Besides, after each failure, Halil Pasha became bolder. The Grand Vizier was whispering among the members of the court that the siege was hopeless and should be abandoned, that the Venetians and the Genoese were sending powerful relief fleets. Only swift success would silence him and in turn, give Mehmed the freedom to silence him forever.

Ismail's instructions were plain. He was to explain to the Greeks the hopelessness of their situation, to convince them that it was not too late for them to make peace and save themselves from certain death. The Sultan's terms would be generous to the Emperor and his court. He was to bring back someone to whom the specific conditions would be given. Ismail stepped forward, bowed, and then addressed the august assembly.

"My lord the Sultan wishes to make peace and spare your people the death and destruction that must surely follow a continuation of hostilities. Have no doubts that my lord Mehmed's forces will break through your defenses and enter the City. When they do, unimaginable suffering must surely follow for your people. But you can avoid this. It must be clear to you all that there is no way for Constantinople to hold out against his majesty's forces.

"Sultan Mehmed is a reasonable man. It is not too late to come to terms with him. The Sultan wishes one of you to come back to camp with me to hear his majesty's terms and report back with them. They are extremely generous. Some of you know me as a man whose father was born a Greek and chose to serve the Sultan. My heritage is Greek, but this has not prevented me from rising in his majesty's service. There is no shame in serving the most powerful lord in the world. I can tell you that we Greeks are just as well respected in the Sultan's court as any other people who pay him homage. I shall leave you to make your decision."

Ismail turned away from the company and made his way to a side room. There was silence when he left. No one wanted to be the first to address the new issue that faced them. Then, the Emperor's cousin, Theophilos Palaeologos spoke.

"We should at least send someone to hear the terms. Perhaps the Sultan realizes that our defenses are too strong and wishes to make peace."

Sphrantzes responded. "I do not believe that the Sultan wishes peace. Nor does he wish to withdraw without conquering the prize he has sought since his childhood. He simply hopes to compel us to surrender to him that which he cannot win by force of arms."

Giustiniani looked at the Emperor. The two soldiers knew that Mehmed's victory was not as improbable as Theophilos or Sphrantzes seemed to think. If anything, they realized that Turkish victory was inevitable unless help arrived soon. Giustiniani, however, thought that there was reason to at least hear the terms. He spoke.

"Whatever the Sultan's intentions, sire, it would be wise to send someone to parlay, if for no other reason than to delay the siege even for a few hours. There are repairs to be made to the walls and the men desperately need rest and treatment for their wounds."

"And whom, Master Giustiniani, do we send on this mission?" demanded Lukas Notaras caustically. "The Sultan has an unflattering reputation for hospitality. I have no desire to see one of our nobles impaled like a lamb on a spit!"

Demetrios Cantacuzenos took the part of the Grand Duke. "I must agree with Lord Notaras, if we send someone to hear the Sultan's terms he cannot be anyone of importance or the barbarian will undoubtedly kill him."

"Then, my lords, if it cannot be anyone of us," chimed Sphrantzes, "whom do you suggest?"

The company had become so engrossed in their deliberations that they completely overlooked the fact that Father Athanasios was still present in the council room. The priest now dared to step forward and speak.

"My lords, if a humble servant might be allowed to speak in this noble company, I offer myself as ambassador to the Sultan to hear his terms. If he should decide to kill me then you shall not have lost anyone of importance, and I will happily accept the martyrdom for my faith and my Emperor."

"This is not your place, Father," responded the secretary. Then to the council he said, "I hardly think the Sultan will put his terms forward to a priest."

There was agreement in the chamber until Cantacuzenos spoke again.

"Master Sphrantzes is correct. However, why should Mehmed know that Father Athanasios is a priest? If we remove his vestments, his ears would be as suitable as any of ours to hear the Sultan's terms." He turned to the priest. "Do you agree, Father?"

Athanasios paused for a moment. He thought of his flock, starving and afraid, of the icon, heavy and covered in mud and grime. His sins needed to be expiated. He felt that he had betrayed the trust that his faith had bestowed upon him. If he died at the hands of the Sultan it would clear the ledger. If he lived, perhaps he could be a small part of bringing peace and saving the lives of his people and the Emperor. Perhaps, through him, the Holy Mary would bring victory to the City after all.

"I agree."

* * *

They trimmed Father Athanasios' beard in order to make him less conspicuous. Suitable clothes were found, and Sphrantzes imparted a few suggestions on courtly deportment so that he would not appear too awkward before the Sultan. The shorter beard made the priest seem a little younger. This worked to their advantage. It would not be good to send too old a man to hear the Sultan's terms.

He rode a small horse next to his nephew. The boy had grown since he had seen him last. Ismail's father had always been a mystery to the priest. He was a good man. Why had he turned away from his people and his faith to serve the barbarian? But Athanasios could not blame his brother entirely. Destiny was with the Sultan, not the Emperor. The family had no future beneath the cross. It was logical to seek a better life under the crescent. His brother's son had become a commander, a prince. Father Athanasios' children, all seven of them, had followed their father into the church. His three daughters had become nuns. Three of his sons had entered monasteries, the forth had become a priest.

He looked at the young nobleman beside him. The pact had been sealed before they left. The Greeks would send Athanasios to hear the Sultan's terms, and Ismail promised not to reveal that the ambassador was in fact a priest and his uncle. They rode slowly so as not to arouse the suspicion of the Turkish sentries. It was better that way, for Father Athanasios was unaccustomed to riding. Had he ventured beyond a walk, the horse would no doubt have thrown him.

Ismail raised a hand to the sentry, and they passed wordlessly into the Turkish camp. Father Athanasios looked around, awed by the number of soldiers. A group of warriors were sharpening their long knives, and the priest shuddered as he listened to the blades rasping against the stones. His imagination sensed the steel across his throat. He overcame the urge to cross himself and instead whispered:

"Father, preserve me. Allow me to accomplish my task. Then do what you will with me."

Ismail looked at his uncle. He could see the fear in his eyes. He wanted to say something to reassure him, but the moment did not allow it. They had arrived at the Sultan's tent. Mehmed, as usual was looking at maps surrounded by generals and viziers. At that moment, the shrill voice of Shahabeddin was raised over the assembly. The eunuch disturbed Ismail, not only because of his voice, and the

221

sacrifice that had achieved it, but because of his avarice. It seemed that the castrator's knife, in robbing the man of his hunger for women, had doubled his appetite for riches and influence. As always, the eunuch pressed for a continuation of the struggle.

The appearance of the Greek emissary arrested the internal discussion. Shahabeddin looked up, and upon seeing Father Athanasios immediately stopped speaking. Ismail Bey came forward and bowed to the Sultan and the Viziers.

"Your majesty, noble lords, I bring an emissary from Emperor Constantine. He has come to hear your terms and to report them back to his master."

All eyes were upon the priest. Four decades of saying mass had accustomed him to the gaze of many, but the company made his heart tremble. He silently prayed that his strength would not fail.

"The terms I offer to your master are these," began Mehmed, in excellent Greek. "I promise him his life and the lives of his followers on the single condition that the City is handed over to me immediately. There will be no plundering, and no one will be harmed. My army will enter peacefully in accordance with the law of Allah. The Emperor, along with anyone who chooses, may leave with their arms and proceed to the Morea. If you do not surrender Constantinople, my army shall attack. Once inside, I shall not be responsible for the behavior of my warriors. The Prophet grants his forces three days to do as they wish to any infidel city that has resisted them. I can do nothing to prevent that. Those are the terms."

Father Athanasios nodded that he had understood. He did not answer for fear that his response might betray his position. He knew, however, that the terms were unacceptable. Constantine would never agree to abandon the City. To leave Constantinople would be to renounce the throne. He could only remain Emperor so long as he held the City. Without it, he would be nothing. Emperor and empire would cease to exist. When it was clear that nothing further would be said, Mehmed turned to Ismail Bey and instructed him to take Father Athanasios from the tent and escort him back to the Turkish lines. Uncle and nephew parted wordlessly.

In Mehmed's tent, the debate was renewed. It continued for several hours until a breathless messenger entered the tent with the Emperor's reply. A herald read from the paper:

From Constantine Palaeologos, King and Emperor of the Romans, king of kings, ruler of rulers, to Mehmed Sultan. My lord, it rests with you to continue to brandish the all consuming torch of war, or to enjoy the bounty of peace. If you wish, you may live peacefully with us as your predecessors did before you. Your ancestors regarded my forefathers as their fathers and honored them as such. They looked upon the City as their homeland and knew that no one who made war against Constantinople enjoyed long life.

To make peace, I say to you, keep the fortresses and the lands which you have unjustly seized, as justly yours. Extract as much tribute annually as we are able to pay and depart in peace. For after all, can you be so certain that victory instead of defeat awaits you here? There is no way to divine the outcome of a battle, and it must be in battle that you win the prize of our City, for no power on earth can compel me to surrender this sacred inheritance to you. The right to surrender the City belongs neither to me, nor to anyone who dwells here. Rather than to have our lives spared, it is our common resolve to die fighting, since neither I nor my people have any desire to submit to the slavery you offer.

For an instant, Constantine's reply hung in the air as the assembly remained silent. Seizing upon the moment, Halil Pasha spoke at last. No one dared to interrupt the Grand Vizier as he made a final push for an end to the siege. Now, hard upon the failure of the mining operations and with the Emperor's eloquent refusal ringing in the council's ears, Halil laid out his argument in smooth and controlled words.

"Sire, hear me. The Emperor speaks the truth. We know not what awaits us before these walls. Your army is powerful, but war is unpredictable. You have done your duty here. You have given battle courageously, but every day great numbers of our men are killed. You can see how strongly the City is defended. It is impossible to storm it. The more men you send forward to the attack, the more corpses are strewn around the walls. Remember that none of your ancestors ever achieved what you have accomplished here, or even expected to. It is to your glory and honor that you have done so much. You have accomplished more than anyone in history. This should satisfy you. Be contented with this and do not destroy the whole of your forces here.

"Venice and Hungary are rising. Their ships and men will come to the City. For the safety of the army and the future of your kingdom you must withdraw. Leave this place of death. Like the great conquerors of the past, leave columns and trophies testifying to the great feats that you have accomplished. It is enough. Let your subjects enjoy peace, sire. Do not continue this war and make enemies of Venice and Hungary, Genoa, and your Christian subjects. Your power is great and is best assured in peace. In the end, war can only diminish what you possess."

The council was murmuring their assent. Many were weary. They had stood encamped outside the honeyed walls for almost two months. Morale had ebbed to its nadir. Here, their fathers and grandfathers had failed. The future of the siege hung in the balance. The Grand Vizier had swayed many hearts. Mehmed, even in his arrogance, felt the uncertainty familiar to youth creeping into his spirit. His fears battled with him, mingling with the warnings of Halil Pasha, his ambition, and the lilting temptation of Gülbahar prophesying "*It must be yours.*" Perhaps Halil Pasha was correct: perhaps it was too much to risk the army and the peace of the empire by remaining in front of the unconquerable Queen of Cities. Then, Zagan Pasha spoke above the hushed assembly.

"I have no faith in the words of the Grand Vizier," he countered. His tone was like fire, cutting into the ice of Halil Pasha's speech. "The princes of Christendom are divided. I do not believe that either Hungary or Venice will come to the City. Your father buried the power of Hungary for a generation and the Venetians are more concerned with commerce than Constantinople. The Christian kings are fractious and mistrustful. No one will come.

"Your majesty, Lord Halil says that you have accomplished more than your ancestors, and he is correct in this, if nothing else. But, sire, if you accomplish more than they, it is because your destiny is far greater than theirs and the power you command, superior to anything they could have imagined. This is your first true expedition. You cannot turn away from the City and leave it unconquered after we have come so far and done so much. The walls are battered and crumbling. With every assault our men move closer to victory. With each day the prize is nearer to our grasp. The Greeks cannot resist you. Give us the chance to fulfill *your* destiny. One more assault, sire, just one more is all that I ask. If that fails, then no power on earth is capable of taking the City. But do not withdraw without making one final attempt. Allah will lend you his help, and we shall win a glorious victory."

Shahabeddin took up the charge. "Why is Lord Halil trying to contaminate us with his fear? You, our unconquered prince, *should* make great plans and attempt great things, greater than anything your forefathers contemplated. Through these trials you must bear yourself magnificently no matter the result. And here, my lord, the result will be victory."

The blood of the generals was rising. The youthful, the proud, and the ambitious carried the council upon a wave of infectious exhilaration. Halil Pasha sat silently as the Sultan made his decision. Mehmed spoke, his eyes dancing with sparks.

"It is decided. We shall make one more full-scale assault against the City." He turned to his commanders. "Make your preparations. We will attack before dawn three days hence. From now until then, the men are to rest in camp. During the day they are to fast. Each night, they must light bonfires and pray to Allah. Have the heralds proclaim it. As the law demands, when the City falls, the men shall have three days to pillage it. By Mohammed and the soul of my father, I swear that they shall be granted the right to everything, every person, male or female, all property and all treasure. I swear it!" Mehmed's words came with the same thunder as a salvo from the giant guns. Halil felt his soul melting in the conflagration. The blaze could only be doused in the blood of failure. In the event of victory, he, Constantinople and any hope of peace for the future, would fall victim to the flames.

Inside the red and gold tent, at last, there was silence. It was done. The Sultan had committed the army to one final assault. Mehmed needed to sleep but did not feel tired. The enormity of the situation weighed on his mind. Three days. In three days it would be his, or he would be forced to withdraw, a beaten man, the arrogance of his youth humbled before the Queen of Cities. He wanted Gülbahar. He needed someone who was neither Vizier nor general to talk to.

"Mustafa!"

The servant, familiar with the shrill petulance of his master, entered and bowed.

"Yes, your majesty?"

"Bring the lady Gülbahar here immediately."

Mehmed turned and paced the room restlessly. He took a cup of wine and drank. Would it be possible for him to wait three days? He wanted the City. He wanted it now.

"Patience," he hissed to himself. "The army is not ready yet. Let them prepare for the challenge, and they will succeed. You are right to have given them three days. Yet three days is an eternity. What if Halil Pasha is right and the Venetians arrived while his army sat mute and inactive in front of Constantinople's walls?

He drained a second cup and continued to pace. It was in this agitated state that Gülbahar found him.

"Good evening, my lord."

He turned on her suddenly and blurted the news. "It is done."

"What is done?"

"I have ordered the assault."

"Assault, why?"

"There is no time left to wait. The Emperor will not surrender, and the defenders will not be starved or bullied into submission."

"But the City, your city, its glory, its riches... What will become of them when your animals are done with it?" she was almost pleading

Mehmed frowned. "It cannot be avoided."

The battle that she had wanted, had sought, had connived for, was here, but not the way she wished. Gülbahar had hoped for a grand entrance into a City untouched by devastation. Now she would have to wait outside the walls while the Sultan's warriors vented their frustrations for three days.

"It must be stopped."

"Stopped? Why? Is this not what you wanted, what you begged me for? Constantinople, capital of the world, and it will be mine!"

"Sire," her voice was soothing, attempting to calm him. "Your generals have pushed for this. They seek only to drain the riches of the City for themselves. Have patience, my lord, and everything will be yours."

He looked at the woman, the Albanian slave who had come so far, who wanted glory, power, and riches for him and for herself. For the first time, he saw the precarious game she had played from the beginning, trying to bring him to this point, to victory, but making sure that the victory would suit her more than it would suit his viziers, his generals, his soldiers, perhaps even more than it would suit himself. For now, in spite of her, he agreed with Zagan Pasha, with Shahabeddin and the rest and wanted nothing more to make Constantinople his.

"There is no time. If we do not attack, we risk losing everything."

"What will be left for you after a three day orgy of destruction?"

"The City will be mine."

"The City will belong to your viziers, your generals, to Zagan Pasha, Shahabeddin, and to a hundred-thousand armed fools."

"The City will belong to me! I will not break the *sharia*[††] for this."

"Ha! You would give in to the wishes of peasants, murders, and ambitious generals for plunder and leave yourself Sultan of smoking ruins? What sort of ruler lets his subjects enjoy the fruit first and takes only the crumbs that are left?" Her words bit him deeply.

"It is the law!"

"It is comical to see a king bound not only by his subjects, but by bits of paper."

"I will be Emperor of Constantinople!" he screamed at her. "Sitting on the throne of the Caesars! I will have the City no matter what it costs!" And she saw in him something not there before, the determination to do anything, to conquer anything, to sacrifice anything, even her, for this obsession.

[††] Islamic law.

What she had created those months ago in Adrianople was now beyond her power to control.

She spoke soothingly again, truly fearful of him for the first time: "It will be yours, sire. Yours." Her hand moved gently to stroke his hair. Mehmed grabbed it, hard at first. Gülbahar's eyes came alive, but she could still see the desire alive in his eyes. He swallowed, then kissed her. She stepped back and let her robe fall. The tent came alive with her perfume as they moved to the red bed draped in silk.

But Mehmed's mind was not on her. His frustration and anxiety removed any trace of gentleness as they joined. He took her as he wanted to take the City, with aggression and force. She tried to turn these emotions to passion, to somehow tame his spirit with the charm of her body, but Mehmed could think only of the City. Constantinople was all that he wanted. In three days it would be his.

6—The Warrior: *May 27, 1453*

Giovanni Giustiniani slowly made his way down the long corridor to the Emperor's quarters. In mind and body, the *condottiere* was a broken man. All that remained whole in him was his spirit. A few hours earlier, during a skirmish at the walls, he had been wounded by a crossbow bolt. It had penetrated his armor and lodged in the bundle of nerves and muscle on the side of his left shoulder. The wound was not deep, but it compelled him to withdraw temporarily from the battle line. Doctor Colombo had put the arm in a sling, and Giustiniani could not lift it more than a few inches from his side. The pain was excruciating.

With the bolt extracted, he returned to the battle line, his shoulder throbbing, to find the Turks in full retreat. Even though the enemy withdrew, he did not rest. Instead, he once more directed the repairs of the walls and the stockade. The flimsy barrels of earth and makeshift wooden beams were somehow holding the most powerful army in the world at bay. The defenders dipped into their last reserves of strength to lift the heavy wooden boards and to shift the stone-filled barrels. Their hands were raw from the constant work and laced with splinters.

Now, the greatest assault of all was coming. Friends in Pera, Genoese spies who moved freely in and out of the Turkish camp, had brought him the news late that night. He listened patiently, and they told him everything. Word for word, they related the events of the Sultan's council. The Turks did not know that the Venetian fleet had not been seen, that the defenders were nearly out of ammunition, and that the scarcity of food in the City had driven the price of a loaf of bread so high that it had to be bought in gold. The Turks had their own problems, no less acute. It was possible that if this last grand assault failed, Mehmed would be compelled to withdraw. To hold the Sultan's myriads back would take a superhuman effort.

This was the moment of decision. Constantine had refused the Sultan's terms for peace. Stalwartly, he had rejected the suggestion that he flee the City and continue to live in the Morea with his brothers. Constantinople was everything. A thousand years before, the Emperor Justinian had been told that the Imperial robes would make a fine shroud. So it would be with Constantine.

Giustiniani found the Emperor in his council chamber. He was seated in the center of the room, exhausted, and surrounded by quarreling nobles. They fell silent as the warrior appeared. Everyone present knew of his wound, but no one dared to speak of it. Instead, they probed him with their eyes, searching for the truth of his condition. Attempting to seem as strong and healthy as possible, the *condottiere* had removed the sling. The arm hung limply at his side. Mustering his strength, he pushed his way through the mass and leaned his mouth towards Constantine's ear.

"I have received word that the assault will come soon, your majesty."

"When?" The reply was barely audible.

"Tuesday, before sunrise."

"Is your information reliable?"

"Yes, sire. The Sultan has ordered three days of rest in his camp. The men will pray and fast in preparation. Then the assault will come."

Constantine closed his eyes. Giustiniani was troubled by the blank expression stamped on his face. Constantine had the look of someone resigned to death. Demetrios Cantacuzenos, who had overheard the *condottiere*'s words, now spoke to his cousin.

"Sire, once more we beseech you, there is yet time for you to escape. Leave the City, take refuge with your brothers, and fight on."

"If I fight, cousin, I fight here. There can be no better place. There is no other place. The City is our Empire. We cannot abandon it."

232

"Think of us sire," Sphrantzes added his voice. "You are our City, our sovereign. Your ancestor Michael returned in triumph to recapture Constantinople--why not you?"

"You too, Yiorgo? Do you, too, wish me to betray my position and abandon my throne?"

"No, my lord," answered the courtier, "we only wish you to live."

"There is nothing for me beyond these walls. My life is the City. I cannot live without it." Once more he stood as he spoke. His voice rose in a crescendo of intensity. "I shall never leave it! Constantinople is my home. I shall defend it with my last breath! Do you hear me? All of you? Do you hear me? I will not abandon my throne! I will not abandon my City!"

The Emperor's visage was contorted with emotion; the calm patrician façade, shattered. He stood before the noble assembly, spittle flying from his mouth, the rage boiling behind his exhausted eyes, the already hoarse voice roaring on, driven by inconsolable sorrow. His legs yielded to the tide, and the once regal figure crumpled to the ground, unconscious.

"Your majesty!" cried Sphrantzes.

Everyone rushed forward towards the Emperor. Sphrantzes lifted his master's head from the ground. Giustiniani and Theophilus Palaeologos raised their lord's arms in an attempt to get him to sit up, but Constantine had fainted. Notaras motioned to two servants, who lifted the exhausted body

"Take his majesty to his chambers. Let him rest," instructed the Grand Duke.

"He is tired," said Sphrantzes.

"So are we all," responded Cantacuzenos.

A surreal silence hung over the assembly of lords. They were shocked by the Emperor's display of human frailty. Cantacuzenos recognized the danger replete in the moment and turned to Giustiniani.

"Is there anything, *protostrator*, that we can do to prepare ourselves?"

The *condottiere*'s mind had wandered off. Fatigue had taken possession of him. He could not control his thoughts. They moved unbidden as if borne on gusts of wind to Pera and Caterina, to the bustling comfort of Chios and the peaceful shores of Genoa. His shoulder was throbbing.

"*Protostrator!*" snapped Cantacuzenos again, bringing Giustiniani back to reality.

He tried to think. Was there anything that he needed? The council waited silently for his reply. The *condottiere*'s eyes passed over the men before him: Sphrantzes, the diplomatic secretary; Cantacuzenos, the imperial *protostrator*; Theophilus Palaeologos, the Emperor's cousin; Lukas Notaras, the arrogant Grand Duke. His mind returned.

"There is one thing, my lord. I would ask that the reserve of mobile cannon under the command of Lord Notaras be transferred to me for use along the *Mesoteichion*."

Notaras' expression erupted. He answered the *condottiere*'s suggestion himself.

"How dare you, sir, presume to give me orders? I am not a mercenary for you to command!"

"The Emperor gave *me* command of the land walls, not you. The main enemy attack will be directed against me, far from the safety of your position." The warrior's heart had begun to beat again. His anger towards the Grand Duke and his frustration spilled out.

"Do you dare to accuse me of cowardice?" demanded Notaras.

"I question a pig-headed arrogance that will condemn your City to the sword of the conqueror! Is this the gratitude that you bestow on me for endeavoring to save you from the Turks?"

"You shall have our gratitude, and your money, mercenary, when the Turks are driven from these walls!"

"I am trying to defend this city, my lord. Would you stop me from providing the strongest possible defense?"

"I would stop you from diverting resources simply to preserve yourself."

"And who," responded Giustiniani furiously, striding towards Notaras, "will stop me from running you through with my sword here and now?" With his good right arm, the *condottiere* reached for the long blade at his side, but the courtiers rushed forward to stop him.

"Keep your temper, mercenary!" scolded Notaras.

"Keep your cannon, Lord Notaras, and lose your City." The hilt of the blade slammed back into its scabbard and the *condottiere* stormed from the room.

The fresh afternoon air hit him suddenly as he emerged. Day had worn on and there was only a short time before sunset. Giustiniani walked swiftly, wanting to put as much distance as possible between himself and the old fool. Did they understand nothing? Could such arrogance still thrive at such a late hour? Perhaps God was right in condemning the City to death. The ancient hubris and duplicitous intrigue which had been the foundations of the Byzantine court for a thousand years would finally be swept away in a torrent of blood.

But what of Caterina? Once more, the full lips and feminine form crept into his thoughts. He could not go to her now. How was she passing these last hours of freedom? Did she know that the assault was coming? Poor Caterina. Her days, and those of Pera, were growing short as well. He would have to do something to save her. But could he save both Caterina and the City? His days, too, were numbered. Was the City worth the sacrifice? Was he throwing his life away? He could not afford such thoughts and willed them from his mind. He had chosen to stay and would now have to fight for his survival.

By now, he was at the walls, or rather at what was left of them. The Sultan's cannon had been hard at work again.

They were still firing, doing more damage all the time. With only three days remaining, the Sultan's gunners made every human exertion. Nothing could stand against such power.

"Marco?" he called.

One of his soldiers pointed him towards a place along the palisade. The youth was nearby, assembling men and material to begin the night's repair work once darkness fell. Giustiniani walked up to his nephew and pulled him aside, out of earshot from the other men.

"Marco, the Turks are planning an assault several hours before sunrise on Tuesday. It will be the end."

"The end?"

"Yes. Either way, it will be the end. If we repulse them on Tuesday, they will withdraw. Otherwise..." his voice trailed off. "Otherwise, the City will be theirs."

Marco was silent. He seemed lost in thought. After a few minutes, he spoke.

"Then this is really it?"

"Yes. It is."

There was silence between them for a moment. Neither knew what to say. The younger man hung his head and paused for a moment. He raised it when he spoke.

"Will we lose, Giovanni?"

The *condottiere* drew breath to reply, but stopped himself. A shiver ran over him. There was such trust in his nephew's eyes. The gaze was too trusting to lie to, too innocent to burden with the truth.

"Victory will not come easily," he hedged.

"Will we lose?" insisted the youth.

"We've never lost before." The spirit of the warrior within him was tired, wounded, but still alive. Marco made no response. "Get some sleep. We shall need it."

Marco nodded. The two men were moving away from the walls when the western horizon began to glow red. The crimson aura enveloped the battlements and spread its glow to the City. They rushed to the battlements to see what was happening. The hillside of the Turkish camp was in flames. The orange and red tongues leapt towards the starry dome above, mixing with the blue moonlight.

"What is it Giovanni? Is the Turkish camp on fire?"

"I can't tell."

"Maybe they are the camp fires of a relieving army from Hungary!" exclaimed Marco.

"I don't know. They seem to be too close for that. Something is going on in the Turkish camp."

The two men stared west trying to determine the source of the fire. Then the cheering began. One hundred thousand voices were raised in a makeshift paean to victory. Cymbals, drums, castanets, all the instruments in the camp came alive. The Sultan's nights of terror were beginning. Giustiniani saw his nephew shiver.

"They are preparing themselves for the assault. Don't let it bother you, Marco. It's empty noise. We'll find a way to silence it. Go and sleep."

Marco nodded, but there was fear in his expression. He returned to his quarters, but his eyes would not close. There were too many fearful thoughts and sleep was impossible.

* * *

Giustiniani awakened his nephew two hours after dawn. His arm was feeling better—hopefully he would be able to use it when the assault came.

"Did you sleep?"

"Not too much." Marco shook his head trying to clear away the haze. He looked at his haggard uncle. "What about you?"

"A little."

"You should try to sleep more, Giovanni."

"I appreciate your concern." He said dourly. "I'll try. In the meantime, here, eat some of this." He brought out some bread and a small cheese.

237

Beyond the walls, the Sultan's guns were already at work. The Constantinopolitans were keeping to their homes and their churches. There were a few workshops in the Venetian quarter making *pavises* and other shields for the palisade. Marco rode from the *Mesoteichon* through the position of the three Bocchiardi brothers from Genoa who were defending the area around the imperial palace. He passed a few words with them, raising his voice over the endless drone of the cannon. Everyone looked tired. Still, they seemed confident. There was almost a sense of relief among them. The end was in sight. It would soon be over.

For the rest of the day, that endless day of waiting and uncertainty, they labored at the walls. There was simply no time left, and Giustiniani was forced to risk performing repairs even while the guns battered the City. It was hard, physical work lifting heavy wooden planks, positioning barrels of stones and earth. Marco's hands were raw from the effort. Splinters of wood tore his flesh. The sweat poured from his forehead and trickled down his neck and glistened on his arms, but he continued as the day dragged on. When darkness fell, the bombardment ceased. Night came and the Turkish camp glowed once more. In the orange light, the men moved to the foss and the outer face of the wall to continue their toil. After several hours, with exhaustion setting in, Giustiniani ordered a halt. The men needed their sleep just as the walls needed their repairs. Tomorrow would be the day of decision.

He went to his home to rest for a few hours. At the doorway, he stood silently in the darkness and stared at the bed against the wall, the bed on which he had loved Caterina only a few days before. Loneliness was all around him, now, and silence. At least he did not mind the silence. He sat at his table, lit a candle, and began to write.

Amore,

As you read this, think of the young man you once knew and loved, who loved you more than life, who you knew before you knew pain and hatred and sorrow, just as you knew him before the world turned his love to acid and his heart to steel. There is darkness around me as I write to you, darkness in the room that was once alive with you and with our love.

I am sending this to you before the battle tomorrow and hope that someday we will smile again and laugh at it. Tomorrow the battle is coming. Our preparations are done, and we are waiting for the enemy. For years, I threw myself into battle, fearless, because losing you had driven fear from me. With nothing to live for, I had no reason to think badly of death.

Tomorrow, I will go into battle once more, but I will not be fearless as I was. That confidence, I now know, was hubris, for the courage of a man who has nothing and fights for nothing cannot compare with the valor of someone who has a full life and is still willing to throw it into the hazard. Tomorrow, you will be with me, and my valor will come from the memory of your touch, the recollection of your beauty, and the inspiration of our love. It is late, amore, and I must sleep, but with my last breath, know that I will beg forgiveness from God for having hurt you. I commend my soul to him and my heart to you.

Giovanni Giustiniani Longo.

With a deep breath, the *condottiere* sealed his letter. Across the back he wrote, "*Caterina Luccio.*" He called the sentry and had him send it along the chain boom to Pera while darkness still reigned.

239

7—The Emperor: *May 28, 1453*

The third day dawned in silence. It was the first morning since the beginning of April that the great cannon did not herald the dawn. Everyone within the Turkish camp knew the importance of the day. Orders came from the Sultan himself that they were to stand at their posts awaiting the command to attack. They were compelled, on pain of death, to remain at their positions.

Engineers moved forward in the early morning light to prepare the way for the assault. Some brought wooden mantles and *pavises* to shield the troops who would make the attack. Others carried tall scaling ladders for warriors to use in ascending the walls. The groundwork for the assaulting warriors was laid and the sappers returned to their positions.

Before noon, the encampment came alive with the blaring of trumpets and the clash of tambourines and castanets. Criers rode along the lines shouting encouragement to the troops. A mounted *imam* wearing a red turban swept past Halil Pasha's tent crying in a clarion voice for all to hear.

"Children of Mohammed, rejoice!"

The warriors stood at their positions and listened.

"Tomorrow, thousands of Christians will be in your hands! You shall sell them into slavery, two for a ducat. Unimaginable riches shall be yours! Our brave Sultan promises you the fruits of victory: women, gold, and slaves. Rejoice, children of Mohammed, and be ready to fight with a firm heart for love of the Prophet!"

The Grand Vizier came to the entrance and stared out at the spectacle before him. Mehmed's *imams* rode everywhere through the camp, whipping the warriors into a frenzy. He could feel the moment of decision nearing. Tension hung around him. The air was charged with expectation. Halil looked at the clouds moving slowly through the humid air. It looked as if it would rain by tomorrow. Tomorrow. By tomorrow morning the deciding attack would be in full swing. The hand of fate would already be pointing to his future. Halil felt the necessity of taking action. He had to do something. He went back into his tent and sat down at his desk. Taking pen in hand he began to write.

"*To his Grace, Grand Duke Lukas Notaras, from Halil Candarli Pasha, Grand Vizier to his Majesty Mehmed Sultan, greetings. If you and your master are unaware, I would inform you that his Majesty the Sultan has decided to make a grand assault against your City late this evening. As his loyal servant, I have always counseled his Majesty against any violence towards your City. I have extolled the merits of peace and the perils of war to no avail. Since childhood, his intention has been the destruction of your Empire and the conquest of the City for his own. I have never been able to dissuade him from this.*

"*You know me to be a fair man who has always sought peace and understanding between us. I have never been an advocate of war. Now, at this late hour, I must inform you that our power, while great, is not overwhelming. Only after long and heated debate was the decision to assault tonight made. Many, led by myself, feel that we should withdraw and allow you to continue to live peacefully. Our army is weary of battle. In spite of our superior numbers and equipment, you have nearly won a great victory. Now, I write not only to inform you of our plans, but to urge you to resist this last assault with all the strength you have left. No matter the odds, do not contemplate surrender. Prepare your defenses and keep guard. Be prepared to give battle at all times. Do not give in to fear. Do not be frightened by the follies of an intoxicated youth. Do not be afraid of an enemy who is largely a mob of unskilled recruits. Do not be cowed by threats.*

"*You must believe my words, my lord, because in speaking out for peace and moderation I have placed myself against the Sultan and his attempt to destroy you.*

As a result we have ended on the same side. If Mehmed is victorious, it will not only mean the end of your City, but also the end of my power, and perhaps the end of my life. Our fates are intertwined. I wish you courage for tomorrow and pray to Allah that he will see fit to grant you life and allow both of us to live on in peace and harmony."

Halil read over the letter and signed it. The Grand Vizier let out a long breath and then called a trusted messenger. The messenger took the letter and wrapped it tightly around an arrow. He moved off towards the Turkish lines opposite the Blachernae quarter and sneaked beyond the now silent guns. The army was quietly at their positions enjoying the midday meal and he slipped past unnoticed. Snaking his way forward towards the edge of the foss, he checked that the letter was tied securely to the shaft. He notched it to his bow, pulled on the string with all his might and arched the arrow over the single Blachernae wall.

It landed harmlessly on the ground well beyond the wall. It was not uncommon for messages to enter the City in this way. Some of the Europeans within Mehmed's army still felt a strange camaraderie for their brothers inside the walls and sent messages and information. A Greek soldier took the letter to his officer, who read it and sent it along to the Grand Duke.

Notaras was at the palace. The Emperor, recovered from his collapse, was once more planning the defense with his council. The Grand Vizier's letter was placed in Notaras's hands. He read. Giustiniani's information was correct. The assault would be tonight. He thought it odd that the Sultan's own Grand Vizier was encouraging them to resist. But he realized that if Halil had opposed his master's choice to make war on Constantinople, success in that operation would prove ruinous to him. He had no desire to share the letter with the rest of the council. Such knowledge concerning Mehmed's most important subject was powerful. He waited until the councilors left before bringing the

matter to the attention of the Emperor in private.
Constantine listened patiently to his Grand Duke. Any
doubts that this was the final day disappeared. The past
nights of cheering and the aberrational silence during this
day were the final proof that the assault was coming.

"We must prepare ourselves, Lord Notaras. I know you
have not always agreed with my actions. Tonight, we must
put all feelings of disunity behind us."

"Your majesty, I have never sought to oppose you."

Constantine waved down his protest.

"It is not my intention to chastise you, my lord. Forgive
me. I am tired. Now it is almost over."

Even the cynical old man was struck by his Emperor's
forlorn tone. He tried to comfort his lord.

"Lord Halil insists that the Sultan is not invincible."

"No one is invincible, but our strength has ebbed to
almost nothing."

"Our men will continue to fight, sire. They will give a
good account of themselves."

"Yes. I have every faith in them. And we must also put our
faith in God. I will call his Eminence the Cardinal and ask
that a mass be said in *Hagia Sophià*. After the ceremony, I
will address our army."

"Yes, your majesty." The Grand Duke bowed and turned
to go.

"Lord Notaras, I would appreciate if you came to the
mass in spite of your objections to the Cardinal."

"I shall be there, sire, just as I was at the mass which
proclaimed our Union."

The old man bowed and left the room. Loneliness crept
over Constantine like a cold sweat. It was not the loneliness
he was familiar with, but cold, like death. There was so much
to be done, and he felt extremely tired. When he shut his
eyes, he felt a thousand pins scratching them. The lids were
heavy. He felt them in constant danger of closing
permanently and turning the world black. This night, the

most important of his life, would be long. Perhaps it was also the last night of his life, but there was not enough time for such thoughts. Much had yet to be done. He gazed out at the city in the afternoon light. Was this the last time he would see Constantinople kissed with sun? He gazed deeply, not knowing how to say farewell for the final time to his home. Wrenching himself from the window, the Emperor went to summon the Cardinal and to prepare himself for his ordeal.

By now the sun was going down. The great orb disappeared behind the Sultan's camp in the West, casting the brilliant light of its dying glow into the eyes of the defenders. The troops along the walls could not see, but beyond the blinding orange radiance, they heard the Turks moving forward once again to fill the foss. The defenders could make out the sound of stones and branches being piled into the ditch in front of the walls. They could not see, and with ammunition low, they held their fire. The great creaking of wheels from the giant siege engines heralded the advance of those weapons. Mehmed's engineers placed the catapults and ballistae on top of the rubble in the foss, bringing the guns and stone throwing machines to less than one hundred yards from the walls.

When the sun had set, it began to rain. Large drops as big as ripe grapes fell upon the ancient stones and holy domes of the City. They fell upon the Sultan's warriors as they strained to fill the ditch. They fell upon the Genoese, Venetians, and Greeks within Constantinople, upon soldiers, women and children. Both within and outside of Constantinople, people prayed. The final battle was drawing near. For all, it could be their last night on earth. Heaven wept at the thought of the carnage to come.

Every church within the City celebrated a special mass. The Emperor and his court, needing to remain close to the walls, attended the service at the Blachernae chapel. Cardinal Isidore celebrated mass in the *Hagia Sophià*. Thousands crowded into the holy place to pray. The desecration of union was forgiven and forgotten. This day was different from other days. At the altar, Catholic and Orthodox priests concelebrated the ceremony. Cardinal Isidore stood before the great altar, flanked by Orthodox priests and Archbishop Leonardo. Communion passed freely between them, Latins to Greeks, Orthodox to Catholics. The Constantinopolitans, so resolute in their faith, no longer cared if the sacrament was given to them by a Latin or a Greek priest. At this final hour, all were brothers. Noble Constantinopolitans, Venetians and Genoese, the common people, men, women and children all thronged the cathedral. Every man, except for a token along the walls, came to the last great service. It was still raining as the last blessings were given and the men left to take their places.

Isidore intoned the final benediction and retreated to remove his vestments and prepare himself for battle. The Orthodox priests would continue to lead the women, children and old men in prayer, but the Cardinal and his suite left to arm themselves for battle. His kissed the jeweled miter as he took it from his head. Servants brought his arming jacket, red velvet studded with metal disks and stuffed with cotton, trimmed with mail around the underarms. Then, they brought the plate armor, gauntlets, *sabatons*, breastplate, backplate, *cuisses*,* and the great helm. Around his neck the Cardinal tied a red scarf. The old man, made the sign of the cross and moved to his position.

Isidore's gunners and archers strapped on their light armor and assembled, before taking up their positions between the *Hagia Sophià* and the Acropolis. Above them stood the Papal banner: the left half golden, the right half white, with the crossed keys of Saint Peter against the white field. The rain had begun to lessen and the fires from the Turkish camp once more cast their aura over the City. The flames reflected off the waning moon and danced with the

---

* Plate armor protecting the thighs.

clouds. The haze above Constantinople glowed like hot blood.

Messengers came to inform the defenders that the Emperor wished to speak with them. The imperial noblemen, the soldiers and their commanders, the foreign captains and their men assembled to hear their Emperor speak. There was an ominous silence as Constantine approached the crowd. Like the men before him, the Emperor was in full battle regalia. The imperial pearl diadem stood out white and pale around his dark hair. His eyes looked over the men who stood between his empire and destruction. They had chosen to stay here and to fight, fully aware of the price they might pay, the price they would almost certainly pay. The Emperor, moved with compassion for their sacrifice and admiration for their courage, spoke.

"Most noble peers, illustrious commanders and generals, noble fellow-soldiers, and all my honorable and faithful people, for two months you have fought to defend this great city. Like heroes, you have stood against a treacherous enemy who has disturbed our peace without cause. He has broken his oaths, violated his treaties, invaded our lands, massacred our farmers, and laid waste to our estates. He has built a cut-throat fortress to swallow us up and brought his army to surround our city, all the while feigning peace. Now he is threatening to capture this city, the city of Constantine the Great, the capital of the world and your home!

"For this reason I speak to you now, beseeching you to bravely resist our enemies as you have always done. We all owe the City a love which makes us prefer to die as free men, rather than to live in slavery. We must fight for our country against the invader, for our faith against the heathens, for our friends and loved ones against those who would defile them. Brothers, we, who would be obliged to fight for any of these causes, must now fight for them all.

"By God's grace, the troops of the enemy have been repulsed from the walls many times with heavy casualties.

Do not fear that our walls have been battered. Our strength lies not in stone, but in the protection of God. We have entrusted ourselves and all our hopes to His invincible glory. The Turks trust in their arms and their horses, their power and numbers; we place our trust in the name of our Lord, in our own hands and the bold strength which the divine power has given us. Use this strength against our enemies, because it is into your hands I give this most illustrious and renowned Queen of Cities.

"In your hands of flesh, you hold the eternal reputation of Christendom. Defend it! Protect it! Nobles of Venice, you have shown your ability numberless times. You have adorned this City as if it were your own with fine and noble men. Now, let your spirits be exalted in preparation for this contest. Brave men of Genoa, who are renowned for your victories, who have always protected this City as though she were your mother, now show your strength and your spirit against those who would destroy her. Finally, my fellow soldiers, show obedience to your superiors in all things. If but a drop of your blood is shed, you will earn for yourselves a martyr's crown and everlasting glory in heaven."

The soldiers knelt and crossed themselves, the Latins left to right and the Orthodox right to left. There was a moment of silence before they rose and in a single voice swore to resolutely make their stand. To this oath, the Emperor replied.

"Tonight, let the world bear witness to your courage, and let your courage lead us to victory!"

In their many voices, the soldiers raised a cheer. It echoed through the ancient stones and monuments of the past, filtering into the lonely houses and deserted streets which feared the outcome of the battle. In the darkness, the defenders took up their positions. Demetrios Cantacuzenos stood furthest to the South at the Postern of Christ. To his right, Giacopo Contarini of Venice and Manuel Catteno of Genoa at Studion, the Venetian, Filippo Contarini at the

Pegae Gate, and Theophilus Palaeologos at the Gate of Rhegium. At the center of the line, the *Mesoteichion*, Constantine set his standard with the double-headed eagle at the Gate of Saint Romanos. To his right, at the Gate of Charisios, stood Giustiniani. Then, at Blachernae, the Bocchiardi brothers of Genoa and beyond them, at Xyloporta, the *bailò*, Girolamo Minotto. Gabriele Trevisano's men had been ordered from their ships and onto the sea walls in the east. They defended from the Phanar quarter to the Imperial Gate where the troops of Cardinal Isidore began.

As the men moved to the land walls, they heard cheering once more from the Turkish lines. The Sultan's warriors filled the night with their screams and their bonfires. An inferno, greater than anything created during the previous two nights, blazed from Mehmed's camp. To the defenders, it seemed that Hell had come to the very gates of Constantinople, threatening to overwhelm it. Silently, the defenders went about their preparations. Lit by the lurid conflagration, Mehmed's gunners once more served their monsters, adding the crash of cannon to the horrifying din. The guns, repositioned at the edge of the foss, slammed their stones against Giustiniani's improvised defenses from point blank range. The defenders, cowering behind wooden barrels and rubble, prayed for the barrage to stop. The hours dragged on, and the defenders waited.

Abruptly, the Turkish camp fell silent. The bonfires were put out. The guns ceased their thunder. It was now midnight. The Turks in the camp, ordinary men like their foes, needed sleep as well. In the night they too feared the battle, wary of throwing their flesh once more against the impregnable stones, the streams of fire, and the wall of steel that had met them time and again. The waning moon commanded a hushed firmament. Silence reigned over Constantinople and roared in the ears of the defenders. With every nerve strained, they heard their lungs nervously draw each breath and felt each clink of steel. An occasional whisper broke the stillness.

Orders arrived from the Emperor. The twelve gates along the Theodosian walls were closed and locked. The soldiers remained at their posts along the battlements while keys turned in the massive locks and sealed the outer fortifications. At the first line, encapsulated from the inner curtain and the City itself, the defenders would fight where they stood until victory or death.

The hour of decision was fast approaching. Constantine walked his horse along the miles of the stone shield making one final assessment. Sphrantzes accompanied him. They moved together wordlessly. The Emperor could sense that the assault was only hours away now. Mehmed would attack before dawn. Constantine wished to inspect the entire length of the land walls personally before it began. In truth, he wanted to see his City once more and to look at the great walls while they still stood guard over his battered Queen.

Giustiniani's men had worked through the night and were still patching the work of Theodosius' architects. Along the *Mesoteichion* he saw little more than wooden boards and barrels built on rubble. The Emperor frowned. The night was cool. A shiver passed over him. Spring was still very much in the air. Summer, that season full of warmth and life, seemed so distant. In his heart, Constantine feared that he would never know the comfort of summer again.

He dismounted and climbed a tower. His feet stepped heavily on the stone stairs. Sphrantzes was behind him. The Emperor reached the parapet and looked out. Night had shrouded the Turkish camp. The fading moon's blue light played along the clouds. Constantine turned and gazed back into the City. He could feel the tears springing from his eyes and sorrow choking his throat.

"The City is beautiful in the moonlight," he whispered. "She is still beautiful." The Emperor turned back to the walls, looking up and down the shattered stones. "Look at

what they have done, how they have wounded her.
Tomorrow they will bring their destruction to our streets,
into our City, our churches, and our homes. Oh God, why
have you made me powerless to stop this? Why are we
condemned to this suffering? Tomorrow, Yiorgo, the City
will fall. Mehmed will walk his horse down the *Mesé* and
stable his cattle in *Hagia Sophià*."

"Surely, sire, this will not be."

"My friend you know the truth as well as I. Only a miracle
can save us now. We stand, five thousand men against a
hundred thousand. There is nothing we can do to deny
Mehmed his prize. Soon the battle will begin, and we shall
never see each other again."

There was a pause. For once, the diplomat could not
summon words suitable to the occasion. Silence commanded
the moment. Then, Constantine spoke again.

"I am glad, Yiorgo, that you failed to find me a bride."

"Why, my lord?" The sudden change in topic took him by
surprise.

"It is well that no wife should suffer the tragedy that will
soon come. I must thank you."

"For failing you, sire?"

"No, Yiorgo. I wish to thank you for succeeding on my
behalf on so many occasions and for serving me so faithfully
for all these years."

Sphrantzes was genuinely moved. With all his heart he
wished to profess his love and admiration for his lord, for his
friend, but the words would not come.

"Sire, do you truly believe that the City will fall?"

"Yes. This is the end. The end of everything. From
tomorrow, the empire will cease to exist. Nothing will
remain. The City will be taken by the heathens. Our
churches will be desecrated and turned into mosques. Our
treasure will be stolen, melted down and destroyed. Our way
of life will vanish from the earth. Our libraries will be
burned; our knowledge destroyed. Our soldiers will be killed

and our people sold into slavery. Only echoes of glory will remain. Memories will live on for a while, held tight by those who survive and passed on in their writings to generations, or by their words to their children and grandchildren, but tomorrow is the end for us."

Sphrantzes wept. He bit his lips to hold back the sobs. His mind's eye filled with the terrors his master described. He thought of his personal concerns, wishing that he had sent his wife and daughters away to safety while there was yet time. Now it was too late, too late for everyone. He turned to his Emperor.

"My lord, do not die," he begged.

"I have given the City my life already. Now I will give her my death. It is the least I can do for my Queen. I shall die defending her."

Sphrantzes was too overcome to reply.

"The battle will soon be upon us. Take yourself to safety. Your place is not on a battlefield. Remember me to your wife and children. Tell them and tell the world what you have witnessed. Go with God."

They embraced. Constantine turned his teary eyes beyond the walls and heard the clang of hoofbeats as Sphrantzes disappeared into the night.

8—The Assault: *May 29, 1453*

It began suddenly. Shouts rose from the darkness, and a wave of humanity surged against the City. The Bashi-bazouks were advancing. The Sultan had chosen these half-wild men to begin the final assault. They filled the night with their screams and rushed over the filled-in foss to drain away the strength of the defenders with their lives. Cymbals, kettle-drums, trumpets and fifes drove the attack forward. The din was heard throughout the City. Constantinople's church bells took up the alarm, calling every man to the walls. Within the church of Holy Wisdom, the weary faithful redoubled their prayers as their fate hung in the balance.

Orders rang out along the walls as officers positioned their men. Bails of straw and cloth soaked in sulfur were set alight and then thrown into the foss to illuminate the battlefield. Near the Gate of Charisios, Giustiniani had already made the final adjustments to his troops. A precious few more handguns and mobile cannon had been brought forward to the position from Lord Notaras' central reserve. Marco was at the *condottiere*'s side. The boy's breath was coming in rapid gasps. He was afraid.

"This is it Marco. If we hold them now, we win. We must survive this night."

Marco, who could not force a response to his lips, nodded. His throat was parched, his mind dizzy with fear for his own life. He felt his heart about to explode.

"You must do your duty. I need you." The *condottiere*'s words had a tenderness that his nephew was not familiar with.

Before Marco could reply, he added one word, "*coraggio*." There was no time for anything else. The battle was upon them.

The Bashi-bazouks reached the walls and threw scaling ladders against them. Giustiniani's men leaned over the ramparts and fired their handguns into the darkness below.

The flares and waning moon cast a surreal light over the battle. Further down the line, at the *Mesoteichion*, Greek fire poured from the towers at the Gate of Saint Romanos. The Emperor was also engaged. The Turks were incinerated by the liquid fire as their cries of aggression turned into screams of agony. The flames leapt from their burning bodies sending flickering shadows and sparks across the killing ground beneath the walls.

At the Gate of Charisios, Giustiniani's troops poured gunfire and arrows into the Bashi-bazouks. Stones had been brought to the wall beforehand, and the *condottiere*'s men hurled them down from the battlements crushing the skulls of the Turks as they climbed up the ladders and pulverizing them to the earth. The axes and swords of the vigilant defenders hacked off arms and heads as soon as they appeared at the crest of the walls. Ladders were overturned, sending their loads into the inferno below.

The enemy, however, kept coming. The smell of plunder was strong in the nostrils of the Sultan's irregulars, and they threw themselves again and again against the ancient masonry. Raggedly armed, and many without armor, they stood little chance against the well equipped defenders. Their high spirits were soon sobered by the unyielding walls and the men of steel who held them. The Bashi-bazouks began to waver. They edged back but were driven forward by troops from the Sultan's regular army, who moved up behind them. These lashed out at them with whips of chain and leather, forcing them to the slaughter once more. A Turkish officer moved towards one running Bashi-bazouk and sliced his head off with a scimitar stroke. He picked up the fallen head by the hair and hurled it towards the walls shouting:

"Back to the battle, dogs! If the Christians don't kill you, we will!" With the flat of his sword he beat at the nearest tribesmen, sending them running after the severed head.

Caught between two fires, the Bashi-bazouks had no choice but to attack again. Mehmed, who had ridden forward from his tent, watched as the attack collapsed amidst the shattered ladders and smoldering bodies of their comrades. The irregulars were broken, but they had served their purpose in sapping the strength of the defenders. The Sultan allowed them to withdraw.

As the pressure eased, the Emperor Constantine came to Giustiniani's position to see the state of the *protostrator's* forces.

"How is the battle, my lord?"

"We're holding, sire. Did they attack you heavily?"

"Not too heavily. Mostly irregulars."

"Here too. They are trying to wear us down. The main forces will attack during the daylight when they can coordinate better. I doubt the Sultan will risk his finest troops in a night assault."

"Then we should expect them in a few hours. We don't have more than that until sunrise."

Giustiniani nodded. He was holding his left arm. Constantine noticed.

"How is your wound?"

"I'll manage, sire." He spoke the words through gritted teeth.

The Emperor looked into his eyes for a moment. He could see the will to fight, to continue the battle, the desire to survive. Constantine hoped that his visage too possessed such determination.

"Let me know if you need anything, *protostrator*. God be with you."

"Thank you, your majesty. And with you."

Giustiniani had become accustomed to the Emperor's pale worn face. The apparent resignation no longer troubled him. Constantine would fight to the death.

The stars were fading as the Bashi-bazouks withdrew and the first pink light of day appeared in the East. The rosy dawn illuminated the Turks as they formed once more for battle. Giustiniani's faint hope that the tribesmen had been part of an isolated night attack were quickly dashed. His information was correct. The attack would continue on a grand scale. The Anatolians under Ishak Pasha were moving forward into the Lycus Valley.

The defenders, already feeling the weight of their exertions prepared to receive the next assault. The position was repaired from the damage caused by the irregulars. The barrels of earth, the timbers and beams were pushed into place. Giustiniani moved along the line encouraging his soldiers to resist, congratulating them on their courage. Guns were reloaded, and archers moved along the lines gathering up arrows. The men sat for a short rest and drank what little water or wine they had kept with them. At least the evening rain had filled their canteens.

All too soon, the clamor began once more. The Turkish lines erupted in smoke as Mehmed's cannon unleashed a volley against the walls. The City shuddered, trumpets blared, the cymbals and drums picked up the cacophony. In the fading darkness, the Anatolians moved forward clashing their weapons. Within the City, the church bells added their alarum to the uproar as the defenders rushed to the walls. The Turks hurled themselves forward in a fury. They knew that this was their last chance to conquer the Queen of Cities. They were met with streams of liquid fire from the walls and riddled with the grape-sized stones fired from the defenders' cannon. The Anatolians threw ladders against the walls and began to scale them. These the defenders cut at with axes and pushed away sending the clambering warriors crashing to the earth. The ground was littered with broken and bloodied bodies.

Near the Gate of Saint Romanos, the Greeks were directing streams of liquid fire. The Turks marched into the firestorm and crumpled, screaming, in a sea of flames. The smoldering bodies beneath the walls continued to blaze and sent smoke up into the faces of those fighting along the ramparts. Dawn had not yet fully broken, and the fighting was confused. Great flaming lances and bundles of combustibles from the Turkish lines cast a nightmarish red and orange hue over the field. The City's honey-colored walls stood splashed with blood amidst the scarlet light and carnage.

The cannon continued their roar, and the Anatolian hand gunners added their fire to that of Orban's great monsters. In the breaches, the fighting went on unabated. Ishak Pasha moved his men forward against the breaches. They clambered over the filled foss and funneled themselves up the gashes in Theodosius' masonry. They were met by fire from Giustiniani's crossbows and hand gunners. Slowly, they forced their way to the crest, where the fighting was hand-to-hand. Scimitar and broadswords clanged off each other. Axes severed arms, while spears were thrust deeply into unprotected bellies or deflected by bucklers and breastplates. Javelins and arrows arched death over the fighters and struck home indiscriminately among friend and foe.

About an hour before sunrise, a ball from one of Orban's largest guns struck the stockade with full force. It smashed down several yards of the improvised work, opening a gaping hole in the City's defenses. A regiment of Anatolians surged forward to take the ground. With Giustiniani heavily engaged to the right of the breach, the Emperor himself, with all the men he could afford to move, rushed forward to seal the gap. The reserves under his cousin, Nikephoros Palaeologos, joined them. Constantine was at the front of the battle slashing and thrusting with his sword and shouting encouragement to his troops.

The Emperor's force closed around the single regiment that had forced itself into the opening, pouring javelins, crossbow bolts and gunfire into the attackers who wavered, and then ran. A few survivors fell back from the walls into the foss. This last failure broke the spirit of the Anatolians, and they began to withdraw all along the line.

Gaining in confidence, the defenders challenged warriors crouching beneath them in the pale dawn:

"Why do you continue to attack? You have come forward many times, and every time we have beaten you back. Give up. You cannot win."

The words struck the hearts of the Anatolians as Ishak's assault petered out. The defenders had won themselves a few more minutes of respite. Once again the ramparts were cleared of the dead and wounded. Again the barrels and planks along the earthworks were brought into position as Giustiniani worked feverishly to make the defenses stand once again. The *condottiere* had been hit again, this time in the foot by a crossbow bolt. The shot had not penetrated far beyond his armor, but there was some blood, and walking was painful. His left arm, out of the sling for combat, was numb and useless. Marco cleaned and wrapped the new wound before Giustiniani once again put on the *sabaton* that protected his left foot. The armor went on painfully, and Giustiniani grimaced. There was no time for pain: the Janissaries were coming.

The Sultan had planned that the deciding assault would be delivered by his elite troops. He had suspected that the Bashi-bazouks and even the Anatolians would not succeed in taking the City. It would be up to his Janissaries, the finest soldiers in the world, to finally breach the walls. They had nearly finished forming for the attack. The Sultan's cannon continued to fire.

Twelve thousand fresh men would now be thrown at the center of the City's walls against the beleaguered defenders who could muster less than two thousand to oppose them. Dawn was coming quickly. The tall white headgear of the Janissaries stood out ghostly pale in the early morning light.

Marco saw the eerie host and turned to his uncle.

"Who are those soldiers with the white headdresses?" he asked.

"Janissaries. They are the Sultan's elite bodyguard made up of Christian boys torn from their families in childhood."

"They're Christians?"

"They were. As part of their training they are converted to the teachings of Mohammed. They have no recollection of their families or their pasts. They train for war isolated from the world. Now they are as zealous as Mehmed himself. Expect no mercy from them."

As he spoke, Giustiniani regretted his statement. Marco's eyes were melting with fear. He tried to soften his words with a joke.

"We do have one advantage over them."

"What's that?"

"They're forbidden from touching women." The *condottiere's* face remained grim.

"I'm afraid, Giovanni." Marco's words were a gasp.

"We're all afraid, Marco. But so are they. And they'll be even more afraid, as they begin to fall before these walls.

The Janissaries advanced at a walk. The white silk of their hats swayed as they moved forward. There was an ominous sound as their chainmail *coifs*‡‡ bounced against twelve thousand advancing necks and shoulders. Then the drums began. Beating in a wild fury, they drove the Janissaries into a run. Cymbals clashed, and the Sultan's Christian-born warriors raised their battle-cry against the City they had come to conquer, the religion they had forgotten and the peoples they had forsaken.

"Fire!" shouted Giustiniani.

The handguns banged. Archers loosed their arrows. Javelins streaked across the pale dawn sky and drilled into the advancing enemy. Men in the first few ranks fell in a sheet of blood. The Janissaries reached the foss and threw

---

‡‡ The chainmail protection for the head and shoulders, extending over the ears and cheeks and spreading to cover the shoulders and neck.

259

themselves across it, striving to reach the walls. More fire poured into them from the ramparts. To his left, the *condottiere* saw the siphons of Greek fire furiously pumping death down onto the enemy. Arrows and bullets were now flying at the defenders as the Janissaries took cover in the foss and fired up at the walls. Giustiniani could see the Sultan, mounted on a black horse prancing along the edge of the ditch engulfed in smoke, shouting his warriors forward. Giustiniani could not hear him.

Groups of Janissaries climbed forward into the breaches, where they were met with arrows and swords. The defenses, by some miracle, were holding. Not even fresh troops, not even the Sultan's finest, were making progress. The fighting was furious. A Janissary swung an axe at the *condottiere*. Giustiniani twisted out of the way and drove his sword between the man's ribs. Another came forward with a scimitar, but Giustiniani parried his blow and caught him under the arm with a thrust. To his right, Marco dodged the blow of an axe and lunged into the stomach of his adversary. A handgunner from Chios standing next to the *condottiere*'s left was killed by an arrow. The *condottiere* picked up the man's gun and fired it at the head of a Janissary as it appeared over the wall. The cranium disappeared in a dark red mist. The breach was a solid mass of white caps wriggling their way forward against the walls. A painfully thin steel line, glittering in the early morning sun, was all that stood between the Janissaries and the Queen of Cities.

Mehmed saw the assault was stalling. From his horse he shouted curses and encouragement at his soldiers. The Janissaries ebbed and flowed, forward and back, relentless like the tide, but could not break through. Along the entire line, the Ottoman army was attacking. The men at the center stood alone against the Sultan's elite. Officers would lead a group of two or three dozen forward into the storm, only to have their men killed off by the indomitable defenders. No attacker had yet been able to force his way to the top of the wall. Mehmed now spurred his horse forward, almost to the edge of the foss, perilously close to the defenders' fire. He had one refrain—"Forward!"

Giustiniani screamed at his men to concentrate their fire. Arrows were in short supply and their store of powder was almost depleted. Another group of Janissaries was pressing forward when Giustiniani spun round and fell to the rampart. He had been hit again. This time, the wound was serious. The ball, fired from a handgun, entered his right side just above the rim of his breastplate and deflected up from his ribs into the soft tissue of his underarm. A great profusion of blood poured through his chain mail, staining the glittering steel plate.

Immediately, Marco was at his side trying to sit him up and tend to him. He took off Giustiniani's helmet. Desperately, he looked around for a surgeon. In the confusion of the battle, none could be found. Marco could hear the Turks pressing forward again. Why had his uncle been struck now, when the battle was at its height? Was there no mercy in the world? Marco called over one of the Greek boys who served as messengers and told the youth to run to the Saint Romanos Gate and inform the Emperor of the *condottiere*'s wound. The firing was slackening. The Turkish battle cries were dying down. The present assault had been repulsed. The defenders pushed the last of the Turks from the breach and reoccupied the shattered walls.

Giustiniani moaned.

"Lie still," hissed his nephew.

But the warrior took no notice and stood, supporting himself upon the sword that he had let fall. From the parapet, in the morning light, he could clearly see another wave of white capped Janissaries moving forward into the assault. The breach was already choked with dead soldiers, but the enemy pressed on without regard. Below the walls, in the foss, the living huddled under the corpses of their comrades, preparing to join the next wave. The mass of humanity squirmed below them like a heap of snakes. Giustiniani swayed and fell into Marco's arms. The Emperor himself was soon at his side. The *condottiere* was extremely pale. He was in a great deal of pain and at the point of physical and mental collapse.

"Are you hurt, *protostrator*?" asked the Emperor.

"Yes, sire. I fear that I am wounded quite badly." His voice was beset with agony.

The Emperor looked at his marshal. The strong handsome man he had met five months before had collapsed into a worn ghost with sunken cheeks and black rings around his eyes. His left foot was wrapped in bloodied rags. The left arm was motionless. Giustiniani's right side was a sheet of blood staunched only by the cloth Marco had stuffed under his arm.

In hoarse tones, choked through pain, the *condottiere* spoke to him.

"My Lord, I must retire to have my wounds treated."

The words struck Constantine like a sword thrust. Could the great and noble Giustiniani be abandoning him at the crisis of the battle?

"*Protostrator*, you cannot leave the field now. We are pressed everywhere. The enemy is coming to make his greatest attack of all. We need you. We need you here."

The Emperor's voice was desperate. Giustiniani tried to respond but could not. He was drifting out of consciousness. Marco answered in his place.

"Your majesty, for the moment the Turks are withdrawing. There is time for the wound to be treated before they come again."

"This is the crucial moment, my lord. You cannot leave the battle now," said the Emperor again, still addressing Giustiniani.

Again, Marco responded for his uncle. His words were laced with anger and frustration.

"No one has done more for the defense of the City than my master. He is well aware of his position and his responsibilities. He is of no value to you dead or in his present state—he is unable to command the defense. Let him retire from the field to have his wound dressed!"

Giustiniani nodded his assent to his nephew's words. The Emperor, knowing that this was hardly the time for an argument, consented. Calling one of his lieutenants, he handed Marco the key to the small gate of the inner wall.

Marco called forward Giustiniani's personal servant, Michiele, and another man. "Take him to the ship and stay with him," he commanded.

The *condottiere* looked up in protest because Marco was not going with him.

"Come back when you are able, uncle."

"But..." Giustiniani's protest was cut off as Mehmed's cannon made the walls shudder once more.

"Get him out of here!" ordered the younger man once more. He met his uncle's eyes for a moment and was chilled by the pain and fear that he saw in them.

"Are you not going with your kinsman?" asked the Emperor.

"No, my lord. The battle is yet to be won."

"The command is yours now, Master Marco. These are your men. God be with you."

"And with you, your majesty." He watched his uncle disappear into the City, then turned to the battle.

The Emperor rode back to his position to face the assault. It was not long before the Janissaries were pressing again. The men of Genoa and Chios struggled to hold off the Turkish horde. The last reserve of strength was being spent by the defenders against the renewed Janissary advance. The white capped ranks were again giving way when the shattering news arrived—the defenses had been breached. The rumor spread like plague through the embattled ranks. The Turks had entered the City. It was not here at the

Mesoteichion, but to the north, at Blachernae. A small party of Turks, no more than fifty, had come through the Kerkoporta postern. There had been a sally from the small gate, and the last defender had failed to close and lock it. Now, green flags and red banners with white crescents waved from a nearby tower. The nerve of the defenders began to give way. Minotto and the Bocchiardis were hard pressed in the Blachernae quarter, but they sent some troops to close the breach.

Word soon reached the Emperor. Immediately, Constantine himself rode to the point. The members of the imperial suite spurred their horses and burst upon the scene. The single company of Turks occupied a tiny section of the wall joining the imperial palace to Blachernae. The Emperor and his retainers surged into the fray. A fury had taken possession of Constantine and, flanked by his kinsmen, he cut into the enemy. The Bocchiardi brothers and their men joined the Emperor's counterattack. The Turkish band crumpled before the onslaught and was massacred. The crescent stamped banners were struck down and the red cross of Saint George and the double-headed eagle were raised once more above the shattered battlements.

But victory had come too late. Around the *Mesoteichion*, rumors that the City had fallen continued to spread unchecked. Giustiniani's Genoese and Chians, their morale already shaken by the loss of their commander, began to fall back. It was not a rout, but by ones and twos they left their posts, scaled the inner wall and fled towards the harbors of the Golden Horn. There, they hoped to board ships and flee to safety. Breathlessly, the bloodied soldiers stomped onto the dock, panicked with terror.

"All is lost!" they screamed.

"The Turks have entered the City!"

"Constantinople has fallen!"

In his bed, aboard ship, Giustiniani sat up. Pushing the surgeon away, he dragged his broken body to the door of the cabin and staggered onto the deck. His men, a few with wounds, some without their arms, all covered in powder and dirt, were chattering, overcome by the horror of their situation. Their resolve was broken. Giustiniani could not blame them. They had suffered beyond human endurance. It was over. He tottered back to the cabin. Now, there was only one thought in his mind.

"My lord, please do not move," cautioned the doctor.

The surgeon had been able to stem the flow of blood, but the shot was still deep in the *condottiere's* body. The physician had felt it too dangerous to probe for the ball under the present circumstances. His patient had the stamp of death upon his face.

"Caterina," he called her name as if it were a prayer. His voice was nothing more than a choked moan. The surgeon did not understand him.

"Calm yourself, my lord. You need quiet and rest." he pleaded.

"Caterina," he moaned again, this time attempting to rise.

"Lie down, commander!"

"She... she...." Giustiniani's world went black.

9—The City: *May 29, 1453, 9 am*

The fighting along the land walls was dying down. The Turkish incursion at the Kerkoporta had been contained and the small force slaughtered. Disaster had apparently been avoided, but the Sultan scented blood and ordered his warriors to move in for the kill. Near the Saint Romanos Gate, the Janissaries were at the crumbled wall once more with Mehmed himself urging them on.

"They are breaking!" he cried. "Forward! Who will be the first of my warriors to enter Constantinople?"

An enormous Janissary, Hasan Ulabad, took up the Sultan's challenge. Brandishing an axe above his head, he led a group against the breach. The company climbed over stones and bodies, slipping on blood. Arrows and bullets tore into them, but the group, inspired by the giant, pressed on until they reached the crest of the embrasure. The colossus, holding a shield with his left hand, struck about with the axe in his right as he made his way through the breach. A Genoese archer was split in two. A man-at-arms struck out with his sword, only to have his head taken off with a single blow. Alone, the giant pushed the defenders back. His comrades, feeding on his strength, followed. Cutting through the makeshift palisade, Hasan finally stood at the top of the wall, the first Turk to reach it alive. A primordial cry of triumph came to his lips and the men behind him cheered as they moved forward.

The defenders moved against the juggernaut. The Janissary warded off a sword cut with his shield, but a Genoese spear took him in the guts. Hasan's axe shattered the spear shaft and then scythed off the arm of the man who had thrust it. An arrow buried itself in his left shoulder. Hasan maneuvered his shield over his head to protect himself from the rain of missiles and stood his ground, holding the breach. A sword cut at his side, wounding him again. The axe of a Chian marine chopped at his legs,

267

bringing the colossus to his knees. A stone from a sling struck him, like Goliath, bringing a stream of blood from his forehead. Another blow came at the back of his head and Hasan fell. Past his body swept the Turkish horde. Janissaries, Anatolians and wild Bashi-bazouks joined together in the attack. Above them, red and black banners flooded through the honey breaches, stained with so much blood. The outer wall was breached.

Around him, Marco saw that all was now lost. The Turks were everywhere.

"Retreat," he called above the din. "Retreat to the ships."

The men threw themselves from the battlements and ran back from the palisades. Running across the open ground between the walls, they battered down the locked gates of the inner wall open and poured into the City with the Turks in hot pursuit. As he ran, Marco heard screams behind him as the slaughter began. Now he had only one objective, the safety of Giustiniani's ship. He ran down the *Mesé*.

From the Blachernae, the Emperor saw the Turks swarming over the wall. There were simply too many for his exhausted forces to stop. The Kerkoporta was secure, but now the Turks were pouring in from everywhere. To his right, he saw Diedo's ditch alive with Turkish bodies. Ottoman warriors streamed over the scaling ladders overwhelming the Venetian and Genoese defenders. To his left, Giustiniani's troops were broken. Everywhere the defenders were in retreat.

Seeing the destruction, Constantine spurred his horse back towards the Gate of Saint Romanos. There, he and four comrades, the Catalan, Don Francisco of Toledo, his cousin Theophilus Palaeologos, and John of Dalmata, all that was left of the imperial suite, tried to stem the rout of the army. The defenders were running. Order had become chaos. The men were not even stopping to guard the inner wall. Cries of panic and defeat spread through the ranks.

Constantine looked about him in despair. It had been less than an hour since the *condottiere* had withdrawn. The four men dismounted and, for a few moments, held the narrow entrance of the gatehouse with their swords against dozens of Turks. Hopelessly outnumbered, they fled, sealing the great doors behind them. All was lost. Constantine looked at his comrades. The last Emperor of the Romans stood before the three men. His sword was stained with blood. His armor was furrowed with slashes from dozens of enemy swords and arrows, but he was miraculously unwounded. The Turks would reach them soon. Already, they were coming over the inner wall and into the City itself. Constantine looked around him and saw the beginning of the destruction of Constantinople. Reaching the battlements of the inner wall, the Turks struck down the banners of Saint Mark, Saint George, and the double-headed eagle. The red and green banners of the Sultan waved above the City of Constantine. It was more than the Emperor could bear. It was the end.

"Is there no Christian who will take my head?" he implored.

His companions looked at him with terrified eyes. He wanted one of them to take his life, to deny that pleasure to the Turks. He wished his life to end at the hands of a friend rather than an enemy. But it was too great a request. They turned their faces away in anguish.

"I can bear this no more!" shouted Theophilus. "I would rather be killed than live to see my master's death. Farewell cousin!" So saying, he charged into the swirl of battle and disappeared.

Constantine now looked again at his comrades, tears in his eyes. They could not move themselves to speak. They would die with him. Constantine tore at the insignia of his office. He cast off the pearl diadem on his head.

"I shall not live an Emperor without an Empire" he cried. "As my City falls, I fall with it!"

Raising his sword, he led Don Francisco and John of Dalmata against a throng of Turks. They screamed as they rushed forward cutting down all who opposed them. They came on with an inhuman strength, tearing into the disordered ranks around them. But there were too many enemies. In the press, they were separated. John of Dalmata struck down one last Janissary, but the axe of a Bashi-bazouk crashed into his arm shattering the plate armor and the bones beneath. A mace swung by a Janissary crushed his skull within his helmet and sent him sprawling onto the blood soaked pavement.

Don Francisco's helmet had been knocked from his head in the struggle. An arrow caught him in the eye before an Anatolian pinned him to the ground and took his head with a swift slash from his dagger. Alone, the Emperor fought on. His city lost, his empire lost, his life was nothing to him. There were no thoughts in his mind as he slashed the beautiful saber against the hordes around him. There was nothing left but enemies surrounding him, bubbling out of the smoke as in a nightmare. He slashed through the throat of a Janissary and felt an enormous heavy blow against the side of his helmet. He threw himself sideways against the man who had struck him, thrusting his sword with both hands into the warrior's abdomen. He managed to bring himself back to his feet before another blow struck him from behind. Not knowing that they had killed the Emperor of the Romans, a Bashi-bazouk hacked his head off and turned to plunder the fallen City.

* * *

The Turks flowed into Constantinople as the dam of resistance broke. As soon as Mehmed's warriors entered, the nightmare of the sack began. Screams of anxiety, shrieks of panic, and the victorious roar of the Sultan's army filled the air. Though most of the soldiers fled towards the sea walls to try and make their escape, a few still offered opposition along the ramparts and in the streets. They were mixed bands of Greeks, Venetians and Genoese, no more than five or six men in any group. The Turks swiftly surrounded them and hacked them to pieces. Pikes capped with their severed heads bobbed above the swirling mass. Decapitated bodies of the defenders lay in gutters.

The banners of Saint Mark, Saint George, and the Palaeologos family were cut down and trampled underfoot as blood ran like rainwater through the drains. The soldiers defending the sea walls found themselves outflanked by the Turkish forces as they breached the land walls. Near the Imperial Gate, Turkish marines broke through Gabriele Trevisano's sailors, cutting off the final defenders along the land walls. Men threw their armor away and dove into the sea attempting to swim to the ships that were already crammed with refugees trying to escape the merciless Turkish knives.

The Sultan's men, unleashed without restraint, acted blindly on their impulses of desire, violence, cruelty, greed and destruction. Wholesale slaughter and pillage began. Warriors pushed down the doors of homes, churches, monasteries and shops indiscriminately. Any article that could prove even remotely valuable was unceremoniously seized. Groups of men began digging up the gardens of private homes in search of booty. Soon the landscape was cratered like the moon. Despite the poverty and hardship in Constantinople, enough wealth remained to make enterprising robbers fabulously rich. Besides, the foremost commodity was not jewels, gold, silver, or rich clothing, but human spoils for the slave markets. Pretty young women and handsome young boys in particular were of great value. The conquered ran in scattered groups to avoid their pursuers, but were soon overhauled and captured.

The citizens who had taken shelter in churches remained cowering in their holy refuges as axes smashed against the

271

bolted doors which flew open from powerful kicks. The wild-eyed conquerors entered. The parishioners were unceremoniously dragged by the hair from their violated sanctuary. Greedy warriors, gone mad with the victory they had sought for almost two months tore at the gold and silver *iconostasis*. Relics were broken from their jeweled cases and cast to the floor to be trampled underfoot. Knives and axes went to work in extracting gems from their settings. Crosses, so prevalent in the Christian city, were destroyed by the warriors of Islam wherever they encountered them. Those hanging above altars were torn down, cut apart by axes, or smashed by heavy boots. Not content with mere physical desecration, the Sultan's zealots defiled the holy symbols of the Passion by drenching them with their urine.

At the church of the Holy Apostles, a savage warrior, covered in blood, amused himself by lighting the beard of a deacon with a votive candle. The old man cried out to God, and with the monk's face still smoking, the Turk hacked his head clean off with one stroke of his axe sending a sheet of blood across the holy icons.

At the great *Hagia Sophià*, a place was cleared in front of the altar so that the prisoners could be inspected by their future owners. A procession of naked young girls and boys, their eyes wild with terror and streaming with tears, was paraded before the altar. The warriors cheered and laughed as each captive was auctioned off. These few were spared the general massacre and reserved for the seraglios of the Viziers and pashas who paid handsomely to satisfy their lust. Some soldiers donned the holy robes of the priests and pranced mockingly amidst the devastation. Others took the luxurious materials and converted them into caparisons for their horses. Food was spilled out on other vestments that were thrown on tables and altars to serve as tablecloths. The churches were no longer houses of God; they had become stables, dining rooms, slave markets, and brothels.

In places, it would have been easy to have mistaken the entire City for a brothel, for the lust of the pashas was matched by the masses of soldiery that had been let loose. From dark alleys and from behind the closed doors, many of which had been smashed from their moorings, the cries of the violated were heard. A young woman staggered unsteadily from one such den into the light. Her dress torn and her lips smeared with blood. The ragged dress revealed her half-naked body. Blood flowed from her ankles, which bore vicious scratches from the spurs of her assailant. The rapist, a cavalry officer, emerged into the light soon after her. Adjusting the red sash around his waist, he mounted the horse a common soldier had been holding and disappeared into the swirl of humanity. The soldier, freed from his duty, took two steps after the girl, grabbed her by the hair and pulled her back into the lair. She had no strength left to resist and mutely accepted the second violation.

Some found no need for such privacy and threw themselves upon their victims in the streets and against the walls of buildings. Nuns, finding their station in no way preserved them from abuse, were taken in their convents, a few on the altar itself. Numbers of women, rather than face the horrors that awaited them, threw themselves down wells or off the battlements of the sea walls to their deaths.

The sea, as much as the land, was a site of horrendous carnage. The Turkish ships were moving in with the sailors eager to participate in the pillaging. Many ships had already moored against the walls and poured their crews over scaling ladders to take part in the plunder. Here, the denuded defenses were quickly overrun. The shore along the sea wall was a writhing mass of humanity. At the harbor's edge, a horde of men, women and children, monks, and nuns, implored those on the ships to take them on-board and spare their lives. They pleaded and sobbed, but to no avail. Soldiers had thrown away their armor and swam out into the Golden Horn hoping to find some ship that would pull them aboard. The ships were already overflowing with refugees and were desperate to escape as swiftly as possible. The Turks were too busy plundering to stop them. Of the prisoners taken back to the Turkish fleet, some were killed, their bodies dumped into the sea. Bodies and heads floated in the water like driftwood.

In the shrine of the *Hodegetria*, Father Athanasios was at his place in front of the holy icon. He could hear the cries of the victors and the screams of the vanquished. As he heard the tide of humanity washing against the walls of the shrine he decided that the icon must be saved from the conflagration. He approached the relic and placed his hands lovingly on the jeweled frame.

"Holy Mary, give me the strength to lift you and carry you to safety. I must take you away from this place of desolation." With all his strength, the old man tried to raise the idol and bring it away from the *iconostasis*, but it was too heavy.

"Please, Holy Mother, let me carry you away with me." As he spoke, the door to the sanctuary flew open and a bloodied Greek soldier entered.

"The City has fallen, Father! The Turks are in the streets, they are killing everyone!"

The young man was badly wounded, blood flowed from his head. There was an arrow stuck in his left arm.

"Come here, my son," said the priest tenderly. "Let me treat your wounds."

Leaving the *Hodegetria*, father Athanasios walked over to the man and began to staunch the flow of blood with a piece of cloth. He had cleared the blood away from the young soldier's face when he heard voices in Turkish at the entrance to the shrine. The youth had collapsed from exhaustion. The priest felt himself faced with a dilemma. He had to flee, but should he take the wounded soldier or the holy icon to safety. He looked at both for a second, first the boy, bloodied and drained, then the painting. He was spared the decision by the Turks as they burst into the room. There were three soldiers and an officer. The sight of the priest checked them for a moment.

"Kill the *gâvur* !" ordered the captain, already covered in blood. "Kill them both!"

Father Athanasios did not understand the Turkish words, but stepped forward to protect the boy.

"We are unarmed. You have won. We are your prisoners."

He was trying to speak gently so as not to antagonize them. He was not sure that they even understood.

"Kill them!" commanded the officer once more.

One of the soldiers obeyed and rushed forward. He pushed the priest aside, placed his knee on the unconscious boy's chest and slashed his head off with a single stroke from his knife.

The priest got up and threw himself at the murderer, but a massive boot took him in the side and kicked him over. He was trying to regain his feet when one of the Turks moved towards the *Hodegetria*.

"Don't touch her!" screamed the old man. "Don't touch her!" His voice was desperate.

The Turks did not understand his words but more than made out their meaning by his frantic tone and gestures.

The men needed no command from their officer to plunder the opulent relic. They tore at the golden *Hodegetria*, plucking the jewels out with their knives. They fought with each other for the golden frame. The officer moved forward towards his men.

"Stop fighting over it! Cut it in four."

Father Athanasios could not make out what had been said, but when he saw one of the men produce an axe and step towards the icon he launched himself with every bit of strength against the Turks. The officer struck him with a mace. The blow shattered his skull and sent him crumpled to the floor. Through glazed eyes, Father Athanasios saw the icon divided into quarters. Blood was seeping into his brain. He could feel life passing from him.

"Leave her alone." His voice was nothing more than a hoarse whisper. No one heard him. To the Turks, he was already dead.

"Let's take his clothes," said one. "They look like they might be worth something."

"Something? Look at those jewels. Those are real gemstones sewn into his cloak."

The second speaker moved towards the dying old man and cut away the vestments with his knife. The careless blade slit Father Athanasios' skin in several places, but the dying man did not react.

"Come on," said the officer. "There's nothing left here that's worth having."

Carrying the desecrated relic and the head of the young Greek, they left. Father Athanasios' was left on the floor wearing only his bloodstained undershirt.

"*Panagia,** Panagia...*" he murmured, and with his last strength brought himself to the desecrated *iconostasis* where the *Hodegetria* had stood. He was able to lift one bloodied hand to the alcove before he breathed his last.

---

* The Greek term for Mary, literally "holiest one."

10—The Ships: *May 29, 1453, 10 am*

From his flagship, Alvise Diedo saw everything with painful clarity. Constantinople had fallen. He had thought that panic might accompany this most tragic moment, but now he felt a strange calmness. It was now his responsibility to save whatever he could of the Venetian fleet, along with as many poor refugees as could make it to his ships. The grief could come later. Now, the captain had an important task to accomplish. Decisive action was necessary if he hoped to avoid death in a cause that was now irretrievably lost.

Staring at the lost city, he weighed his options. The fleet could head immediately for the open sea, but that would condemn hundreds, if not thousands of refugees to death or slavery. The ships were badly undermanned. The incessant fighting and detachments to the City had left many vessels with skeleton crews. With so many non-combatants on board, fighting their way out would not be much of an option. Moreover, Gabriele Trevisano was still at the walls trying to keep the Turks at bay, and so were Minotto and hundreds of other Venetians. Diedo felt that it was his responsibility to try and save those men from the destruction of Constantinople. If they were prisoners, he could attempt to negotiate their ransom. He could not do that from the deck of his flagship.

Diedo looked out towards the chain boom. It was keeping him and the Venetian ships in just as much as it was keeping Hamza Bey's fleet out. The Turkish fleet had moved off from *Diplokionion*, failed to force the boom and withdrawn to the south, around the Acropolis Point. Within the Horn, Zagan Pasha's longboats had already moved against the sea walls to participate in the sack. The time for action had come. He looked across the sea to Pera. The Genoese ships lying at anchor there might offer some protection. Perhaps they might even be able to negotiate with the Sultan for their safe passage.

He called out to the sailing master. "Niccolò, make sail for Pera! Send word for our Venetian ships to follow us."

"Yes, sir."

The great galley turned and moved out directly into the northerly wind. The galleys commanded by Girolamo Morosini, Dolfin Dolfin, who had replaced Giacomo Coco, and Silvestrio Trevisano followed. Four smaller galleys from Crete moved out behind the Tana fleet. The Genoese boats along the chain boom had not moved. Giustiniani's two ships remained at anchor near the walls. On the Venetian flagship, Diedo remained on deck and called an orderly to him. He would go ashore to Pera and discuss the situation with the *podestà*, Angelo Lomellino.

"Find Bartolo Fiuriani and Doctor Barbaro. Tell them that they will be coming ashore with me." He said to his sailing master.

"Ashore sir?"

"At Pera, Niccolò. I'm going to see what the Genoese think about the situation. It could be war with the Sultan for both Venice and Genoa after today. I don't know which way they'll jump. At the very least, I might be able to buy us safe passage using them as an intermediary."

The sailing master did not respond.

"If we're not back in an hour, Niccolò, I want you get our ships to safety. The Genoese will have betrayed us to the Sultan. Understand?"

"Yes, sir. I understand."

"Good man."

The two men presented themselves to the captain. Both were tired. Fiuriani was the armorer for the Tana fleet. The endless days of action had left him exhausted. Barbaro too, was tired. As the ship's surgeon, he had had an endless stream of wounded to treat. This final day was far from done and he was sure that before it was out, he would be extremely busy once more. They looked up at their captain through bloodshot eyes that betrayed their fatigue.

278

Diedo's ships traversed the narrows swiftly and anchored off Pera. Genoa's colony was very quiet. The citizens were keeping to their homes. News was spreading quickly that Constantinople had fallen. Many feared for the lives of friends and relatives who had gone to the City in her hour of need. They also now feared for themselves. Pera's merchant ships, which had given no aid during the struggle, remained idle at anchor as the world around them was consumed by flames. Diedo's flagship docked, and the captain, followed by his two companions, entered the city of their ancient enemy.

A lookout had spotted the ships, and a delegation from the *podestà* met the men as they disembarked. They were immediately brought before Angelo Lomellino. The *podestà* had a profound concern etched on his face. He looked at the haggard soldiers with genuine sympathy. Diedo spoke first.

"Sir, my name is Alvise Diedo, captain of the Venetian fleet from Tana and commander of the naval forces defending the City of Constantinople. I come with heavy tidings. The City has fallen to the Turks."

Lomellino, whose expression was already dour, frowned.

"I have come to determine your intentions, sir. My ships are ready to sail or to fight depending on your choice. If Genoa finally wishes to oppose this murderous Sultan while his hands reek with the blood of your brave citizens who chose to fight for freedom, we are here to join you. If you seek peace and self preservation, allow us to depart in peace."

The *podestà*'s eyes flickered around the room, to the captain's and to those of his councilors.

"Wait here, captain, and I shall send an ambassador to the Sultan. We shall see whether he wishes war or peace with us."

"As you wish, sir."

The *podestà* departed the room. Behind him the door slammed shut. Lomellino turned to a guard outside.

"Don't let those men out without my orders."

The guard nodded. Lomellino went to discuss the situation with his council. Within the room, the Venetians waited.

"What do you think he intends, sir?" asked the armorer.

"I do not know."

"He seemed less than pleased about fighting with us," volunteered Barbaro, the surgeon.

"I cannot blame him for that," answered Diedo wearily. "They are but one step from falling into the chasm. We must be careful. I do not trust these Genoese."

"Nor do I, captain. If they can further their position by sacrificing us, they will not hesitate to do so," said Fiuriani.

Diedo did not respond. He felt uneasiness spreading over him. He paced back and forth as the minutes ticked away, all the time feeling a noose tightening around his neck. They had to leave. The Genoese had no right to hold them. He moved to the door and opened it. The guard stood, stone-faced, in front of him.

"I wish to speak to *podestà* Lomellino immediately!" he demanded in his most commanding voice.

"The *podestà* is not here."

"Then take me to him!"

"That is not possible, sir."

"Not possible? Damn it, I demand to speak with his Excellency immediately!" Diedo tried to push his way past. The guard stopped him.

"His Excellency has requested that you wait here until he returns."

"How dare you! You have no right to keep us here like prisoners."

"I have my orders, sir."

The guard closed the door.

"What's going on, sir?" asked the surgeon.

"That Genoese bastard has betrayed us to the Turks. They refuse to release us, or to let me speak with anyone."

"Then we are doomed. Our ships will leave without us, unless we return soon. We must act."

The two men nodded to their captain. At that moment they heard the *podestà*'s voice through the door. Lomellino was agitated. Knowing that this was their opportunity, the men rushed at the door, overpowered the guard and stood in the hallway opposite the governor of Pera.

"*Signor* Lomelino," cried Diedo, "what do you intend to do with us?"

The *podestà* stared coldly at the captain.

"You cannot have it in mind to hand us over to the Turks, can you?"

Lomellino replied to the guard. "Take those men back inside. Lock the door behind them."

"This is an outrage against Venice! How can you do this to us?" screamed Diedo as he struggled with the guards.

Barbaro and Fiuriani also shouted in protest, but their captain's voice roared over them.

"Master Lomellino, do not betray us! So many brave men have died today, following the heroes who gave their lives during the past two months. Do not betray their sacrifices, our sacrifices, with this dishonorable course. Your citizens of Pera fought with us, bled with us, died with us. Do not let their gallantry be forever stained by your choice now. My men and I are ready to depart. Aboard our ships are not only Venetians, but Genoese, Florentines, Catalans, citizens of Constantinople, merchants from Ancona and soldiers from Chios."

Lomellino listened. His heart felt weak. Diedo's words were full of truth. He looked at the haggard captain. The Venetian's face was pale, drawn with fatigue and pain. The *podestà* feared the Turks would not honor their word. Sacrificing the brave captain to the Sultan would not assure the safety of Pera. Enough good men had died. But leaving was still a risky proposition. Perhaps there was still a chance to come to terms with Mehmed.

"Captain, please. We have no intention of 'betraying' you to the Sultan. Our intention is to negotiate an arrangement that will allow you to leave in peace without further harm to yourselves or to this city."

"No such arrangement is possible, and you know it. The Sultan wishes us in chains, and you suborned to his will. Do you honestly believe that he will honor any promises that they have given you? You will turn us over to them, and they will turn on you before our blood is dry on their swords. We came here in peace and friendship. If you will not fight with us, in the name of Christ, allow us to go in peace."

Wearily, Lomellino acquiesced. He did not have the heart to do otherwise. Besides, he did not wish to complicate relations between Venice and Genoa with Turkish power in the ascendant. With a solemn gaze, he turned to the captain of the Tana fleet.

"Very well, captain. Go in peace. Take your men with you and escape while there is still time."

"Thank you, *signore*. God be with you."

"God, I fear, Captain Diedo, no longer cares for Constantinople."

Without additional words, the three Venetians left the room and went to their ships.

Confidence returned to Diedo with the deck of his flagship once more beneath his feet. He snapped orders to Niccolò, the sailing master, to raise the sails. Niccolò Barbaro, the surgeon, was still at the captain's side.

"I was afraid that the *podestà* would not allow us to go."

"We are fortunate. As much as our departure will displease the Sultan, our capture would have displeased Venice more."

"I can't believe that the City has fallen, sir."

"Neither can I. Now we must leave quickly before we become a permanent part of this disaster."

The sail was raised. The golden lion of Saint Mark fluttered over the galley.

"Niccolò, set course for the chain!"

"Aye-aye, sir!" responded the sailing master.

The ships got under way. There were seven in all: Diedo's flagship, the galleys commanded by Morosini and Dolfin, Gabriele Trevisano's light galley under a different master, a large galley from Crete and three smaller Cretan ships. The small force sailed from beneath the safety of Pera's walls and struck out towards the boom. Hamza Bey had sent his fleet south to harass the far sea walls and encircle the City. The Genoese ships defending the chain had scattered, and · Diedo's ships reached the boom unopposed. The barrier that had protected them for two months now kept them from freedom. They could not pass.

"Niccolò!" barked Captain Diedo, "get a couple of men with axes and cut through that damn chain!"

"Yes, sir!"

The ships were practically touching the obstruction. Diedo glanced back at Constantinople. Fire and smoke rose from the Queen of Cities. He could make out a mass of people still jostling along the harbors, desperate to escape. The once placid waters of the Golden Horn were choppy with the flailing arms of hundreds of refugees attempting to swim to friendly ships. Niccolò and the captain's own son, Marco Diedo, jumped down from the ship and began to hack at the blocks supporting the enormous metal links. In a possessed fury they struck the wood trying to cut their way to freedom and safety. Soon, the blocks gave way and were pulled aside. Niccolò and the younger Diedo climbed back aboard. Deprived of its buoy, the heavy chain slackened and sank. The ships would now be able to pass. One after another, they poured over the gap.

Now in open water, Diedo was faced with another choice: to run for safety or to wait for other survivors. An idea struck him.

"Niccolò, take us to *Diplokionion*. We'll wait there for any sign of other ships that manage to escape."

"*Diplokionion*, sir? asked the sailing master, not sure if he had heard correctly. "That's where the Turkish fleet was anchored."

"Yes, Niccolò, I know. But has it occurred to you that since they have moved to attack the City, their anchorage is the last place that they will be? The lion must leave its den to hunt."

"I understand sir."

"We'll wait there for any other survivors and sail for Tenedos at nightfall."

The other six ships followed behind Diedo's galley. As they moved off from the harbor, Marco arrived, panting with the remnant of Giustiniani's army at the *condottiere*'s ships. He saw the Venetians leaving and realized that they must do the same. Boarding the ship, he immediately called on the ship's captain to follow the Venetians. The *condottiere*'s ships raised anchor and sailed towards the boom. The hulls scraped the chain, but the ships pushed over and broke into open water.

"Captain," cried Marco, "set sail for Chios!"

He ran down to the cabin to see his uncle. The physician had left, gone to help other men whose wounds were not beyond the power of his skills. Giustiniani lay on the bed in his blood-soaked shirt, with his eyes rolled back, his head tilted sickeningly to one side.

Inclining his mouth to his kinsman's ear, Marco whispered:

"It's done Giovanni. We're past the chain. We've escaped. The Turkish fleet is engaged against the City walls, they are not following us."

The *condottiere* tried to speak. His lips had lost all color, and between them, his breath came in uneven gasps, like puffs of wind. His face was ashen.

"No. Rest, rest. We'll be in Chios soon." Marco put his hand on his uncle's head to comfort him. Giustiniani was cold; life was already deserting him. Against his uncle's hair,

Marco saw his own hand, blackened by dirt and smoke, bloody and ghastly. Tears were coming to his eyes. "Stay with me, stay with me, uncle," he pleaded. But his uncle's eyes were glazed over. Marco held him in desperation, realizing slowly that his uncle's time had come. They would reach safety, but Giustiniani would not live to see it. The ships would escape, but they would never be able to return to Constantinople. The Queen of Cities had fallen.

11—The Conqueror: *May 29, 1453, noon*

"Oh City head of all cities! Oh City, the center of the four corners of the earth! Oh City, the pride of Christians and ruin of barbarians! Oh City, a second Paradise laden with spiritual fruits. Where is your beauty, oh Paradise?"
(Lament of the Greek historian Doukas)

From beyond the walls, Mehmed saw his soldiers stream through the breaches. He saw his banners raised over the battlements and heard the victorious shouts of his army as they entered the City. The sun stood at its apex—noon—before the wholesale slaughter began to ebb. The conquerors, exhausted from battle, rape and pillage, turned to consolidating the wealth they had plundered. Word was brought to the Sultan that the City was completely his. Mounted on an immaculate white charger, and accompanied by a full entourage of viziers, pashas, and sheiks, the conqueror entered the City through the great Gate of Charisios. The way was lined by a host of cheering warriors who cleared a path for the royal retinue.

Anyone who stepped back from the enormity of the events unfolding to observe the Sultan's horse would surely have noticed its discomfort. The animal lifted its hooves hesitantly and twitched its head about, snorting loudly. The palpable smell of blood and the tangle of fallen bodies through which the creature passed was, no doubt, the source of its anxiety. Strewn before the conqueror lay the ruins of the conquered. Many of the bodies had been decapitated, and blood flowed from the severed necks between the paving stones. Through this scene of carnage, the suite pranced forward.

The Sultan was relishing his moment of glory. The moment he had dreamed of his entire life had arrived. He had never set foot in the City, and now his eyes marveled at the splendor that they encountered. Even now, amid the orgy of pillage, at the moment of her rape, the Queen of

Cities was strikingly beautiful. The proud horses rode into the Forum of Theodosius and down the imperial road to the *Hagia Sophià*. Much of the destruction wrought to the great building had been corrected. The blood of the priests had been mopped up, and the slave market had been moved outside the holy walls.

When he reached the outside of the church, the Sultan dismounted. Walking forward a few steps, he knelt on the ground. He took a handful of earth in his fist and raised it above his head. He paused for a moment and slackened his fingers so that the black earth ran through his palm onto his white turban. An enormous weight lifted from his soul. Mehmed took a deep breath. He stood and walked to the doorway of the great cathedral. Standing there he was swept away by the beauty of what he beheld. It was greater than anything imagination could have created. Gold mosaics shimmered and the porphyry columns blazed. Four great angels sat in their pendentives looking down on unearthly beauty. The dome stood huge and all encompassing, lit by a mystical light from the noonday sun. The conqueror raised his head to try to view the top of the dome, doubling his neck back before he could see it.

A deafening clatter interrupted the Sultan's silent reflections. A soldier was slashing violently at the mosaic floor with his axe. Immediately, Mehmed approached the man and demanded angrily:

"Why are you doing that?"

"For the Faith!" replied the zealot, and he continued his assault on the graven images.

Enraged, the Sultan responded:

"You have got enough by pillaging the City and taking the citizens for slaves. The buildings are mine! Leave them to me."

As he spoke, he struck the man in the head with his mace, knocking him unconscious to the floor. Bodyguards came forward quickly to remove the corpse. As Mehmed advanced into the church, streams of bound captives were being lead past him, but the conqueror's eyes were enthralled by the beauty that surrounded him.

Six priests who had not been able to flee came before him and uttered one word—*"Amman"*—be merciful. He gestured for them to rise.

"Do not be afraid of my wrath, nor of death, nor of pillage." He turned to his viziers and pashas. "Send public criers through the City. Prohibit all further molestation of the people. Now, in peace, and in safety, let every man go to his own home."

There had been enough destruction. He turned to one of the members of the *ulema* in his party and gestured for the man to mount the pulpit. There was a hushed silence as the cleric climbed the steps to re-consecrate the church as a mosque. All present held their breath. The *imam* had reached the pulpit. In a clarion voice he proclaimed, for all the world to hear:

"Lâ ilâha illallâh; Muhammad rasûllallâh!" There is no God but God. Mohammed is God's Prophet!

With this formality complete, the conqueror threw his prayer mat onto the altar. Vaulting on top of it, he bent his head towards Mecca and intoned a prayer to the Prophet. After he finished, he leapt from the altar to the adulation of his retainers. He strode out of the mosque still thronged with people. To all who could hear, he proclaimed:

"May the House of Osman continue forever! May success be eternally graven on its seal!" The men cheered.

Leaving the *Hagia Sophia* behind, news was brought to the Sultan that the Greek Grand Duke had been captured. He ordered the prisoner brought to him. Immediately, Lukas Notaras was before the Sultan. There were two servants with him, each carrying a large chest. The proud old man was forced into a humble bow by the sword of a Janissary.

Mehmed assessed his captive, running his eyes over the worn skin beneath the locks of silver hair. Was there anything to fear in this creature? Was there any place for this man? Perhaps the elderly statesman could be put to use, installed as a figurehead to maintain a link with the past. Mehmed knew stories of the Grand Duke, tales of avarice, duplicity, and parsimony, everything that was basest among the Greeks. Yet, this relic was reputed to possess a fortune in spite of his City's travails. Now the old man was on his knees amidst destruction worthy of Troy. Revolted by the devastation around him, the Sultan snapped at his captive.

"Did you do well to not surrender the City?" The voice was full of sarcasm and scorn. He continued before any reply could be made. "Behold the damage and ruin. Behold the captivity of so many!" His arms spread to encompass the desolation before them. His words rang with power and a hint of sorrow. Lukas Notaras raised his head to reply.

"Your majesty, I have brought you gifts. These treasures I have preserved for you. At my home there is more wealth, everything I own, which I give to you." As he spoke, the servants opened the strongboxes to reveal a hoard of gold and jewels.

Mehmed and his court were amazed at the riches in the Grand Duke's coffers. The Sultan looked at the gold and gemstones, the treasure with which this man was attempting to buy his life.

"You cowardly, cunning contriver. You had so much wealth, and yet you did not use any of it to serve the Emperor, your master, or to save your City or your country. You are a disgrace. *The wealth a man hordes is nothing but evil.** Now, with this treasure, you hope to save your own life and escape the fate to which you have condemned yourself?"

"My lord..."

Mehmed cut him off. "Tell me, wicked man, who has given your wealth and this City into my hands?"

---

* From the *Koran*, 3:180: "Let those who hoard the wealth which God has bestowed upon them out of His bounty never think it good for them: it is nothing but evil."

"God."

"God? Then, if God has given me all, including you and everyone else in the City as my slaves, these goods are not yours to give me. They are already mine." Before the Grand Duke could muster a reply the conqueror spoke again. "Why did you not send me this treasure before I came to attack the City, or before I succeeded in taking it? Then, you would have been in a position where I would show favor to you. Now you do not own these things. As you have said yourself, God has given them to me, just as He has delivered you into my hands."

The Grand Duke did not answer, so the Sultan continued.

"Are those questions too hard for you? Then perhaps you will answer this. Why did you not counsel your master to surrender the City and spare his people this misery?"

The answer came with all the pride that the noble old man could command. Tears were in his eyes as he spoke.

"Lord, we did not have the authority to give you the City. Even my master, the Emperor himself, did not have that authority." He spoke with the calmness of a proud man who having lost everything, fears nothing. "The Venetians along with the Genoese of Pera encouraged my lord to resist. They fed him with promises of a rescue fleet."

Mehmed turned away in disgust.

"We were also urged to continue our resistance by officials from your own court." The Grand Duke was playing his hand to somehow survive the disaster around him, attempting to ingratiate himself with the conqueror.

Mehmed paused and cast an accusing glance at his Grand Vizier, who met it with steady eyes. That could wait until later. Mehmed's success made the fall of Halil Pasha certain. This last accusation only served to strengthen his conviction that the Grand Vizier would lose his head. The conqueror's mind returned to the matters at hand.

"What has become of your master the Emperor? Did he escape by ship?"

"I do not know where my lord the Emperor is. I was not with him when your troops entered the City." His words were heavy, weighed as they were with sincere grief.

Mehmed questioned the men around him.

"Does anyone here know what became of the Emperor?"

There was a moment of silence, before two warriors came forward and prostrated themselves before the conqueror.

"Speak."

"We saw the Emperor, your majesty. He was struck down near the Gate of Romanos. We can show you where the body is."

"Very well. Mustafa, have these men show you the Emperor's body. I want to see his head."

The servant bowed and left with the two warriors. Mehmed turned his horse and spoke once more to the Grand Duke.

"Take us to your home."

The Grand Duke nodded and rose. He was helped into the saddle of a nearby horse, and the Sultan and his suite set off towards Notaras' palace. They soon reached their objective and dismounted. Notaras led the conqueror into his home.

"Here, your majesty, are the remains of my fortune. All that I have is yours."

Mehmed found himself surrounded by gold and silver, gemstones and pearls. It was a spectacular treasure. Two younger men approached the Sultan and bowed.

"These are my sons, my lord."

The Grand Duke caught a glimpse of surprise in the conqueror's eyes.

"God was generous enough to grant me children even at my time of life. My older son is a man, but my second son is only fourteen."

Mehmed's eyes were drawn to the younger boy. He was handsome, fair like his father, with delicate features that betrayed both his youth and his nobility. In seductive tones the conqueror addressed the Grand Duke.

"It would please us greatly, if you and your sons would dine with us and our court this evening."

Though the Sultan's manner made him cringe, Notaras voiced his consent. "Yes, your majesty."

"Very well." Mehmed swung himself into the saddle. After a final glance at Notaras' younger son, the conqueror spurred his horse away to see the rest of the City that was now his.

It was afternoon, and the day had grown hot. The once golden City of Saint Constantine was desolate. Smoke billowed in ominous gray clouds from abandoned buildings. Terrified captives stained with blood and tears, wearing filthy, torn clothes, were led by their new masters on leashes like dogs. A steady procession of severed heads passed in review before Mehmed, but there was only one head that the conqueror truly desired—the head of Constantine Palaeologos.

After an intensive search, the body of the Emperor was found near the Gate of Saint Romanos. The fine armor made the corpse conspicuous, and though Constantine had thrown away his crown of pearls, his greaves bore the stamp of the double-headed eagle of the House of Palaeologos. Even more obvious were the purple slippers revealed beneath the body's steel *sabatons*. Only the Emperor was allowed to wear the royal purple. Heralds were sent out among the troops who had taken the Saint Romanos gate crying that there would be a reward for the head of the Emperor of the Romans, and describing the body from which it had been taken. Greedily, the warriors set about washing their gruesome trophies in hopes of discovering the object of their master's desires.

Eventually, a head was brought before the Sultan. Mehmed was at dinner, celebrating the conquest of the City with a feast in the imperial palace. He was drinking heavily in celebration. As requested, Grand Duke Notaras was in attendance with his sons. A servant entered, carrying the head on a charger of gold. A hush fell over the banquet hall as the solitary figure approached the conqueror. The man bowed and offered the salver to his master. Mehmed looked at the face. The eyes had been closed. There was a beard of dark brown, interspersed with silver strands. Clotted blood remained in the once well groomed hairs. Mehmed turned to the Grand Duke.

"Tell me truthfully, is this the head of your master, the Emperor?"

Notaras stared at the pallid face, drained of blood, drained of life, mute and mutilated, the head of Constantine Palaeologos, King and Emperor of the Romans.

"It is his, my lord." The words came out like an appeal to God.

Mehmed smiled the scornful and glutted smile of a sated predator.

"Take the head and place it on top of the column of the Augustaion for all to see. Let it stand there until nightfall tomorrow. Then, take it and have it stuffed with straw so that we may send it throughout our kingdom to bear witness to our victory."

The Turks cheered their victorious Sultan and drank. The castanets, pipes, and drums resumed their wild song of celebration. Great skewers loaded with beef and lamb paraded into the banquet hall on trays of gold and silver. The conqueror and his court ate and drank. Circassian dancing girls, their red veils undulating with each seductive motion, thrilled the pashas with their performance. Mehmed drained cup upon cup in celebration. The wine was going to his head. He could feel the artificially induced warmth spreading through his body. Enthralled, he followed the sensuous movements of the Circassians with his eyes. Their black hair stood out against the red silk, which glowed warmly from the light of the torches in the hall. Mehmed's eyes danced with the twisting of their voluptuous abdomens. Gülbahar was sitting at his side. Jealously, his mistress watched his eyes as they fawned over the dancing girls. She moved to caress his face, but he ignored her. Her hand slipped down to his neck. He grabbed it sharply and turned a drunken face towards her. His gaze was dulled by wine. She recoiled from it. She stood up from the table, and without asking permission, departed. The Sultan watched her go, but did nothing. Over the flickering candles and torches, his eyes found the younger son of Lord Notaras. The boy's face shined like cool white marble amidst the hot orange light of the flames. Mehmed began to feel the heat of lust contending with the warmth of intoxication. Shahabeddin's shrill voice tore him from the object of his desire.

"Halil Pasha has left the banquet, your majesty."

"Hmm?" Mehmed's mind, awash with alcohol, reacted slowly as he turned reluctantly to look at his chief eunuch.

"The Grand Vizier has left, sire. He has no stomach to witness the destruction of the Greeks he loved so well."

"Later, later."

He waved down his councilor's words with slurred speech and immediately turned his eye back to the handsome boy. But the youth was not there. Furiously, he swung his eyes across the hall searching out the delicate features and white skin. There was no sign of the boy. Was *everyone* leaving? With a sudden burst of energy, Mehmed stood and scanned the room once more. They had gone; father and sons, all gone. He turned savagely to Shahabeddin.

"Go to the home of the Grand Duke and tell him that his ruler commands him to send his younger son back to the banquet immediately!"

The eunuch looked at his master with uncertainty.

"Do it!"

Shahabeddin bowed and went to fulfill his mission. It did not take him long to reach the home of the Grand Duke. Notaras and his sons had retired, but Shahabeddin entered the villa with his guards and summoned the Grand Duke from his bed.

"His majesty the Sultan requests that your younger son return to the banquet immediately." The old man shuddered with fear.

"Why does his majesty request this?"

"It is not your position to question, my lord. I have express orders from the Sultan that your son come immediately."

"But why?" shouted the old man. Even bereft of temporal power, his voice, so accustomed to authority, carried enough weight that the eunuch answered him.

"I believe his majesty has chosen to honor your son with a place in his *seraglio*."

"Honor? It is not *our* custom to hand over our children to be despoiled!" The Grand Duke's voice shook with pride and anger.

"My lord, I would caution you that his majesty is firm in his desires. Opposing him in this can only bring harm to you and to your family."

"What greater harm can we suffer than the ruin of our honor and the death of our souls? It would be far better for me if the executioner were sent to take my head."

"I advise you to surrender the boy, my lord. You have already seen the scope of my master's wrath. Do not invite it against your house."

"If you want my son, you will have to take him by force. I will never surrender him to you." He held the eunuch's gaze for a moment. "Goodnight."

The Grand Duke turned and left. Shahabeddin remained speechless at the door. As much as he detested the Greeks, he admired Notaras's courage and resolve. With trepidation of his master's reaction, he returned to the feast. Mehmed had collapsed, drunk with wine and worn out from lack of sleep. The news would have to wait until morning. With Notaras' refusal echoing in his ears, the chief eunuch retired to his quarters giving orders to be awakened at dawn or as soon as the Sultan rose.

* * *

Dawn broke for the first time over the conquered City. Attendants roused Shahabeddin. The Vizier left his bed and prepared himself for his master's wrath. He did not have long to wait. A little after dawn Mehmed awoke. He had slept at the banquet table. His head was still humming, swimming with wine. As it began to clear, he remembered Notaras' handsome son. He had commanded that the boy be brought to him. Where was he?

"Mustafa! Where is Shahabeddin? Bring him to me immediately! And bring wine!"

Mehmed looked down at his robe. It was stained with vomit. He called again to his servant.

"And bring me another robe!"

The wine arrived first. Mehmed drained the cup and ordered it refilled. Shahabeddin arrived before the change of clothes, but at that moment, the Sultan was not concerned with his appearance.

"Eunuch, last night I ordered you to bring me the son of Lord Notaras! Why is he not here?"

Shahabeddin's head was bowed. He raised his eyes slightly as he spoke. "Your majesty, the Grand Duke refused to hand his son over to you. Despite my urging, he refused to have his son 'despoiled' by you."

Mehmed threw the cup away in rage. "Refused? Despoiled? How dare he?"

"He said it would be better if you sent your executioner for him than ask him to give you his child."

"So be it!" cried the conqueror. "If he desires the executioner, he shall have him! Summon Hassan the swordsman. Take him with you to the Grand Duke's home and bring back the old man and both his sons!"

"As you command, sire."

The eunuch hurried off and made his way back to Notaras' house. The Grand Duke was already awake. Once more the Vizier stood before him. This time, the giant executioner stood at his side. Notaras looked at the two men and knew why they had come. Shahabeddin spoke first.

"My lord, the Sultan has sent me again. This time he asks that you and your sons come with me immediately to the palace."

"I understand. May I say farewell to my wife and daughters?"

"You may."

"Thank you." Notaras returned to the courtyard of his home, emerging several minutes later with both his sons.

"We are ready," said the Grand Duke.

The men were led from their home to the palace. Around them, morning broke over the fallen City. Everything was quiet. Turkish soldiers, gorged on wine, treasure and blood, lay in the streets. Homes and shops were completely deserted. The entire population of the City had seemingly disappeared. Solemnly, the small party reached the palace. At the gate, they stopped.

"You men remain here. The boy will come with me."

"Courage, my child," Notaras called after his son.

The eunuch and the boy entered the palace and climbed the steps of the inner courtyard leading to the Sultan's chambers. Mehmed was wearing new robes.

"Your majesty, here is the son of Lord Notaras, as you requested. His father and brother await your pleasure at the palace gate."

The conqueror strode towards the boy. Wine made his legs unsteady, and he stumbled forward. There was a cup of wine in his left hand. With his right, he reached out towards the boy and caressed his face.

"What a handsome child."

The boy shrank back from the touch, trembling with fear and uneasiness.

"Thank you, lord Vizier, for bringing me this beautiful boy. He shall have a place of great honor in my house."

Notaras' son cringed as the conqueror's hand moved to stroke his hair. Unable to bear the humiliation further he cried out.

"Father! Help me, father!" and tried to run away.

Shahabeddin's guards grabbed him immediately. Mehmed strode forward and slammed his right fist into the boy's stomach.

"Cut off his head! Cut off his head! Execute his father and brother as well! Cut their heads off immediately, here on the palace grounds! Kill the children first and let their father watch in horror as the headsman's sword severs their delicate necks!"

He took hold of the boy as he spoke and propelled him from the room, down the stairs of the courtyard and towards the gate. The father saw them. His heart, already broken, sobbed within his chest. He moved forward to embrace his child.

"Courage, my sons." The Grand Duke's voice was full of love. There was sincerity in his words. That virtue, so long abandoned in his speech, returned in his final hour.

"Yesterday in a fleeting moment of time, you witnessed the undoing of all our works. Our wealth, the wondrous glory we enjoyed in this great City, a glory envied by the entire world, all were lost. Now, in this hour, nothing is left us but our honor and our faith." He lifted the tearstained visage of his younger son and gazed deeply into the boy's eyes. "This life will not continue forever, my child. We must all die sometime. And how will we die? Deprived of our goods, robbed of our glory, our honor, our authority, despised by all, scorned and harassed until Death comes to us. Where is our Emperor? Was he not slain yesterday? All our friends, everyone we love has perished. We should have died with them. However, this hour is sufficient unto us. Let us sin no more. The stadium is ready, the match must be played."

His sons had stopped crying. Their father had given them the courage to face death. The Grand Duke turned to the executioner.

"Carry out your orders."

Notaras' eldest son knelt and bared his neck. The sword struck through it with a single stroke.

"Thou art just, Lord," murmured the Grand Duke.

The boy knelt before his father and again the terrible sword sang through the air, bringing the handsome head to the earth.

Notaras continued to pray. "Father in heaven, grant us mercy."

The Grand Duke opened his eyes and saw the bloodied trunks of his two sons. Turned to the executioner he asked:

"May I pray for a moment?"

Hassan nodded. Upon the earth stained with the blood of his sons, the Grand Duke knelt and prayed. He mumbled the words peacefully and bowed his head before the swordsman. A single blow took his life. The executioner picked up the heads and brought them to the Sultan. Mehmed was continuing to feast in celebration. The executioner laid the heads before him. The boy was still pretty. Why had he refused? Seeing the severed skull did not assuage the conqueror's temper. Instead, it made him hungrier for blood.

In the slurred speech of a drunkard he commanded, "Have the prisoners brought to Hasan. He is to behead them all! Spare the maidens and the boys for my seraglio, but the men are to die, here and now."

All the nobles Mehmed had ransomed, Greeks, Venetians, and Genoese, passed before the sword of the headsman. Still, the conqueror felt empty. The head he sought was not among these helpless captives but on the shoulders of his greatest enemy, his own Grand Vizier. Soon the disapproving gaze would stare at him for the last time over a neck of congealed black blood. The conqueror laughed a wild drunken laugh, drunk with wine, drunk with power, drunk with glory. He had come and conquered his Troy. Like Alexander, he had destroyed an ancient and fabulous empire. Like the Caesars, he would rule the greatest empire the world had ever seen from behind the eternal walls of the City of Cities. The laughter of the conqueror carried beyond the noisy banquet hall, through the deserted corridors of forgotten power that echoed with the glories of the past, and into the sun-drenched City. It was nearly June, and the sun was warm. The spring flowers shone at the apex of their splendor, a moment removed from the beginning of their decay. Amidst the blossoms, like a body laid out in state, the Queen of Cities lay desolate, naked, and mute, stripped of her form, her beauty and her glory.

Character List

Niccolò Barbaro: The surgeon of the Tana fleet survives the siege and escapes aboard Alvise Diedo's flagship. Upon reaching Venice, Barbaro writes his *"Diary of the Siege of Constantinople, 1453"* which serves as one of the best eyewitness accounts of the events described in this book.

Alvise Diedo: The captain of the Tana fleet safely escapes the Turkish forces and returns with his sons and the other surviving Venetians to Venice. Exhausted from his ordeal, he dies a few months after the taking of the City.

Fabrizio Cornaro: The one time ambassador is killed by the Turks during the final assault.

Doge Francesco Foscari: The aged Doge of Venice is deposed in 1457. He dies shortly thereafter.

Halil Pasha: The Grand Vizier is stripped of his office on May 30, the day after the fall of the City. In his place, Mehmed appoints Zagan Pasha, whose views are closer to those of his ruler. On June 1, the former Grand Vizier is imprisoned. Still under arrest, Halil returns with Mehmed to Adrianople in the middle of June. On July 10, 1453 he is executed for treason.

Cardinal Isidore: During the sack, he exchanges his clothes with a beggar. The beggar is captured and killed. His head is displayed as that of the Cardinal. Isidore is also taken prisoner, but is not recognized. A merchant, who does recognize him, ransoms him and Isidore returns to Italy. Upon the death of Patriach Gregory in 1459, the Pope appoints him Patriarch of Constantinople. He never returns to the City and dies in 1463.

Giovanni Giustiniani: The wounded *condottiero* escapes the City's destruction aboard his flagship and sails for his home on the island of Chios. He dies there only a day after his arrival.

Archbishop Leonardo: Escapes the destruction of the City and returns safely to Lesbos. He is still there when the Turks conquer the island in 1462. He is taken captive and returns to Constantinople as a prisoner. He is quickly ransomed and goes to live in Italy where he dies in 1482.

Angelo Lomellino: After the fall of Constantinople, Lomellino remains *podestà* of Pera in spite of his desire to return to Genoa. In the days that follow the events of May 29, Mehmed orders the walls and towers protecting Pera destroyed. The colony retains its nominal autonomy but a Turkish administration is put in place. He is unable to ransom his nephew, Imperiali, who becomes a member of the Sultan's court. On June 23, he writes a short and mournful letter to his brother with some description of the occurrences following the fall of the City.

Giacomo Loredan: The Captain-General's fleet is delayed by weather and circumstance at every stage of its voyage. Two days after Constantinople falls, the fleet makes contact with the fleeing survivors near the island of Tenedos.

Giovanni Loredan: is captured at the land walls by the Turks. He is executed by Mehmed.

Sultan Mehmed: Following his triumph at Constantinople, the conqueror re-installs the Greek Orthodox Church with all its privileges. A monk, Gennadius, is appointed patriarch. All Latin Catholic organizations are banned from his kingdom. Between 1454 and 1455, Mehmed launches several campaigns against Serbia annexing the entire country with the exception of Belgrade in 1459. Between 1458 and 1460 Mehmed takes advantage of internal quarrels between Demetrios and Thomas Palaeologos to annex the Morea including Athens. In 1461, the conqueror moves on the final Byzantine city of Trebizond, on the Black Sea. It falls to his troops after a short siege. In 1463, his relentless armies conquer Bosnia. During the same year, Venice, apprehensive of the spectacular Ottoman expansion allies with Hungary and declares war on the Sultan. Initial successes are swept away by Mehmed's ferocious counterattack. Parts of Albania fall in 1468. Negroponte is captured in 1470. A peace treaty in 1479 recognizes Ottoman rule in all of Albania and the Aegean islands. Venice agrees to pay an annual tribute of 10,000 ducats. Mehmed's power is at its apex. In 1480 Ottoman forces move against the island of Rhodes and are repulsed by the Knights of Saint John. Later that year, the Sultan's armies take the city of Otranto in southern Italy. On May 3, 1481, Mehmed dies suddenly. Soon after his death, Otranto is re-conquered. The Turks never return to Italy. The conqueror's death heralds an end to an age of Ottoman conquest.

Girolamo Minotto: The Venetian *bailò* is captured in Blachernae by the Turks and executed along with his sons Zorzi and Polo.

Girolamo Morosini: safely escapes the Turkish forces aboard his galley and returns to Venice. Several months later when Niccolò Barbaro writes his account of the siege, Morosini is dead. His cause of death is not known.

George Sphrantzes: Constantine's faithful secretary is captured after the siege and becomes a slave in the household of Mehmed's Master of Horse. His son, John, is put to death for refusing to become Mehmed's lover. His daughter dies in the Sultan's seraglio. After months of captivity, he succeeds in ransoming himself and travels to the Morea, then ruled by Constantine's brothers. In 1454 he is able to travel to Adrianople and ransom his wife. He visits Venice during an embassy from the Despot Thomas in 1455 but returns to see the Morea conquered by Mehmed in 1460. He leaves the service of the Palaeologos family and retires to a monastery in Corfu. He dies there in 1477.

Gabriele Trevisano: is captured at his post along the sea walls. He dies a few months later still in the hands of the Turks.

Made in the USA
Lexington, KY
20 September 2010